# THE
# QUEEN'S
# RISING

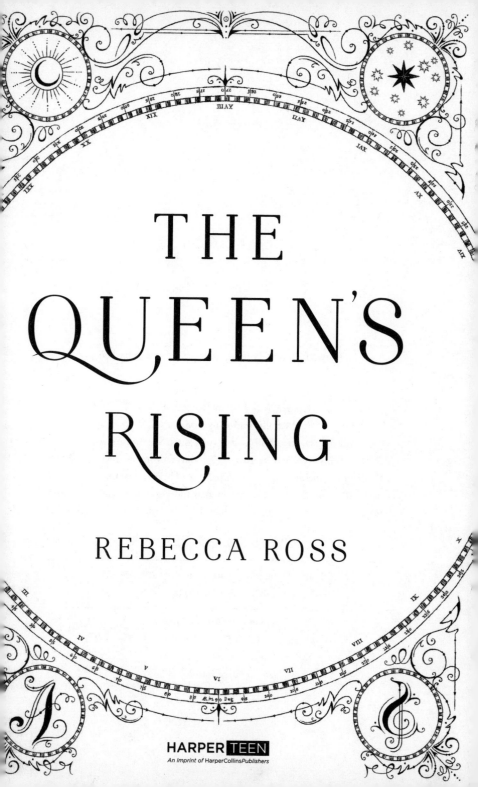

# THE QUEEN'S RISING

REBECCA ROSS

HARPER TEEN
*An Imprint of HarperCollins Publishers*

HarperTeen is an imprint of HarperCollins Publishers.

The Queen's Rising
Copyright © 2018 by Rebecca Ross LLC
Map illustration by Virginia Allyn
www.epicreads.com

Library of Congress Control Number: 2017939005
ISBN 978-0-06-247134-5

Typography by Aurora Parlagreco
17 18 19 20 21   CG/LSCH   10 9 8 7 6 5 4 3 2 1
❖
First Edition

*For Ruth and Mary,*
*Mistress of Art and Mistress of Knowledge*

# TABLE OF CONTENTS

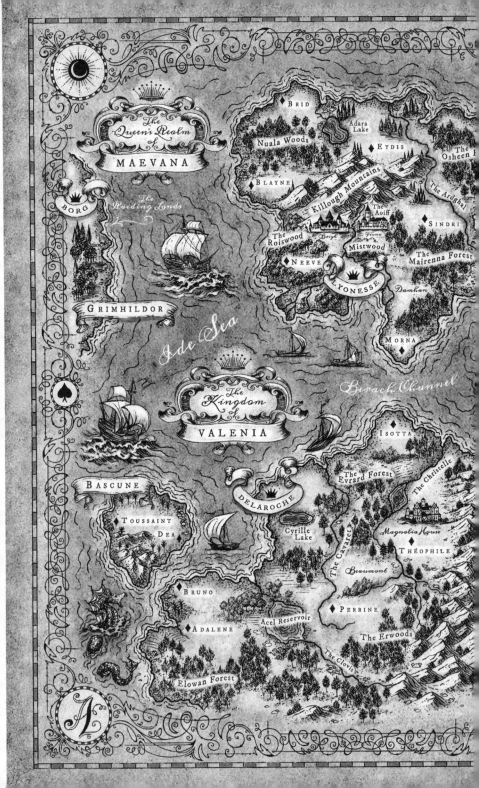

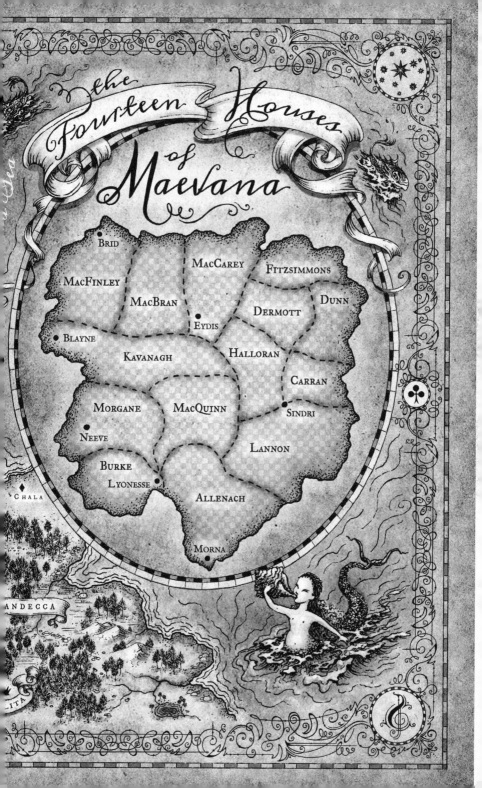

# CAST OF CHARACTERS

## MAGNALIA HOUSE

The Dowager of Magnalia

*Magnalia's Arials:*

Solene Severin, mistress of art

Evelina Baudin, mistress of music

Xavier Allard, master of dramatics

Therese Berger, mistress of wit

Cartier Évariste, master of knowledge

*Magnalia's Ardens:*

Oriana DuBois, arden of art

Merei Labelle, arden of music

Abree Cavey, arden of dramatics

Sibylle Fontaine, arden of wit

Ciri Montagne, arden of knowledge

Brienna Colbert, arden of knowledge

*Others Who Visit Magnalia:*

Francis, courier

Rolf Paquet, Brienna's grandfather

Monique Lavoie, patron

Nicolas Babineaux, patron

Brice Mathieu, patron

## JOURDAIN HOUSE

Aldéric Jourdain

Luc Jourdain

Amadine Jourdain

Jean David, lackey and coachman

Agnes Cote, chamberlain

Pierre Faure, chef

Liam O'Brian, thane

*Others Involved with Jourdain*

Hector Laurent (Braden Kavanagh)

Yseult Laurent (Isolde Kavanagh)

Theo d'Aramitz (Aodhan Morgane)

## ALLENACH HOUSE

Brendan Allenach, lord

Rian Allenach, firstborn son

Sean Allenach, second-born son

*Others Mentioned*

Gilroy Lannon, king of Maevana

Liadan Kavanagh, the first queen of Maevana

Tristan Allenach

Norah Kavanagh, third-born princess of Maevana

Evan Berne, printmaker

# THE FOURTEEN HOUSES OF MAEVANA

Allenach the Shrewd

Kavanagh the Bright*

Burke the Elder

Lannon the Fierce

Carran the Courageous

MacBran the Merciful

Dermott the Loved

MacCarey the Just

Dunn the Wise

MacFinley the Pensive

Fitzsimmons the Gentle

MacQuinn the Steadfast*

Halloran the Upright

Morgane the Swift*


*Denotes a fallen House

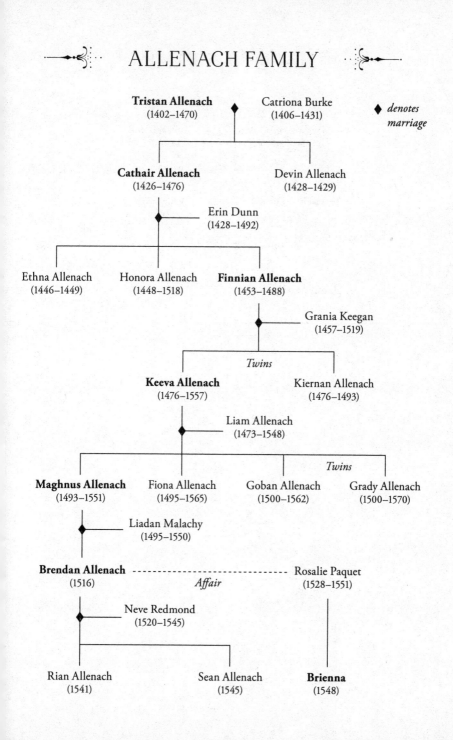

# ALLENACH FAMILY

◆ *denotes marriage*

**Tristan Allenach** (1402–1470) ◆ Catriona Burke (1406–1431)

**Cathair Allenach** (1426–1476)   Devin Allenach (1428–1429)

◆ Erin Dunn (1428–1492)

Ethna Allenach (1446–1449)   Honora Allenach (1448–1518)   **Finnian Allenach** (1453–1488)

◆ Grania Keegan (1457–1519)

*Twins*

**Keeva Allenach** (1476–1557)   Kiernan Allenach (1476–1493)

◆ Liam Allenach (1473–1548)

**Maghnus Allenach** (1493–1551)   Fiona Allenach (1495–1565)   *Twins*   Goban Allenach (1500–1562)   Grady Allenach (1500–1570)

◆ Liadan Malachy (1495–1550)

**Brendan Allenach** (1516) ------------ *Affair* ------------ Rosalie Paquet (1528–1551)

◆ Neve Redmond (1520–1545)

Rian Allenach (1541)   Sean Allenach (1545)   **Brienna** (1548)

# MACQUINN FAMILY

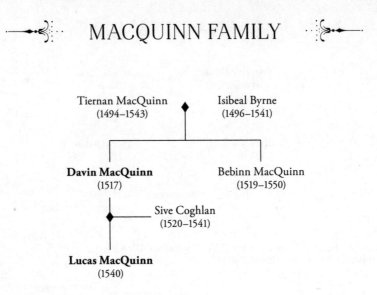

Tiernan MacQuinn (1494–1543) ◆ Isibeal Byrne (1496–1541)

**Davin MacQuinn** (1517)

Bebinn MacQuinn (1519–1550)

◆ Sive Coghlan (1520–1541)

**Lucas MacQuinn** (1540)

# MORGANE FAMILY

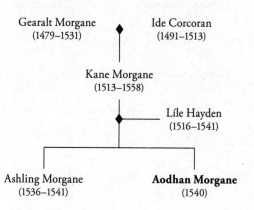

Gearalt Morgane
(1479–1531)

Ide Corcoran
(1491–1513)

Kane Morgane
(1513–1558)

Líle Hayden
(1516–1541)

Ashling Morgane
(1536–1541)

**Aodhan Morgane**
(1540)

# KAVANAGH FAMILY

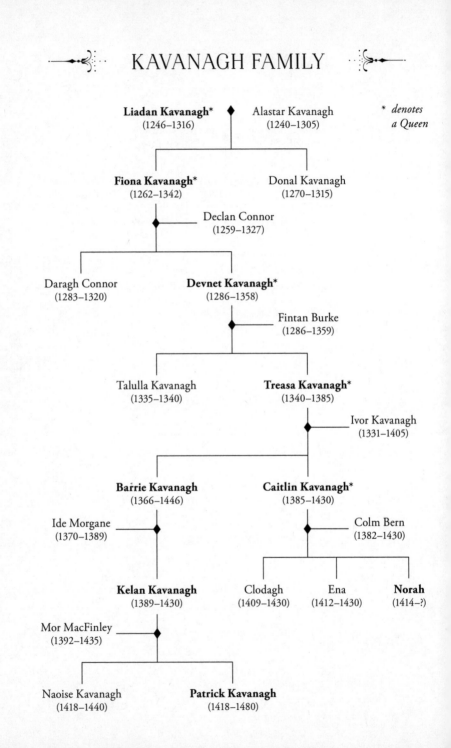

**Liadan Kavanagh*** (1246–1316) ◆ Alastar Kavanagh (1240–1305)

*\* denotes a Queen*

**Fiona Kavanagh*** (1262–1342)

Donal Kavanagh (1270–1315)

Declan Connor (1259–1327)

Daragh Connor (1283–1320)

**Devnet Kavanagh*** (1286–1358)

Fintan Burke (1286–1359)

Talulla Kavanagh (1335–1340)

**Treasa Kavanagh*** (1340–1385)

Ivor Kavanagh (1331–1405)

**Barrie Kavanagh** (1366–1446)

**Caitlin Kavanagh*** (1385–1430)

Ide Morgane (1370–1389)

Colm Bern (1382–1430)

**Kelan Kavanagh** (1389–1430)

Clodagh (1409–1430)

Ena (1412–1430)

**Norah** (1414–?)

Mor MacFinley (1392–1435)

Naoise Kavanagh (1418–1440)

**Patrick Kavanagh** (1418–1480)

# KAVANAGH FAMILY
## *(continued)*

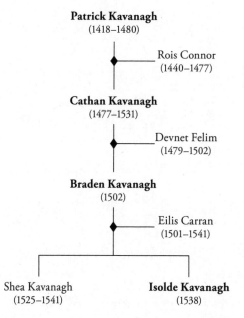

**Patrick Kavanagh**
(1418–1480)

Rois Connor
(1440–1477)

**Cathan Kavanagh**
(1477–1531)

Devnet Felim
(1479–1502)

**Braden Kavanagh**
(1502)

Eilis Carran
(1501–1541)

Shea Kavanagh
(1525–1541)

**Isolde Kavanagh**
(1538)

# THE
# QUEEN'S
# RISING

# ⸺⊰ PROLOGUE ⊱⸺

*Midsummer 1559*
*Province of Angelique, Kingdom of Valenia*

Magnalia House was the sort of establishment where only wealthy, talented girls mastered their passion. It wasn't designed for girls who were lacking, for girls who were illegitimate daughters, and certainly not for girls who defied kings. I, of course, happen to be all three of those things.

I was ten years old when my grandfather first took me to Magnalia. Not only was it the hottest day of summer, an afternoon for bloated clouds and short tempers, it was the day I decided to ask the question that had haunted me ever since I had been placed in the orphanage.

"Grandpapa, who is my father?"

My grandfather sat on the opposite bench, his eyes heavy from the heat until my inquiry startled him. He was a proper man, a good yet very private man. Because of that, I believed he was ashamed of me—the illegitimate child of his beloved, dead daughter.

But on that sweltering day, he was trapped in the coach with me, and I had voiced a question he must answer. He blinked down at my expectant face, frowning as if I had asked him to pluck the moon from the sky. "Your father is not a respectable man, Brienna."

"Does he have a name?" I persisted. Hot weather made me bold, while it melted the older ones, like Grandpapa. I felt confident that he would at long last tell me who I had descended from.

"Don't all men?" He was getting crabby. We had been traveling for two days in this heat.

I watched him fumble for his handkerchief and mop the sweat from his crinkled brow, which was speckled like an egg. He had a ruddy face, an overpowering nose, and a crown of white hair. They said my mother had been comely—and that I was her reflection—yet I could not imagine someone as ugly as Grandpapa creating something beautiful.

"Ah, Brienna, child, why must you ask of him?" Grandpapa sighed, mellowing a bit. "Let us talk instead of what is to come, of Magnalia."

I swallowed my disappointment; it sat in my throat like a marble, and I decided I did not want to talk of Magnalia.

The coach took a turn before I could bolster my stubbornness, the wheels transitioning from ruts to a smooth stone drive. I glanced at the window, streaked from dust. My heart quickened at the sight and I pressed closer, spread my fingers upon the glass.

I admired the trees first, their long branches arched over the drive like welcoming arms. Horses leisurely grazed in the pastures, their coats damp from the summer sun. Beyond the pastures were the distant blue mountains of Valenia, the backbone of our kingdom. It was a sight to salve my disappointment, a land to grow wonder and courage.

We rambled along, under the oak boughs and up a hill, finally stopping in a courtyard. Through the haze, I stared at the decadent gray stone, glistening windows, and climbing ivy that was Magnalia House.

"Now listen, Brienna," Grandpapa said, rushing to tuck away his handkerchief. "You must be on your absolute best behavior. As if you were about to meet King Phillipe. You must smile and curtsy, and not say anything out of line. Can you do that for your grandpapa?"

I nodded, suddenly losing my voice.

"Very good. Let us pray that the Dowager will accept you."

The coachman opened the door, and Grandpapa motioned for me to exit before him. I did, on trembling legs, feeling small as I craned my neck to soak in the grand estate.

"I will speak to the Dowager first, privately, and then you will meet her," my grandfather said, pulling me along up the stairs to the front doors. "Remember, you must be polite. This is a place for cultured girls."

He examined my appearance as he rang the doorbell. My navy dress was wrinkled from travel, my braids coming unwound, the hair frizzy about my face. But the door swung open before my grandfather could comment on my unkemptness. We entered Magnalia side by side, stepping into the blue shadows of the foyer.

While my grandfather was admitted into the Dowager's study, I remained in the corridor. The butler offered me a place on a cushioned bench along the wall where I sat alone, waiting, my feet swinging nervously as I stared at the black-and-white checkered floors. It was a quiet house, as if it was missing its heart. And because it was so quiet, I could hear my grandfather and the Dowager speaking, their words melting through the study doors.

"Which passion does she gravitate toward?" the Dowager asked. Her voice was rich and smooth, like smoke drifting up on an autumn night.

"She likes to draw. . . . She does very well with drawing. She also has a vivid imagination—she would do excellent in theater. And music—my daughter was very accomplished with the lute, so surely Brienna inherited a bit of that. What else . . . oh yes, they say she enjoys reading at the orphanage. She has read all of their books two times over." Grandpapa was rambling. Did he even know what he was saying? Not once had he seen me draw. Not once had he listened to my imagination.

I slipped from the bench and softly padded closer. With my ear pressed to the door, I drank in their words.

"That is all very good, Monsieur Paquet, but surely you understand that 'to passion' means your granddaughter must master *one* of the five passions, not all of them."

In my mind, I thought of the five. *Art. Music. Dramatics. Wit. Knowledge.* Magnalia was a place for a girl to become an arden—an apprentice student. She could choose one of the five passions to diligently study beneath the careful instruction of a master or mistress. When she reached the height of her talent, the girl would gain the title of a mistress and receive her cloak—an individualized marker of her achievement and status. She would become a passion of art, a passion of wit, or whichever one she was devoted to.

My heart thundered in my chest, and sweat beaded along my palms as I imagined myself becoming a passion.

Which one should I choose, if the Dowager admitted me?

But I couldn't mull over this, because my grandfather said, "I promise you, Brienna is a bright girl. She can master any of the five."

"That is kind of you to think such, but I must tell you . . . my House is very competitive, very difficult. I already have my five ardens for this passion season. If I accept your granddaughter, one of my arials will have to instruct *two* ardens. This has never been done. . . ."

I was trying to figure out what "arial" meant—"instructor," perhaps?—when I heard a scuff and jumped back from the twin doors, expecting them to fly open and catch me in my crime. But it must have only been my grandfather, shifting anxiously in his chair.

"I can assure you, Madame, that Brienna will not cause any trouble. She is a very obedient girl."

"But you say she lives in an orphanage? And she does not bear your last name. Why is that?" the Dowager asked.

There was a pause. I had always wondered why my last name did not match my grandfather's. I stepped close to the doors again, laid my ear to the wood. . . .

"It is to protect Brienna from her father, Madame."

"Monsieur, I fear that I cannot accept her if she is in a dangerous situation—"

"Please hear me, Madame, just for a moment. Brienna holds dual citizenship. Her mother—my daughter—was Valenian. Her father is from Maevana. He knows she exists, and I was concerned . . . concerned that he might seek her out, find her by my last name."

"And why would that be so horrible?"

"Because her father is—"

Down the hall, a door opened and closed, followed by the click of boots entering the corridor. I rushed back to the bench and all but fell on it, provoking its squat legs to scrape along the floor as nails on a chalkboard.

I didn't dare look up, my cheeks flushed with guilt, as the owner of the boots walked closer, eventually coming to stand before me.

I thought it was the butler, until I conceded to glance up and see it was a young man, horribly handsome with hair the color of summer wheat fields. He was tall and trim, not a wrinkle on his breeches and tunic, but more than that . . . he wore a blue cloak. He was a passion, then, a master of knowledge, as blue was their signifying color, and he had just discovered that I was eavesdropping on the Dowager.

Slowly, he crouched down, to be level with my cautious gaze. He held a book in his hands, and I noticed that his eyes were as blue as his passion cloak, the color of cornflowers.

"And who might you be?" he asked.

"Brienna."

"That is a pretty name. Are you to become an arden here at Magnalia?"

"I don't know, Monsieur."

"Do you want to become one?"

"Yes, very much, Monsieur."

"You do not need to call me 'monsieur,'" he gently corrected.

"Then what should I call you, Monsieur?"

He didn't answer; he merely looked at me, his head tilted to the side, that blond hair spilling over his shoulder as captive sunlight. I wanted him to go away, and yet I wanted him to keep talking to me.

It was at that moment that the study doors opened. The master of knowledge stood and turned toward the sound. But my gaze strayed to the back of his cloak, where silver threads gathered—a constellation of stars among the blue fabric. I marveled over it; I longed to ask him what they meant.

"Ah, Master Cartier," the Dowager said from where she stood on the threshold. "Do you mind escorting Brienna to the study?"

He extended his hand to me, palm up with invitation. Carefully, I let my fingers rest in his. I was warm, he was cold, and I walked at his side across the corridor, where the Dowager waited for me. Master Cartier squeezed my fingers just before he let go and continued his way down the hall; he was encouraging me to be brave, to stand tall and proud, to find my place in this House.

I entered the study, the doors closing with a soft click. My grandfather sat in one chair; there was a second one beside his, meant for me. Quietly, I surrendered to it as the Dowager walked around her desk, settling behind it with a sigh of her dress.

She was a rather severe-looking woman; her forehead was high, bespeaking years of pulling her hair back beneath tight wigs of glory. Now, her white locks of experience were almost completely concealed beneath her gabled headdress of black velvet, which was elegant upon her head. Her dress was a deep shade of red with a low waist and a square neckline trimmed with pearls. And I knew in that moment as I soaked in her aged beauty that she could usher me into a life that I would not have been able to achieve otherwise. To become impassioned.

"It is nice to meet you, Brienna," she said to me with a smile.

"Madame," I returned, wiping my sweaty palms on my dress.

"Your grandfather says many wonderful things about you."

I nodded and awkwardly glanced at him. He was watching me, a fastidious gleam in his eyes, handkerchief gripped in his hand once more, like he needed something to hold on to.

"Which passion are you drawn to the most, Brienna?" she asked, attracting my attention back to her. "Or perhaps you have a natural inclination toward one of them?"

Saints above, I didn't know. Frantically, I let my mind trace them again . . . *art . . . music . . . dramatics . . . wit . . . knowl-edge*. I honestly had no natural inclinations, no intrinsic talent for a passion. So I blurted the first one that came to mind. "Art, Madame."

And then, to my dismay, she opened a drawer before her and procured a fresh square of parchment and a pencil. She set it down on the corner of her desk, directly before me.

"Draw something for me." The Dowager beckoned.

I resisted looking at my grandfather, because I knew that our deceit would become a smoke signal. He knew I wasn't an artist, I knew I wasn't either, and yet I grasped that pencil as if I were.

I took a deep breath and thought of something that I loved: I thought of the tree that grew in the backyard of the orphanage, a wise, gangly old oak that we adored to climb. And so I said to myself . . . anyone can draw a tree.

I drew it while the Dowager conversed with my grandfather, both of them trying to grant me a measure of privacy. When I was finished, I set the pencil down and waited, staring at what my hand had born.

It was a pitiful rendition. Not at all like the image I held in my mind.

The Dowager stared intently at my drawing; I noticed a slight frown creased her forehead, but her eyes were well guarded.

"Are you certain you wish to study art, Brienna?" There was no judgment in her tone, but I tasted the subtle challenge in the marrow of her words.

I almost told her no, that I did not belong here. But when I thought about returning to the orphanage, when I thought about becoming a scullery maid or a cook, as all the other girls at the orphanage eventually did, I realized this was my one chance to evolve.

"Yes, Madame."

"Then I shall make an exception for you. I already have five girls your age attending Magnalia. You will become the sixth arden, and will study the passion of art beneath Mistress Solene. You will spend the next seven years here, living with your ardens-sisters, learning and growing and preparing for your seventeenth summer solstice, when you will become impassioned and gain a patron." She paused, and I felt drunk on all she had just poured over me. "Does this sound acceptable to you?"

I blinked, and then stammered, "Yes, yes indeed, Madame!"

"Very good. Monsieur Paquet, you should bring Brienna back on the autumn equinox, in addition to her tuition sum."

My grandfather rushed to stand and bow to her, his relief like overpowering cologne in the room. "Thank you, Madame. We are thrilled! Brienna will not disappoint you."

"No, I do not think that she will," the Dowager said.

I stood and dropped a crooked curtsy, trailing Grandpapa to the doors. But just before I returned to the corridor, I glanced behind to look at her.

The Dowager watched me with a sad gaze. I was only a girl, but I knew such a look. Whatever my grandfather had said to her had convinced her to accept me. My admittance was not of my own merit; it was not based on my potential. Was it the name of my father that had swayed her? The name I did not know? Did his name truly even matter, though?

She believed that she had just accepted me out of charity, and I would never passion.

I chose that moment to prove her wrong.

# PART ONE
# MAGNALIA
*Seven years later*

## ONE

# LETTERS AND LESSONS

*Late spring of 1566*

Twice a week, Francis hid amid the juniper bush that flour-ished by the library window. Sometimes I liked to make him wait; he was long-legged and impatient, and imagining him crouched in a bush was cordial to my mind. But summer was a week away, and that provoked me to hurry. It was also time to tell him. The thought made my pulse tumble as I entered the quiet afternoon shadows of the library.

*Tell him this will be the last time.*

I lifted the window with a gentle push, catching the sweet fragrance of the gardens as Francis emerged from his gargoyle-inspired position.

"You like to make a man wait," he grumbled, but he always greeted me this way. His face was sunburned, his sable hair escaping from its plait. The brown courier uniform was damp with sweat, and the sun glinted off the small accrual of achievement badges hanging from the fabric over his heart. He boasted he was the fastest courier in all of Valenia despite his rumored twenty-one years.

"This is the last time, Francis," I warned, before I could change my mind.

"Last time?" he echoed, but he was already grinning at me. I knew such a smile. It was what he used to get what he wanted. "Why?"

"Why!" I exclaimed, swatting a curious bumblebee. "Do you really need to ask?"

"If anything, this is the time I need you the most, mademoiselle," he responded, retrieving two small envelopes from the inner pocket of his shirt. "In eight days comes the summer solstice of fate."

"Exactly, Francis," I retorted, knowing he was only thinking of my arden-sister Sibylle. "Eight days and I still have much to master." My gaze rested on those envelopes he held; one was addressed to Sibylle, but the other was addressed to me. I recognized the handwriting as Grandpapa's; he had finally written. My heart fluttered to imagine what that letter might hold within its creases. . . .

"You are worried?"

My eyes snapped back up to Francis's face. "Of course I'm worried."

"You shouldn't be. I think you will do splendidly." For a

change, he wasn't teasing me. I heard the honesty in his voice, bright and sweet. I wanted to believe as he did, that in eight days, when my seventeenth summer marked my body, I would passion. I would be chosen.

"I don't think Master Cartier—"

"Who cares what your master thinks?" Francis interrupted with a nonchalant shrug. "You should only care about what *you* think."

I frowned as I pondered that, imagining how Master Cartier would respond to such a statement.

I had known Cartier for seven years. I had known Francis for seven months.

We had met last November; I had been sitting before the open window, waiting for Cartier to arrive for my afternoon lesson, when Francis passed by on the gravel path. I knew who he was, as did all of my arden-sisters; we often saw him delivering and receiving the mail to and from Magnalia House. But it was that first personal encounter when he asked if I would give a secret letter to Sibylle. Which I had, and so I had become entangled in their letter exchanges.

"I care about what Master Cartier thinks, because he is the one to claim me impassioned," I argued.

"Saints, Brienna," Francis replied as a butterfly flirted with his broad shoulder. "*You* should be the one to claim yourself impassioned, don't you think?"

That gave me a reason to pause. And Francis took advantage of it.

"By the way, I know the patrons the Dowager has invited to the solstice."

"What! How?"

But of course I knew how. He had delivered all the letters, seen the names and addresses. I narrowed my eyes at him just as his dimples crested his cheeks. Again, that smile. I could see perfectly well why Sibylle fancied him, but he was far too playful for me.

"Oh, just give me your blasted letters," I cried, reaching out to pluck them from his fingers.

He evaded me, expecting such a response.

"Don't you care to know who the patrons are?" he prodded. "For one of them is to be yours in eight days . . ."

I stared at him, but I saw beyond his boyish face and tall gangly frame. The garden was dry, yearning for rain, trembling in a slight breeze. "Just give me the letters."

"But if this is to be my last one to Sibylle, I need to rewrite some things."

"By Saint LeGrand, Francis, I do not have time for your games."

"Just grant me one more letter," he pleaded. "I don't know where Sibylle will be in a week's time."

I should have felt sympathy for him—oh, the heartache of loving a passion when you are not one. But I should have remained firm in my decision too. Let him mail her a letter, as he should have been doing all this time. Eventually I sighed and agreed, mostly because I wanted my grandfather's letter.

Francis finally relinquished the envelopes to me. The one from Grandpapa went straight to my pocket, but Francis's remained in my fingers.

"Why did you write in Dairine?" I asked, noting his sprawling script of address. He had written in the language of Maevana, the queen's realm of the north. *To Sibylle, my sun and my moon, my life and my light.* I almost burst into laughter, but caught it just in time.

"Don't read it!" he exclaimed, a blush mottling his already sunburned cheeks.

"It's on the face of the envelope, you fool. Of course I'm going to read it."

"Brienna . . ."

He reached toward me and I relished the chance to finally taunt him when I heard the library door open. I knew it was Cartier without having to look. For three years, I had spent nearly every day with him, and my soul had grown accustomed to how his presence quietly commanded a room.

Shoving Francis's letter into my pocket with Grandpapa's, I widened my eyes at him and began to close the window. He understood a moment too late; I caught his fingers on the sill. I clearly heard his yelp of pain, but I hoped the hasty shutting of the window concealed it from Cartier.

"Master Cartier," I greeted, breathless, and turned on my heel.

He was not looking at me. I watched as he set his leather satchel in a chair and pulled several volumes from it, laying the lesson books on the table.

"No open window today?" he asked. Still, he had not met my gaze. It might have been in my best interest, for I felt the way my face warmed, and it was not from the sunlight.

"The bumblebees are pesky today," I said, discreetly glancing over my shoulder to watch Francis hurry down the gravel path to the stables. I knew Magnalia's rules; I knew that we were not to create romantic entanglements while we were ardens. Or, more realistically, be caught doing such. I was foolish to transport Sibylle's and Francis's letters.

I looked forward to find Cartier was watching me.

"How are your Valenian Houses coming?" He motioned for me to come to the table.

"Very well, Master," I said, taking my usual seat.

"Let us begin by reciting the lineage of the House of Renaud, following the firstborn son," Cartier requested, sitting in the chair across from mine.

"The House of Renaud?" Saint's mercy, of course he would request the expansive royal lineage. The one I struggled to remember.

"It is the lineage of our king," he reminded with that unflinching gaze of his. I had seen that look of his many times. And so had my arden-sisters, who all complained about Cartier behind closed doors. He was the most handsome of Magnalia's arials, the instructor of knowledge, but he was also the strictest. My arden-sister Oriana claimed that a rock dwelled in his chest. And she had drawn a caricature of him, depicting him as a man emerging from stone.

"Brienna." My name rolled off his tongue as his fingers snapped impatiently.

"Forgive me, Master." I tried to summon the beginning of the royal line, but all I could think of was my grandfather's letter, waiting in my pocket. What had taken him so long to write?

"You understand that knowledge is the most demanding of the passions," Cartier spoke when my silence had extended far too long.

I met his gaze and wondered if he was trying to tactfully imply that I did not have the fortitude for this. Some mornings, I thought the same myself.

My first year at Magnalia, I had studied the passion of art. And since I had no artistic inclinations, the next year I squandered in music. But my singing was beyond redeeming and my fingers made instruments sound like caterwauling felines. My third year I had attempted dramatics until I discovered my stage fright could not be overcome. So my fourth year was given to wit, a very fretful year that I tried not to remember. Then, when I was fourteen, I had come to stand before Cartier and asked him to accept me as his arden, to make me into a mistress of knowledge in the three years I had remaining at Magnalia.

Yet I knew—and I suspected the other arials who instructed me knew this as well—that I was here because of something my grandfather had said those seven years ago. I was not here because I deserved it; I was not here because I was brimming with talent and capacity as were the other five ardens, who I loved as my true sisters. But perhaps that made me want it even more, to prove that passion was not just inherently gifted as some people believed, but that passion could be earned by anyone, commoner or noble, even if they did not have intrinsic skill.

"Maybe I should go back to our first lesson," Cartier said, breaking my reverie. "What is passion, Brienna?"

The passion catechism. It echoed in my thoughts, one of the first passages I had ever memorized, the one all the ardens knew by heart.

He was not patronizing me by asking this now, eight days from the summer solstice, but all the same, I felt a twinge of embarrassment until I bravely met his gaze and saw there was more to this question.

*What do you want, Brienna?* His eyes quietly asked as they held mine. *Why do you want to passion?*

And so I gave him the answer I had been taught to say, because I felt it would be safest.

"Passion is divided into five hearts," I began. "Passion is art, music, dramatics, wit, and knowledge. Passion is wholehearted devotion; it is fervor and agony; it is temper and zeal. It knows no bounds and marks a man or woman no matter their class or status, no matter their heritage. The passion becomes the man or woman, as the man or woman becomes the passion. It is a consummation of skill and flesh, a marker of devotion, dedication, and deed."

I couldn't tell if Cartier was disappointed with my learned answer. His face was always so carefully guarded—not once had I ever seen him smile; not once had I ever heard him laugh. Sometimes, I imagined he was not much older than me, but then I always reminded myself that my soul was young and Cartier's was not. He was far more experienced and educated, most likely the product of a childhood cured too soon. Whatever his age, he held a vast amount of knowledge in his mind.

"I was your last choice, Brienna," he finally said, disregarding my catechism. "You came to me three years ago and asked me to prepare you for your seventeenth summer solstice. Yet instead of having seven years to make you into a mistress of knowledge, I only had *three*."

I could hardly bear his reminders. It made me think of Ciri, his other arden of knowledge. Ciri soaked in knowledge with envious depth, but she had also had seven years of instruction. Of course I would feel inadequate when I compared myself to her.

"Forgive me for not being as Ciri," I said before I could swallow the sarcasm.

"Ciri began her training when she was ten," he reminded me calmly, preoccupied with a book on the table. He picked it up and passed through several pages that were dog-eared—something he fervently detested—and I watched him gently straighten the bends from the old paper.

"Do you regret my choice, Master?" What I really wanted to ask him was, *Why didn't you refuse me when I asked you to become my master three years ago? If three years was not enough time for me to passion, why didn't you tell me no?* But maybe my gaze expressed this, because he looked at me and then glanced languidly away, back to the books.

"I only have a few regrets, Brienna," he answered.

"What happens if I am not chosen by a patron at the solstice?" I asked, although I knew what became of young men and women who failed to reach impassionment. They were often broken and inadequate, neither here nor there, belonging to no group, shunned by passion and common folk alike. To dedicate years, time, and mind to passion and not accomplish it . . . one became marked as *inept*. No longer an arden, never quite a passion, and suddenly forced to merge back into society to become useful.

And as I waited for his answer, I thought of the simple metaphor Mistress Solene had taught me that first year in art (when she realized I was in no way artistic). Passion moved in phases. One began as an arden, which was like a caterpillar. This was the time to devour and master as much of the passion as one could manage. It could happen as short as two years if one was a prodigy, and as long as ten if one was a slower learner. Magnalia House was a seven year program and fairly rigorous compared to other Valenian passion Houses, which often went to eight or nine years of study. And then came impassionment—marked by a cloak and a title—and the phase of the patron, which was like the cocoon, a place to hold and mature the passion, to support her as she readied for the final phase. Which was the butterfly, when the passion could emerge out in the world on her own.

So I was thinking of butterflies when Cartier replied, "I suppose you will be the first of your kind, little arden."

I did not like his response, and my body sank deeper into the brocade of the chair, which smelled of old books and loneliness.

"If you believe you will fail, then you most likely will," he continued, his blue eyes sparking against my brown ones. Dust motes crossed the chasm between us, little swirling eddies in the air. "Do you agree?"

"Of course, Master."

"Your eyes never lie to me, Brienna. You should learn better composure when you fib."

"I shall take your advice to heart."

He tilted his head to the side, but his eyes still rested on mine. "Do you want to tell me what is truly on your mind?"

"The solstice is on my mind," I answered, a bit too quickly. It was a half-truth, but I could not imagine telling Cartier about my grandfather's letter, because then he might ask me to read it aloud.

"Well, this lesson has been futile," he said and rose to his feet.

I was disappointed that he was cutting it short—I needed every lesson he was willing to give me—yet I was relieved—I couldn't focus on anything with Grandpapa's letter resting in my pocket as a coal.

"Why don't you take the rest of the afternoon to study independently," he suggested, waving his hands to the books on the table. "Take these, if you want."

"Yes, thank you, Master Cartier." I stood as well, to grant him a curtsy. Without looking at him, I gathered the books and strode from the library, anxious.

I made my way out into the gardens, walking into the hedges so Cartier would not be able to see me from the library windows. The sky above was rippled and gray, warning of a storm, so I sat on the first bench I came across and set his books carefully to the side.

I retrieved my grandfather's letter and held it before me, his crooked penmanship making my name look like a grimace over the parchment. And then I broke his red wax seal, my hands trembling as I unfolded the letter.

June 7, 1566
My Dearest Brienna,

Forgive me for taking so long to respond. I fear the pain in my hands has worsened, and the physician has instructed me to keep my writings brief, or else procure a scribe. I must say that I am very proud of you, that your mother—my sweet Rosalie—would be proud as well to know you are mere days away from becoming impassioned. Please write to me after the solstice and tell me the patron you choose.

To answer your question . . . I fear you will be familiar with my response. Your father's name is not worthy to note. Your mother was swayed by his handsome face and saccharine words, and I fear it would only harm you to learn his name. Yes, you have dual citizenship, which means you are part Maevan. But I do not want you to seek him out. Rest assured that you would find the same faults in him as I do. And no, my dear, he has not inquired after you. Not once has he sought for you. You must remember that you are illegitimate, and most men flee when they hear that word.

Remember that you are indeed loved, and that I stand in place of your father.

Love, Grandpapa

I crumpled the letter in my hand, my fingers as white as the paper, my eyes swarming with tears. It was folly to cry over such a letter, to once more be denied the name of the man who was my father. And it had taken me weeks to muster the courage to write that letter and ask again.

I decided that it would be the final time I asked. The name did not matter.

If my mother had lived, what would she say about him? Would she have married him? Or perhaps he was already married, and that was why my grandfather was so mortified by the mere thought of my father. A shameful extramarital affair between a Valenian woman and a Maevan man.

Ah, my mother. Sometimes, I thought I could remember the musical cadence of her voice, that I could remember how it felt to be held in her arms, the scent of her. Lavender and clover, sunshine and roses. She died from the sweating sickness when I was three, and Cartier had once told me that it was rare for one to remember memories that early. So perhaps it was all in my mind, what I wanted to remember of her?

Why did it hurt, then, to think of one I didn't truly know?

Shoving the letter into my pocket, I leaned back and felt the scalloped leaves of the hedge stroke my hair, as if the plant were trying to comfort me. I should not be dwelling on fragments of my past, pieces that did not matter. I needed to think of what was to come in eight days, when the solstice arrived, when I should master my passion and finally receive my cloak.

I needed to be reading Cartier's books, pressing the words into my memory.

But before I could so much as twitch my fingers toward the pages, I heard a soft tread on the grass, and Oriana appeared on the path.

"Brienna!" she greeted, her black hair captured in a tangled braid to her waist. Her brown skin and arden dress were speckled with paint from the endless hours she spent in the art studio. And while her dress told of enchanting creations of color, mine was boringly clean and wrinkled. All six of Magnalia's ardens wore those drab gray dresses, and we unanimously loathed them, with their high collars and long plain sleeves and chaste fit. To shed them soon would feel passionate, indeed.

"What are you up to?" my arden-sister asked, closing the gap between us. "Has Master Cartier driven you to frustration yet?"

"No, I think it's the other way around this time." I stood and took the books in one hand and looped my other arm with Oriana's. We walked beside each other, Oriana petite and slender compared to my height and long legs. I had to slow down to remain in stride with her. "How are your final paintings coming?"

She snorted and gave me a wry smile as she plucked a rose from a bush. "They are coming along, I suppose."

"Have you picked which ones to display at the solstice?"

"Yes, actually." She began to tell me which paintings she had chosen to display for the patrons, and I watched as she nervously twirled the rose.

"Don't worry," I said and eased her to a stop so we could look upon each other face-to-face. In the distance, thunder rumbled, the air swelling with the scent of rain. "Your paintings are exquisite. And I can already see it."

"See what?" Oriana gently tucked the rose behind my ear.

"That the patrons will fight over you. You will bring the highest price."

"Poppies, no! I do not have the charm of Abree, or the beauty of Sibylle, or the sweetness of Merei, or the brains of you and Ciri."

"But your art creates a window into another world," I said, smiling at her. "That is a true gift, to help others see the world in a different way."

"Since when did you become a poet, my friend?"

I laughed, but a clap of thunder swallowed the sound. As soon as the storm's complaint quieted, Oriana said, "So, I have a confession." She pulled me back along the path as the first drops of rain began to fall, and I followed, mystified, because Oriana was the one arden who never broke the rules.

"And . . ." I prompted.

"I knew you were here in the gardens, and I came to ask you something. You remember how I drew portraits of the other girls? So I can have ways to remember each of you after we part ways next week?" Oriana glanced at me, her amber eyes gleaming in anticipation.

I tried not to groan. "Ori, I cannot sit still that long."

"Abree managed it. And you know she is constantly in motion. And what do you even mean, *you cannot sit still that long*? You sit all day long with Ciri and Master Cartier, reading book after book!"

I pressed a smile to my lips. For an entire year, she had asked to draw me, and I had simply been too overcome with my studies to have the leisure time for something like a portrait. I had lessons with Cartier and Ciri in the mornings, but then come the afternoon, I typically had a private lesson with Cartier, because I was still struggling to master everything I should. And while I sat through grueling lessons and watched the sunlight melt across the floor, my arden-sisters had the afternoons to themselves; many days I had listened to their laughter and gaiety fill the house while I flogged my memory beneath Cartier's scrutiny.

"I don't know." I hesitated, shifting the books in my arms. "I am supposed to be studying."

We rounded the hedge's corner only to plow into Abree.

"Did you convince her?" Abree asked Oriana, and I realized that this was an ambush. "And don't look at us like that, Brienna."

"Like what?" I countered. "You both know that if I want to receive my cloak and leave with a patron in eight days, I need to spend every minute—"

"Memorizing boring lineages, yes, we know," Abree interrupted. Her thick auburn hair sat free upon her shoulders, a few stray leaves caught within the curls as if she had been crawling through the bushes and brambles. She was known to practice her lines outside with Master Xavier, and several times I had watched her through the library windows as she tossed and turned on the grass and crushed berries to her bodice as fake blood, projecting her lines to the clouds. I saw evidence of mud on her arden skirts now, the stain of berries, and knew she had been in the throes of rehearsal.

"Please, Brienna," Oriana pleaded. "I have drawn everyone else's but yours. . . ."

"And you will *want* her to draw it, especially after you see the props I found for you," Abree said, wickedly smiling down at me. She was the tallest of us, taller than me by an entire handbreadth.

"Props!" I cried. "Now, listen, I do not—" But the thunder came again, drowning out my weak protests, and before I could stop her, Oriana stole the books from my hands.

"I'll go ahead and get things set up," Oriana said, taking three eager steps away from me, as if my mind could not be changed once she got out of earshot. "Abree, bring her to the studio."

"Yes, Milady," Abree returned with a playful bow.

I watched as Oriana dashed across the lawn, in through the back doors.

"Oh, come now, Brienna," Abree said, the rain fully breaking through the clouds, dappling our dresses. "You need to enjoy these final days."

"I cannot enjoy them if I worry that I will become inept." I began to walk toward the house, yanking the ribbon from my braid to let my long hair unwind about me, running my fingers anxiously through it.

"You are *not* going to become inept!" But there was a pause, which was followed by, "Does Master Cartier think you will?"

I was halfway through the lawn, drenched and overwhelmed with the impending expectations when Abree caught up to me, grabbed my arm, and spun me about. "Please, Brienna. Do the portrait for me, for Oriana."

I sighed, but a small smile was beginning to touch the corners of my lips. "Very well. But it cannot take all day."

"You really will be excited to see the props I found!" Abree insisted breathlessly, dragging me across the remaining strip of lawn.

"How long do you think it will take?" I panted as we opened the doors and stepped into the shadows of the back hall, soaked and shivering.

"Not long," Abree replied. "Oh! Remember how you were helping me plot the second half of my play? The one where Lady Pumpernickel gets thrown in the dungeon for stealing the diadem?"

"*Mm-hmm.*" Even though I was no longer studying dramatics, Abree continued to solicit my help when it came to plotting her plays. "You don't know how to get her out of the dungeon, do you?"

She sheepishly blushed. "No. And before you say it . . . I don't want to kill her off."

I couldn't help but laugh. "That was years ago, Abree."

She was referring to the time when I had been an arden of dramatics and we had both written a skit for Master Xavier. While Abree had authored a comical scene of two sisters fighting over the same beau, I had penned a bloody tragedy of a daughter stealing her father's throne. I killed off all the characters save for one by the end, and Master Xavier had obviously been shocked by my dark plotting.

"If you do not wish to kill her," I said as we began to walk down the hall, "then make her find a secret door behind a skeleton, or have a guard shift his allegiance and help her out, but only at a twisted, unexpected cost."

"Ah, a secret door!" Abree cried, linking her arm with mine. "You plot like a fiend, Bri! I wish I schemed like you." When she smiled down at me, I felt a drop of remorse, that I had been too frightened of the stage to become a mistress of dramatics.

Abree must have felt the same, for she tightened her hold on me and murmured, "You know, it's not too late. You can write a two act play in eight days, and impress Master Xavier, and—"

"Abree." I playfully hushed her.

"Is this how two of Magnalia's ardens behave a week before their solstice of fate?" The voice startled us. Abree and I stopped in the hall, surprised to see Mistress Therese, the arial of wit, standing with her arms crossed in blunt disapproval. She looked down her thin, pointed nose at us with eyebrows raised, disgusted by our drenched appearance. "You act as if you are children, not women about to gain their cloaks."

"Much apologies, Mistress Therese," I murmured, giving her a deep curtsy of respect. Abree mimicked me, although her curtsy was quite careless.

"Tidy up right away, before Madame sees you."

Abree and I tripped over each other in our haste to get away from her. We stumbled down the corridor into the foyer, to the mouth of the stairs.

"Now, *that* is a demon in the flesh," Abree whispered, far too loudly, as she flew up the stairs.

"Abree!" I chided, slipping on my hem just as I heard Cartier behind me.

"Brienna?"

I caught my fall on the balustrade. My balance restored, I whirled on the stair to look down at him. He stood in the foyer, his stark white tunic belted at his waist, his gray breeches nearly the same shade as my dress. He was fastening his passion cloak about his neck, preparing to depart in the rain.

"Master?"

"I assume you will want another private lesson Monday after our morning lecture with Ciri?" He stared up at me, waiting for the answer he knew I would give.

I felt my hand slide on the railing. My hair was uncommonly loose, falling about me in wild, brown tangles, my dress was drenched, my hem dripped a quiet song over the marble. I knew I must look completely undone to him, that I looked nothing like a Valenian woman on the verge of passioning, that I looked nothing like the scholar he was trying to mold. And yet I raised my chin and replied, "Yes, thank you, Master Cartier."

"Perhaps there will be no letter to distract you next time?" he asked, and my eyes widened as I continued to stare down at him, trying to read beyond the steady composure of his face.

He could punish me for exchanging Francis's and Sibylle's letters. He could impart discipline, because I had broken a rule. And so I waited, waited to see what he would require of me.

But then the left corner of his lips moved, too subtle to be a genuine smile—although I liked to imagine it might have been—as he bestowed a curt bow of farewell. I watched him pass through the doors and melt into the storm, wondering if he was being merciful or playful, desiring that he would stay, relieved that he had departed.

I continued my way up the stairs, leaving a trail of rain, and wondered . . . wondered how Cartier always seemed to make me want two conflicting things at once.

## —◄ TWO ►—

# A MAEVAN PORTRAIT

The Art Studio was a chamber I had avoided since my first failed year at Magnalia. But as I tentatively entered it that rainy afternoon, my wet hair wound in a bun, I was reminded of the good memories that room had hosted for me. I remembered the mornings I spent sitting beside Oriana as we sketched beneath the careful instruction of Mistress Solene. I remembered the first time I tried to paint, the first time I tried to illuminate a page, the first time I attempted an etching. And then came the darker moments that still sat in my mind as a bruise, such as when I realized my art lay flat on the page while Oriana's breathed and came to life. Or the day Mistress Solene had pulled me aside and said gently, *Perhaps you should try music, Brienna.*

"You're here!"

I glanced across the room to see Oriana readying a place for me, a new streak of red paint on her cheek. This room had always been overwhelming with clutter and mess, but I knew it was because Oriana and Mistress Solene made their own paints. The longest table in the room was completely covered with jars of lead and pigments, crucibles and earthenware bowls, pitchers of water, chalkstone, stacks of vellum and parchment, a carton of eggs, a large bowl of ground chalk. It smelled of turpentine, rosemary, and of the green weed they boiled to mysteriously render pink paint.

Carefully, I wended my way around the paint table, around chairs and cartons and easels. Oriana had set a stool beside the wall of windows, a place for me to sit in the stormy light while she drew.

"Should I be concerned about these . . . *props* Abree is so excited about?" I asked.

Oriana was just about to respond when Ciri entered the chamber.

"I found it. This is what you wanted, right, Oriana?" Ciri asked, leafing through the pages of a book she held. She almost tripped over an easel as she walked to our corner, passing the book to Oriana as she looked at me. "You look tired, Brienna. Is Master Cartier pushing you too hard?"

But now I did not have time to respond, for Oriana let out a cry of delight, which drew my eyes to the page she was admiring.

"This is perfect, Ciri!"

"Wait a moment," I said, reaching for the book. I plucked it from Oriana's hands. "This is one of Master Cartier's Maevan history books." My eyes rushed over the illustration, my breath hanging in my chest. It was a gorgeous illustration of a Maevan queen. I recognized her because Cartier had taught us the history of Maevana. This was Liadan Kavanagh, the first queen of Maevana. Which also meant she had possessed magic.

She stood tall and proud, a crown of woven silver and budding diamonds resting on her brow as a wreath of stars, her long brown hair flowing loose and wild about her, blue dye that Maevans called "woad" streaked across her face. Hanging from her neck was a stone the size of a fist—the legendary Stone of Eventide. She wore armor fashioned like dragon scales—they gleamed with gold and blood—and a long sword was sheathed at her side as she stood with one hand on her hip, the other holding a spear.

"It makes you long for those days, doesn't it?" Ciri asked with a sigh, peering over my shoulder. "The days when the queens ruled the north."

"Now is not the time for a history lesson," Oriana said, gently easing the book away from me.

"You don't intend to draw me as that?" I asked, my heart beginning to pound. "Ori . . . that would be presumptuous."

"No, it wouldn't," Ciri retorted. She loved to argue. "You are part Maevan, Brienna. Who is to say you have not descended from queens?"

My mouth fell open to protest, but Abree walked in bearing an armload of props.

"Here they are," she announced and dropped them at our feet.

I watched, stunned, as Ciri and Oriana sifted through pieces of cheap armor, a dull sword, a dark blue cloak the color of midnight. They were props from the theater, no doubt smuggled from Master Xavier's stash in the dramatics wardrobe.

"All right, Brienna," Oriana said, straightening with the breastplate in her hands. "Please let me draw you as a Maevan warrior."

They all three waited, Oriana with the armor, Abree with the sword, Ciri with the cloak. They looked at me, expectant and hopeful. And I found that my heart had quieted, thrilled by the thought, my Maevan blood stirring.

"Very well. But this cannot take all day," I insisted, and Abree victoriously whooped and Oriana smiled and Ciri rolled her eyes.

I stood still and patient as they dressed me. The portrait would only be from the waist up, so it did not matter that I still wore my arden dress. The breastplate enclosed about my chest, vambraces about my forearms. A blue cloak was draped about my shoulders, which made my stomach clench as I inevitably thought of my passion cloak, and Ciri must have read my mind.

She stood and liberated my hair from its bun, braided a small plait, and said, "I told Abree to choose a blue cloak. You should wear your color. *Our* color." Ciri stepped back, pleased with how she had arranged my hair.

When an arden became impassioned, their master or mistress would present them with a cloak. The color of the cloak depended on the passion. Art received a red cloak, dramatics black, music purple, wit green, knowledge blue. But it wasn't a mere marker of achievement and equality, that the arden was now on the same level as their master or mistress. It was a unique commemoration, a symbol of the relationship between the master and the arden.

But before my thoughts could become too entangled with cloaks, Sibylle rushed into the studio, drenched from the rain. A jubilant smile was on her face as she held up a crown of white flowers. "Here!" she cried, slinging water and attracting our attention. "This is the most starlike crown I could make before the rain came!"

Indeed, all five of my arden-sisters must have been in on this portrait ambush. But Merei, my roommate, was the only one missing, and I felt her absence like a shadow had fallen upon the chamber.

"Where is Merei?" I inquired as Sibylle brought her flower crown to me.

Sibylle, graceful, buxom, and coy, set the crown upon my brow. "You look like you could take off a man's head," she said, her rosebud lips opening with a wide, satisfied smile.

"Can't you hear her?" Abree responded to my inquiry, and held up a finger. We all fell silent, and over the tickling of rain on the windowpanes, we could hear the faint, determined song of a violin. "Merei said she is furiously working on some new composition, but she'll come as soon as she can."

"Now, Brienna, take up the sword and sit on the stool," Oriana requested as she held a shell of blue paint.

I watched her, warily, as I eased myself to the stool, the sword awkwardly blooming from my grip. With my hand coaxed to my right thigh, the sword crossed my chest, its dull point near my left ear. The armor was pliant but still felt odd on my body, like a set of unfamiliar arms had come about my chest, embracing me.

"Ciri, will you hold the illustration up next to Brienna's face? I want to make sure I do this perfectly." Oriana waved Ciri closer.

"Do what perfectly?" I stammered.

"The woad. Hold still, Bri."

I had no choice; I held myself still as Oriana's eyes flitted from the illustration to my face, back to the illustration. I watched as she dipped her fingertips into her blue paint, and then closed my eyes as she dragged her fingers diagonally across my face, from my brow to my chin, and felt as if she was opening up some secret part of me. A place that was supposed to lie hidden and quiet was waking.

"You can open your eyes."

My eyes fluttered open, my gaze anxiously meeting my sisters' as they looked me over with pride and approval.

"I think we are ready." Oriana reached for a rag to wipe the paint from her fingers.

"But what about that stone?" Sibylle asked as she braided her honey-brown hair away from her eyes.

"What stone?" Abree frowned, upset that she'd missed a prop.

"That stone about the queen's neck."

"The evening stone, I think," Ciri said, examining the illustration.

"No, that would be the Stone of Eventide," I corrected.

Ciri's milk white face blushed—she hated to be corrected—but she cleared her throat. "Ah yes. Of course you would know Maevan history better, Brienna. You have a reason to listen when Master Cartier drones on and on about it."

Oriana dragged a second stool before mine, her parchment and pencil ready. "Try to hold still, Brienna."

I nodded, feeling the blue paint begin to dry on my face.

"I wish I held dual citizenship," Abree murmured, stretching her arms. "Are you ever going to cross the channel and see Maevana? Because you absolutely should, Brienna. And take me with you."

"Perhaps one day," I said as Oriana began to sketch upon her paper. "And I would love for you to come with me, Abree."

"My father says Maevana is very, *very* different from Valenia," Ciri remarked, and I could hear the pinch in her voice, like she was still upset that I had corrected her. She set Cartier's book down and leaned against a table, her gaze wandering back to mine. Her blond hair looked like moonlight spilling over her shoulder. "My father used to visit once a year, in the fall, when some of the Maevan lords opened their castles for us Valenians to come stay for the hunt of the white hart. My father enjoyed it whenever he went, said there was always good ale and food, epic stories and entertainment, but of course would never let me go with him. He claimed that the land was too wild, too dangerous for a Valenian girl like me."

Sibylle snorted, unbuttoning the high collar of her dress to rub her neck. "Don't all fathers say such, if only to leave their daughters 'safe' at home?"

"Well, you know what they say about Maevan men," I said, helplessly quoting Grandpapa.

"What?" Sibylle was quick to demand, her interest suddenly burning as stars in her hazel eyes. I forgot that Francis's letter to her was still in my wet arden dress, which I had left discarded on the floor of my room. That poor letter was most likely drenched through and smeared.

"They are smooth-talking, skilled, dastardly lovers," I said, using my best imitation of Grandpapa's scratchy voice.

Sibylle burst into laughter—she was the most confident with the opposite sex—and Abree covered her mouth, like she didn't know if she should be embarrassed or not. Ciri made no response, although I could tell she was trying not to smile.

"That's enough talk," Oriana playfully scolded, waving her pencil at me. "If one of the mistresses happened to walk by and hear that, you'd be given kitchen duty for the final week, Brienna."

"They would *have* to be skilled, dastardly lovers to be worthy of women who look like that!" Sibylle continued, pointing to the illustration of the queen. "By the saints, whatever happened to Maevana? Why is there now a king on her throne?"

I exchanged a glance with Ciri. We had both had this lesson, two years ago. It was a long, tangled story.

"You would have to ask Master Cartier," Ciri finally responded with a shrug. "He could tell you, as he knows the entire history of every land that ever was."

"How cumbersome," Abree lamented.

Ciri's gaze sharpened. "You do recall, Abree, that Brienna and

I are about to become passions of knowledge." She was offended, yet again.

Abree took a step back. "Pardon, Ciri. Of course, I meant to say how enthralled I am by your capacity to hold so much knowledge."

Ciri snorted, still not appeased, but thankfully left it at that as she looked back at me.

"Are you ever going to meet your father, Bri?" Sibylle asked.

"No, I do not think so," I answered honestly. It was ironic to me that on the day I vowed to never inquire of him again I would be dressed as a Maevan queen.

"That is very sad," Abree commented.

Of course it would be sad to her, to all my sisters. They all came from noble families, from fathers and mothers who were in some measure involved in their lives.

So I claimed, "It truly doesn't matter to me."

A lull settled in the room. I listened to the rain, to Merei's distant music mellowing the corridor, to the scratch of Oriana's pencil as she replicated me on parchment.

"Well," Sibylle said brightly, to smooth away the wrinkles of discomfort. She was an arden of wit, and was skilled to handle any manner of conversation. "You should see the portrait Oriana drew of me, Brienna. It is the exact opposite of yours." She retrieved it from Oriana's portfolio, held it up so I could get a good glimpse of it.

Sibylle had been staged as the perfect Valenian noblewoman. I gazed, surprised at all the props Abree had scrounged for this one. Sibylle had worn a daring, low-cut red dress studded with pearls, a necklace of cheap jewels, and a voluptuous white wig. She even had a perfect star mole on her cheek, the marker of feminine nobility. She was beautifully polished, Valenia incarnate. She was etiquette, poise, grace.

And then here was mine, the portrait of a queen who wielded magic and wore blue woad, who lived in armor, whose constant companion was not a man but a sword and a stone.

It was the stark difference between Maevana and Valenia, two countries that I was broken between. I wanted to feel comfortable in the fancy dress and the star mole, but I also wanted to find my heritage in the armor and the woad. I wanted to wield passion, but I also wanted to know how to hold a sword.

"You should hang Brienna's and Sibylle's portraits side by side," Abree suggested to Oriana. "They can teach future ardens a good history lesson."

"Yes," Ciri concurred. "A lesson as to who you should never offend."

"If you offend a Valenian, you lose your reputation," Sibylle chirped, picking dirt from beneath her nails. "But if you offend a Maevan . . . then you lose your head."

# → THREE ←

# CHEQUES AND MARQUES

It took Oriana another hour to complete my sketch. She didn't dare ask me to linger any longer as she began to color it; she could sense I was anxious to shed the costume and resume my studies. I handed the cloak, the armor, the flower crown, and the sword back to Abree and left my sisters' laughter and conversation behind in the studio, seeking out the quiet shadows of Merei's and my room.

Traditionally, Magnalia's arden of music was the one student privileged with a private bedchamber, to accommodate the instruments. The other four ardens were paired as roommates. But since the Dowager had done the unexpected and accepted me as her sixth student, the arden of music's bedchamber had become a shared space.

As I swung the door open, the smell of parchment and books greeted me as loyal friends. Merei and I were messy, but I would blame it upon our passions. She had reams of music scattered in all places. I once found a bundle of music in her quilts, and she claimed she had fallen asleep with it in hand. She told me she could hear the music in her head when she silently read the notes; such was the depth of her passion.

As for my part, I was books and journals and loose papers. Shelves were carved in the wall next to my bed, crowded with volumes I had brought up from the library. Cartier's books also had several shelves, and as I looked upon their soft- and hard-bound spines, I wondered what it would feel like to return all of them back to his possession. And realized that I owned not one book.

I bent to retrieve my discarded dress on the floor, still drenched, and found Francis's letter. It was smeared into unintelligible ink.

"Did I miss it?" Merei declared from the doorway.

I turned to look at her standing with her violin tucked beneath her arm, the bow extending from her long fingers, the storm spilling lavender light over her brown complexion, over her rosin-smeared dress.

"Saint LeGrand, *what* did they do to your face?" She moved forward, wide-eyed with intrigue.

My fingers traced my profile, feeling the cracked trail of blue paint. I had forgotten all about that. "If you had been there, this would never have happened," I teased her.

She set her instrument aside and then took my chin in her fingers, admiring Oriana's handiwork. "Well, let me guess. They dressed you up as a Maevan queen fresh off the battlefield."

"Do I look *that* Maevan?"

Merei led me over to our commode, where a pitcher of water sat before the mullioned window. I tucked Francis's letter back in my pocket as she poured water into a waiting porcelain bowl and took a washcloth. "No, you look and act very Valenian. Didn't your grandfather claim you were the image of your mother?"

"Yes, but he could be lying."

Merei's dark eyes quietly scolded me for my lack of faith. And then she began to wipe away the paint with the washcloth.

"How are your lessons coming, Bri?"

This was the one question we continued to ask each other, over and over, as the solstice grew closer. I groaned and shut my eyes as she began to vigorously scrub. "I don't know."

"How can you not know?" She paused in her washings until I relented to open my eyes again. She gazed at me with an expression trapped somewhere between alarm and confusion. "There are only two more official days of lessons."

"As I know. But do you want to know what Master Cartier asked me today? He asked, 'What is passion?' as if I were ten and not seventeen." I sighed and took the washcloth from her, dunking it back into the water.

I had told Merei my suspicions. I had told her how I believed the Dowager had accepted me for some mysterious reason, not because I held potential. And Merei had witnessed firsthand that second year I had struggled in music. She had sat beside me and tried to help coach me when Mistress Evelina seemed overwhelmed by how poorly I played. Never had a violin sounded like it wanted to die.

"Why didn't he refuse me when I asked him to take me on as his arden?" I continued, scrubbing my face. "He should have said that three years was not enough time for me to master this. And if I had been smart, I should have chosen knowledge from the very beginning, when I was ten and had plenty of time to learn all these wretched lineages." The blue paint was not coming off. I tossed the washcloth aside, feeling like I had peeled half of my face away, revealing the true bones of who I was: inept.

"Need I remind you, Bri, that Master Cartier hardly makes mistakes?"

I cast my gaze to the window, watching the rain streak as tears on the glass, knowing that she was right.

"Need I remind you that Master Cartier would not have accepted you as his arden if he thought for one moment that you could not passion?" She took my hand, to draw my attention back to her. She smiled, half of her curly black hair caught by a ribbon, the rest loose about her shoulders. "If Master Cartier believes you can passion in three years, then you can. And so you will."

I squeezed her fingers in silent gratitude. And now it was my turn to ask after her passion. "How is your latest composition coming? I heard a bit from the Art Studio. . . ."

Merei dropped my fingers and groaned. I knew from the sound that she felt as I did . . . overwhelmed and worried. She turned and walked back to her bed and sat, propping her chin in her palm.

"It's horrible, Bri."

"It sounded lovely to me," I said, remembering how her music had trickled down the halls.

"It's horrible," she insisted. "Mistress Evelina wants me to have it ready in time for the solstice. I don't think it's possible. . . ."

I knew from my seven years of rooming with Merei that she was a perfectionist when it came to her music. Every note had to be exquisitely placed, every song must be played with fervor and rapture. If her fingers or bow so much as let a screech slip over the strings, she was irritated by her performance.

"Do you know what this means?" I asked, smiling as I reached for the elaborately carved box on one of her shelves.

Merei lay back on her bed, overly dramatic as she claimed, "I am too tired to play."

"We have a pact," I reminded her as I opened the box on our communal table, drawing forth the checkered board and the marble pawns.

Her father had sent this game of cheques and marques for both of us, a game Merei adored and had grown up playing on the island of Bascune. As the years had gone by at Magnalia, as Merei and I had become progressively more preoccupied with our impassionment, we hardly had time to play anymore. Save for the evenings when we were both overwhelmed and worried. We had vowed to bring forth the game then, as a way to remind ourselves that the impending solstice wasn't everything.

"All right." She relented, as I knew she would. She rose from the bed and walked to our table, gathering a few loose sheets of music and setting them aside.

We sat across from each other, our colorful pawns gleaming as I lit the candles and Merei flipped a ducat to see who had the first move.

"You start, Bri," she said.

I stared at my pawns, lined up obediently. Cheques and marques was a game of strategy, the goal being to remove all three of the opponent's red pawns. I decided to begin on the edge, shifting my yellow pawn forward to the first marque.

We always started the game quietly, granting ourselves time to adjust to moving in rhythm with each other. I tended to make the bold moves, Merei the cautious moves. Our pawns were scattered all over the board when Merei broke our silence by asking, "Have you heard from your grandfather?"

I claimed her first red pawn, one she had defiantly floating toward our line of impact. "Yes. I'll have to let you read it later."

She began to shift toward one of my red pieces. "Did he tell you a name?"

"No name. The usual response."

"That your father is unworthy to note?"

"Yes, those very words." I watched as she swiped one of my red pawns. She also had me blocked with her yellow pieces. I began to weave between them. . . . "What about your father?"

"He wrote a few days ago. He says hello, and that he hopes you come with me to visit him after the solstice."

I watched her jump over my blue pawns, landing in the middle of my territory. A bold move from her always baffled me; she tended to play so carefully. I retaliated, mirroring her, and asked,

"Would you rather have a very handsome patron who had bad breath, or a very ugly patron who always smelled good?"

Merei laughed. "Nice try, Bri. I am not that easily distracted."

"I am not distracting you," I insisted, trying to hide a smile. "These are very important things to think about."

"Mm-hmm." She swiped my second red pawn. "I would have to go with the ugly patron, then."

"Same," I responded, trying to break through yet another ring of her yellow pawns.

"If we are going to play this game, then you have to answer a question." She moved her black pawn to an odd marque. "Would you rather fall in love with your master or your patron?"

"Both are horrible, foolish choices," I muttered.

"You must answer."

I stared at the board, trying to see a way out of the knot she had me in. "Fine, then. I would rather fall in love with my patron." My face warmed, but I kept my eyes on the marques. I was almost to her second red pawn. . . .

"I have to say I would go with the master."

I glanced up, surprised at her answer. She smiled; her eyes locked with mine as she effortlessly claimed my final red pawn.

"You always beat me at this game," I lamented.

"You lose because you never protect your side, Bri. It's your one weakness. I beat you with an oblique move." She waggled my defeated red pawn. "Shall we play again?"

I made a noise of objection, but she knew that I wanted to. We reset our pawns on their origin marques, and then I waited for Merei to move first.

We asked no questions this round; I was too focused on trying to outwit her, by employing this oblique tactic she always
championed me with. So when she cleared her throat, I looked up,
startled to see she was about to claim my last red pawn.

"Now," Merei said. "On to a very important question."

"And what is that?"

She paused, trying to hold back her laughter as she defeated
me yet again. "What are you going to tell Master Cartier when he
asks why your face is stained blue?"

## → FOUR ←

# THE THREE BRANCHES

I was the first one to reach the library Monday morning, waiting for Ciri and Cartier to arrive for the lesson. Despite Merei's faithful scrubbing and a dose of Oriana's turpentine, I still had a faint shadow of blue paint on my face. So I decided to leave my hair unbound and drawn to the front; it spilled down my chest, long and ornery, the color of mahogany, but it felt like a shield for me to hide behind, to guard my face and the lingering memory of war paint.

Ciri arrived next and took her seat across from me, on the other side of our table. "I can still see the paint," she murmured. "But maybe he won't notice."

Master Cartier entered not two breaths after that. I pretended to pick at my nails as he set his books down on the table, my hair falling forward even more. I realized my mistake only when I felt his eyes rest on me, his hands go still. Of course he would notice my hair was loose. I always bound it in a braid for lessons, to keep it out of my eyes.

I heard him walk about the table, to Ciri's side, so he could get a full look at me.

"Brienna?"

I silently swore. And then relented to lift my face and meet his gaze. "Master?"

"May I ask why . . . it looks as if you painted half of your face blue?"

My eyes shifted to Ciri, who was pressing her lips together, trying not to giggle.

"You may ask, Master," I responded, kicking Ciri beneath the table. "I sat for a portrait. Oriana decided to, ah, paint my face."

"It was because we dressed her as a Maevan queen, Master," Ciri rushed to explain, and then I watched, mortified, as she leafed through the history book to find the illustration of Liadan Kavanagh. "Here, this is the one."

Cartier turned the book around so he could get a closer look at it. He stared at Liadan Kavanagh, and then he stared at me. I couldn't tell what he was thinking, if he thought this was humorous or offensive—if he thought I was bold or childish.

He gently pushed the book back to Ciri and said, "Tell me about Liadan Kavanagh, then."

"What about her?" Ciri was quick to respond, always eager to answer everything before me.

"Who was she?"

"The first queen of Maevana."

"And how did she become queen?" He walked about the table, his voice settling into that deep, rich cadence that made me think of a summer night crowded with stars. It was the sort of voice a storyteller might harbor.

"Well, she belonged to the Kavanagh clan," Ciri answered.

"And why does that matter?"

Ciri hesitated. Did she truly not remember? I was a bit amazed by this, by watching the frown mar her brow, her blue eyes sweeping the table before us as if the answers were in the marks of the wood. She never forgot the things Cartier told her.

"Brienna?" Cartier prompted me when she took too long.

"Because the Kavanaghs are the descendants of dragons," I replied. "They hold magic in their blood."

"But the other thirteen Houses of Maevana do not?" he questioned, even though he knew the answer. This was how he taught Ciri and me; he entered into conversations with us, asked us to tell the little pieces of history that he had once fed us.

"No," I said. "The other Houses do not possess magic. Just the Kavanaghs."

"But why a *queen*, then, and not a king?" He stopped his walking before the great map on the wall, his finger brushing the four countries that composed our hemisphere: the island of Maevana to the north, Grimhildor to the far frozen west, Valenia and

Bandecca to the south, the ocean breaking them into three pieces of mountainous lands. As he touched them, he said, "Valenia has a king. Bandecca has a king. Grimhildor has a king. All the countries in our realm do. Why, then, would Maevana—a warrior, clannish land—build its throne on a queen?"

I smiled, letting my fingers trace a mark in the wood. "Because the Kavanagh women are naturally stronger in magic than their men." And I thought of that glorious illustration of Liadan Kavanagh; I remembered her proud stance, the blue woad on her skin and the blood on her armor, the silver crown of diamonds on her brow. Might it be possible that I had descended from one such as her?

"You are right, Brienna," Cartier said. "Magic always flows stronger in woman than in man. Sometimes I think the same of passion, until I am reminded that passion is in no way magical or inherited. Because some of us choose our passion"—and here he looked at me—"and sometimes, the passion chooses us"—and here he looked to Ciri. It was only then that I realized how different Ciri and I were, how flexible Cartier had to be in his teachings, to ensure his two ardens learned by the methods that best suited them. I preferred stories; Ciri preferred facts.

"So." He resumed his slow walk about the library. "You have told me that Liadan Kavanagh held magic. But why was she appointed queen, then, three hundred years ago?"

"Because of the Hilds," Ciri hastened to say, rejoining the conversation. "The raiders of Grimhildor plagued the Maevan coast."

"Yes," I added. "Little did the raiders know that they didn't scatter or intimidate the fourteen clans of Maevana. Rather, the Hilds' violence united them beneath a queen."

"And Liadan was chosen because . . ." Cartier prodded.

"Because she held magic," Ciri said.

"Because she united the clans," I responded. "It wasn't just because Liadan wielded the magic of her ancestors. It was because she was a warrior, a leader, and she brought her people together as one."

Cartier stopped his pacing. His hands were linked behind his back, but his eyes found mine through the morning sunshine and shadows. For a moment, one slender wondrous moment, he almost smiled at me.

"Well said, Brienna."

"But Master Cartier," Ciri protested. "Both of you just said that she was chosen because of the magic."

Any hint of a smile was gone as his eyes moved from me to her. "She held powerful magic, yes, but need I remind you of how the Kavanaghs' magic behaved in battle?"

"It went astray," I said softly, but Cartier and Ciri heard me. "Magic gained a will of its own during battle and bloodshed. It turned on the Kavanaghs; it corrupted their minds, their motivations."

"So what did Liadan do?" Cartier asked me.

"She did not fight the Hilds with magic. She fought with sword and shield, as if she were born of another House, as if she did not possess magic at all."

Cartier did not need to affirm my response. I saw the pleasure in his eyes, that I had remembered a lesson from so long ago, a lesson he probably gave thinking we had not listened.

Ciri hefted a loud sigh, and the moment was broken.

"Yes, Ciri?" Cartier inquired with raised brows.

"This has been pleasant, listening to the two of you recount the story of the first queen," she began. "But Maevan history does not mean much to me, not like it does to Brienna."

"So what would you like to talk about, then?"

She shifted in her chair. "Perhaps you can prepare us for the solstice. Who are these patrons attending? What can Brienna and I expect?"

As much as I enjoyed talking to Cartier about Maevan history, Ciri was right. I was, once again, trapped by things of the past instead of looking to the coming days. Because knowledge about Maevan queens was probably not the sort of thing that hooked a Valenian patron. As far as I knew, Maevana recognized the passions but did not embrace them.

Cartier pulled back his chair and finally sat, lacing his fingers as he looked at us. "I fear that I cannot tell you much about the solstice, Ciri. I do not know the patrons the Dowager has invited."

"But, Master—"

He held up his finger and Ciri quieted, although I could see the indignant red rise in her cheeks.

"I may not be able to tell you much," he said. "But I can give you both a little hint about the patrons. There will be three of them seeking a passion of knowledge, one for each branch."

"Branch?" Ciri echoed.

"Think back to our very first lesson, a long time ago," Cartier said. "Remember how I told you that knowledge is broken into three branches?"

"The historian," I murmured, to whet her memory.

She glanced at me, the knowledge slowly trickling back to her. "The historian, the physician, and the teacher."

He nodded in affirmation. "Both of you need to prepare your approach for each of these three patrons."

"But how do we do that, Master Cartier?" Ciri asked. She tapped her fingers over the table anxiously, and I wanted to tell her she had nothing to worry over; she would undoubtedly impress all three of the patrons.

"For the historian, you should have an impressive lineage memorized; you should be able to talk of any member of that lineage. Preferably, you should focus on the royal kindred," Cartier explained. "For the physician, you should be prepared to talk about any bone, any muscle, any organ of the body, as well as trauma and wounds. And for the teacher . . . well, this one is more difficult. The best advice I could give you both is to exemplify that you can conquer any subject as well as instruct any student."

He must have seen the glazed look in our eyes. Again, he *almost* smiled as he crossed his legs and said, "I've overwhelmed you. Both of you take the rest of the morning and prepare for the solstice."

Ciri at once pushed back from her chair, eager to get away and mull over what he had just told us. I was slower to rise, once more feeling that strange confliction . . . the need to stay with him and ask him to teach me *more* warring against the desire to sit alone and try to sort it all out on my own.

I had just walked past his chair, heading to the open door when I heard his voice, soft and gentle, say my name.

"Brienna."

I paused. Ciri must have heard it too, for she stopped on the threshold to frown over her shoulder. She watched me retreat back to him before she vanished down the corridor.

"Master?"

He looked up at me. "You are doubting yourself."

I drew in a deep breath, ready to deny it, to feign confidence. But the words withered. "Yes. I worry that a patron will not want me. I worry that I do not deserve my cloak."

"And why would you believe such?" he asked.

I thought about telling him all the reasons why, but that would require me to extend back to that fateful day when I had first sat in Magnalia's hall, eavesdropping. The day I had first met him, when his unexpected entrance had drowned out the name of my father.

"You remember what I told you," Cartier said, "the day you asked me to become your master, to teach you knowledge in three years?"

I nodded. "Yes, I remember. You said I would have to work twice as hard. That while my sisters were enjoying their afternoons, I would be studying."

"And have you done such?"

"Yes," I whispered. "I have done everything you have told me to do."

"Then why do you doubt yourself?"

I glanced away, looking to the bookshelves. I didn't feel like explaining it to him; it would bare far too much of my heart.

"Would it encourage you to know that I have chosen your constellation?"

That bold statement brought my eyes back to his. I stared down at him, a prince on his throne of knowledge, and felt my pulse quicken. This was his gift to me, a master to his student. He would chose a constellation for me, have it replicated on the heart of my passion cloak. Stars that would belong only to me, to mark my impassionment.

He wasn't supposed to tell me that he was preparing my cloak. Yet he had. And it made me think of his own cloak, blue as the wild cornflower, and the stars that belonged to him. It was the constellation of Verene, a chain of stars that foretold triumph despite loss and trials.

"Yes," I said. "Thank you, Master Cartier." I began to leave, but felt hung once more between the door and his chair.

"Is there something else you long to ask me, Brienna?"

I came back around to him, meeting his gaze. "Yes. Do you have a book about the Stone of Eventide?"

His brows rose. "The Stone of Eventide? What makes you ask about it?"

"That illustration of Liadan Kavanagh . . ." I began shyly, remembering how she had worn the stone about her neck.

"Ah yes." Cartier rose from his chair and opened his leather satchel. I watched as he sifted through the books he carried, at last bringing forth an old tattered volume wrapped in a protective sheet of vellum. "Here. Pages eighty through one hundred will tell you all about the stone."

I accepted the book, minding its fragile binds. "Have you always carried this book around?" I found it odd that he would, because I saw the Maevan printing emblem on it. And who bothered to tote around a tome on Maevan lore?

"I knew one day you would ask for it," Cartier responded.

I didn't know what to say. So I curtsied to him, dismissing myself without another word.

## → FIVE ←

# THE STONE OF EVENTIDE

That afternoon did not find me with Cartier in a private lesson, because we both forgot that the tailor was coming to measure the ardens for our solstice dresses. But I was never one to be seen lacking a book. I stood in the hall beside Ciri as we waited for our measurements, my fingers turning the delicate, speckled pages of the Maevan lore book Cartier had given me.

"Listen to this, Ciri," I said, my eyes rushing over the words. "'The origin of the Stone of Eventide is still largely speculated about, but legends claim that it was found at the bottom of a cave pond in the Killough Mountains. It was retrieved by a Kavanagh maiden, who took the stone to the clan elders. After many deliberations, the Kavanaghs decided to bind their magic to the stone, which slowly led to the digression of their ability to shapeshift into dragons.'"

I was enchanted by the lore, but when Ciri continued to remain quiet, my eyes drifted to her, to see her standing rigid against the wall, her gaze stubbornly fastened to the wainscoting.

"Ciri?"

"I do not care about the Stone of *Eventide*," she said. "In fact, I do not wish to hear about it at all. I have enough things to crowd my mind these days."

I shut the book, my thoughts quickly sifting through my memory of that morning, trying to find the source of her irritation. "What is wrong, Ciri?"

"I cannot believe I never saw it until now," she continued.

"Saw what?"

At last, she turned her eyes to me. They were cold, the blue of ice ready to crack. "That Master Cartier favors you."

I stood, frozen by her claim. And then my words rushed forward, incredulous. "He does not! Ciri, honestly . . . Master Cartier does not like anyone."

"For seven years, I have striven to impress him, to gain his favor, to try and get even a tiny smile out of him." Her face was exceptionally pale, the envy burning bright and hot within her. "And then you come along. Did you see how he looked at you today? How he wanted to smile at you? It was as if I was not in that room as you both prattled on and on about Maevan queens and magic."

"Ciri, please," I whispered, my throat suddenly hoarse as her words sank into me.

"And then he couldn't help himself," she continued. "He had to hold you back and tell you that he had chosen your constellation. Why would he tell you that? Why wouldn't he say the same to me? Oh, that's right—you're his pet, his favorite."

My cheeks warmed as I realized she had been eavesdropping on us. I didn't know what to say; my own temper was roused, but arguing with her would be as foolish as banging my head against the wall. All the same, she stared at me, daring me to oppose her.

That was when the tailor opened the door and called for Ciri.

I felt the brush of her passing, breathed in the fragrance of lilies that trailed her as she disappeared into the dressing room, the tailor shutting the door.

Slowly, I slid to the floor, my legs feeling like water. I pulled my knees up and held them close to my chest, staring at the wall. My head began to throb, and I wearily rubbed my temples.

I had never thought that Master Cartier favored me. Not once. And it baffled me that Ciri would think such rubbish.

There were certain rules that masters and mistresses followed very closely at Magnalia House. They did not show favoritism to one of the ardens. They evaluated us by a certain rubric at the solstice, far removed from bias and prejudices, although they could provide some level of guidance. They did not bestow a passion cloak if an arden failed to master. And while their modes of teaching ranged from dancing to mock debates, they abided by one cardinal rule: they never touched us.

Master Cartier was nigh perfect. He wouldn't dare break a rule.

I was thinking of this, my eyes shut, pressing my hands to my flushed cheeks, when I smelled a faint tendril of smoke. I drew it in, deep to my heart . . . the scent of roasting wood, of crushed leaves, of long, tangled grass . . . the metallic aroma of steel being warmed over fire . . . wind carved from bright blue skies free of clouds . . . and opened my eyes. This was not a scent of Magnalia House.

The light seemed to have shifted around me, no longer warm and golden but cool and stormy. And then came a distant voice, the voice of a man.

*My lord? My lord, she is here to see you. . . .*

I rose shakily to my feet and leaned against the wall, staring down the corridor. It sounded like that voice was coming toward me, the weathered and raspy words of an older man, yet I stood alone in the hall. I briefly wondered if there was a secret door I didn't know about, if one of the servants was about to emerge from it.

*My lord?*

My assumption faded when I realized he was speaking in Dairine, Maevana's tongue.

I was one moment from stepping forward, to search and discover who was speaking, when the dressing room door groaned open.

Ciri emerged, ignoring me as she walked down the hall, and the light returned to summer gold, the cloying scent of burning things evaporated, and the stranger's beckoning fizzled into dust motes.

"Brienna?" the tailor inquired.

I forced myself to walk across the hall to him, to step inside the dressing room. I carefully set Cartier's book aside, made sure that I stood still and quiet on the pedestal as the tailor began to take my measurements. But within, my head was pounding, my pulse darting along my wrists and neck as I stared at my reflection in the mirror.

I looked pale as bone, my brown eyes sadly bloodshot, my jaw clenched. I looked as if I had just seen a ghost.

Most Valenians would claim that they were not superstitious. But we were. It was why we sprinkled herbs on our thresholds at the start of every season, why weddings only took place on Fridays, why no one ever wanted an odd number of sons. I knew that saints could appear to sinners, but this . . . this almost seemed as if Magnalia House was haunted.

And if it was, then why was I just *now* hearing voices?

"All right, Mademoiselle, you are free to go."

I stepped down from the pedestal and reclaimed the book. The tailor undoubtedly thought me rude, but my voice was tangled deep in my chest as I breathed and opened the door. . . .

The corridor was normal, as it should be.

I stepped into it, smelled the yeast of freshly baked bread drift from the kitchens, heard Merei's music float on the air as a cloud, felt the polished black-and-white floor beneath my slippers. Yes, this was Magnalia.

I shook my head, as if to clear the gossamer that had gathered between my thoughts and perceptions, and glanced down to the book in my hands.

Through the protective sheet of vellum, its maroon cover

gleamed bright as a ruby. It no longer looked ancient and worn; it looked freshly bound and printed.

I stopped walking. My hand gently removed the vellum, letting it drift to the floor as I stared at the book. *The Book of Hours*, its title read with embossed gold. I hadn't even noticed the title on the cover when Cartier had given it to me, so worn and tattered was the book; it had seemed more like a smudge of stardust before. But now, it was strikingly clear.

What would I tell him when I returned it? That this crafty little Maevan book of lore had turned back time?

No sooner did I think such than did my curiosity sprout as a weed. I flipped open the cover. There was the Maevan publishing emblem, and there was the year of its first print. *1430.*

And the fingers on the page—the hands holding this book—were no longer mine.

They were the hands of a man, broad and scarred, with dirt beneath his nails.

Startled, I released the book. But the volume remained in the man's grip—my grip—and I realized I was anchored to him. As my senses became aware of his body—he was tall, muscular, strong—I felt the light shift around us, gray and troubled, and the smoke trickled down the hall again.

*"My lord? My lord, she is here to see you."*

I glanced up; I no longer stood in Magnalia's hall. This was a corridor built of stone and mortar, with flickering torches sitting in iron brackets along the wall. And there was a man standing patiently before me, the owner of the voice I had first heard.

He was old and bald with a crooked nose. But he bowed to me, dressed in black breeches and a leather jerkin that was worn about the edges. A sword was sheathed at his side.

*"Where is she?"* The voice that warmed my throat was nothing like my own; it rumbled as tamed thunder, masculine and deep.

I was no longer Brienna of Magnalia House. I was a strange man standing in some distant hall of the past, our bodies and minds linked by this book. And while my heart was wild within my chest, terrified, my soul settled comfortably into his grooves. I watched him, from within, through his eyes and his perceptions.

"In the library, my lord," the chamberlain said, bowing his bald head once more.

The man I was anchored to shut the book, mulling over what he had just read—what I had just read—as he made his way down the corridor, down the winding stairs to the library. He paused, just before the twin doors, to look once more at *The Book of Hours*. There were some moments he wanted to believe in such lore, that he wanted to trust magic. But today was no such moment, and he abandoned the book on a chair and pushed open the doors.

*The princess stood with her back to him before the arched windows, the light sweetening her dark hair. Of course, she had come to visit him in full armor with her long sword sheathed at her side. As if she had come to wage war against him.*

*Norah Kavanagh pivoted to look at him. She was the third-born daughter of the queen, and while she was not the most beautiful, he still had a difficult time looking away from her.*

"Princess Norah." He greeted her with a respectful bow. "How can I help you?"

They met in the center of the vast library, where the air grew deep and their voices would not be overheard.

"You know why I have come, my lord," Norah said.

He stared at her, took in her delicate nose, the sharp point of her chin, the scar down her cheek. She was not lazy as her oldest sister, the heiress. Nor was she wasteful and cruel as her second sister. No, he thought, her eyes so blue they seemed to burn. She was grace and steel, a warrior as well as a diplomat. She was a true reflection of her ancestor, Liadan.

"You have come because you are concerned about the Hilds," he said. It was always the Hilds, Maevana's one true nemesis.

Norah glanced away, to the shelves burdened with books and scrolls. "Aye, the Hilds' raids have provoked my mother to declare war on them."

"And the princess does not desire to wage war?"

That brought her gaze back to him, her eyes narrowing with displeasure. "I do not desire to see my mother use her magic for evil."

"But the Hilds are our enemy," he argued. Only in a private space would he challenge her like this, if only to test how deep her beliefs ran. "Perhaps they deserve to be sundered by battle magic."

"Magic is never to be used in battle," she murmured, taking a step closer to him. "You know this; you believe this. You have been spouting such ideology since I can remember. I have grown up beneath your warnings, trained myself to master sword and shield as you suggested. I have prepared myself for the day when I would need to protect my land by my own hand, by my blade, not my magic."

His heart slowed, feeling the space between them tighten. She was only sixteen years old, and yet who would have thought that the third-born princess, the one who would never inherit the crown, the one many forgot about, would be the only one to heed his words?

"Your mother the queen does not believe such," he said. "Nor your sisters. They see their magic as an advantage in battle."

"It is not an advantage," Norah said, shaking her head. "It is a crutch and a danger. I have read your pamphlets on the matter. I have studied Liadan's war and have come to my own conclusions. . . ."

She paused. He waited, waited for her to speak the words.

"My mother must not be allowed to enter this war wielding it."

He turned away from her, her declaration making him drunk on his own ambitions, his own pride. Because of that, he would need to tread this very carefully, lest he turn her against him.

"What do you want me to do, Princess Norah?"

"I want you to advise me. I want you to help me."

He stopped before the great map nailed to the wall. His gaze traced the island of Maevana, her edges and mountains, her forests and valleys. To the far west was the cold land of Grimhildor. To the south were the kingdoms of Valenia and Bandecca. And an idea seeded in his thoughts, grew roots, and bloomed off his tongue. . . .

"You could tell the queen that Valenia would never come to Maevana's aid if we wield battle magic." He turned back around to look at Norah. "In fact, they would most likely sever our alliance."

"We do not need Valenia's aid," the princess replied. There was the haughtiness, which all Kavanaghs seemed to possess.

*"Do not dismiss the Valenians so quickly, Princess. They are our strongest ally, our faithful brother. It would be folly to estrange them from us, all because your mother has decided to wage a magical war."*

*Norah's face did not soften; she did not blush or apologize for her arrogance.*

*He walked back to her, stood so close his chest nearly brushed her breastplate, so close that he could smell the fragrance of mountain air in her hair, and he whispered, "You do realize that your mother could annihilate Grimhildor? Could turn Valenia into her slaves? Could cast Bandecca in eternal darkness? That your mother could shatter the realm into pieces with her battle magic?"*

*"Yes," she whispered in return.*

*It wasn't fair, he thought. It wasn't fair that the Kavanaghs were the only magical House, that the other thirteen were decidedly frail, weak, and human. That the slender woman before him could burn his land with a mere snap of her fingers, that she could stop his heart with a mere word. And yet he would have to kindle the fire to burn the land; he would have to draw a blade to end her. He could feel the magic teem about her, as tiny flecks of diamonds in her armor, as stardust in her hair, as moonlight on her skin.*

*Ah, he had always resented the Kavanaghs.*

*He thought back to what he had just read in* The Book of Hours, *about the Stone of Eventide's ancient origins. Why should he believe such a foolish myth, that the Kavanagh elders would actually shackle their magic to the stone? Either they were foolish, or they were afraid of their own power. So they tempered it.*

*And he was about to make a great assumption—she would probably laugh when he told her—yet this was what he had wanted for quite some time.*

"*You must bring me the Stone of Eventide,*" *he said to her, watched a frown pull along her brow.*

"*What? Why?*"

"*Your mother's magic, your sisters' magic, your magic, Princess, is contingent that one of you wear the stone over your heart, against your flesh. That if the stone is separated from the Kavanaghs, your magic will go dormant.*"

*She drew in a deep breath through her teeth, but he could tell this was no surprise to her. So she knew? She knew that her House required wearing the stone in order to wield magic? And yet her clan, the Kavanaghs, had kept that secret. Who had begun it? Liadan herself?*

"*How do you know this, my lord?*"

*He smiled down at her; it tasted sour on his lips.* "*Years and years of reading your lore, Princess. It is an assumption of mine, but I can see in your eyes that I have stumbled onto truth.*"

"*I cannot take the Stone of Eventide,*" *Norah all but growled.* "*It never leaves my mother's neck.*"

"*You cannot or will not?*" *he countered.* "*You are afraid of feeling the magic dim in your blood, aren't you?*"

*Norah glanced to the window, where the storm finally broke, lashing the glass.* "*My mother would behead me if she caught me taking the stone. If she knew I handed it to . . . to you.*"

"*You think I could destroy such a thing?*" *he snapped, his patience*

*waning. "Lest you forget, Princess Norah, that the Stone of Eventide*
*would burn me if I dared to touch it."*

*"She will think I have conspired with you," she went on, paying*
*him no heed.*

*He sighed, weary of trying to coax her. "I think you need more*
*time to think on this. Return to the castle, Princess. Consider what*
*I have said to you, what I ask of you. If you think you can temper*
*your mother's magic another way, then we shall consider a different*
*approach. But if not . . . you must bring the stone to me. Or else we*
*will witness your mother's battle magic sunder the world."*

*Norah's face was carefully guarded; he could not read what she*
*was thinking, what she was feeling.*

*He watched her leave, the library doors banging behind her.*

*She would return, he knew it. She would return because there*
*was no other way. She would return because she was afraid of her*
*own magic.*

I was hardly aware of him leaving me, of his body dissolving as
mist about mine, drifting out the open window. But my eyes
cleared, as if I were blinking away the sand of sleep, finding myself
standing in Magnalia's familiar library. My hands still gripped
*The Book of Hours—* it was old and tattered and threadbare again.
But this book had once been his, the man I had shifted into. This
book had once been in the hall of a Maevan castle one hundred
and thirty-six years ago.

I winced, the sunlight deepening the ache in my head. I
grappled for the door and shuffled down the hall, up the stairs,

clenching my jaw when Sibylle's sudden laughter rattled my ears.

It felt as if I had just slammed my head upon a rock. I was halfway tempted to feel my skull, to see if there was a crack.

Into my room I went, closing the door behind me.

I should be studying. I should be preparing.

But all I could do was set the book aside and lie down on my bed, closing my eyes and willing the pain in my mind to go away, trying to calm the alarm that began to thrum in my heart.

I retraced what I had seen, over and over, until all I could wonder was *why* and *who*. Why had I seen this? And who was this man?

Because I had never discovered his name.

# SIX

# THE FALL

The next morning, I arrived to Cartier's lesson half an hour late. That might have been a little excessive; I had never been late, not even when I was an arden of the other four passions. But I couldn't bear to imagine that Ciri thought Cartier favored me. I couldn't bear to let this come between her and me, between our sisterhood and friendship. I wanted to ease Ciri's mind; I wanted to prove to her that Cartier would not treat me any differently from her. And the best way to get under his skin was to be tardy.

I walked into the library, my gaze resting on him first. He stood by the table reviewing with Ciri, his flaxen hair captured by a ribbon, his white shirt soaking in the sunlight. My heart was racing—agonizingly thrilled—when he turned to look at me.

"And what are the bones of the skull?" he asked Ciri as I slipped into my chair.

Ciri, for the first time since I had shared lessons with her, was speechless. Her eyes were wide, blue as a summer sky to fall into. "Th-the frontal bone, the parietal bone, the zygomatic bone . . ."

Cartier walked toward me—he often paced during lessons, this was nothing new—but I could hear it in his tread, the calm before the storm. He came to stand near my elbow, close enough that I could feel the air spark between us.

"You are late, Brienna."

"Yes." I dared to look up at him. His face was well guarded; I could not tell if he was angry or relieved.

"Why?" he asked.

"Forgive me, Master. I do not have a good reason."

I waited—waited for him to punish me, to assign some horrible writing assignment in which I described in detail the folly of tardiness. But it never came. He turned away and resumed his languid walk about the table, about the library.

"Now, recite to me the bones of the arm, Ciri."

Ciri rolled her eyes at me when his back was to us. I knew what she was trying to say to me: *See, Brienna? You can get away with anything.*

I listened to her begin to dissect the arm bones—she had always been brilliant with human anatomy—as I thought of another way to push Cartier's boundaries. Ciri had just reached the humerus when I interrupted, my voice rudely cutting her off.

"Humerus, radius, ulna, ossa capri . . ."

"I did not ask you, Brienna." Cartier's voice was smooth as glass. It was a warning, his eyes meeting mine from across the room.

I held my tongue; I tried to make my guilt dissipate. I wanted this, remember. I wanted to anger him, to annoy him.

"Now, Ciri," he said, closing his eyes and pinching the bridge of his nose as if he was exhausted, "please recite the bones of the leg."

Her fingers were absently tracing the tabletop as she stared at me, confused. "Lateral condyle, medial condyle, tib—"

"Tibial tuberosity," I overpowered her again. "Tibia, fibula—"

"Brienna," he said, his voice quickly tangling with mine. "You are dismissed."

I stood, dipped a curtsy, and departed without looking at him, without looking at her. I raced up the stairs, my heart quivering like a plucked harp string.

I sat on my bed and stared at *The Book of Hours*, which continued to rest on my bedside table, untouched since the vision, looking tattered and harmless. After an inward debate, I decided to pick it up and read another passage, expecting *him* to pull me back to 1430. But the hours passed, and I remained sitting quietly, safely on my bed reading Maevan lore.

When I heard the faint chime of the grandfather clock in the foyer, I carefully closed the book and wrapped it in the vellum. The last lesson was officially over, and I had made a fool of myself.

I heard my sisters' voices as they emerged from their lecture rooms . . . jubilant, lively. They were finished, ready for the solstice. And yet I thought about all the things I still needed to conquer before Sunday and I absently, reluctantly pulled a random book from my shelf. It so happened to be the tome of royal lineages, which I was supposed to have memorized.

The door swung open, and Merei rushed in carrying her lute. She was startled to see me.

"Bri? What are you doing?"

"I'm studying," I replied with a lopsided smile.

"But lessons are over," she argued, setting the lute on her bed and striding over to mine. "We are going on a celebration picnic. You should come."

I almost did. I was one breath from shutting the tome and forgetting the list of things I needed to memorize, but my gaze drifted to *The Book of Hours*. I needed, perhaps more than anything, to talk to Cartier about it. About what I had seen.

"I wish I could," I said, and I thought Merei was about to pull me up and drag me down the stairs when Abree hollered for her from the foyer.

"Merei!"

"Brienna. Please come," Merei whispered.

"I have to talk to Master Cartier about something."

"What about?"

"*Merei!*" Abree continued to shout. "Hurry! They are leaving us!"

I stared up at her, my sister, my friend. She might be the one person in the world I could trust, the one person who would not think I had lost my wits if I told her what had happened, how I had shifted.

"I will have to tell you later," I murmured. "Go, before Abree loses her voice."

Merei stood a breath longer, her dark eyes steady over mine. But she knew arguing with me was futile. She left without another word, and I listened to the sound of her descending the stairs, the front doors latching with a shudder.

I stood and walked to our window, which overlooked the front courtyard. I watched my arden-sisters gather into one of the open coaches, laughing as their entourage traveled down the drive, disappearing beneath the boughs of the oaks.

Only then did I grab *The Book of Hours* and rush down the stairs in a tumble. I nearly collided with Cartier in the foyer; his cloak was draped over his arm, his satchel in hand as he prepared to depart.

"I thought you had left," Cartier stated.

"No, Master."

We stood and stared at each other, the house unusually quiet, as if the walls were watching us. It felt like I was taking in a breath, about to plunge into deep waters.

"May I request an afternoon lesson?"

He shifted his satchel and snorted. "I dismiss you from one, and now you want another?"

A smile warmed my lips as I held up his book. "Perhaps we can discuss this?"

His gaze flickered to the book, then back to me and my soft, repentant eyes. "Very well. If you agree to act as yourself."

We walked into the library. As he began to set down his things, I stood at my chair, sliding *The Book of Hours* onto the table.

"I wanted you to dismiss me," I confessed.

Cartier glanced up, one eyebrow cocked. "So I concluded. Why?"

I pulled out my chair and sat, lacing my fingers as an obedient arden. "Because Ciri thinks you favor me."

He took Ciri's chair, sitting directly across from me. Propping his elbows on the table, he rested his chin on the valley of his palm, his eyes half-lidded with poorly concealed mirth. "What makes her think that?"

"I don't know."

He was quiet, but his gaze touched every line and curve of my face. I remembered how easily he could see through me, that my face was like a poem he could read. So I tried to keep from smiling, or frowning, but he still insisted, "You do know. Why?"

"I think it is because of the things we talk about. Yesterday, she felt left out."

"When we talk of Maevana?"

"Yes." I wasn't about to tell him of the suspected smile. "And I think she is worried about the patrons, about . . . competing with me." This is what *I* was most worried about—that Ciri and I would inevitably turn the solstice into a competition, that we would want the same patron.

His gaze sharpened. Any glimmer of mirth faded, and he straightened in the chair. "There should be no need for you and her to compete. You have your strengths, she has hers."

"What would you call my strengths?" I tentatively asked.

"Well, I would claim you are similar to me. You are naturally a historian, attracted to things of the past."

I could hardly believe his words, how he had just opened the door to what I was anxious to talk about. Gently, I unwrapped *The Book of Hours* and set it between us.

"Speaking of the past," I began, clearing my throat, "where did you come by such a book?"

"Where I come by most of my books," he smartly replied. "The bookseller."

"Did you purchase it in Maevana?"

He was quiet, and then he said, "No."

"So you do not know who owned it before you?"

"These are strange questions, Brienna."

"I am merely curious."

"Then no, I do not know who owned it before me." He leaned back in the chair, that half-lidded expression returning. But he did not fool me; I saw the gleam in his eyes.

"Have you ever . . . seen or felt things when you read this book?"

"Every book makes me see and feel things, Brienna."

He made me sound foolish. I began to mentally retreat, slightly stung by his sarcasm, and he must have sensed it, because he instantly softened, his voice like honey.

"Did you enjoy reading about the Stone of Eventide?"

"Yes, Master. But . . ."

He waited, encouraging me to speak my mind.

"Whatever happened to it?" I finished.

"No one knows," Cartier answered. "It went missing in 1430, the year of the last Maevan queen."

1430. The year I had somehow stepped into. I swallowed, my mouth suddenly dry, my pulse skipping. I remembered what the princess had said, what the man had said.

*Bring me the Stone of Eventide.*

"The last Maevan queen?" I echoed.

"Yes. There was a bloody battle, a magical battle. As you already know from reading about Liadan, the Kavanaghs' magic in war turned wild and corrupt. The queen was slain, the stone lost, and so came the end of an era." He tapped his fingers on the table, gazing at nothing in particular, as if his thoughts ran as deep and troubled as mine.

"But we still call Maevana the *queen's realm*," I said. "We do not call her a 'kingdom.'"

"King Lannon hopes to change that soon, though."

Ah, King Lannon. There were three things I thought of at the sound of his name: greed, power, and steel. Greed because he had already minted Maevan coins with his profile. Power because he heavily restricted travel between Maevana and Valenia. And steel, because he settled most opposition by the sword.

But Maevana had not always been so dark and dangerous.

"What are you thinking?" Cartier asked.

"I am thinking of King Lannon."

"Is there that much to think of when he comes to mind?"

I gave him a playful look. "Yes, Master Cartier. There's a man on Maevana's throne when there should be a queen."

"Who says there is supposed to be a queen?" And here came the banter; he was challenging me to flex my knowledge as well as my articulation.

"Liadan Kavanagh said so."

"But Liadan Kavanagh has been dead two hundred and fifty years."

"She may be dead," I said, "but her words are not."

"What words, Brienna?"

"The Queen's Canon."

Cartier leaned forward, as if the table cast too much distance between us. And I found myself leaning closer too, to meet him in the middle of the oak, the wood that had witnessed all my lessons. "And what is the Queen's Canon?" he asked.

"Liadan's law. A law that declares Maevana should be ruled only by a queen, never a king."

"Where is proof of this law?" he asked, his voice dropping low and dark.

"Missing."

"The Stone of Eventide, lost. The Queen's Canon, lost. And so Maevana is lost." He leaned away, settling back into his chair. "The Canon is the law that keeps the power from kings, granting the throne and the crown to the noble daughters of Maevana. So when the Canon went missing in 1430, right after the Stone of Eventide was lost, Maevana found herself on the brink of civil war until the king of Valenia decided to step in. You know the story."

I did know it. Valenia and Maevana had always been allies, a brother and a sister, a kingdom and a queen's realm. But Maevana, suddenly void of a queen and magic, became a divided land, the fourteen Houses threatening to splinter off into clans again. Yet the Valenian king was no fool; from the other side of the channel, he watched the Maevan lords fight and squabble over the throne, over who should rise to power. And so the Valenian king came to Maevana, told each of the fourteen northern lords to paint their House sigil on a stone and to toss their stones into a cask, that he would draw who should rule the north. The lords agreed—each of them was hindered by pride, believing he had the right to rule— and anxiously watched as the Valenian king's hand descended into the cask, his fingers shifting the stones. It was Lannon's stone that he drew forth, a stone graced with a lynx.

"The king of Valenia put the Lannon men on the throne," I whispered, regret and anger entwining in my heart whenever I thought of it.

Cartier nodded, but there was a spark of anger in his eyes as he said, "I understand the Valenian king's intentions: he thought what he was doing was right, that he was saving Maevana from a civil war. But he should have stayed out of it; he should have let Maevana come to her own conclusions. Because Valenia is ruled by a king, he believed Maevana should also embrace a kingdom. And so the noble sons of Lannon believe they are worthy of Maevana's throne."

It wasn't lost on me that Cartier would probably lose his head if loyal Maevans heard him speak such treason. I shivered, let the fear gnaw on my bones before I reassured myself that we were tucked into the deep pocket of Valenia, far from Lannon's tyrannical grip.

"You sound like the *Grim Quill*, Master," I stated. The *Grim Quill* was a quarterly pamphlet that was published in Valenia, paper inked with bold beliefs and stories written by an anonymous hand that loved to poke at the Maevan king. Cartier used to bring the pamphlets for me and Ciri to read; we had laughed, blushed, and argued over the belligerent claims.

Cartier snorted, obviously amused by my likening. "Do I, now? 'How shall I describe a northern king? By humble words on paper? Or perhaps by all the blood he spills, by all the coins he gilds, by all the wives and daughters he kills?'"

We stared at each other, the *Grim Quill*'s bold words settling between us.

"No, I am not *that* brave to write such things," he finally confessed. "Or that foolish."

"Even so, Master Cartier . . . surely the Maevan people remember what the Queen's Canon says?" I argued.

"The Queen's Canon was authored by Liadan, and there is only one of them," he explained. "She carved the law magically into a stone tablet. That tablet, which cannot be destroyed, has been missing for one hundred and thirty-six years. And words, even laws, are easily forgotten, eaten by dust, if they are not passed from one generation to the next. But who is to say a Maevan won't inherit their ancestor's memories, and remember these powers of the past?"

"Ancestral memories?" I echoed.

"An odd phenomenon," he explained. "But a passion of knowledge did extensive research on the matter, concluding that all of us carry them in our minds, these select memories of our ancestors, but we never know of them because they lie dormant. That being said, they can still manifest in some of us, based on the connections we make."

"So maybe Liadan's will be inherited one day?" I asked, only to taste the hope of the words.

The gleam in his eyes told me it was wishful thinking.

I mulled on that. After a while, my thoughts circled back to Lannon, and I said, "But there must be a way to protect the Maevan throne from . . . such a king."

"It's not so simple, Brienna."

He paused and I waited.

"Twenty-five years ago, three lords tried to dethrone Lannon," he began. I knew this cold, bloody story, and yet I did not have the heart to tell Cartier to stop speaking. "Lord MacQuinn. Lord Morgane. Lord Kavanagh. They wanted to put Lord Kavanagh's eldest daughter on the throne. But without the Stone of Eventide and without the Queen's Canon, the other lords would not follow them. The plan fell to ashes. Lannon retaliated by slaughtering Lady MacQuinn, Lady Morgane, and Lady Kavanagh. He also killed their daughters, some who were mere children, because a Maevan king will always fear women while Liadan's Queen's Canon lies waiting to be rediscovered."

The story made my heart feel heavy. My chest ached, because

half of my heritage came from such a land, a beautiful, proud people that had been driven into darkness.

"Brienna."

I blinked away the sadness, the fear, and looked at him.

"One day, a queen will rise," he whispered, as if the books had ears to eavesdrop. "Perhaps it will be in our lifetime, perhaps the one to follow us. But Maevana will remember who she is and unite for a great purpose."

I smiled, but that emptiness didn't fade. It perched on my shoulders, roosted in my chest.

"Now then," Cartier said, tapping his knuckles on the table. "You and I are easily distracted. Let us talk of the solstice, how I can best prepare you."

I thought back on his suggestions of the three patrons, of what I needed to have prepared. "My royal lineage is still lacking."

"Then let us begin there. Pick a noble as far back as you can, and recite the line through the inheriting son."

This time, I did not have Grandpapa's letter sitting in my pocket to distract me. All the same, I got several sons into my recitation before I felt a yawn creep up my throat. Cartier was listening to me, his gaze focused on the wall. But he forgave my yawn, let it pass by unacknowledged. Until it came again, and I finally resolved to take a hardback book from the table and stand on my chair with a swirl of my skirts.

He glanced up at me, startled. "What are you doing?"

"I need a moment to revive my mind. Come, Master. Join me," I invited as I balanced the book on my head. "I shall continue my recitations, but the first one whose book falls from their head loses."

I only did it because I was weary, and I wanted to feel a jolt of risk. I only did it because I wanted to challenge him—challenge him after he had challenged me these three years. I only did it because we had nothing to lose.

I never thought he would actually do it.

So when he grabbed *The Book of Hours* and stood on his chair, I was pleasantly surprised. And when he balanced the book on his head, I grinned at him. He no longer seemed so old, so infinite, with his sharp, crisp edges and infuriating depth of knowledge. No, he was far younger than I'd once believed.

There we were, face-to-face, standing on chairs, books on our heads. A master and his arden. An arden and her master.

And Cartier smiled at me.

"So what are you going to give me when you lose?" he teased.

"Who says I am going to lose?" I countered. "You should have chosen a hardback book, by the way."

"Aren't you supposed to be reciting to me?"

I held still, my book perfectly balanced, and continued where I left off in the lineage. I misspoke once; he gently corrected me. And as I continued to descend the rungs of noblemen, that smile of his eased, but it never faded.

I was nearing the end on the lineage when Cartier's book *finally* began to slip. His arms flew out, outstretched as a bird, eager to regain his balance. But he had moved too suddenly, and I watched—a wide-eyed victor—as he tripped down from the chair with a tremendous crash, sacrificing his dignity in order to catch *The Book of Hours.*

"Master, are you all right?" I asked, trying in vain to control my chuckling.

He straightened; his hair had fallen loose from his ribbon, spilling around his shoulders as gold. But he looked at me and laughed, a sound I had never heard, a sound that I would yearn to hear again once it faded.

"Remind me to never play games with you," he said, his fingers rushing through his hair, refastening his ribbon. "And what must I sacrifice for my loss?"

I took my book and eased down from my chair. "Hmm . . ." I walked around the table to stand near him, trying to sort through the mayhem that had become my thoughts. What, indeed, should I ask of him?

"Perhaps I might ask for *The Book of Hours,*" I breathed, wondering if it was too valuable to request.

But Cartier only set it into my hands and said, "A wise choice, Brienna."

I was about to thank him when I noticed a streak of blood on his sleeve. "Master!" I reached for his arm, completely forgetting that we were not supposed to touch each other. I caught my fingers just in time, before I grazed the soft linen of his shirt. My hand jerked back as I awkwardly said, "You're . . . you're bleeding."

Cartier glanced down to it, plucking at his sleeve. "Oh, that. Nothing more than a scratch." And he turned away from me, as if to hide his arm from my gaze.

I hadn't seen him hurt himself when he fell from the chair. And his sleeve had not been ripped, which meant the wound had already been there, reopened from his tumble.

I watched him begin to gather his things, my heart stumbling over the desire to ask him how he had hurt himself, the desire to ask him to stay longer. But I swallowed those cravings, let them slide down my throat as pebbles.

"I should go," Cartier said, easing his satchel over his good shoulder. The blood continued to weep beneath his shirt, slowly spreading.

"But your arm . . ." I almost reached for him again.

"It'll be fine. Come, walk me out."

I fell into step beside him, to the foyer, where he gathered his passion cloak. The river of blue concealed his arm, and he seemed to relax once it was hidden.

"Now then," he said, all stern and proper again, as if we had never stood on chairs and laughed together. "Remember to have your three approaches prepared for the patrons."

"Yes, Master Cartier." I curtsied, the movement ingrained within me.

I watched him open the front door; the sunshine and warm air swelled around us, laced with scents of meadows and distant mountains, stirring my hair and my longings.

He paused on the threshold, half in the sun, half in the shadows. I thought he would turn back around—it seemed like there was more he wanted to say to me. But he was just as good at swallowing words as I was. He continued on his way, passion cloak fluttering, his satchel of books swinging as he moved to the stables to fetch his horse.

I didn't watch him ride away.

But I felt it.

I felt the distance that widened between us as I stood in the foyer shadows, as he rode recklessly beneath the oaks.

## ⊷ SEVEN ⊶

# EAVESDROPPER

The summer solstice descended upon us like a storm. The patrons were to lodge in the western quarters of the grand house, and every time one of their coaches pulled into the courtyard, Sibylle shouted for us to rush to her room window so we could catch a glimpse of the guests.

There were fifteen of them in all—men and women of varying ages, some who were passions, some who were not.

I became so nervous that I couldn't bear to watch them arrive. I tried to slip from Sibylle and Abree's room, but Sibylle caught my hand before I could vanish, drawing me back around to face her.

"What's wrong, Brienna?" she whispered. "This is one of the most exciting nights of our lives, and you look like you are about to go to a funeral."

That coaxed a little laugh from me. "I'm only anxious, Sibylle. You know that I am not as prepared as you and our sisters."

Sibylle glanced to the sheen of the window, where we could hear yet another patron arrive to the courtyard, and then she returned her gaze to me. "Don't you remember the first lesson Mistress Therese gave you when you were an arden of wit?"

"I try to block all such memories from my mind," I said drily.

Sibylle squeezed my fingers with an exasperated smile. "Then let me refresh your memory. You and I were sitting on the divan, and it was storming outside, and Mistress Therese said 'to become a mistress of wit, you must learn how to wear a mask. Inside your heart, you may rage as the storm beyond the walls, but no one must see such in your face. No one must hear such in your voice. . . .'"

Slowly, I began to remember.

To be a mistress of wit, one must have perfect command over their expressions, over their aura, over what they concealed and what they revealed. It truly was like donning a mask, to hide what actually lay beneath the surface.

"Perhaps that is why I did so poorly in wit," I said, thinking of how Cartier could always read my face, as if I wrote my feelings on my skin.

Sibylle smiled, tugging on my fingers to regain my attention. "If you remember anything of wit, remember the mask. Wear confidence instead of worry tonight."

Her suggestion was comforting, and she kissed my cheeks before letting me go.

I retreated to my room, pacing around Merei's instruments and my piles of books, reciting over and over the three approaches

I had diligently prepared. By the time the maids came to dress us, I was sweating.

I knew that every noble and passionate Valenian woman wore a corset.

Even so, I was not prepared to shed the comfortable innocence of my arden dress for a cage of whalebone and complicated laces.

Neither was Merei.

We stood facing each other as our corsets were laced, the maids tugging and pulling on us. I could see the pain on Merei's face as she readjusted her breathing, her posture, trying to find symbiosis with it. I mirrored her—she knew better how to hold herself from all those years of playing instruments. My posture had always been poor, stooped by books and writing.

*There is no passion without pain,* Cartier had once told me when I had complained of a headache during lessons.

And so I embraced it that night, the agony that was married to the glory.

I was, not surprisingly, short of breath by the time my solstice dress emerged from its parcel in three elaborate pieces.

The first was the petticoats, layered in lace. Then came the kirtle, which was low-cut and spun from silver fabric, and last, the actual gown, a steel-blue silk that opened up to reveal coy glimpses of the kirtle.

Merei's kirtle was a rosy shade of gold, overlaid by a mauve gown. I realized that she was wearing her color—the purple of musical passion—and I was wearing mine—the blue depths of knowledge. Obviously, this was arranged so the patrons would know who we were by the colors of our gowns.

I gazed at her, her brown skin glistening in the warmth of early evening, the maids brushing the last of the wrinkles from our skirts. My roommate, the friend of my heart, was stunning, her passion as light radiating from her.

She met my gaze, and it was in her eyes as well; she was looking at me, seeing me as if I had just taken my first breath. And when she smiled, I relaxed and settled into the dusk of summer, for I was about to passion with her, a moment that had taken seven years in the making.

While Merei's hair was intricately braided with tendrils of gold ribbon, I was surprised when one of the maids brought me a laurel of wildflowers. It was a whimsical array of red and yellow blossoms, a few shy pink petals, and a brave ring of blue cornflowers.

"Your master had this made for you," the chambermaid said, setting the flowers as a crown in my hair. "And he has requested your hair remain down."

My hair remain down.

It was untraditional and a bit perplexing. I looked to my blue-and-silver dress, to the long brown waves of my hair, and wondered why he would make such a request.

I moved to stand before the window and waited for Merei, forcing myself not to think of Cartier but to mentally recite my chosen lineage again. I was whispering the ninth-born son when the maids departed from our room and I heard Merei sigh.

"I feel like I should be ten," she said, and I turned to look at her. "Or eleven, or even twelve. Is this truly our seventeenth summer, Bri?"

It was strange to think of, how slowly time had moved until we had reached a certain point. And then the days had flowed as water, rushing us along to this night. I still didn't feel wholly prepared. . . .

"Where did the time go?" she asked, glancing to where her lute sat on the bed. Her voice was sad, for come Tuesday, we would both leave this place. She might to be pulled to the west, me to the east, and we might not ever see each other again.

It bruised my heart, made a knot well in my throat. I could not think of such possibilities, of the good-byes that loomed on our horizon. So I walked to stand before her and took her hands in mine. I wanted to say something, but if I did, I might shatter.

And she understood. Gently, she squeezed my fingers, her dimples kissing her cheeks as she smiled at me.

"I think we are probably late," she whispered, for the house around us was quiet.

We held our breath, listening. I could hear the faded sounds of the party melt through the windows, a party that was flourishing outside on the back lawn, beneath the stars. Punctures of laughter, the hum of conversations, the clink of glasses.

"We should go," I said, clearing the aches from my throat.

Together, Merei and I left our room only to discover we were not the last ardens to the solstice. Abree stood at the top of the stairs, her dress as a cloud of midnight, her red hair piled up high on her head with curls and jeweled barrettes. She clutched the railing in a white-knuckled grip and looked at us in relief.

"Thank the saints," she panted, her hand clawing at the corset. "I thought I was the last one. This dress is horrid. I can't breathe."

"Here, let me help you," Merei offered, easing Abree's hand from her waist.

I was just as inclined to fall down the stairs as Abree, so I took my time behind them, familiarizing myself with the wide arc of my petticoats as I descended. My sisters reached the foyer and turned into the corridor, their footsteps fading as they walked through the shadows to the back doors.

I would have caught up to them, but my hem snagged on the last iron rung of the balustrade and it took me a good minute to untether myself. By then, I was annoyed by the dress and shaky with hunger, a few stars dancing in the corners of my sight.

Slowly, I turned into the corridor, moving down its long passage to the back doors, when I heard Ciri's voice. She sounded upset, her words muffled until I walked closer, realizing she was standing just inside the Dowager's study, speaking to someone. . . .

"I don't understand! I was your arden first."

"What don't you understand?" Cartier. His voice was low, a rumble of thunder in the shadows. I stopped walking, just before the study doors, which were cracked.

"Are you going to hold her hand all evening and forget about me?"

"Of course not, Ciri."

"It's not fair, Master."

"Is anything in life fair? Look at me, Ciri."

"I have mastered everything you have ever asked of me," she hissed. "And you act as if . . . as if . . ."

"As if what?" He was becoming impatient. "As if you have not passioned?"

She fell quiet.

"I do not want us to quarrel," Cartier said in a softer tone. "You have done exceedingly well, Ciri. You are by far the most accomplished of all my ardens. Because of that, I will simply stand back and watch you passion tonight."

"And what of Brienna?"

"And what of her?" he responded. "You should not worry about Brienna. If I see you compete with her, you will wish that I had never been your master."

I heard her sharp intake of breath. Or perhaps it was my own. My fingers curled into the wall, into the carvings of the wainscoting; I felt my nails bend as I tried to hold on to something solid, something reassuring.

"You may be my master for one more night," she said in a dark tone. "But if the patron I want is interested in her . . ."

His voice dropped so low it was nothing but a growl to me. I made my feet move forward, as silently as I could, praying they did not hear me pass the doors.

Through the glimmer of the bay windows, I could see the white tents of the solstice on the lawn. I watched the servants circulating with platters of drinks, heard the laughter floating amid the night. I caught a glimpse of Sibylle's green dress as she meandered beside a patron, her beauty warbled by the mullioned windows when she moved. I was almost to the threshold, a threshold scattered with herbs to welcome the new season.

But I didn't walk through the back doors.

I turned to the right, to the safe shadows of the library.

Gently, as if my bones might break, I sat in the chair in which I had withstood all of Cartier's lessons. And I thought about what I had just overheard, wishing that I had not stopped to listen.

At Magnalia, there was never supposed to be two ardens of one passion. There was only supposed to be one of each, and now I understood why the Dowager had structured her house this way. We weren't supposed to compete, but how could we not? The arials were not supposed to favor one over the other, but what if they did?

Should I say something to Ciri?

Should I leave Ciri be?

Should I avoid Cartier?

Should I confront Cartier?

I sat there, letting those four questions pick at my thoughts until I felt the urgency of the night. I could not continue to sit there as a coward.

Rising in a swell of silk, I left the library; I passed through the terrace doors, trembling until I glanced up. The night sky was ruled by a golden sickle moon, welcoming stars and dreams. One of those constellations would soon become mine.

I walked mindfully, my dress swallowing the last of my childhood as it whispered over the grass.

I had prepared years for this one night, I thought, and breathed in the fragrance of summer.

Where had time gone?

There was no answer as I welcomed the solstice.

## — EIGHT —

# THE SUMMER SOLSTICE

There were six tents in all—a large one billowed from the center, surrounded by five smaller tents that resembled the white petals on a rose. Every timber beam dripped with ivy; every passageway was crowned with boughs of blushing peonies, creamy hydrangeas, and wreaths of lavender. Silver lanterns bobbed on strings, hovering as fireflies, their candles filling the night with scents of honeysuckle and rosemary.

I came to a stop on the lawn, hesitant, the grass crinkling beneath my slippers until I heard the slow, seductive plucking of Merei's lute. Her music drew me to the first tent, invited me to part and enter the fluttering white cambric as if I were slipping into a stranger's bed.

Rugs had been laid down over the grass, divans and chairs arranged to facilitate conversations. But this was wholly for Merei, I soon realized, for her instruments were scattered about—her gleaming harpsichord, her violin, her reed flute all waited their turn to feel her touch. She sat on a cushioned bench, playing her lute for two women and one man. Her three patrons.

I kept to the mouth of the tent, where the night could trickle in and the shadows could hold me. But there, off to the right, was Merei's mistress, Evelina. The arial of music stood where she could observe quietly, her eyes lined with the silver of tears as she listened to Merei play.

The song was rich and slow; it made me want to shed my heavy dress for a lighter one, to dance in the pastures, to swim in the river, to taste every piece of fruit, drink every stream of moonlight. It made me feel old and young, wise and naïve, curious and satisfied.

Her music had always been such to me, something that had filled me to overflowing. There had been countless evenings when she had played for me in our room, when I was weary and discouraged, when I felt as if I didn't belong and would never belong.

Her music was like bread and wine . . . nourishing, emboldening.

I found that I too was wiping tears from my eyes.

My movement must have attracted her gaze. Merei looked up and saw me; her song never faltered, no, rather her song seemed to find a new chorus and she smiled. I hoped that I inspired her as much as she did me.

And so I slipped from her tent to the next, following the ivy and the flowers, feeling as if I were stepping into the honeycomb of a dream.

This tent was also laid with rugs and fitted with chairs and divans. But there were three easels, each displaying a magnificent oil painting. I walked about the edge of the tent, once more keeping to the shadows as I admired Oriana's masterpieces.

She stood in a dark red dress, her black hair swept off her neck by a net of hammered gold, a patron on each side as she told them about her work. They were talking of oils. . . . What was her recipe for ultramarine, for umber? And I passed quietly into the next tent, smiling as I knew my prediction would come true: the patrons were bound to fight over Oriana.

This third tent was Sibylle's. There was a table set in the center of the rugs, where Sibylle sat in her emerald taffeta gown, playing a game of cards with her three potential patrons. Her laughter was like the tinkling of a bell as she engaged her guests in nimble conversation.

Wit was the one passion I had, honestly, despised. I was poor at debate, intimidated by speeches, and a lousy conversationalist. Struggling through that year as an arden had made me realize that I preferred quiet spaces and books over a room full of people.

"What are you doing here?"

I turned to look at Mistress Therese, who had snuck up on me as a wraith. And that was the other reason why I had been so miserable as an arden of wit. Therese had never warmed to me as her student.

"You should be in your own tent," she hissed, snapping out a delicate lace fan. Sweat was pouring down her face, making her muddy blond hair stick to her forehead as if she had been splattered with grease.

I didn't waste words on her. I didn't even waste a curtsy.

I moved into the next tent, which was Abree's. There was a shallow, octagonal stage in the heart of the tent, low-lit lanterns and a ring of smoke that made it seem as if I were in the middle of a cloud. But there was my Abree, her hair red as flame, standing among her three patrons and Master Xavier. I was happy to see her laughing and carrying on, completely at ease, even in so uncomfortable a dress.

But the dramatics were always friendly; their company was lively and fun. If they caught sight of me lurking, they would undoubtedly call me over to their gathering, and I knew I was short on time.

I slipped out to the slender patch of grass between tents, grateful for the night breeze that lifted the hot curtain of my hair. I stood and breathed, my hands pressed to the bodice of my gown, watching the fabric door of the tent ripple with invitation, like foam on a current.

This was mine and Ciri's tent; this was where I should have been an hour ago.

And if I bent just a little bit, defying my corset, I could see into the tent, see the rugs laid on the ground and the foot of one of the patrons . . . a spit-polished boot . . . and I could hear the low hum of conversation. Ciri was speaking, saying something about the weather. . . .

"You are late."

Cartier's voice made me startle. I straightened and whirled about to find him standing behind me on the grass, his arms crossed.

"The night is still young," I responded, but a traitorous blush nipped my cheeks. "And you should know better than to startle me like that."

I resumed my clandestine observation, hesitant to part the linen and enter. It was even worse now that he was here, witnessing my qualm.

"Where have you been?" Cartier stepped closer to me; I felt his leg brush my skirts. "I was beginning to think you had called a coach and fled."

I gave him a wry smile, although the thought of fleeing was horribly tempting at that moment. "Honestly, Master . . ."

I was going to say more, but the words faded when my eyes caught on his clothes. I had never seen him dressed so elegantly. He wore knee-high boots, velvet breeches, a black doublet studded with fancy buckles and silver-stitched trim. His sleeves were long and loose and white, his hair slicked back in his usual queue, his face freshly shaven and golden in the lantern light. His passion cloak faithfully guarded his back, a captive piece of blue sky.

"Why are you looking at me like that?" he asked.

"Like what?"

"Like you have never seen me wear proper clothes."

I snorted, like he was being ridiculous. But thankfully, a server passed by right at that moment, bearing a tray of cordial. I reached for one, a blessed distraction, holding the glass tumbler with a tremor in my fingers, and took a gulp, then another.

Maybe it was the cordial, or maybe it was the dress, or the fact that he was standing far too close to me. But I met his gaze, the glass rim brushing my lip, and murmured, "You don't have to hold my hand all evening."

His eyes darkened at my words. "I am not planning to hold your hand, Brienna," he said tartly. "And you know what I think of eavesdropping."

"Yes, I know very well," I responded with a lilt of a smile. "What will it be tonight? The hangman's noose, or the stocks for two days?"

"I will mercifully pardon you tonight," Cartier said and took the tumbler from my fingers. "And let's do away with cordial for now, until you have eaten."

"That is fine. I shall get another," I stated as my hands rushed down my dress, wiping the perspiration away. It was a warm evening; I could feel every bit of underclothing swelter against my skin. "Why did you have to pick such a heavy dress?"

He drank the remainder of my cordial before responding. "All I chose was the color. And your flowers . . . and that your hair remain down."

I decided not to answer, and my pause provoked him to look at me. I felt his blue gaze touch the crown of my head, my flowers, then along my jaw, down my neck to my aching waist. I imagined he thought me beautiful and then reprimanded myself for entertaining such an absurd fancy.

"Now then," Cartier said, his eyes returning to mine. "Are

you going to stand out here with me all night, or find yourself a patron?"

I glared at him before I finally mustered the courage to step into the tent, leaving him behind to the night.

I felt four sets of eyes rest on me and my sudden entrance. There was Ciri, sitting in a navy gown, her hair curled into ringlets with a wreath of red flowers crowning her head, her cheeks romantically flushed from her high spirits. Beside her sat a woman, dark-skinned and handsomely middle-aged, dressed in a splendid array of yellow silk. And opposite them sat two men in chairs, cordial sparkling in their hands. One was older, his auburn hair streaked through with silver, his nose and chin pointedly sharp as if he had been chiseled from pale marble. The other was younger, with a dark beard, ruddy skin, and jaunty posture.

Ciri rose to greet me. "Brienna, let me introduce you to our guests. This is Mistress Monique Lavoie." The woman in yellow smiled. "And then we have Master Brice Mathieu." The haughty bearded man stood and raised his cordial with a half bow. "And Master Nicolas Babineaux." The stoic, auburn-haired man also stood with a curt bow. All three of the patrons had blue cloaks fastened at their collars; all three of them were passions of knowledge.

"A pleasure," I said, giving them my deepest curtsy. Despite Ciri's seamless introductions, I felt like my bones had come out of their sockets, that I was an imposter in this silk gown.

"Perhaps I might steal you first," Monique Lavoie said to me.

"Of course," Ciri responded, but I saw the reservation in her eyes as she stepped away so I could take her place on the divan. This was the patron she wanted. And so I decided that I would tread gently.

I sat beside Monique as Ciri stood between the two masters, engaging them in a conversation that had them both chuckling.

"So, Brienna," Monique began, and I let all other noise fade to the background. "Tell me about yourself."

I had several points of introductory conversation prepared. One was my dual citizenship, one was learning beneath Master Cartier, one was the splendor of Magnalia. I decided to choose the first thread.

"I am an arden of knowledge, Mistress. My father is Maevan, my mother Valenian. I was raised in Colbert's orphanage until I was brought here my tenth summer. . . ." And so my words flowed, short and pinched as if I could not draw a proper breath. But she was kind, her eyes interested in all that I said, encouraging me to tell her more of my lessons, of Magnalia, of my favorite branch of knowledge.

Finally, after what felt like days of me rambling about myself, she opened up.

"I am a physician on the island of Bascune," Monique said, accepting a fresh glass of cordial from a server. "I grew up on the island, but I passioned when I was eighteen and became an assistant to a physician. I have had my own infirmary and apothecary for ten years now, and I am seeking to gain a new aide."

So she belonged to the physician branch of knowledge, and she was seeking a passion to assist her. She was offering a partnership.

And no sooner did I let her offer tempt me than I felt Ciri's concerned gaze drift to us.

"Perhaps I should ask you first how you respond to blood," Monique said, sipping her cordial with a smile. "For I see it quite often."

"Blood does not affect me, thankfully," I responded, and here was my chance to integrate my story, as Cartier had told me to do.

I told her about Abree's wounded forehead, an injury she had acquired after tripping off the practice stage during her rehearsal. Instead of calling the physician, Cartier had allowed Ciri and me to stitch our friend's wound, walking us through the motions as he looked over our shoulders and Abree had remained—amazingly—calm.

"Ah, Ciri has told me the same story," Monique said, and I felt my face warm. I hadn't thought to check my story against Ciri's. "How wonderful, that the two of you could work together to mend your friend."

Ciri was trying not to stare at me, but she had heard my duplicate story and Monique's response. The air crackled with tension, and there was only one way I could think to smooth it.

"Yes, indeed, Mistress Monique. But Ciri is far more skilled than I with needles. We compared our stitches afterward, and mine were not as cleanly placed as hers."

Monique smiled sadly, knowing what I was doing, that I was withdrawing myself from her contention. That she should choose Ciri, and not me.

A shadow tumbled over my skirts as I realized the young

bearded patron had come to stand at my side. He was dressed in clean-cut black and silver; he smelled of cardamom and peppermint as he extended a pale, manicured hand to me.

"Might I steal you now?"

"Yes, Master Brice," I responded, thanking Monique for her time as I let my fingers rest in his, as I let him draw me up from the divan.

I could not remember the last time I had touched the opposite sex.

No, wait, I did remember. The autumn my grandpapa had surrendered me to Magnalia, seven years ago. He had hugged me, kissed my cheek. But since that moment, the only affection I had ever felt had come from my arden-sisters, when we laced fingers or hugged or danced.

I couldn't help but feel uncomfortable as Brice continued to hold my hand, leading me over to a quieter corner of the tent where two chairs were arranged in tender candlelight.

I sat and resisted the urge to wipe my palm on my skirts as he brought me a tumbler of cordial. That was when I saw Cartier had finally returned to the tent. He had taken Brice's abandoned seat and was talking to the red-haired patron, my master appearing at ease as he crossed his legs.

"I hear you are quite the historian," Brice stated, settling into the chair at my side.

I withdrew my eyes from Cartier and said, "May I ask how you came to know such, Master Brice?"

"Ciri said such of you," he answered. I tried to guess his age, casting him in his early thirties. He was attractive, his eyes bright and friendly; his voice was polished, as if he had only attended the nicest of schools, ate at the richest of tables, danced with the loveliest of women. "Which, I confess, interests me because I am a historian myself."

Ciri had called me one. As had Cartier, who had confessed that he aligned himself with this branch, even though he had chosen to teach. Helplessly, my eyes drifted to Cartier again.

He was already looking at me, regarding me with absolutely no expression in his face as I sat in this corner with Brice Mathieu. It was as if I was a stranger to Cartier, until I realized that auburn-haired Nicolas was saying something, and Cartier didn't hear a word of it.

Brice was saying something to me as well.

I turned back to the patron, my skin soaking in the heat of the night. "Forgive me, Master Brice. I did not hear what you said."

"Oh." He blinked. He was not accustomed to being ignored, I could tell. "I asked if you would like to talk of your favorite lineage. I am currently employed by the royal scribes, ensuring their historical records are accurate. And I need an assistant, one who is just as sharp and keen as me, who knows genealogy as the lines on her palm."

Another partnership.

This interested me. And so I pretended like Cartier was not in that tent, and smiled at Brice Mathieu.

"Of course, Master. I am fond of Edmond Fabre's lineage."

So we began to talk of Edmond Fabre and his three sons, who in turn had had three more sons. I was keeping up well, despite the sweat that began to trace down my back, despite the corset that ate all my comfort, despite the way Cartier's gaze continued to touch me.

But then I misspoke. I didn't even realize I had said the wrong name until I watched Brice Mathieu frown, as if he had smelled something distasteful.

"Surely you mean Frederique, not Jacques."

I hung in that moment, trying to reconcile what I had said to what he was saying. "No, Master Brice. I believe it was Jacques."

"No, no, it was Frederique," Brice countered. "Jacques was not born until two generations later."

Had I honestly skipped generations? But, more important, did I honestly care?

My memory went limp, and I chose to laugh, to cover it up. "Of course, I misspoke." I drained the cordial before I could make a further fool of myself.

I was saved by the entrance of a servant, who announced dinner was now being served in the grand central tent.

I rose on shaky legs, my nerves strung so tight I seriously considered bolting back to the house until the third patron arrived at my side, his lean, great height nearly brushing the wisp of tent.

"Might I escort you to dinner, Brienna?" the auburn-haired master asked. His voice was very soft and delicate, but I was not fooled; there was steel in this one. I recognized it, because Cartier was very similar.

"Yes, Master Nicolas. I would be honored."

He offered me his arm and I took it, once more feeling hesitant about touching a strange man. But he was older, perhaps the age my father would be. So this touch felt proper, not as dangerous as holding Brice Mathieu's hand.

We left before the others, heading for the central tent.

There were three round tables, nine chairs per circle, and no seating chart. A dinner intended to let the passions mingle, I thought with renewed dread as Nicolas chose a place for us to sit. I eased into my chair, my gaze roaming the tent as my arden-sisters, their patrons, and their arials wandered in.

The tables were draped with white linens, their centers blossomed with candles and wreaths of roses and glossy leaves. The plates, flatware, and chalices were all spun from the finest silver, set in wait to be touched, gleaming as a dragon's hoard. Above us, lanterns hung, their panels fashioned from delicately pierced tin, and the light cascaded on us as little stars.

Nicolas did not speak a word to me, not until the rest of our table was filled and introductions had been exchanged. Ciri, naturally, had chosen *not* to sit at my table. She had drawn Monique with her, and Brice Mathieu had decided to be sociable and sit among the cluster of dramatics. My table was filled by Sibylle (which reassured me as she could keep the conversation flowing), two of her patrons, Mistress Evelina, Mistress Therese (to my dismay), a patron of art, and a patron of music. An odd, mismatched table, I thought as the wine was poured and the first course set down.

"Your master speaks very highly of you, Brienna," Nicolas said, his voice so muted I could hardly hear him over Sibylle's chatter.

"Master Cartier has been a very good instructor," I responded, and realized I had no idea where he was.

My eyes flickered about the other two tables, and found him almost instantly, as if a channel had been forged between us.

He had sat beside Ciri.

I wanted to be hurt by this, that he had chosen to sit with her instead of me. But then I realized his decision had been brilliant, for Ciri was enthused by his choice; indeed, she seemed to glow as she sat between Cartier and Monique. And if he had sat beside me, it would have heightened my reservations; I would not feel the freedom to talk to Nicolas Babineaux, who was likely the final hope I had of securing a patron.

"Tell me more about yourself, Brienna," Nicolas said, dicing his salad.

And so I did, relying on the same conversation thread I had done before with Monique. He listened as he ate; I wondered who he was, what he wanted, and if I would be a good match for him.

Was he too a physician? A historian? A teacher?

By the time the main course came, pheasant and duck drowning in apricot sauce, Nicolas finally revealed himself.

"I am the headmaster of a House of knowledge," he said, dabbing his mouth with a napkin. "I was thrilled when the Dowager extended her invitation to me, for I am currently in need of an arial to teach my ardens."

I should have expected this. Nevertheless, my heart plummeted at the revelation.

This was, perhaps, the one source of patronage that made me the most anxious. For I had only been applying myself to knowledge for three years, and how could I be expected to quickly turn around and teach it to others? I felt like I needed more time, time to expand my mastery, time to gain my confidence. If I had just chosen Cartier from the very first year, if I had not been so foolish to claim I was art . . . then I could easily see myself as a teacher, pouring my passion into others.

"Tell me more of your House," I said, hoping my hesitations were not evident in my voice, in my expression.

Nicolas began to illustrate it for me, a House he had founded west of here, near the city of Adalene. It was a House that instructed only knowledge, a six-year program, teaching girls and boys alike.

I was pondering all of this, wondering if I was being unreasonable by considering myself unprepared for such a task, when I heard my name on Sibylle's tongue.

"Oh, Brienna is excellent at wit, even if she claims she is not!"

My fingers tightened on my fork as I stared at her across the table.

"And how is that?" one of her patrons asked, smiling at me.

"Why, she spent an entire year studying wit alongside me, and I wish she had stayed!" Sibylle had drunk one too many cordials. She was glassy-eyed, unable to read the darts my gaze was trying to send her.

Nicolas turned to me, a frown creasing his brow. "You studied wit?"

"Ah yes, Master Nicolas," I responded, trying to keep my voice low so no one else could hear, for an awkward lull had frosted our table. Even Mistress Therese appeared concerned for me.

In vain, I tried to wear my confidence instead of my worry,

but my treacherous heart started to hammer, breaking my mask to pieces.

"And why is that? I thought you were knowledge," he remarked.

The solstice began to unravel around me, as if it were a spool of midnight, and I could not catch it. Nicolas looked perplexed, as if I had lied to him. It was no secret that I had studied all of the passions, but he apparently had not known. I suddenly realized how I must appear to him.

"I began my time at Magnalia studying art," I said, keeping my voice level, but the shame was there, in the undercurrent of my words. "Then a year in dramatics, then one in music, and one in wit before I began to study knowledge."

"A well-rounded arden!" one of Sibylle's patrons cried, lifting his wine goblet to me.

I ignored him, my gaze on Nicolas, willing him to understand.

"So how many years have you been applying yourself to knowledge?" he asked.

"Three."

It was not the answer he wanted. I was not the passion he wanted.

The night ended for me then.

I continued to sit at Nicolas's side through the remainder of courses served, but his interest had wilted. We talked with those gathered about our table, and after the marzipan confections were served for dessert, I forced myself to mingle with the others. I forced myself to talk and laugh until it was well past midnight and half of the patrons had retired to bed, and only a few of us remained in Merei's tent, listening to her play song after song.

Only then did I slip from the tents and stare at the gardens, drenched in quiet moonlight. I needed a moment alone, to process what had just happened.

I walked along the paths, letting the hedges and roses and ivy swallow me until the night felt peaceful and gentle again. I was standing before the reflection pond, kicking a few pebbles into the dark water, when I heard him.

"Brienna?"

I turned. Cartier stood a good distance away, smudged in the shadows like he was unsure if I wanted him here or not.

"Master Cartier."

He walked to my side, and I had just determined not to tell him anything when he asked, "What happened?"

I sighed, my hands resting on the rigid bones of my corset. "Ah, Master, am I so easy to read?"

"Something happened at dinner. I could see it in your face."

I had never heard regret in his tone, until that moment. I could taste the sorrow in his voice, like sugar melting on my tongue, sorrow that he had not sat beside me. And if he had, perhaps it might have been different. Perhaps he would have been able to keep Nicolas Babineaux's interest piqued.

But most likely not.

"I look uneducated to Mathieu, and inexperienced to Babineaux," I finally confessed.

"How so?" His words were sharp, angry.

I tilted my head, my hair pouring over my shoulder as I mournfully smiled at him in the moonlight. "Do not take it personally, Master."

"I take everything personally when it comes to you and Ciri. Tell me, what did they say?"

"Well, I forgot two entire generations in my genealogy. Brice Mathieu was much alarmed by this."

"I do not care for Brice Mathieu," Cartier swiftly retorted. I wondered if he was the slightest bit jealous. "What of Nicolas Babineaux? He is the patron I want for you."

I realized now that he had wanted me to become an arial. And he must have also known Ciri was going to branch to the physician. He had read her effortlessly, but me? I shivered despite the warmth, feeling like he did not know me at all. And it wasn't supposed to be what he desired; it was what I wanted for myself.

We had two different images in mind, and I wasn't sure if it was possible to align them into something beautiful.

"I thought you said I was a historian, not a teacher," I remarked.

"I did," he replied. "All that being said, you and I are very much alike, Brienna. And I feel as if all historians should begin as teachers. My time here at Magnalia has in no way stanched my love of history. Rather, it has breathed upon it, as if my mind was a mere ember before."

We stared at each other, the starlight sweetening the shadows that had fallen between us.

"Tell me what he said," Cartier softly persisted.

"He was not impressed with my three years."

He sighed and roughly drew his fingers through his hair, his frustration tangible. The buckles on his doublet winked in the dim light as he said, "Then he is not worthy of you."

I wanted to tell him that was kind of him to say. But my throat had tightened, and different words came out instead.

"Perhaps it was never meant to be," I whispered, and began to walk away from him.

His hand took my elbow before I could stray, as if he knew words were not enough to keep me there. And then his fingertips slowly traced down the inside of my bare forearm, exploring all the way to my palm, to catch the curve of my fingers. He held me there before him on the grass—steady, resolute, celestial. It reminded me of another time, long ago, when his fingers had encompassed mine, when his touch had encouraged me to stand and earn my place in this House. When I was but a girl, and he was so far above me I never thought it possible to catch him.

I closed my eyes as the memory haunted me, a jasmine breeze weaving between us, trying to knit us closer.

"Brienna." His thumb brushed my knuckles. I knew he wanted me to open my eyes, to look at him, to acknowledge what was unfolding between us.

He is breaking a rule, I thought. He is breaking a rule for me, and I let that truth gild my heart as I drew in a deep breath.

I opened my eyes; I parted my lips to tell him that he should let me go when we heard laughter on the other side of the hedges.

At once, his fingers released mine and we stepped farther apart.

"Bri! Bri, where are you?"

It was Merei. I turned to the sound just as she emerged from the path, Oriana with her.

"Come, it's time for bed," she said, not seeing Cartier until she took a step closer. She halted when she recognized him, as if she had walked into a wall. "Oh, Master Cartier." She and Oriana instantly curtsied.

"Good night, Brienna," Cartier murmured, bowing to me, bowing to my sisters as he strode away.

Oriana gazed after his retreat with a frown, but Merei kept her eyes on me as I moved to join them.

"What was that about?" Oriana inquired with a yawn as we began to weave our way to the back of the house.

"A deliberation about patrons," I answered.

"Is everything all right?" Merei asked.

I linked my arm with hers, exhaustion suddenly snaking up my back. "Yes, of course."

But her eyes were regarding my face as we emerged back into the candlelight.

She knew that I was lying.

## ·✦· NINE ·✦·

# SONG OF THE NORTH

Monday arrived with rain and restlessness. The Dowager was in her study, conversing with interested patrons for most of the day. The ardens had nothing to do but pace the second floor. We were told to remain nearby, because the Dowager would soon request our presence to discuss our offers.

I sat with my sisters in Oriana and Ciri's room, listening to their conversations excitedly flicker back and forth as the lightning that raged outside.

"Were all three patrons interested in you?"

"Who are you going to pick, if they are?"

"How much do you think they will offer?"

So the questions spun about me, and I listened to my

arden-sisters share their experiences, their hopes and dreams. I listened but didn't speak, because as the hours stretched thin and the afternoon progressed, I began to prepare for my greatest fear to come alive: a creature molded from the shadows of my dismay and failures.

When the clock struck four, the Dowager sent for the first girl. Oriana. As soon as she left the room for her meeting, I retreated to the library. Sitting in the chair by the window, I watched the rain streak the glass with *The Book of Hours* in my lap. I was afraid to read about the Stone of Eventide again, afraid that I might shift into the nameless Maevan lord once more. And yet I wanted to read about the stone, about the shackled magic. I wanted to see Princess Norah again for no other reason than to discover if she had truly been the one to steal the stone from her mother's neck.

I trembled as I read it, waiting for the shift, caught between dread and desire. But the words remained words on a ripened, speckled page. And I wondered if I would ever shift to the past again, if I would ever see him again, if I would ever know why it had happened to me, and if Princess Norah had truly been the one to hand the stone over.

There were so many questions, and no satisfying answers.

"Brienna?"

Thomas, the butler, spoke into the darkness of the library. He caught me off guard and I rose to my feet, my legs prickling with pins and needles as I saw him standing on the threshold.

"Madame would like to see you in her study."

I nodded and set *The Book of Hours* on the lesson table.

Following him, I tried to gird myself with courage. I dwelled on the image of Liadan Kavanagh, imagined her giving me a tiny measure of her victory and bravery. Yet I still trembled when I entered the Dowager's study, because this was the moment I had spent seven years trying to champion, and I knew that I had failed.

The Dowager sat at her desk, warmed by the light of flickering candles. She smiled at the sight of me.

"Please, come sit, Brienna." Her hand extended to a chair before her.

I walked to it and sat with stiff knees. My hands were as ice, and I folded them together over my lap and waited.

"How did you find the solstice last night?" she asked.

It took me a moment to choose the proper response. Should I act as if nothing was wrong? Or should I make it evident that I knew none of the patrons had contended for me?

"Madame, I must apologize," I blurted. This was certainly not the answer I had prepared, but once it had broken from my lips, it rushed forth. "I know that I failed to passion last night. I know I have failed you, and Master Cartier, and—"

"My dear girl, please don't apologize," she gently interrupted. "That is not why I have called you in."

I drew in a deep breath, my teeth aching, my eyes resting on hers. And then I found a tiny seed of courage and acknowledged my fear. "I know that I have no offers, Madame."

Nicolas Babineaux and Brice Mathieu had both found fault in me. But before this truth could further blister my confidence, the Dowager said, "No offers were made, but do not let this distress you. I know the challenges you have faced here over the years, Brienna. You have worked harder than any other arden I have ever admitted."

*Ask her now*, a dark voice whispered in my mind. *Ask her why she accepted you; ask her for the name of your father.*

But to ask would require more courage, more confidence, and mine had waned. I twisted my arden dress in my hands and said, "I will leave tomorrow, with the others. I do not wish to be a burden on your House any longer."

"Leave tomorrow?" the Dowager echoed. She stood and walked the length of the room, coming to a resting place by her window. "I do not want you to depart tomorrow, Brienna."

"But Madame—"

"I know what you are thinking, dear one," she said. "You are thinking that you do not deserve to be here, that your passion is contingent on securing a patron at the solstice. But not all of us travel the same path. And yes, your other five sisters have chosen their patrons and will leave on the morrow, but that does not make you less worthy. On the contrary, Brienna, it makes me believe there is more to you, and I misjudged the proper patrons for you."

I think I must have been gaping at her. For she turned to look at me and smiled.

"I want you to remain the summer with me," the Dowager continued. "During that time, we will find you the right patron."

"But Madame, I . . . I could not ask such of you," I stammered.

"You are not asking for it," she said. "I am offering it."

We both fell quiet, listening to our own thoughts and the chorus of the storm. The Dowager resumed her seat and said, "It is not my choice to say whether you have passioned or not. For that is Master Cartier's decision. But I do think a little more time here will benefit you tremendously, Brienna. So I hope that you will stay the summer. By autumn, we will have you in the graces of a good patron."

Isn't this what I wanted? A little more time to polish myself, to measure the true depths of the passion I was claiming. I would not have to face my grandfather, who would be ashamed of my shortcomings. Nor would I have to embrace the title of inept.

"Thank you, Madame," I said. "I would like to stay the summer."

"I am happy to hear such." When she stood again, I knew she was dismissing me.

I wandered up the stairs to my room, pain blooming with each step as I began to realize what this summer would be like. Quiet and lonely. It would just be the Dowager and me, and a few of the servants. . . .

"Who did you choose?" Merei's enthusiasm greeted me the moment she heard me enter. She was on her knees, busy packing her belongings into the cedar trunk at the foot of her bed.

My own cedar trunk sat in the shadows. I had already packed my possessions, with the expectation I would depart tomorrow with the others. Now I needed to unpack it.

"I had no offers." The confession was liberating. It felt as if I could finally move and breathe, now that it was in the open.

*"What?"*

I sat on my bed and stared at Cartier's books. I needed to remember to give them back to him tomorrow, when I bid him good-bye with the others.

"Bri!" Merei came to me, settled beside me on the mattress. "What happened?"

We had not had a chance to talk. Last night, we had been so weary and bruised from our corsets that we had tumbled into bed. Merei had begun snoring at once, although I had lain in bed and stared into the darkness, wondering.

So I told her everything now.

I told her of what I had overheard in the corridor, of the three patrons, of Ciri's draw to the physician, of my blunders and my spoiled dinner. I told her of the Dowager's offer, of my chance to stay through the summer, of how I honestly wasn't sure what to feel.

The only thing I withheld was that starlit moment with Cartier in the gardens, when he had touched me, when our fingers had been linked. I couldn't expose his decision to willingly break a rule, even though Merei would guard and protect such a secret for me.

She brought her arm around me. "I am so sorry, Bri."

I sighed and leaned into her. "It's all right. I actually do believe the Dowager is correct, as far as patrons. I do not think Brice Mathieu or Nicolas Babineaux were good matches for me."

"Even so, I know you are disappointed and hurt. Because I know I would be."

We sat side by side quietly. I was surprised when Merei stood and retrieved her violin, the wood lustrous in the evening light as she brought it to her shoulder.

"I wrote a song for you," she said. "One I hope will help you remember all the good memories we shared here, and remind you of all the great things still to come."

She began to play, the music soaring through our chamber, eating the shadows and cobwebs. I leaned back on my hands and closed my eyes, feeling the notes fill me, one by one, as rain in a jar. And when I reached that point of overflowing, I beheld something in my mind.

I was standing on a mountain; below me, lush green hills rolled around as the waves on the sea, the valleys veined with sparkling streams and bordering woods. The air here was sweet and sharp, like a blade that cuts to heal, and the mist hung low, as if she wanted to touch the mortals who lived in the meadows before the sun burned her away.

I had never been here, I thought, and yet I belonged.

That was when I became aware of a slight pressure around my neck, a humming over my heart, as if I wore a heavy necklace. And as I stood on this summit looking down, I felt a dark thread of worry, like I was searching for a place to conceal me. . . .

Her song ended, and the vision faded away. I opened my eyes, watched Merei lower her violin and smile at me, her gaze glistening with passion and fervor. And I wanted more than anything else to tell her how exquisite her music was—that this was my song, and somehow she had known the very notes to string together to encourage my heart to see where it should be.

The hills and the valleys, the mountain in the mist, had not been Valenia.

It had been another glimpse of Maevana.

"Did you like it?" Merei asked, fidgeting.

I rose and embraced her, the violin trapped between us as a complaining child. "I love it, Merei. You know and love me so well, sister."

"After I saw Oriana's portrait of you," she said as I let her go, "I thought of your heritage, that you are two in one, north and south, and how marvelous yet challenging that must be. And so I asked Master Cartier if he could find some Maevan music for me, which he did, and I wrote you a song inspired from the passion of Valenia but also the courage of Maevana. Because I think of both when I think of you."

I was not one to cry. Growing up at the orphanage had taught me that. But her words, her revelations, her music, her friendship punctured the stubborn dam I had built a decade ago. I wept as if I had lost someone, as if I had found someone, as if I was breaking, as if I was healing. And she wept with me, and we held each other and laughed and cried and laughed some more.

Finally, when I had no more tears left, I wiped my cheeks and said, "I have a gift for you too, although it is not nearly as marvelous as yours." I opened the lid of my chest, where six little booklets rested, each one bound by leather and red thread. They were filled with poems, written by an anonymous passion of knowledge I had long admired. And so I had bought the booklets with the small allowance Grandpapa sent me every birthday, one for each of my arden-sisters, so they could carry paper and beauty around in their pockets and remember me.

I set one in Merei's hands. Her long fingers turned the pages as she smiled at the first poem, reading it aloud after clearing the trace of tears from her throat.

"'How shall I remember thee? As a drop of eternal summer, or a blossom of tender spring? As a spark of autumn's stirring fire, or perhaps as the frost of winter's longest night? No, it shall not be as one of these, for these shall all come to pass, and you and I, though parted by sea and earth, will never fade.'"

"Again," I said, "not as beautiful as your gift."

"It doesn't mean I will cherish it any less," she responded, gently closing the booklet. "Thank you, Bri."

It was only then we realized the state of our chamber, which looked as if a windstorm had passed through.

"Let me help you pack," I offered. "And you can tell me of the patron you have chosen."

I began to help her gather her music and fold her dresses, and Merei told me of Patrice Linville and his traveling consort of musicians. She had received offers from all three of her patrons, but had decided to choose a partnership with Patrice.

"So you and your music are bound to see the world," I said, awed, as we finished at last with her packing.

Merei closed her cedar chest and sighed. "I don't think it has quite caught up to me, that tomorrow I will receive my cloak and leave this place for constant travel. All I know is I hope that it was the right decision. My contract with Patrice is for four years."

"I am sure it is right," I answered. "And you should write to me, about all the places you see."

"Mmm." She made that sound when she was worried, nervous. "Your father will be very proud of you, Mer."

I knew she was close to her father; she was his only daughter, and had inherited the love of music from him. She had grown up beneath his lullabies, his chansons, and his harpsichord. So when she had asked to attend Magnalia when she turned ten, he had not hesitated to send her, even though it put vast distance between them.

He wrote her faithfully every week, and oftentimes Merei would read his letters to me, because she was determined I would meet him one day, that I would visit her childhood home on the island.

"I hope so. Come, let's get ready for bed."

We donned our night shifts, washed our faces, and braided our hair. Then Merei climbed into bed with me, even though it was a narrow slip of a mattress, and we began to reminisce all of our favorite memories, such as how shy and quiet we had once been our first year rooming with each other. And how we had climbed onto the roof with Abree one night to watch an asteroid shower, only to discover Abree was terrified of heights and it had taken us until dawn to get her back in through the window. And about all the holy day celebrations, when we had a week free from lessons, and the snow arrived just in time for snowball fights, and our masters and mistresses suddenly felt more like older brothers and sisters during the festivities.

"What does Master Cartier think, Bri?" Merei asked around a yawn.

"About what?"

"About you staying through the summer."

I fiddled with a loose thread in my quilt and then responded, "I don't know. I haven't told him yet."

"Will he still give you your cloak tomorrow, then?"

"Probably not," I said.

Merei blinked at me through the watery moonlight. "Did something happen between the two of you, last night in the garden?"

I swallowed, my heart quieting as if it wanted to hear what I might say. I could still feel that agonizing trace of his fingertips down my arm, feather soft and wildly deliberate. What had he been trying to say to me? He was my master, and I was his arden, and until I passioned there was to be nothing more between us. So maybe he was only trying to reassure me, and I had completely misread the touch? That seemed more reasonable, because this was Master Cartier, the strict law abider who never smiled.

Until he had.

"Nothing important," I finally murmured, and then forced a yawn to hide the deceit in my voice.

If she hadn't been so tired, Merei would have pressed me. But two minutes later, she was softly snoring.

I, on the other hand, lay awake and thought about Cartier and cloaks and the unpredictable days to come.

# TEN

## OF CLOAKS AND GIFTS

By nine the following morning, the patrons were beginning their departures from Magnalia. The footmen started to ascend the stairs, gathering each girl's cedar chest and packing it away in the coach of her new patron. I stood amid the flurry in the sunlight of the courtyard and watched, waiting with my basket of poetry booklets. By then, it was no secret that I had not been chosen. And each of my sisters had reacted in the same manner during breakfast. They had hugged me with sympathy, reassured me that the Dowager would find me the perfect patron.

As soon as breakfast was cleared away, I retreated outside, knowing that my arden-sisters were about to receive their cloaks. It wasn't that I didn't want to see them officially gain impassionment; I merely thought it best if I was not there. I did not want to be the awkward observer when Cartier gave Ciri her cloak.

Sweat was beginning to dampen my dress by the time I heard Ciri's voice. She was descending the front stairwell, her pale blond hair tamed in a braided crown. At her back fluttered a blue cloak, a color for midsummer days. She and I came together without words; we didn't truly need them, and when I smiled she turned about, so I could see the constellation Cartier had chosen for her.

"Yvette's Bow," I murmured, admiring the silver threads. "It suits you, Ciri."

Ciri spun back around and gave me a toothless smile, her cheeks flushed. "I only wish that I could see what he picks for you." And there was no longer spite in her voice, no envy, although I heard the words she didn't say. Master Cartier did favor me, and we both knew it.

"Ah, well, perhaps when we meet again," I said.

I gave her the book of poetry, which made her eyes alight. And then she gave me a beautiful writing quill, which swarmed me with a sad pleasure.

"Good-bye, Brienna," Ciri whispered.

We embraced, and then I watched her walk to Monique Lavoie's coach.

I bid farewell to Sibylle and Abree next, who both gave me bracelets as their departing gifts as I admired their cloaks.

Sibylle's green cloak had the stitched emblem of a spade, for wits adorned their cloaks with one of the four suits according to their strengths: hearts for humor, spades for persuasion, diamonds for elegance, clubs for opposition. So Mistress Therese had given Sibylle a spade, and I had to confess it suited my sister very well.

Abree's black cloak had a golden crescent moon nestled in the sun—the dramatics' crest—stitched over the center. But I also noticed that Master Xavier had sewn pieces of her past costumes along the trim of her cloak, to commemorate the roles that had gotten her to this moment. So it was like beholding a sumptuous story of colors and threads and textures. Perfect for my Abree.

Oriana emerged next for the farewell. Her red cloak was extremely detailed and personalized; all passions of art had a bold *A* stitched to the backs of their cloaks, which commemorated Agathe, the first passion of art. But a master or mistress of art would then design something to be stitched within that *A*, and Mistress Solene had outdone herself. For Oriana, Solene had designed the story of a girl ruling an underwater kingdom, complete with sunken ships and treasure. It glistened in silver thread as I gazed at it in awe, honestly not knowing what to say.

"I have a gift for you," Oriana said, shyly withdrawing a sheet of paper from the portfolio she carried. She set the parchment in my hands. It was the portrait she had drawn of me, illuminating my Maevan heritage.

"But Ori, I thought this was for you."

"I made a copy. I felt like you should have one." And then to my surprise, she pulled out yet another sheet. "I also want you to have this." The caricature of Cartier she had drawn years ago, the one of him emerging from rock when we all thought him mean.

I started to laugh, until I questioned why she was presenting this to *me*. "Why not give this to Ciri?"

Oriana grinned. "I think it would fare better in your hands."

Saint LeGrand, was it that obvious? But I had no time to ask her further about it, because her patron was waiting for her in the coach. I slipped the poetry into her hands and watched her leave, my heart trembling as the weight of these good-byes spread an ache in my bones.

Patrice Linville's coach was the only one remaining in the courtyard. I set Oriana's drawings into my basket and turned to the front doors, to the stairs, where Merei stood waiting for me, a glorious purple cloak fastened about her collar.

She was weeping by the time she reached the final stair, as she rushed to meet me on the cobblestones.

"Don't cry!" I fussed, folding her into an embrace. My hands tangled with her passion cloak, and if I hadn't already emptied myself the night before, I would have wept again.

"What am I doing, Bri?" she whispered, dashing the tears from her cheeks.

"You are going to see and play for the realm, sister," I said, tucking a curl of her dark hair away from her eyes. "For you are a passion of music, Mistress Merei."

She laughed, because it was so odd to know she now had a title fastened to her name. "I wish you could write to me, but I . . . I do not think I shall be in one place for too long."

"You should, of course, write to me from wherever you are, and perhaps I can get Francis to track you down with my letters."

She drew in a deep breath, and I knew she was calming her heart, girding herself for this next phase. "Here, this is your song. In case you would like to hear it played by another." Merei handed me a roll of music, bound by a ribbon.

I accepted it, although it hurt to imagine another instrument, another set of hands, playing this song that she had borne. That was when I felt the fissure in my heart. A shadow was creeping up my back, making me shiver in broad daylight, because this farewell might mark something everlasting.

I might never see her again.

"Let me see your cloak," I said, my voice thick.

She turned.

There was music stitched upon the violet fabric, a song Mistress Evelina had written just for Merei. I let my fingertip trace the notes—some of them I remembered; some were now a mystery.

"It is lovely, Mer."

She spun back around and said, "I shall play it for you, when you come to visit me on the island."

I smiled, taking hold of the fragile hope she extended of future visits and music. Let me believe such, I thought, if only to get me through this farewell.

"I think Patrice Linville is ready for you," I whispered, feeling his eyes on us.

I walked her to the coach, to her new patron, a middle-aged man with thistledown hair and a charming smile. He greeted us both and offered his hand to help Merei up into the open coach.

She settled on the bench across from Patrice, her eyes finding mine. Even as the coach began to clatter over the stones, she watched me as I watched her. I stood in the courtyard, as if my feet had grown roots, and watched until I could no longer see her beneath the shadows of the oaks, until she truly was gone.

I should return to the house. Acclimate myself with how quiet it now would be, how bare, how lonely. I should go back and flood myself with books and studies, with anything to keep me distracted.

I walked to the stairs, hollowly looked up at the front doors. They still sat open; I could hear the murmuring of voices—the Dowager and the arials debriefing, no doubt. And I suddenly could not bear to be enclosed within walls.

I couldn't even bear to hold my basket any longer.

I set it on the stairs and walked, walked until I craved to go faster, and then I ran deep into the gardens. I tore open my collar, too impatient to fuss with the buttons, and then decided to also rip the buttons from my sleeves, forcing the ugly gray fabric up my forearms.

I finally came to a stop at the farthest acre, deep in the maze of hedges, where the roses bloomed wild and bright, and there I surrendered wholly to the grass, lying down on the damp earth. But I still wasn't satisfied, so I conceded to yank off my boots and my stockings and pull my dress up to my knees.

I was watching the clouds, listening to the quiet murmur of the bees, the rustling wings of the birds, when I heard him.

"She walks with grace upon the clouds, and the stars know her by name."

I should have been flustered. Here my master had found me,

boots and stockings gone, my legs revealed, my collar broken and my dress muddied. And he had just recited the poem that I loved best. But I felt nothing. And I did not even acknowledge him until he had done the impossible and lain down beside me on the grass.

"You will get muddy, Master."

"It has been far too long since I have lain on the grass and watched clouds."

I still had not looked at him, but he was near enough to me that I could smell the spice of his aftershave. We lay in the quiet for a while, both of our eyes to the sky. I wanted to put some distance between us, let a wide expanse of grass grow betwixt our shoulders, and I wanted to draw close to him, to let my fingers rush over him as his had done to me. How was it that I could want two conflicting things at once? How was it that I did neither of them but remained, unmoving, breathing, captive in my own body?

"Did the Dowager tell you?" I eventually asked, when the desires became so entangled that I needed to speak to loosen them.

Cartier took his time responding. For a moment, I thought he had not heard me. But he finally said, "About you staying on for the summer? Yes."

I wanted to know what he thought about the arrangement. But the words caught in my throat, and so I remained quiet, my fingers weaving through the grass.

"It eases my mind, knowing you will be here," he said. "We do not need to rush. The right patron will come in time, when you are ready."

I sighed, time no longer hastening about me but stalling,

moving slow as honey in winter.

"In the meantime," he continued, "you should resume your studies, keep your mind sharp. I will not be here to guide you, but I have faith that you will continue to master on your own."

I tilted my chin so I could look at him, my hair spreading out around me. "You will not be here?" Of course, I knew this. All the arials left for the summer after a passion cycle, to vacation after seven solid years of teaching. It was only right to let him go and relax, go and enjoy himself.

He angled his face to meet my gaze. A hint of a smile was on his lips when he said, "No, I will be away. But I have already told the Dowager to alert me as soon as she finds your patron. I want to be here when you meet them."

And I wanted to exclaim that I would never get a patron. That I should never have been accepted to Magnalia. But it was the grief that wanted my voice, and I would not give it power to speak. Not when Cartier had given so much to me.

"That is kind . . . that you would want to be here," I said, casting my eyes back to the clouds.

"Kind?" he snorted. "Saints, Brienna. You realize that I wouldn't dare let you leave with a patron I have not met face-to-face?"

I glanced back to him, wide-eyed. "And why is that?"

"Must I answer that?"

A cloud passed over the sun, covering us with gray, drinking away the light. I decided I had lain here long enough and rose to my feet, brushing clumps of grass off my skirts. I didn't even bother with my shoes and stockings; I left them and began to walk, choosing the first path that opened to me.

Cartier was quick on my heels, drawing close to my side. "Will you walk with me, please?"

I slowed, inviting him to adjust to my pace. We took two turns in the path, the sunlight returning with vengeful humidity, before he spoke again.

"I desire to be here to meet your patron because I care about you, and I want to know where your passion leads you." He glanced at me; I kept my eyes ahead, afraid to yield to that gaze of his. But my heart was like a wild creature inside of me, desperate to escape its cage of bone and flesh. "But also, and perhaps more important, so I can give you your cloak."

I swallowed. So he was not going to give it to me yet. Part of me had hoped that he would. Part of me had known that he wouldn't.

The thought of my cloak came about me as gossamer, and I stopped in the grass, trapped in a web of my own making.

"I cannot help but tell you, Brienna," he murmured to me, "that your cloak is made and is tucked away in my satchel at the house, waiting for when you are ready for this next step."

I looked up at him. He wasn't much taller than me, but in that moment, I felt hopelessly small and fragile.

I would not be impassioned until I received my cloak. I would not receive my cloak until I gained a patron. I would not gain a patron unless the Dowager actually found one who saw my value.

My thoughts fell into this downward spiral and I forced myself to keep walking, if only to give me something to do. He followed, as I knew he would.

"Where will you go this summer?" I asked, eager to move on to a different topic. "Will you visit any family?"

"I plan to go to Delaroche. And no, I do not have any family."

His words made me pause. Never had I imagined that Cartier was alone, that he did not have parents who fawned over him, that he did not have brothers or sisters who loved him.

I met his gaze, my hand moving to my neck, to the broken collar of my dress. "I am sorry to hear that, Master."

"I was raised by my father," he said, opening his past to me as if he were a book, as if he—at last—wanted me to read him. "And my father was very good to me, even though he was a grieving man. He lost my mother and my sister when I was very young, so young I don't remember them. When I turned eleven, I began to beg my father to let me passion in knowledge. Well, he did not like the thought of sending me off to a House, away from him, so he hired one of the finest passions of knowledge to teach me privately. After seven years, when I turned eighteen, I became impassioned."

"Your father must have been so proud," I whispered.

"He died, just before I could show him my cloak."

It took everything within me not to reach out to him, to take his hand and lace my fingers with his, to comfort him. But my spine remained locked in place, my status still a student beneath his mastery, and to touch him would only unfetter the longings we both felt. "Master Cartier . . . I am so sorry."

"You are kind, Brienna. Saints know I have grown up quickly, yet I was saved from much. And I found a home here at Magnalia."

We stood together in the quiet incandescence of morning, a time made for new beginnings, a time spun between youth and maturity. I could have stood with him for hours, hidden among green living things, sheltered by clouds and sun, speaking of the past.

"Come, we should return to the house," he said softly.

I fell into step beside him. We walked back around to the front courtyard, where I saw in horror that the caricature of him was sitting upright in my basket. I rushed to turn it over as I looped the basket on my arm, praying he did not see it as we ascended the stairs into the quiet foyer.

His leather satchel sat on the entry bench, and I tried not to look at it, knowing my cloak was tucked within, as he took the bag into his hands.

"I have a gift for you," I said, reaching beneath the parchment to find the last poetry booklet in my basket. "You probably do not remember, but one of the first lessons you gave me was on poetry, and we read this one poem that I loved. . . ."

"I remember," Cartier said, accepting the booklet. He leafed through the pages, and I watched as he silently read one of the poems, pleasure flickering over his expression as sun over water. "Thank you, Brienna."

"I know it is a simple gift," I stammered, feeling as if I had removed a layer of clothing, "but I thought you would like it."

He smiled as he slipped it into his satchel. "And I have something for you." He brought forth a small box, letting it rest in the hollow of his palm.

I took the box and slowly eased it open. A silver pendant with a long chain sat on a square of red velvet. And as I examined it closer, I saw that a Corogan flower was carved into the pendant, a silver drop of Maevan whimsy to rest against one's heart. I smiled as my thumb traced the delicate etching.

"It's lovely. Thank you." I shut the box, unsure of where to look.

"You can write to me, if you want," he said, smoothing over the awkwardness we both felt. "To let me know how your studies fare over the summer."

I met his gaze, a smile quirking the corner of my mouth. "You can write to me as well, Master. To make sure I am not dwindling in my studies."

He gave me a wry look, one that made me wonder what he was thinking, as he slipped his satchel over his shoulder. "Very good. I will be awaiting word from Madame."

I watched him step into the flood of morning, his passion cloak snapping behind him as he departed. I could not believe he had left so swiftly—he was worse at good-byes than I was!—and I hurried to the threshold.

"Master Cartier!"

He stopped halfway down the stairs and turned to look at me. I leaned on the door frame, the small pendant box clutched in my fingers.

"Your books! They are still upstairs on my shelf."

"Keep them, Brienna. I have far too many as it is, and you will need to start your own collection." He smiled; I lost my thread of thought, until I realized he was about to spin around and continue on.

"Thank you."

It felt far too simple for what he had given me. But I could not allow him to leave without hearing it from my lips. Because I felt that fissure again, a cleaving of my heart. It was an admonition, as I had felt saying good-bye to Merei, a warning that I may never see him again.

He did not speak, but he bowed. And then he was gone, like the rest of them.

# ❖ ELEVEN ❖

# BURIED

*July 1566*

The next month passed quietly. I longed for Merei's music, for Abree's laughter. I missed Oriana's spontaneous art, Sibylle's games, and Ciri's company. But even with loneliness for a companion, I was faithful to my studies; I filled my hours with books and lineages, with anatomy and herb lore, with histories and astronomy. I wanted to be able to branch any way I desired with knowledge.

Every Monday, I wrote to Cartier.

At first it was only to ask for his advice about my studies. But then my letters became longer, eager for a conversation with him, even if it was made of ink and paper.

And his letters reflected mine; at first he was succinct, giving me lists of things to study, as he had often done in the past, and then asking me for my thoughts and opinions. But I gradually began to encourage more words and stories out of him, until his letters required two pages, and then three. He wrote about his father, about growing up in Delaroche, about why he'd chosen the passion of knowledge. And soon, our letters were not so much concerned with lessons but about discovering more of each other.

It astonished me that for three years, I had sat nearly every day in his presence and there was still so much I did not know about him.

The month elapsed with letters and studies, with the Dowager sending inquiries to potential patrons, all of which were kindly rejected. But at last, in that fourth week of waiting, something finally happened.

I was walking the long drive one afternoon, beneath the oaks and the threat of a thunderstorm, waiting on the mail. When I was out of sight of the house, I chose one of the oaks to sit beneath, leaning against the trunk, closing my eyes as I thought about how much time I had left of summer. That was when the rain came, gently through the rustling branches above me. Sighing, I rose and caught my sleeve on a small branch.

I felt the sting of a cut in my arm.

The storm broke loose above me, drenching my dress and hair, as I begrudgingly examined my cut. I had torn my sleeve and blood oozed forth. Gently, I touched the wound, the blood staining my fingertips.

There was a buzzing in my ears, a shiver over my skin, the sort of premonition lightning might give before it strikes. The storm no longer smelled like sweet meadows but like bitter earth, and

I watched as the hands before me widened into those of a man, crooked knuckles smudged by dirt and blood.

I glanced up, and the orderly oaks of Magnalia twisted into a dark forest of pines and alders, aspens and hickories. I felt like the woods were spreading me thin; my ears popped and my knees ached until the shift had fully overcome me.

He had cut his arm on a branch too. The same place as mine. And he had stopped to examine it, to smudge his blood on his fingertips.

*He didn't have time for this.*

*He continued weaving through the forest, his tread soft, his breath slightly ragged. He wasn't out of shape; he was nervous, anxious. But he knew the tree that he wanted, and he continued to let branch after branch claw at him to get there.*

*At last, he reached the old oak.*

*It had been here long before the other trees, had sprouted upward with a massive canopy. He had often come to this tree as a boy, climbed and rested in her branches, carved his initials within her wood.*

*He fell to his knees before her now, the twilight dying blue and cold as he began to dig. The loam was still soft from the spring rains, and he furrowed a deep hole among the weaker roots.*

*Slowly, he drew the wooden locket up from beneath his tunic, away from his neck. It dangled from his fingers in a slow, burdened circle.*

*He had had his carpenter render it, just for this purpose, an ungainly wooden locket the size of a fist. It was a locket designed for one purpose: to hold and guard something. A casket for a stone.*

*His fingers were stained with soil as he flicked open the latch, just to look at it one final time.*

*The Stone of Eventide sat within its coffin, translucent save for a tiny flare of red. It was like watching a heart slowly cease beating, the last of the blood drip from a wound.*

*He latched the locket and dropped it into the darkness of the hole.*

*As he buried it—packed down the earth, scattered the pine straw and leaves—he doubted himself again. He had wanted to hide it in the castle—there were so many secret passages and crannies—but if it was ever found among his walls, he would lose his head. It needed to be given back to the earth.*

*Satisfied, he rose with a pop to his knees. But just before he turned away, he searched over the deep ridges of the trunk. And there . . . his fingers found it, traced the old carving of his initials.*

*T.A.*

*He smiled.*

*Only one other person knew of this tree. His brother, and he was dead.*

*He left the tree to the shadows, weaving through the forest just as darkness fell, until he could no longer see.*

*He felt his way out.*

I ran the remainder of the drive, up the hill to the courtyard through sheets of rain. I was sore for breath, because—unlike *him*—I was not in shape, and I nearly busted my shin as I slipped on the front stairs.

I could still feel his thoughts in my own, like oil slipping over water, inspiring a sharp ache in my head; I could still feel the weight of the locket, dangling from my fingers.

The Stone of Eventide.

He had hidden it, tucked it away in the soil.

So the princess *had* stolen it from the queen's neck, after all.

But more important . . . was the stone still buried there, beneath that old oak?

I burst in through the front doors, shocking the sleepy-eyed butler, and then raced down the corridor to the Dowager's study. I knocked, slinging water all over the doors.

"Come in."

I entered her study; she immediately rose to her feet, startled by my drenched appearance, the blood dribbling down my arm.

"Brienna? What is wrong?"

I didn't truly know. And I didn't even know what I was going to tell her, but I was burdened with the need to tell it to someone. Had Cartier been here, I would have told it all to him. Or Merei. But it was just the Dowager and me, and so my boots squeaked over her rug as I sat in the chair opposite her desk.

"Madame, I must tell you something."

She slowly sank back to her seat, her eyes wide. "Did someone hurt you?"

"No, but . . ."

She waited, the whites of her eyes still showing.

"I have been . . . seeing things," I began. "Things of the past, I believe."

I told her of the first shift, channeled by *The Book of Hours*. I told her of Merei's music, with its Maevan influences granting me a glimpse of some northern mountain. And then I told her of my wound and his wound, of the woods and the burial of the stone.

She abruptly stood, the candles on her desk trembling. "Do you know this man's name?"

"No, but . . . I saw his initials, carved on the tree. T.A."

She paced her study, her worry hanging in the air like smoke. I could hardly draw breath as I waited. I thought she would challenge my claim, tell me that I was slowly losing my wits. That what I had said was fantastical, improbable. I expected her to laugh, or become condescending. But the Dowager did none of those things. She was quiet, and I marveled with dread as I waited for her to speak her mind. Eventually, she came to a stop at her window. Facing the glass to watch the storm, she asked, "What do you know of your father, Brienna?"

I was not expecting this question; my heart flared with surprise as I responded, "Not much at all. Only that he is Maevan and that he wants nothing to do with me."

"Your grandfather never told you what your paternal name is?"

"No, Madame."

She walked back to the desk but seemed too agitated to sit. "Your grandfather told me the day he first brought you here. And I swore to him that I would never reveal it to you, out of his concern and protection for you. So I am about to break my word, but only because I feel like your father's blood is calling out to you. Because your paternal name could potentially match this . . . man's last initial, the man you have been shifting to."

I waited, twisted rain from my skirts.

"Your father bears the name of Allenach," she confessed. "I will not speak his first name, so at least I will honor your grandfather on that account."

Allenach.

The name rolled and writhed, ending with a harsh syllable.

Allenach.

It was one of the fourteen Houses of Maevana.

Allenach.

Long ago, Queen Liadan had granted them the blessing of "shrewd" when the clans united into Houses beneath her rule. Allenach the Shrewd.

And yet after all this time, learning the latter half of my father's name didn't affect me how I'd thought it would. It was simply another sound, one that failed to stir much emotion within me. Until I thought of T. Allenach, and how he was pulling me back. Or, now that I reflected on it, how his memories were overlaying with mine.

Cartier had mentioned this, the oddity of ancestral memory. And at the time, I had been more concerned with Lannon and the Queen's Canon to entertain the possibility that it was happening to me.

But it began to come together. For T.A. and I had held and read the same book, had listened to a thread of the same music, and had felt the same pain amid the trees. And so I laid my hands on the armrests of the chair, looked at the Dowager, and said very calmly, "I think I have inherited this man's memories."

The Dowager sat.

It sounded fanciful; it sounded magical. But she listened to me as I told her of what Cartier had randomly said one day in lessons.

"If you are right, Brienna," she said, spreading her hands over her desk, "then what you have seen might be the key to bring about reform for Maevana. What you have seen is . . . very dangerous. Something that King Lannon has ruthlessly tried to keep from happening."

At the mention of Lannon, I stifled a shiver. "Why would this stone be dangerous?"

In my mind, it was a beautiful artifact of ancient Maevana, a channel for magic that was no more. It was a drop of history, painfully lost, which should, of course, be recovered if possible.

"I am sure Master Cartier has taught you the history of the queen's realm," she said, her voice dropping to a whisper, as if she was afraid we would be overheard.

"Yes, Madame."

"And I am sure he has also taught you the current state of politics? That there is a strain between Maevana and Valenia? Our King Phillipe no longer condones King Lannon with his violent affairs, even though King Phillipe's forefather was the very one to set Lannon House as a regal imposter to the northern throne."

I nodded, wondering where she was guiding this conversation. . . .

But the Dowager said nothing as she opened one of her drawers and retrieved a pamphlet, bound by red thread. I recognized the emblem on the front—the unmistakable illustration of a quill that was bleeding.

"You read the *Grim Quill*?" I asked, surprised that she would peruse satire.

"I read everything, Brienna." And she extended it to me. I accepted it, my heart beginning to nervously pound. "Read the first page."

I did as she beckoned, opening the pamphlet. This was an edition I had not read before, and I took it in, word by word. . . .

## HOW TO DETHRONE AN UNRIGHTEOUS NORTHERN KING:

STEP ONE. Find the Queen's Canon.

STEP TWO. Find the Stone of Eventide.

STEP THREE. If step 1 cannot be accomplished, jump to step 2.

If step 2 cannot be accomplished, proceed to . . .

STEP FOUR. Find the Queen's Canon.

STEP FIVE. Find the Stone of Eventide. . . .

It was a set of instructions that continued to circle back upon itself, over and over. I sat quietly, staring at the page, until the Dowager cleared her throat.

"So the Canon . . . or the stone . . ." I began. "One of them is enough to remove Lannon?"

"Yes."

By law, or by magic, a northern king would come undone.

"But magic can only be wielded by the Kavanaghs," I

whispered. "And that House has been destroyed."

"Not destroyed," she corrected. "Many of them, yes, have been ruthlessly hunted and killed by the Lannon kings over the years. But there are some who survived. There are some who found refuge in Valenia. And Lannon knows it. Simply another reason for him to close his borders to us, to gradually turn Valenia into his enemy."

I thought of what she had just told me, what I had just read, what Cartier had taught me, what T.A.'s memories had illuminated. I drew in a deep breath and then said, "If I found the stone and gave it to a surviving Kavanagh . . ."

The Dowager smiled, our thoughts entwining.

Magic would return. And a magical queen could overcome Lannon.

"What am I to do?" I asked.

The Dowager folded her hands, as if in prayer, and pressed them to her lips. Her eyes closed, and I thought maybe she truly was praying, until she suddenly yanked open another drawer of her desk, a determined line creasing her brows.

She had forgone wearing her gable, now that it was just the two of us. Her hair was as a stream of silver in the candlelight, her eyes darkly lucid as she brought forth a sheet of parchment and opened her vial of ink.

"There is an old acquaintance of mine," she began, lowering her voice. "He will find your memories extraordinary. And he will know how to wield them." She took her quill but hesitated just before dipping it in the ink. "He would offer you ready patronage,

Brienna. I would ask that he adopt you into his family, to become your patron father. But before I do this and invite him here to meet you . . . I want you to understand the cost of recovering the stone."

She didn't have to voice the cost; I knew that Lannon was a vicious, cruel king. I knew that he killed and maimed any who opposed him. I was silent, so the Dowager softly continued, "Just because you have seen these things does not mean you must act on them. If you desire the true life of a passion, I can find a safer patron for you."

She was giving me a choice, a way out. I didn't chafe at her warning. But nor did I quail.

I weighed the memories, the name of Allenach, and my own desires.

I knew that sometimes a patron would adopt a passion into their family, usually years after patronage if the bond became very deep. So what the Dowager was offering was odd; she would ask this acquaintance to readily adopt me, without a previously established relationship. This felt strange to me at first, until I began to unravel what I wanted.

What did I want?

I wanted a family. I wanted to belong, to be claimed, to be loved. Furthermore, half of me was hungry to see Maevana, the land of my father. I wanted to become impassioned; I wanted my title and my cloak, which I would not receive until I took a patron. And deep within, in some quiet corner of my heart, I wanted to see King Lannon fall; I wanted to see a queen rise from his ashes.

All of these desires could be answered, one by one, if I was brave enough to choose this path.

And so I answered her without a vestige of doubt.

"Write to him, Madame."

I listened to her quill bite the paper as she invited him to come and meet me. Her letter was short, and as she sprinkled sand over the drying ink, I felt strangely at peace. My past failures did not seem to weigh so heavily upon me any longer. That difficult, uncertain night at the solstice suddenly felt like years ago.

"You know what this means, Brienna."

"Madame?"

She set down the quill and looked at me. "Your grandfather cannot know of this. Cartier cannot know of this."

My mind went blank, and my fingers tightened on the armrests. "Why?" The word scraped up my throat.

"If you choose Aldéric Jourdain as your patron," the Dowager explained, "you will begin a very precarious mission to recover the stone. If Lannon so much as catches wind of this, your life is forfeit. And I cannot let you leave my protection, my House, with the fear that someone may inadvertently expose you. You must leave Magnalia House quietly, secretly. Your grandfather, your master, and your arden-sisters must not know who you are with, or where you are."

"But Madame," I began to protest, only to feel my arguments die, one by one, in my heart. For she was right. No one must know the patron I accepted, especially if that patron was going to use my memories to find the stone that would bring down a cruel king.

Not even Cartier.

The cut on my arm flared when I remembered what he had said to me in the garden, the day he departed. *I wouldn't dare let you leave with a patron I have not met face-to-face.*

"Madame, I worry that Master Cartier . . ."

"Yes, he will be exceedingly vexed to discover you have left without word. But once all of this is resolved, it will be explained to him, and he will understand."

"But he has my cloak."

The Dowager began to fold the letter, preparing to address it. "I fear you will have to wait to receive it, until all this passes."

There was no certainty that it would pass, or how long it would take. A year? A decade? I swallowed as I watched the Dowager warm her wax over a candle.

I imagined Cartier returning to Magnalia at the start of autumn, wondering why I had not written to him, wondering why he had not been summoned. I could see him step into the foyer, the leaves trailing him; I could see the blue of his cloak and the gold of his hair. Saints help me, I could hardly bear to think of him discovering that I had left without a word, without a trace. As if I did not appreciate the passion he had sparked in me, as if I did not care for him.

"Brienna?"

She must have sensed my turmoil. I blinked away the glaze of my agony and met her gentle stare.

"Do you wish for me to recant this letter? As I said, you can easily choose another path." She held the edge of it to the flame, to burn it if I so wanted.

Recant the letter and disregard my ancestor's memories. It was like a forbidden piece of fruit, dangling on the vine, now that I knew how many I would have to leave in the dark. My grandpapa. Merei. Cartier. I might not ever receive my cloak. Because Cartier might shred it.

"Do not recant the letter," I determined, my voice rasping.

As she poured a dab of wax on the envelope, she said, "I would not take such strict precautions—I would not ask you to leave so quietly—if Lannon's spies did not lurk about Valenia. With the tensions rising between our two countries, with publications like the *Grim Quill* . . . Lannon feels threatened by us. He has men and women who dwell among us, ready to whisper names of Valenians who openly oppose him."

"Lannon has spies *here*?" I countered, hardly able to believe it.

"You have been very sheltered at Magnalia, dear one. King Lannon has eyes everywhere. Now you might understand why your grandfather was so adamant about sheltering you from the name of Allenach. Because he did not want you to be claimed unto their House. Because he wanted you to look and feel as Valenian as possible."

Oh, I understood. It didn't make it any sweeter to digest.

My father must be one of Lannon's staunch supporters. He could be anyone, from the groom to the yeoman to the castle chamberlain. Many lords' vassals took on his last name to show their unwavering allegiance. Which meant I was about to wage war against him; I was about to become his enemy before I even knew him. And so I leaned forward and took the edge of the Dowager's table, until she met my gaze.

"I would ask only one thing of you, Madame."

"Speak it, child."

I drew in a deep breath, looked down at the dried blood on my arm. "Swear to me you will not tell Aldéric Jourdain the full name of my father."

"Brienna . . . this is not a game."

"As I know," I said, keeping my voice respectful. "My patron will know I hail from Allenach's House, that my father's allegiance is to that House, but that does not mean my patron needs to know my father's identity."

The Dowager hesitated, her eyes sharpening over mine as she tried to understand my request.

"I have never seen my father," I continued, my heart twisting deep in my chest. "My father has never seen me. We are utter strangers, and our paths most likely will never cross. But if they do, I would prefer my patron not to know who he is, since I will never know who he is."

She was still debating.

"I have grown up here with you knowing, with my grandfather knowing, with such knowledge withheld from me," I whispered. "Please, do not give it to another to hold over me, to judge me by."

She finally softened. "I understand, Brienna. So I will swear to you: I will speak your father's name to no other."

I leaned back into the chair, shivering against the dampness of my dress.

I thought of these old, faded memories, of the patron who was very soon coming to meet me.

I thought of Grandpapa.

Merei.

My cloak.

The Dowager pressed her seal into the wax.

And I resolved to think of Cartier no more.

# PART TWO

# JOURDAIN

# —⫷ TWELVE ⫸—

# A PATRON FATHER

*August 1566*

Aldéric Jourdain arrived to Magnalia on a hot stormy evening a fortnight after the Dowager had sent her letter in the post. I remained in my room watching the rain streak the window, even after I heard the sounds of the grand doors opening below and the Dowager greeting him.

She had sent all of the servants away for a brief vacation, leaving behind only her faithful Thomas. This was to ensure that Jourdain and I left in utter secrecy.

As I waited for her to send word to come downstairs, I walked to my bureau. Cartier's latest letter sat open, weighed down by the pendant's box, his penmanship elegant in the candlelight.

Ever since the Dowager and I had made our resolution about

Aldéric Jourdain, I had begun to gradually shorten my letters to Cartier, preparing for this moment when I would quietly leave. And he had felt it—my distance, my retreat, my desire to talk only of knowledge and not of life.

*Are you worried about a patron? Talk to me, Brienna. Tell me what is drawing you away. . . .*

So he had written to me, his words smoldering as an ember in my heart. I hated to think that he would never receive a proper response, that I had written my final letter to him days ago, claiming all was well.

There was a gentle rap on the door.

I crossed the floor, smoothing the wrinkles from my arden dress, tucking my hair behind my ears. Thomas stood on the other side of my door, holding a candle to burn away the evening shadows.

"Madame is ready for you, Brienna."

"Thank you, I will be right down." I waited until he had melted back into the darkened corridor before I began my descent down the stairs, my hand trailing behind me on the balustrade.

The Dowager had told me nothing of this Aldéric Jourdain. I did not know his profession, how old he was, or where he lived. So I followed the light to the Dowager's study with a tremor of apprehension.

Pausing before the door, the place of all my eavesdropping transgressions, I listened to his voice, a rich baritone, polished around the vowels. He spoke too low for me to catch every word, but from the sound of him, I imagined he was a well-educated man in his early fifties. Perhaps he was a fellow passion.

I stepped forward into the candlelight.

He was sitting with his back to me, but he saw my entrance in the softness of the Dowager's face as her eyes shifted to me.

"Here she is. Brienna, this is Monsieur Aldéric Jourdain."

He immediately stood and turned to face me. I met his stare, carefully taking in his height and strong build, his russet hair streaked with gray. He was clean-shaven and handsome even with a crooked nose, although in the dim lighting I could see the scar of an angry wound along his right jaw. Despite his travel, his clothes hardly held a wrinkle. The scent of rain still hovered about him, along with the tang of a spice I did not recognize. There was no passion cloak.

"A pleasure," he said, giving me a casual bow.

I returned it with a curtsy, moving to sit in the chair that had been set for me, adjacent to his. The Dowager was perched behind her desk, per usual.

"Now, Brienna," Jourdain said, resuming his seat and retrieving his glass of cordial. "Madame has told me only a glimpse of what you have seen. Tell me more of your memories."

I glanced to the Dowager, hesitant to share something so personal with an utter stranger. But she smiled and nodded at me, encouraging me to raise my voice.

I told him all that I had told to her. And I expected him to snort, to scoff, to say that I was making absurd claims. But Jourdain did nothing but quietly listen, his eyes not once leaving my face. When I was done, he set his glass down with an eager clink.

"Could you find this tree?" he asked.

"I . . . I am not sure, monsieur," I replied. "I saw no other distinguishing landmarks. It was a very dense forest."

"Is it possible for you return to the memories? Revisit them just as vividly?"

"I do not know. I have only experienced the shift three times, and there is little I can do as far as controlling them."

"It seems that Brienna must make a connection to her ancestor," the Dowager inputted. "Through one of her senses."

"Hmm." Jourdain crossed his legs, his finger absently stroking the scar on his chin. "And your ancestor's name? Do you, at least, know that?"

My eyes flickered to the Dowager once more. "His first name begins with a T. As for his last name . . . I believe it was Allenach."

Jourdain went very still. He was not looking at me, but I felt the ice of his gaze, a bitterness so cold it could sunder bone. "Allenach." The name—my name—sounded very rough on his tongue. "I take it you hail from that House, Brienna?"

"Yes. My father is Maevan, serves beneath that House."

"And who is your father?"

"We do not know his full name," the Dowager lied. She lied, for me, and I could not help but sag in relief, especially after seeing Jourdain's apparent disdain for the Allenachs. "Brienna was raised here in Valenia, with no ties to her paternal family."

Jourdain settled deeper in his chair and took his glass once more. He swirled the rosy liquid about, deep in his own thoughts. "Hmm," he hummed again, a sound that must mean he was perturbed by his contemplations. And then he looked at me, and I swore there was a touch of wariness in his gaze, as if I was not nearly as innocent as I had once been upon entering, now that he knew half of my heritage.

"Do you think you could guide us to the location of the Stone of Eventide, Brienna?" he asked after what felt like a season of silence.

"I would do my best, Monsieur," I murmured. But when I dwelled on what he was asking, I felt the weight of an uncertain territory come to rest on my shoulders. I had never seen Maevana. I hardly knew anything about the Allenachs, or their land and woods. The old oak was marked by a *T.A.*, but there was no assurance that I could comb through a forest and find such a tree.

"I want to make myself very clear," Jourdain said after draining the last of his cordial. "If you accept my offer of patronage, it will be nothing as you expect. Yes, I would honor the binds of patronage, and I would take you as my own daughter. I would care for you and protect you, as a good father should. But my name comes with risks. My name is a shield, and beneath it are many secrets that you might never learn but all the same must guard as if they were yours, because it could mean something as vital as life or death."

I stared back at him steadily, and asked, "And who are you, Monsieur?"

"To you? I am merely Aldéric Jourdain. That is as far as you need to know."

By the Dowager's shifting, I knew that she knew. She knew

who he truly was, who the man beneath Aldéric Jourdain was.

Was he refusing to tell me for my own protection? Or because he did not trust me, with my Allenach roots?

How could I accept a patron if I did not know who he truly was?

"Are you a Kavanagh?" I dared to ask. If I was about to find the Stone of Eventide, I wanted to know if my patron father had the old dragon blood. Something sat wrong in my mind when I thought about recovering the stone only to restore his magic. I was not going to take the crown from Lannon only to give it to another king.

A smile softened his face; a gleam sparked in his eyes. I could tell I had amused him when he replied, "No."

"Good," I responded. "If you were, I don't think this arrangement would be wise."

The room seemed to grow colder, the candlelight receding as my implication clearly manifested. But Aldéric Jourdain hardly flinched.

"You and I want the same thing, Brienna," he said. "We both desire to see Lannon removed, to see a queen ascend. This cannot happen if you and I do not unite our knowledge together. I need you; you need me. But this choice is ultimately yours. If you feel that you cannot trust me, then I think it best we part ways here."

"I need to know what will happen once I find the stone," I insisted, worry crowding my thoughts. "I need your word that it will not be misused."

I expected a long-winded explanation. But all he said was, "The Stone of Eventide will be given to Isolde Kavanagh, the rightful queen of Maevana, who is currently in hiding."

I blinked, stunned. I had not expected him to give me her name; it was an extraordinary measure of trust, since I was as much a stranger to him as he was to me.

"I know what I am asking you to do is precarious," Jourdain continued gently. "The queen knows this as well. We would not expect any more than for you to help us find the location of the stone. And afterward . . . we would pay you abundantly."

"Do you think I want riches?" I asked, my cheeks warming.

Jourdain merely stared at me, which made my blush deepen. Then he asked, "What do you want, Brienna Allenach?"

I had never heard my first and last name vocally acknowledged, linked together as summer and winter, given to the air, musical as it was painful. And I hesitated, battling what I thought I should say and what I desired to say.

"Would you want to join your father's House?" Jourdain asked, very carefully, as if we were standing on ice. "If you do, I would honor your wishes. We can revoke the adoption after our mission. And I would not hold any ill will toward you for it."

I couldn't drown the small glimmer of desire, of hope. I couldn't deny that I did want to see my blood father, that I wanted to know who he was, that I wanted him to see me. But all the same . . . I had grown up with the belief that illegitimate children were burdens, lives no one wanted. If I did ever come across my father, he most likely would turn his back on me.

And that image drove a blade into my heart, made me pitch forward slightly in the chair.

"No, monsieur," I said once I knew my voice was steady. "I want nothing with the Allenachs. But I do ask for one thing."

He waited, cocked his brow.

"Whatever plans you forge," I began, "I want a voice in them. After the Stone of Eventide is found, it remains with me. I am the one to give it to the queen."

Jourdain seemed to hold his breath, but his eyes never broke from mine. "Your input will be needed and appreciated in the plans. As for the stone . . . we need to wait and see as to what is the wisest strategy. If it is best for it to remain with you, it will. If it is best for it to remain with another, it will. All that being said, I can promise that you will be the one to present it to the queen."

He was crafty with words, I thought as I picked apart his response. But my greatest worries were for the plans to proceed without my input, that the stone would fail to be given to the queen. On these two matters, I had his word, so I finally nodded and said, "Very well."

"Now," Jourdain said, glancing back to the Dowager as if I had never doubted his intentions. "The legality of this must wait. I cannot risk putting my name or hers through the royal scribes."

The Dowager nodded, although I could tell she did not like this. "I understand, Aldéric. As long as you hold to your word."

"You know that I will," he replied. And then to me, he said, "Brienna, would you accept me as your patron?"

I was to become this man's daughter. I was to take his name as my own, without knowing what it meant, what it had bloomed from. It felt wrong; it felt right. It felt dangerous; it felt liberating.

And I smiled, for I was accustomed to feeling two conflicting desires at once.

"Yes, Monsieur Jourdain."

He nodded, not quite smiling, not quite frowning, as if he was just as disharmonized as I was. "Good, very good."

"There is one last thing you should note, Aldéric," the Dowager said. "Brienna has not yet received her cloak."

Jourdain cocked his brow at me, just now realizing I wore no passion cloak at my collar. "How come?"

"I am not impassioned yet," I responded. "My master was going to provide me with my cloak when I took a patron."

"I see." His fingers thrummed along the armrests. "Well, we can work around that. I take it that every precaution has been extended to this arrangement, Renee?"

The Dowager inclined her head. "Yes. No one will know Brienna has departed in your care. Not even her grandfather, or her master."

"Well, we can replicate a cloak for you," Jourdain said.

"No, Monsieur, I do not think that wise," I dared to say. "For you see . . . you would have to choose a constellation to also replicate on the cloak, and that constellation would need to be registered in my name at the Astronomy Archives in Delaroche, and—"

He held up his hand in peace, a mirthful smile quirking the corners of his lips. "I understand. Forgive me, Brienna. I am not well versed in your passionate ways. We will think of an explanation for this tomorrow."

I quieted, but a lump formed in my throat. A lump that emerged whenever I thought of my cloak, of Cartier, and what I was having to leave behind. The past fortnight, I had lain awake in bed, my room unbearably quiet without Merei's snores, and wondered if I had just applied seven years of my life for nothing. Because it was very possible that Cartier might disown me in this space of time when I could not contact him.

"Are you packed, Brienna?" my new patron inquired. "We should leave at dawn."

I did well at concealing my surprise, even though it flared in me like breathing on a flame. "No, Monsieur, but it will not take me long. I do not have much."

"Get some rest, then. We have a two-day journey ahead of us."

I nodded and rose, returning to my room, hardly feeling the floor beneath my feet. Kneeling, I opened my cedar chest and began to gather my belongings, but then I looked to my shelves, at all the books Cartier had given me.

I stood, let my fingers caress each of their spines. I would take as many as I could fit in my chest. The others I would place in the library, until I could return for them.

Until I could return for him.

## ‑‑❧ THIRTEEN ❧‑‑

## AMADINE

"You need a new name."

I had been riding in his coach for an hour, the dark slowly blushing into dawn, when Aldéric Jourdain finally spoke to me. I was sitting opposite him, my back already sore from the bump and jerk of the cab.

"Very well," I conceded.

"Brienna is a very Maevan-inspired name. So you need to sound as Valenian as possible." A pause, and then he added, "Do you have a preference?"

I shook my head. I had slept a scant two hours last night; my head was aching and my heart felt like it had tangled with my lungs. All I could think of was the Dowager, standing on the cobbles to bid me farewell, her gentle hand resting on my cheek.

*Do not worry about Cartier. He will understand when all of this passes. I will do my best to ease his mind. . . .*

"Brienna?"

I snapped from my reverie. "You can pick, Monsieur."

He began to rub his jaw, mindlessly tracing his scar as he regarded me. "What about *Amadine*?"

I liked it. But I didn't know how I was going to train myself to respond not only to the surname of Jourdain, but to Amadine as well. It felt like I was putting on clothes too small for me, trying to stretch the fabric until it fit, until it conformed to my body. I would either have to lose pieces of myself, or let out a few seams.

"You approve?" he prompted.

"Yes, Monsieur."

"Another thing. You must not call me Monsieur. I am your father."

"Yes . . . Father." The word rolled around my mouth like a marble, unfamiliar, uncomfortable.

We rode another half hour in silence; my eyes strayed to the window, watching the green hills gradually begin to flatten into fields of wheat as we traveled west. This was a quiet, pastoral piece of Valenia; we passed only a few simple stone houses, dwellings of solitary farmers and millers.

"Why do you want this?" I asked, the question rising before I could check it for politeness. My eyes returned to Jourdain, who was watching me with a calm, bemused expression. "Why do you want to rebel against a king who would kill you if he discovered your plans?"

"Why do you want this?" he countered.

"I asked first, Father."

He looked away from me, as if he was weighing the words. And then his eyes returned to mine, darkly gleaming. "I have witnessed enough of Lannon's cruelties in my lifetime. I want to see him obliterated."

So he hated King Lannon. But *why*? That is what I wanted to know. What had Aldéric Jourdain seen, what had he witnessed, to elicit such a strong desire?

Father and daughter we may be now, but that didn't mean he was going to divulge his secrets.

"Most would say this is not a Valenian's fight," I responded carefully, trying to encourage more out of him.

"But isn't it?" he answered. "Was it not our glorious King Renaud the First who put the Lannons on the throne in 1430?"

I mulled on that, unsure if we were about to argue over Valenia's past involvement or not. Rather, I shifted our conversation by saying, "So . . . we can *obliterate* Lannon's power by the Stone of Eventide?"

"Yes."

"What about the Queen's Canon?"

He snorted. "Someone taught you thoroughly."

"Is the stone enough? Don't we need the law as well?"

He leaned back, hands resting on his knees. "Of course we need the law as well. Once magic is restored and Lannon has fallen, we will reestablish the Canon."

"Where do you think the original is?"

He didn't speak; he merely shook his head, as if he had

wondered this so often it wearied him. "Now it is your turn to answer. *Why* do you want this, mistress of knowledge?"

I glanced down to my fingers laced together on my lap. "I once saw an illustration of Liadan Kavanagh, the first queen." My gaze met his again. "Ever since then . . . I have wanted to see a queen rise, to take back what is hers."

Jourdain smiled. "You are Maevan on your father's side. That northern blood in you desires to bow to a queen."

I thought of that as we rode a half hour in silence, until another question pulled my voice.

"Do you have a profession?"

Jourdain shifted on the cushion but gave me a sliver of a smile.

"I am a lawyer," he began. "My home is Beaumont, a little river town that makes some of the finest wine in all of Valenia. I am a widower, but I live with my son."

"You have a son?"

"Yes. Luc."

So I was to have a brother as well? My hand rose to my neck, feeling the chain of Cartier's pendant that hid beneath my dress, as if it were an anchor, or a charm for courage.

"Do not worry," Jourdain said. "You will like him. He is . . . quite the opposite of me."

If I had felt more comfortable, I might have teased Jourdain for his wry comment about not liking him. But my patron was still a stranger. And I couldn't help but wonder how long it would take for me to feel at ease with my new life. But then I dwelled on how this all came about—far from traditional roots of patronage—and

I thought, No, I cannot expect to feel the least bit relaxed.

"Now then," he said, once more breaking the depths of my reflections. "We need to flesh out your background. Because no one can know you come from Magnalia."

"What do you suggest?"

He sniffed, glanced out the window.

"You passioned in knowledge beneath Mistress Sophia Bellerose, of Augustin House," he said.

"Augustin House?"

"Have you heard of it?"

I shook my head in decline.

"Good. It's rural and unknown to minds that would be too interested in you." He frowned, as if he was still trying to weave together my story. Then he said, "Augustin House is an all-girls' establishment, hosting all five of the passions, and is a ten-year program. You entered the House at the age of seven, when you were selected out of the Padrig Orphanage, based on your sharp mind."

"Where is this Augustin House?"

"Eighty miles southwest of Théophile, in the province of Nazaire."

The silence swelled again, both of us lost in our own thoughts. I began to lose track of time—how long had I been riding with him? How much longer did we have to go?—when he cleared his throat.

"Now it is your turn to come up with a story," Jourdain said.

I met his gaze, waiting warily.

"You need a viable explanation as to why you lack your cloak. Because, for all our purposes, it is to be known you are my passion daughter, adopted into the Jourdain family, a mistress of knowledge."

I eased out a breath, rolled my shoulders to feel my back pop. He was right; I needed to have an explanation prepared. But this was going to require some creativity and confidence, because passions never lost their cloaks, never stepped out in public lacking their cloaks, and guarded their cloaks as a mythical dragon guarded her hoard of gold.

"Keep in mind," he said, watching the lines furrow on my brow, "that lies can easily catch you in their webs. If you can remain close to the truth, then you will have a beacon to help you out of any incriminating conversation."

Before I could share my ideas, the coach gave a lurch, nearly bucking us from our benches.

I looked at Jourdain, wide-eyed, as he shifted to peer out the window. Whatever he saw made a curse I had never heard before fly from his tongue. It was followed by our coach coming to a rough halt.

"Stay in this coach, Amadine," he ordered, his hand patting the front of his doublet. He was reaching for the door when it swung open, and we were greeted by a sallow, narrow face, leering at us.

"Out! Both of you," the man barked.

I let Jourdain take my hand and draw me out behind him. My pulse was skipping as I stood on the muddy road, Jourdain trying to keep me tucked out of sight behind him. Peeking out from behind his great height, I saw our coachman—Jean David—held at knifepoint by another greasy-looking man with hair the color of rotten mutton.

There were three of them. One had Jean David, one was circling about Jourdain and me, and the other was rifling through my cedar chest.

"Saint's bones, there's nothing but blithering books in here," one with a bald head and a jagged scar exclaimed. I winced as he tossed my books, one right after the other, onto the road, the pages protesting all the way down to the mud.

"Keep looking," the sallow-faced leader said as he walked yet another circuit around me and Jourdain. I tried to remain small and unworthy, but the thief pulled me out anyway, taking hold of my elbow.

"Do not touch her," Jourdain warned. His voice was cold and smooth as marble. I think it frightened me more than witnessing the thievery unfold.

"She's a little young for you, don't you think?" the leader said with a dark chuckle, dragging me even farther away. I fought him, trying to slip from his fingers. He merely prodded Jourdain in the stomach with a knife to make me cease. "Quit pulling, Mademoiselle, or else I disembowel your husband."

"That is my daughter." Again, Jourdain's voice and composure were deathly calm. But I saw the fury in his eyes, a spark of a blade whetted along a stone. And he was trying to tell me something with those eyes, something I couldn't understand. . . .

"I'll enjoy becoming acquainted with you," the thief said, his eyes blatantly undressing me until they discovered my necklace. "Ah, what do we have here?" He set the point of his blade to my throat. He pricked me, just enough to make a bead of blood well. I began to tremble, unable to contain my fear as his blade traced down the length of my neck, smearing my blood, drawing forth Cartier's silver pendant. "Mmm." He jerked it free; I gasped as the chain cut into the back of my neck, as my pendant left me for this vile scum of the earth. But it was the moment Jourdain was waiting for.

My patron moved like a shadow, a blade suddenly flashing in his hand. I don't know where the dagger came from, but I stood, frozen, as Jourdain stabbed the thief in the back, right in the kidney and then sliced his neck, blood spewing up into his face as the thief roiled on the ground at my feet.

I tripped backward as Jourdain went for the second one, the one destroying all of my books. I didn't want to watch, but my eyes were riveted to the bloodshed, watching him effortlessly kill the second thief, taking care to do it away from my books. And then Jean David was scuffling with his captor, grunts and blood spilling onto the road.

It was over so quickly. I don't think I breathed until Jourdain slipped his dagger back into the inside pocket of his doublet, until he strode to me, freckled in blood. He reached down and plucked my pendant from the thief's clawlike hand, cooling in death, Jourdain's thumb wiping away the lingering carnage.

"I shall get you a new chain when we get home," he said,

extending the pendant to me.

Hollowly, I accepted it, but not before I noticed the arch of his brow. He had recognized the carving of the Corogan flower. He knew it was a Maevan symbol.

I didn't want him to ask me where I got it. But all the same, I didn't want him suspecting it had come from the Allenachs.

"My master gave this to me," I said, my voice hoarse. "Because of my heritage."

Jourdain nodded, and then kicked the closest corpse out of the way. "Amadine, quickly gather your things. Jean David, help me with the bodies."

I moved like I was ninety years old, sore and feeble. But every time I recovered another book, my shock gave way to anger. A simmering, dangerous anger that made it feel like ash was coating my tongue. I wiped the mud from the pages and set them back inside my chest as Jourdain and Jean David tossed the bodies over the ridge, out of sight from the road.

By the time I had finished, the men had changed their doublets and shirts, and had washed the blood from their faces and hands. I latched my cedar chest and met Jourdain's gaze. He was waiting for me, the door of the coach open.

I walked to him, scrutinized his clean-shaven face, his perfectly groomed hair that he had plaited back in a noble queue. He looked so refined, so trustworthy. And yet he had not hesitated to kill the thieves; he had moved as if he had done it before, a dagger sprouting from his fingers as if it were part of him.

"Who *are* you?" I whispered.

"Aldéric Jourdain," he replied, handing me his handkerchief so I could wipe the blood from my neck.

Of course. Irritated, I took the square of linen and settled back into the coach, my thumb rushing over my pendant. As Jourdain climbed in behind me, shutting the door, I thought of only one thing.

Who, indeed, had I just become the daughter to?

The rest of the day passed uneventfully. We made good time, arriving to a small town just over the Christelle River as the sun sank behind the treetops. While Jean David delivered the horses and coach to the communal stables, I followed Jourdain to his carefully selected inn. The scent of roasting fowl and watery wine met us, permeating my hair and dress as we found a table in the corner of the tavern hall. There were a few clusters of other travelers, most of whom looked windblown and sunburned, most of whom hardly spared us a second glance.

"We shall have to get you some new clothes when we reach home," Jourdain said after the servant girl had delivered a bottle of wine and two wooden cups.

I watched him pour it, a trickle of red that made me think of blood. "You've killed before."

My statement made him stiffen, like I had tossed a net over him. He purposefully plopped down the bottle of wine, then set down my cup before me and chose not to answer. I watched him drink, the light of the fire casting long shadows over his face.

"Those thieves were vile, yes, but there is a code of justice here in Valenia," I whispered. "That crimes are to be brought before a magistrate and a court. I should think you would know such, being a lawyer."

He gave me a warning glance. I knitted my lips together as the servant girl delivered seedy bread, a wheel of cheese, and two bowls of stew to our table.

Only when the girl had returned to the kitchens did Jourdain square up to me, set down his cup with frightening gentleness, and say, "Those men were going to kill us. They would have slain Jean David, then me, and saved you for their pleasure before giving you the blade. If I had merely injured them, they would have pursued us. So tell me again why you are upset that we lived?"

"All I am saying is you dealt a Maevan justice," I responded. "An eye for an eye. A tooth for a tooth. Death before trial." Only then did I lift my cup to him and drink.

"Are you likening me to *him*?" "Him" obviously being King Lannon. And I heard the hatred in Jourdain's voice, the indignation that I would even string him and Lannon on the same thought.

"No," I said. "But it makes me wonder . . ."

"Wonder what?"

I tapped my fingers on the tabletop, drawing the moment out. "Perhaps you are not as Valenian as you seem."

He leaned forward, his tone sharp as he stated, "There is a time and place for such a conversation. This tavern is not it."

I bristled under his reprimand—I was unaccustomed to it, this fatherly chiding. And I would have rebelliously kept talking had Jean David not entered and joined our table.

I don't think I had heard the coachman speak one word since I had met him that morning. But he and Jourdain seemed able to communicate with mere glances, gestures. And they did such as they began to eat, holding wordless conversations since I was in their presence.

It bothered me at first, until I realized I could sit and focus on my own mulling without interruption.

Jourdain looked and sounded Valenian.

But then again, so did I.

Was he a dual citizen as well? Or perhaps he was a full-blooded Maevan who had once served beneath Lannon and fled in defiance, weary of serving a cruel, unrighteous monarch? It was only a matter of time before I found him out, I thought as I salvaged the last of my stew.

Jean David unexpectedly rose with a bump to the table, finished with dinner. I watched him leave the hall with his gentle gait, his black hair so oily it looked wet in the rosy light, and realized Jourdain must have silently dismissed him.

"Amadine."

I turned back around to meet Jourdain's calm stare. "Yes?"

"I am sorry you had to witness that today. I . . . I realize you have led a very sheltered life."

Part of this was true; I had never seen a man die. I had never seen that much blood spilled. But in other ways . . . books had prepared me more than he realized. "It's all right. Thank you for your protection."

"One thing you should know about me," he murmured, nudging his empty bowl aside. "If anyone so much as threatens my family, I won't hesitate to kill them."

"I am not even of your blood," I whispered, surprised by his steely resolve. I had only been his adopted daughter for one day.

"You are part of my family. And when the thieves tore apart your things, threw your books in the mud, threatened you . . . I reacted."

I didn't know what to say, but I let my gaze remain on his face. My embers of defiance and irritation faded into darkness, because the longer I looked upon him, my patron father, I sensed that something in his past had made him this way.

"Again, I am sorry you had to see such of me," he said. "I do not want you to fear me."

I reached across the table, offering my hand. If we were going to succeed in whatever plans we authored, we would have to trust each other. Slowly, he set his fingers in mine; his were warm and rough, mine were cold and soft.

"I do not fear you," I whispered. "Father."

He squeezed my fingers. "Amadine."

## —⊰ FOURTEEN ⊱—

# PASSION BROTHER

*Town of Beaumont, Province of Angelique*

We reached the river town of Beaumont just as the sun was setting on the second day of travel. This was the farthest west I had ever ventured, and I was enchanted by the vast miles of vineyards that graced the land.

Beaumont was a large town, built along the banks of the lazy Cavaret River, and I intently watched as we passed the market square and the atrium of a small cathedral. All the buildings appeared the same to me, built from bricks and marbled stones, tall and three-storied, hugging narrow cobbled roads.

The coach eventually stopped before a brick town house. A pebbled walkway to the front door was choked with moss and flanked by two cranky sweetgum trees, whose branches rattled against the windows.

"Here we are," Jourdain announced as Jean David opened the coach door.

I took the coachman's hand and stepped down, and then I accepted Jourdain's arm when he offered it, surprised by how thankful I was to have his support. We walked in stride along the path, up the stairs to a red door.

"They are all eager to meet you," he murmured.

"Who?" I asked, but he had no time to respond. He guided me over the threshold and we were met by two waiting faces in the foyer, their eyes latching to me with polite inquisition.

"This is the chamberlain, Agnes Cote, and this is the chef, Pierre Faure," Jourdain introduced.

Agnes gave me a well-rehearsed bob of a curtsy in her simple black dress and starched apron, and Pierre smiled behind the flour smudged on his face, and bowed.

"This is my daughter, Amadine Jourdain, adopted through passion," Jourdain continued.

Agnes, who had the aura of a mother hen, came forward to hold both my hands in her warm ones, an intimate greeting. She smelled of citrus and crushed pine needles, betraying her obsession with keeping all things clean and orderly. Indeed, from what I could see of the mahogany paneled walls and white tiled floors, this was a rigorously tidied house. And I could not help but feel as if I was beginning a fresh life—a blank slate with endless possibilities—and returned her smile.

"If you need anything at all, you simply call for me."

"That is very kind of you," I answered.

"Where is my son?" Jourdain inquired.

"With the consort, monsieur," Agnes was swift to respond, dropping my hands. "He apologizes in advance."

"Another late night?"

"Yes."

Jourdain appeared dissatisfied, until he noticed I was carefully watching him and his face lightened. "Pierre? What is on the menu tonight?"

"We have trout for tonight, so I hope you like fish, Mistress Amadine," the chef responded. His tenor voice was raspy, as if he had spent far too many hours singing while he cooked.

"Yes, I do."

"Excellent!" Pierre bustled back down the hallway.

"Dinner is at six," Jourdain informed me. "Agnes, why don't you give Amadine a tour of the house? And show her to her room?"

Just as Jean David entered carrying my trunk, Agnes led me around the first floor, showing me the dining hall, the small parlor, Jourdain's austere office, and the library, which was crammed with books and instruments. I knew Jourdain was a lawyer, yet his house was eclectically grand and polished, bespeaking one who was educated and seemed to favor the passions. It felt like home, and relief washed over me; it was the last thing I expected, to feel at ease in a new place.

"Is Jourdain's son a musician?" I asked, taking in the scattered sheets of music over the covered spinetta, the piles of books on the floor that my skirts threatened to upset, and a very old lute, which sat upright in a chair as a faithful pet waiting for its master to return.

"He is indeed, Mistress," Agnes answered, her voice thick with pride. "He is a passion of music."

Fancy that. Why hadn't Jourdain mentioned such to me?

"And he is part of a consort of musicians?" I looked to the hasty scrawl of his handwriting, the broken quills, and the vials of inks with half-plugged corks.

"Yes. He is very accomplished," Agnes continued, beaming. "Now let me show you to the second floor. That is where your room will be, as well as Master Luc's and Monsieur Jourdain's."

I followed her from the library, up a set of horribly creaky stairs to the second floor. There was a linen room, Jourdain's and Luc's rooms, which she did not open but pointed to their closed doors so I would know where they were, and at last she took me down the hall to a chamber that sat at the back of the house.

"This is your room, Mistress," Agnes said and swung open the door.

It was beautiful. There was a pair of windows overlooking the river, with thick rugs over the wooden floors and a canopy bed that could comfortably sleep two people. It was simple, yet perfect for me, I thought as I approached a small desk before one of the windows.

"Monsieur says you are a passion of knowledge," Agnes commented from behind me. "I can bring you any book from the library, or I can fetch paper and ink if you wish to write."

I had no one to write to, I thought somberly, but smiled anyway. "Thank you, Agnes."

"I will go and draw you water so you can freshen up before

dinner." She bobbed another curtsy and then was gone.

Jean David had already set my cedar chest at the foot of the bed, and while I knew that I should begin to unpack, I felt far too tired. I lay down on my bed, staring up at the gauzy canopy. Did Agnes and Pierre know about my situation? Did Jourdain trust them enough to tell them about my memories? And what of his son, this Luc? Did he know?

I wondered how long I was to live here, how long before we pursued the stone. A month? Half a year?

Time, my old nemesis, seemed to laugh at me as I closed my eyes. The hours began to move unbearably slowly, mocking me. A day would feel like a month. A month, like a year.

I wanted to rush; I wanted to hasten and reach the end of this journey.

I fell asleep with such desires tumbling through my heart as stones down a well.


I woke just before dawn, in the belly of night's coldest hour.

I sat forward with a jolt, unsure of where I was. On the desk, a candle was burning, its wax almost completely eaten. Blearily, I soaked in the surroundings by the fragile light, and I remembered. This was my new chamber at Jourdain's. And I must have slept through dinner.

A quilt had been laid over me. By Agnes, most likely.

I slipped from the bed and took the candle, my hunger complaining in my empty stomach. Barefoot, I descended the stairs, learned which ones creaked so I could avoid them in the future. I was about to make my way to the kitchens when the velvet darkness of the library—the rich scent of books and paper—caught me in the hall.

I entered it, taking care to look where I stepped. The bizarre piles of books stroked my interest. I had always been the same, aggregating strange clusters of books ever since I had chosen knowledge. Kneeling down to examine which titles lived in one stack, I set my candle aside and began to go through them. Astronomy. Botany. Musical theory. The History of the Renauds . . .

I had read most of these already, I thought. I was just reaching for the next pile when a strange voice spoke through the darkness. . . .

"Oh, hello."

I whirled about, unsettling the stack of books and nearly catching the house on fire. I caught the candle just before it plummeted and stood up, my heart pounding.

In the dim light of my candle, I saw a young man sprawled in a chair, the lute cradled in his arms. I had not even noticed him sitting there.

"Forgive me, I did not mean to startle you," he apologized, voice dusty from sleep.

"You must be Luc."

"Yes." He sleepily smiled and then rubbed his nose. "You must be my sister."

"Were you sleeping in here?" I whispered. "I am so sorry. I should not have come down so early."

"Don't be sorry," he reassured me, and set the lute down to stretch. "Sometimes I sleep in here when I get home late. Because the stairs creak."

"So I discovered."

Luc yawned, leaning back into the chair to regard me by the light of the sputtering candle.

"You are lovely."

I stood frozen, unsure of how to respond. And then he baffled me even further when he lumbered to his feet and folded me into a tight embrace, as if he had known me his entire life and we had been separated for years.

My arms were stiff as I slowly returned the affection.

He was tall and skinny, and he smelled of smoke and something spicy that he must have eaten for dinner and spilled on his shirt. He pulled away from me but his hands remained on my arms.

"Amadine. Amadine Jourdain."

"Yes?"

He smiled down at me. "I am happy you are here."

His tone told me that he knew. He knew of my memories and my purpose.

"As am I," I returned with a faint smile.

He was not handsome. His face was plain, his jaw a bit crooked, his nose a touch too long. And his mop of dark brown hair stood up in all the wrong angles. But there was something very gentle about his gray eyes, and I found the more he smiled, the more endearing he became.

"At long last, I get a passion sister. My father says you are knowledge?"

"Y-yes." Well, almost a passion of knowledge. But I think he knew that as well, because he didn't press me further about it. "And you are a master of music, are you not?"

"What gave it away?" he teased. "My clutter or the instruments?"

I smiled, thinking of Merei. She and Luc would get along quite nicely. "Do all of these books belong to you?" I indicated the piles.

"Three-quarters of them do. The rest are my father's. Which, speaking of him, how was the journey here? I heard there was . . . an altercation of sorts."

The last thing I wanted was to appear nervous and cowardly among these people. So I brushed the hair away from my eyes and said, "Yes. Your father handled it rather . . . what is the word?"

"Violently?" he provided.

I didn't want to confirm or oppose, so I let silence fill my mouth.

"I am sorry that was your first impression of him," Luc said with a little huff, "but he has never had a daughter before. I hear it is far more worrisome than having a son."

"Worrisome?" I repeated, my voice rising with indignation. Saints, was I really about to fight with Luc Jourdain not ten minutes into knowing him?

"Don't you know that daughters are far more precious and revered than sons?" he returned, his brows cocked but his eyes still gentle. "That fathers are, yes, content with a son or two, but it is daughters they truly want? And as such, a father would slay any who even dare to think of threatening her?"

I held his stare, questions stirring in my mind. I still wasn't comfortable, or brave enough, to speak my thoughts. But I dwelled on what he said, knowing this was no Valenian concept. Daughters were loved in the southern kingdom, but it was the sons who inherited everything. Titles, money, estates. So what Luc was expressing happened to be a very old Maevan way of thinking, the desire to have and raise up daughters, to love and esteem them. All because of Liadan Kavanagh's influence.

"That is, of course," he rambled on, "until fathers can teach their daughters to defend themselves. Then they do not have to worry so much over them."

Yet another Maevan sensibility—a woman with a sword.

"Hmm," I finally hummed, borrowing the sound from Jourdain.

Luc recognized it and his smile broadened. "We are already rubbing off on you, I see."

"Well, I am your sister now."

"And again, I am very happy you are here. Now, make yourself at home, Amadine. Any book you want, feel free to enjoy. I'll see you at breakfast in an hour." He winked at me before he departed. I heard the stairs creak as he took them, two at a time, up to his room.

I finally selected a book and sat in a chair hidden behind the spinetta, watching dawn's first light steal into the room. I tried to read, but the house was beginning to come to life. I listened to Agnes's gait as she opened shutters and swept the floor and set the china on the dining table. I heard Pierre whistle and the clink of pots hitting one another, the aromas of frying eggs and sizzling mutton spreading through the house. I listened as Jean David walked down the hall in his creaking leather boots, sniffing his way into the kitchen as a hound to a bone. And then I heard Jourdain's tread as he descended the stairs, clearing his throat as he passed the library and entered the dining chamber.

"Is Amadine awake yet?" I heard him ask Agnes.

"I have not checked on her. Should I? The poor girl looked so exhausted last night. . . ." She must be pouring him a cup of coffee. I could smell it—dark, rich sustenance—and it made my stomach rumble so fiercely I don't know how the entire house didn't hear it.

"No, leave her be. Thank you, Agnes."

Next, I heard Luc descend the creaky stairs, light-footed and energetic. I heard him step into the dining chamber, greet his father, and then ask, "Well, where is this new sister of mine?"

"She'll be along. Have a seat, Luc."

A chair scraped the floor. I could hear the clink of china, and I watched as my candle ate the last of its wick, finally dying with a trail of smoke. Then I rose, realizing my hair was tangled and my dress hopelessly wrinkled from sleep and travel. I did my best to braid my tresses, hoping I didn't look like a wraith as I entered the dining room.

Luc stood at the sight of me—one of those noble Valenian customs—but he rattled everything on the table in his haste.

"Ah, there you are," Jourdain said, placing his hand on the shivering china before something spilled. "Amadine, this is my son, Luc."

"Pleased to meet you Amadine," Luc said with an amused

smile and a half bow. "I hope you slept well your first night here?"

"Yes, thank you for asking," I responded, settling in the chair across from his.

Agnes arrived to pour me a cup of coffee. I all but groaned in delight, thanking her as she set a pot of cream and a bowl of sugar cubes by my plate.

"So, Amadine," Luc said, spreading jam on his toast. "Tell us more about you. Where did you grow up? How long were you at Magnalia?" He had washed and combed his hair back, and it struck me odd how different he appeared in the fullness of light. But I suppose shadows have a way of changing how one remembers a stranger's face.

I hesitated, glancing to Jourdain.

My patron father's eyes were already resting on me. "It's all right," he murmured. "You can trust everyone in this house."

So everyone in this house was involved, or would soon be, with whatever plans we made to find the stone.

I took a sip of coffee, to slick away the cobwebs of my exhaustion, and then began to tell them as much as I felt comfortable sharing. Most of this, Jourdain already knew. But he still listened intently as I rummaged through my past. My time in the orphanage, my grandfather's plea to the Dowager, seven years at Magnalia, each passion attempted but only one nearly mastered . . .

"And who is your master?" Luc asked. "Maybe I know him."

Most likely not, I thought as I remembered how quiet and reserved Cartier was, how he had spent seven years of his life wholeheartedly serving Magnalia, pouring his knowledge into Ciri and me. "His name is Cartier Évariste."

"Hmm. Never heard of him," my passion brother said, scraping the last of the eggs from his plate. "But he must be very accomplished, to be an arial at a House as revered as Magnalia."

"He is very passionate," I agreed, taking another sip of coffee. "He is a historian as well as a teacher."

"Does he know you are here?" Luc licked his fingers. Definitely not Valenian table manners, but I let it pass as if I had not noticed.

"No. No one knows where I am, who I am with." I felt Jourdain's gaze on me again, as if he was beginning to understand how painful this arrangement was for me.

"It is difficult for us to predict when we will be able to recover the stone," Jourdain said. "Part of it will rely on you, Amadine, and this is not to pressure you, but we really do need another one of your ancestors' memories to manifest, one that will hopefully give us solid evidence as to what forest the stone is buried in. Because there are four major forests in Maevana, not to mention all the other little thickets and woods not worthy to note on a map."

I swallowed, feeling a piece of toast scrape all the way down my throat. "How would you like me to do this? I . . . I have little control over them."

"As I know," Jourdain replied. "But when the Dowager first sent her letter, stating she had an arden of knowledge who had inherited ancestral memories . . . I began to do my own research on the matter. Luc found some documents at the archive at Delaroche, which proved to be useless, but one of my clients—a fellow passion of knowledge who is a renowned physician—has done some fascinating research on the topic." I watched as Jourdain reached within the inner pocket of his doublet. But instead of fetching a dagger, this time he brought forth a bouquet of papers, extending them to me. "This is his dossier, which he generously loaned to me. Here, have a look."

I accepted them carefully, feeling the wear of them. The penmanship was sharp and slanted, and crowded page after page. As Agnes began to clear away the china, I let my eyes move over the words.

*The experience with the ancestral memories of my five patients differ greatly, from age of onset to how deep and extensive the memories flow, but one thing I have found constant: the memories are difficult to control, or subdue, without prior knowledge of the ancestor.*

*The memories cannot be commanded to start without a bond (sight, smell, taste, sound, or any other sensory pathway), and there is difficulty in halting them once the stream begins.*

I paused, my gaze still hovering on the words as I tried to absorb this. I looked to the next page and read:

*A boy of ten, fallen from his horse, concussion, odd memories surfacing and compelling him to climb the highest bell tower. His ancestor had been a notorious thief, living in the crooks and shadows of the steeple. A young woman, an inept passion of wit, whose ancestral memories were conjured after she jumped from a bridge in Delaroche to drown herself . . .*

"You want me to try and force a bond?" I said, glancing up to Jourdain.

"Not necessarily force," he amended. "But encourage one. Luc is going to help you with this."

My passion brother smiled and raised his cup of coffee to me. "I have no doubt we can accomplish this, Amadine. Father has already mentioned the other bonds you have made, one through the book, one through music, and one through your wound. I think we can easily manifest another memory."

I nodded, but I didn't feel as confident as him. Because my ancestor had lived a good one hundred and fifty years before me. He was not only a man, he was a full-blooded Maevan. He had not grown up among polite society, but in a world of swords and blood and gloomy castles. There truly was not much we could have in common.

But this was why I was here. This was why I was sitting at this table with Aldéric Jourdain, who was really someone else I was not supposed to know, and with his sanguine son, Luc. Because the three of us were going to recover the Stone of Eventide, uproot King Lannon, and set Isolde Kavanagh on the throne.

So I poured a little more cream into my coffee and then took up my cup and said, as vibrantly as I could, "Excellent. When do we start?"

## —❧ FIFTEEN ❧—

## ELUSIVE BONDS

The most obvious place to start would be music. Because I had already shifted, albeit very weakly, to the sound of a Maevan melody, and Luc was a musician.

We began right after breakfast, retreating to the library, which was bound to become our exploratory chamber. I brought him the roll of Merei's song, her red ribbon still fastened over her perfectly inked notes. I watched as Luc sat on a stool and unrolled it, eagerly reading the notes, and I felt that lump lodge in my throat. I missed her, and this song was not going to sound the same, not even played by a fellow passion of music.

"An interesting title," he remarked, glancing up at me.

I had not even seen the title. Frowning, I stepped closer so I could read it over his shoulder.

*Brienna, Two in One.*

I turned away, pretending to find something fascinating on the crowded shelves. But it was only to give me a moment to tame my emotion. I would not weep here; I would cry only once my jar of tears refilled, and that would hopefully be a long time from now.

"Why don't you play it for me?" I suggested and sat in the chair by the spinetta again.

Luc stood and gently smoothed the pages, weighing each of the corners down with a river rock. I watched as he took his violin and his bow and leaped into the song, the notes dancing in the air about us as will-o'-the-wisps, or fireflies, or maybe even how magic might have saturated a room, had it not been dead for so long.

I closed my eyes and listened. This time, I could find those Valenian pieces—spritely, lively, something Merei called allegro— and then I found those Maevan influences—strong and deep, mellow, rising as smoke, building to a victorious crescendo. But I remained in my chair, my mind wholly my own.

I opened my eyes once he had ceased playing, the memory of the song still sweet in the air.

"Did you see anything?" he asked, unable to conceal his hope.

"No."

"Let me play it again, then."

He played it through two more times. But T.A.'s memories remained sheltered. Perhaps I had inherited only three of them? Perhaps a bond could be used only once?

I was beginning to feel discouraged, but Luc's energy and

determination was like a cool breeze on summer's worst day.

"Let's try *The Book of Hours* again," he said, laying his violin safely on its side. "You said reading the passage on the Stone of Eventide inspired the first shift. Perhaps your ancestor read more of that book."

I didn't want to tell him that I had read many other chapters of that volume, to no avail. Because everything must be attempted again, just to ensure it was a dead end.

Time, for all her previous mockery, suddenly eased and the hours began to move with speed. An entire week passed. I hardly took notice, for Luc kept me busy trying anything he could think of.

We tested all my senses; he had me taste Maevan-inspired food, run my fingers through bolts of northern wool, listen to Maevan music, smell pine and clove and lavender. But I failed to manifest a new memory.

He eventually sat me at the table in the library and unrolled a bolt of maroon linen, a red so dark it almost looked black. In the center there was a white diamond, and in the diamond was the emblem of a stag leaping through a ring of laurels.

"What is this?" Luc asked me.

I stared at it but eventually conceded to shrug. "I don't know."

"You've never seen this?"

"No. What is it?"

He yanked his fingers through his hair, finally displaying a measure of worry. "These are the colors and the coat of arms for the House of Allenach."

I studied it again, but I sighed. "I'm sorry. There is nothing."

He pushed the banner to the side and then unrolled a large map of Maevana; it depicted the cities and landmarks as well as the boundaries of the fourteen territories.

"Here are the forests," he said. "To the northwest, we have Nuala Woods. Then to the far northeast, the Osheen Forest." He pointed to each. My eyes followed his fingertip. "Then we have the slender strip of coastal Roiswood, on the southwestern side. And last, the Mairenna Forest, in the southern heart of the land. This is the one where I think your ancestor has buried the stone, since it sprawls through the northern half of Allenach's territory."

I had never seen a map of Maevana divided into her fourteen territories. My gaze touched each of them before coming to rest on the land of Allenach, which claimed a vast southern territory of Maevana. It was Allenach's land that came closest to touching Valenia; the Berach Channel was the only thing separating the two countries. But I didn't need to be looking at the water. I shifted my eyes to the Mairenna Forest, which spread as a dark green crown over the land of my father's birth.

"I . . . I don't know. I don't see anything," I all but moaned, burying my face in my hands.

"It's all right, Amadine," Luc was quick to say. "Don't worry. We'll come up with something." But he eased himself into a chair, as if his bones had turned to lead. And we sat at the table in the dying light of the afternoon, the map spread between us as butter, one week already gone.

There had to be an explanation for the memories I had been

given. If the Allenach armorial banner had struck nothing within my mind—and my ancestor had undoubtedly looked upon that sigil countless times during his life—then there had to be a reason why I had inherited some memories but not others.

I thought back to the three shifts I had experienced—the library, the summit, and the burial beneath the oak. The library and the burial were both clearly centered on the stone. But the view from the summit . . .

I traced back through it, the weakest of the shifts, and remembered how I had felt a weight about my neck, just over my heart. How I had been searching for a place to hide . . .

My ancestor must have stood on that summit with the stone hanging about his neck, seeking the location where he would eventually bury it.

So the memories I had inherited centered only on the Stone of Eventide.

My gaze strayed to the map, taken with the path of the river Aoife, which wound through southern Maevana as an artery, and it made me think of the Cavaret River, just beyond Jourdain's back door.

"Luc?"

"Hmm."

"What if we found a river rock, one the size of the Stone of Eventide? Maybe holding it would manifest something. . . ."

That perked him up. "It's worth a try."

We rose from the table, and I followed him out into the street. I didn't want to tell him that I was beginning to feel like a prisoner in that library, in that house; I had not walked outside since I had arrived, and I slowed my pace, tipping my head back to the sun.

It was the middle of August, a month bloated on heat and stale air. Yet I drank in the sunlight, the slight breeze that smelled of fish and wine. A part of me missed the clean meadow air of Magnalia, and I realized only then how much I had taken that place for granted.

"Are you coming, Amadine?"

I opened my eyes to see Luc waiting for me a few yards away, an amused smile on his face. I fell into stride beside him as we wound our way through the street, taking the road that led to the riverbank. We passed by the market, which was teeming with life and smells, but I didn't give myself the luxury to be distracted. And Luc set a hardy pace; he led me to where the Cavaret River ran wide and shallow, where the currents danced over the backs of rocks.

He pulled off his shoes and rolled up his breeches, wading to the center of the rapids while I was content to search along the banks. A rock the size of a fist, I had told him. And as I continued to meander down the shore, stopping here and there to scrutinize a few rocks, I wondered if this was going to be another futile attempt. . . .

"Lady?"

I glanced up, startled to see a man watching me. He was only two arm lengths away, leaning against the trunk of a river birch. He was middle-aged with shoulder-length dark hair; his face was wrinkled and weathered, his clothes ratty and filthy, but his eyes were as two coals that had just felt breath upon them. They gleamed at the sight of me.

I halted, unsure what to do, and he pushed off the tree and took one step closer, the shade dappling his shoulders and face. He meekly extended a hand, his dirty fingers trembling.

"Lady, what is the name of the man who you live with?"

I took a step back, jarring my ankle in a deep eddy of the river. The stranger was speaking Middle Chantal—the language of Valenia—but his voice held an obvious accent, a betraying brogue. He was Maevan.

Saints, I thought, my tongue sticking to the roof of my mouth. Was he one of Lannon's spies?

"Please, tell me his name," the man whispered, his voice going hoarse.

That was when I heard the splashing. Luc had finally seen him, and I cast a half glance over my shoulder to see my brother come crashing toward us, his breeches fully drenched, a dagger in his hand. So he was more like his father than I'd realized, sprouting steel and blades like weeds.

"Get away from her," he growled, stepping between me and the stranger.

But the bedraggled man held his ground, his eyes gone wide as he stared at Luc.

"Go on! Away with you!" Luc impatiently flicked the dagger toward him.

"Lucas?" the stranger whispered.

I felt the air change, the wind pull back as if she were fleeing.

Luc's back stiffened, and a cloud stole the sunlight as the three of us stood, unmoving, uncertain.

"Lucas? Lucas Ma—"

Luc was on the stranger, snapping from his web of shock. He took the man by the collar and shook him, holding the tip of the steel to the man's grubby neck.

"Do not dare speak such a name," my brother ordered, so low I could hardly catch the words.

"Luc? Luc, please," I cried, moving closer.

But Luc hardly heard me. He was staring at the man; the man stared right back, although tears were lining his eyes, dripping down his bearded cheeks.

"How long have you been here?" Luc hissed.

"Six years. But I've waited . . . waited twenty-five years . . ."

There was a loud splash from behind us. We turned to look, to see a group of children on the other side of the bank. Two of the boys were warily watching us, and Luc lowered his dagger, but it still remained sheathed between his fingers.

"Come, we can give you a hot meal for the night," Luc said loudly, so the children could hear. "But you will have to go to the cathedral if you need alms." He glanced at me, wordlessly telling me to follow close behind him as he hauled the stranger forward, keeping the blade tucked sightlessly against the man's back.

It was an awkward, hasty walk to the house. We entered through the back door, and I remained in Luc's shadow all the way to Jourdain's office door, which was abruptly closed in my face. I stood in the hall, unbalanced, and listened to the rumble of Jourdain's voice, of Luc's, of the stranger's, as they conversed behind the heavy door. No chance of eavesdropping, but I didn't need to as I found a seat on the creaky stairs. Because the pieces were slowly coming together.

Cartier had once spoken to me of a revolution-turned-massacre that had happened twenty-five years ago in Maevana. I closed my eyes, remembering the cadence of my master's voice. *Twenty-five years ago, three lords tried to dethrone Lannon . . . Lord Kavanagh, Lord Morgane, and Lord MacQuinn. . . .*

I dwelled on all the fragments that I had been gathering since I'd met Aldéric Jourdain. A widower with a son. A lawyer skilled with a blade. Twenty-five years, with a last name that began with *M*. A man who desired to see Lannon obliterated.

I finally knew who Jourdain was.

## —❖ SIXTEEN ❖—

# THE GRIM QUILL

I waited on the stairs, watching the afternoon light fade into dusk, an ache pounding in my head. But I wasn't going to move, not until I could catch Jourdain and set a few things straight. So when the office door finally opened, spilling candlelight into the hall, I quickly stood, the stair creaking beneath me.

Luc and the stranger emerged first, heading down the corridor to the kitchen. And then came Jourdain. He stood on the threshold and felt my gaze, glancing up to where I stood.

"Father?"

"Another time, Amadine." He began to follow Luc and the stranger to the kitchen, willfully ignoring me.

Ire boiled up my throat as I cleared the last stair, following him into the hall. "I know who you are," I said, my words pelting him as rocks in the back. "You may not be Lord Kavanagh the Bright, but perhaps you are Lord Morgane the Swift?"

Jourdain halted as if I had pressed a blade to his throat. He didn't turn around; I could not see his face, but I watched his hands curl into fists at his sides.

"Or might you be Lord MacQuinn the Steadfast?" I finished. That name had scarcely had time to leave the tip of my tongue when he rounded on me, his face pale with fury as he took my arm and pulled me into his office, slamming the door behind us.

I should be afraid. I had never seen him look so furious, not even when he took on the thieves. But there was no room for fear in my mind, because I had spoken truth—I had spoken his name to him, the one he had never wanted me to know. And I let that name sink into me, let the truth of who he was settle in my heart.

MacQuinn. One of the three Maevan lords who had boldly attempted to reclaim the throne twenty-five years ago. Whose plans to dethrone Lannon and crown Kavanagh's oldest daughter had fallen to ashes, and as a consequence, whose wife had been slaughtered, who had fled with his son, to hide and quietly endure.

"Amadine . . ." he whispered, his voice choking on my name. The white wrath was gone, leaving exhaustion in its wake as Jourdain collapsed in his chair. "How? How did you guess?"

I sat slowly in one of the other chairs, waiting for him to look at me. "I've known you were Maevan ever since I saw you so effortlessly cut down the thieves."

He finally met my gaze, his eyes bloodshot.

"It makes sense to me now, why you reacted so violently. How you will protect your family at all cost, because I now know you have lost someone very precious to you. And then this . . . stranger . . . mentioned that he had waited twenty-five years," I continued, lacing my cold fingers together. "Twenty-five years ago, three courageous Maevan lords stormed the castle, hoping to place a rightful daughter on the throne, to reclaim it from a cruel, unrighteous king. Those lords were Kavanagh, Morgane, and MacQuinn, and though they may be hiding, their names are not forgotten—their sacrifice is not forgotten."

A sound came from him, a tangle of laughter and weeping, and he covered his eyes. Oh, it broke my heart to hear the sound come from such a man, to realize how long he had been hiding, carrying the guilt of that massacre.

He lowered his hands, a few tears still clinging to his lashes, but he chuckled. "I should have known you would be shrewd. You are an Allenach, after all."

My heart turned cold at the sound of that name, and I corrected him by saying, "It's not that, but because I am a passion of knowledge, and I was taught the history of Maevana. Were you ever going to tell me the truth?"

"Not until Isolde was crowned. But it was only out of protection for you, Amadine."

I could not believe it. I could not believe my patron father was one of the rebellious Maevan lords—that a name I had once heard Cartier merely talk about was now sitting before me in the flesh.

I glanced to the papers scattered on his desk, overwhelmed. My gaze caught on something familiar . . . a piece of parchment with a drawing of the unmistakable bleeding quill. I reached for it; Jourdain watched as I held up the illustration with a tremor in my fingers.

"You're the *Grim Quill*," I whispered, my eyes darting to his.

"Yes," he responded.

I was flooded with awe, worry. I thought back to all those pamphlets I had read, how bold and persuasive his words were. And I suddenly understood the "why" of it all . . . why he wanted to obliterate the northern king. Because he had lost his wife, his land, his people, his honor because of Lannon.

I read the words he had scrawled beneath the drawing, a messy first draft of his upcoming publication:

*How to ask pardon for rightfully rebelling against a man who thinks he is king: Offer your head first, your allegiance second. . . .*

"I . . . I cannot believe it," I confessed, setting the paper down.

"Who did you think the *Grim Quill* was, Amadine?"

I shrugged. "I honestly don't know. A Valenian who liked to poke fun at Lannon, at current events."

"Did you think that I fled here to hide and cower, to sit on my hands, to try to become Valenian and forget who I was?" he asked.

I didn't answer, but my gaze held his, my emotions still running the gamut.

"Tell me, daughter," he said, leaning forward. "What does every revolution need?"

Again, I was quiet, because I honestly didn't know.

"A revolution needs money, belief, and people willing to fight," he replied. "I began writing the *Grim Quill* almost two decades ago, hoping that it would stir Valenians as well as Maevans. Even if the Dowager had never told me about you and what your memories could unleash . . . I would have continued writing and publishing the *Grim Quill* for however long it took, until I was ninety and frail, until people—Valenian, Maevan, or both united—eventually rose, with magic or without it."

I wondered what that would feel like—he had spent over twenty years in hiding, letting his anonymous words slowly chip away at Valenian ignorance and Maevan fear. And he would spend twenty more doing it, if that's what it required, until he had the money, the belief, and the people to make it possible.

"So without me and the promise of the stone," I said, clearing my throat. "What were you planning to do?"

Jourdain steepled his fingers, propped his chin on them. "We currently have persuaded three Valenian nobles to our cause, who have provided funds, who have promised men to fight. Based on that, we project that we could successfully revolt in four years' time."

In twenty-five years, he had only garnered the support of *three* Valenian nobles. I shifted in my chair. "Wouldn't that spark a war, Father?"

"It would. A war that has been one hundred and thirty-six years in the making."

We stared at each other. I kept my face carefully guarded, even though the image of war made my heart wither. And suddenly, I was besieged with fear of conflict, of battles and spilled blood and death.

"What if you asked Lannon to pardon you?" I dared to ask. "Would he be open to change? To negotiations?"

"No."

"Surely he has advisers there? At least one person who would listen to you?"

He sighed. "Let me tell you a little story. Thirty years ago, I used to attend the royal hearings. Once a week, Lannon would sit on his throne and listen to the people's complaints and requests. I stood among the crowd, bearing witness with the other lords. And I cannot tell you how many times I saw men and women—*children*—cut to pieces at the footstool of the throne, fingers and tongues and eyes and heads. All because they dared to ask something of him. And I watched it, afraid to speak out. We were all afraid to speak out."

I struggled to imagine his story, struggled to fathom that such violence was happening north of here. "There is no peaceful way to do this?"

He finally understood my questions, the glaze in my eyes. "Amadine . . . your procuring the stone and reviving magic is the most peaceful route to justice. I cannot promise there will not be conflict or a battle. But I do want you to know that without you, war would eventually come."

I broke our gaze, glancing down to the pleats of my dress. He was silent, giving me time to process the revelations that had begun to unfold, knowing I was simmering with more questions.

"How do you know the Dowager?" I asked.

Jourdain drew in a deep breath, and then poured himself a glass of cordial. He poured one for me as well. I saw it as a long-awaited invitation, that he was about to tell me some dark things, and I graciously accepted the drink.

"Twenty-five years ago," he began. "I joined Lord Morgane and Lord Kavanagh in their plans to upset Lannon, to place Kavanagh's eldest daughter on the throne. She had a trace of that ancient, magical blood, according to their lineage, which distantly draws from the first queen, Liadan, but more than that . . . we were finished with serving a wicked king such as Lannon, who manipulated us, who oppressed our women, who slayed anyone, even a child, should they look at him the wrong way. You know that we failed, that the other lords would not unite behind us because we lacked the Stone of Eventide, and we lacked the Queen's Canon. If we had possessed just one of those artifacts, I have no doubt the other Houses would have rallied behind us."

He took a sip of cordial, turning the glass tumbler in his hands. I did the same, preparing for the hardest part of the story.

"We were betrayed by one of the other lords who had promised to join us. If not for his treachery, we might have overpowered Lannon, for our plans were contingent on surprising him. We had quietly gathered the forces of our three Houses, our men and our women, and were planning to storm the castle, to do things as peaceably as we were able, to give Lannon a proper trial. But he caught wind of it and sent his forces out to meet us in the field. What ensued was a bloody battle, one that saw our wives cut down, our daughters slaughtered. Yet he wanted us to live, his rebelling lords, to be brought to him for torturous punishment. And if not for Luc . . . if I did not have my son, who I had sworn to protect as my wife died in my arms . . . I would have let them capture me.

"But I took Luc and fled, as did Lord Kavanagh and his youngest daughter, as did Lord Morgane and his son. We had lost everything else: our wives, our lands, our Houses. And yet we lived. And yet our Houses were not dead, because of our sons and daughter. We fled south, to Valenia, knowing we might start a war by fleeing into another country, that Lannon would never cease looking for us, because Lannon is no fool. He knows one day we will return for him, to avenge the blood of our women."

He drained the cordial. I drained mine, feeling the fire flow through every bend and corner of my body. A righteous anger was stirring, the thirst for revenge.

"We pressed as far south into Valenia as we could, keeping to the forests, to the pastures, to the land," Jourdain continued, his voice rasping. "But Luc fell ill. He was only one year old, and I watched him slowly get weaker and weaker in my arms. So on a stormy night, we dared to knock on the door of a beautiful estate in the center of a field. It was Magnalia."

I felt the tears line my eyes as he looked at me, as I realized what he was about to say.

"The Dowager took us in, without question," he said. "She must have known we were fleeing, that we might bring trouble upon her. The news of the massacre had not crossed the channel yet, but we told her who we were, what the cost would be to shelter us. And she let us sleep in safety; she clothed us, fed us, and sent for a physician to heal my son. And then she gave us each a purse of coins, and told us to split up and set down Valenian roots, that the day of reckoning would come soon if we played our cards wisely, patiently."

He poured another cup of cordial and rubbed his temples. "We did as she advised. We took Valenian names and went our separate ways. I settled in Beaumont, became a reclusive lawyer, hired a master of music to instruct my son to become a passion, to make Luc appear as Valenian as possible. Morgane settled in Delaroche, and Kavanagh went south, to Perrine. But we never lost contact. And I never forgot the kindness of the Dowager. I repaid her, wrote to her, let her know that I owed her a mighty debt." His eyes flickered to mine. "So it looks as if she was right; the cards have finally aligned."

I helped myself to the decanter of cordial, only because I felt the weight of that hope. He needed me to find the stone. And what if I couldn't do it? What if the plans fell to ashes again?

"Father," I breathed, meeting his gaze. "I promise you that I will do all that I can to recover the stone, that I will help you achieve justice."

He drew his hand through his auburn hair, the gray gleaming as silver in the candlelight. "Amadine . . . I do not plan to send you to Maevana."

I all but spurted on my cordial. "What? I am supposed to retrieve the stone, am I not?"

"Yes and no. You will tell us how to find it. I will send Luc to retrieve it."

This did not please me. At all. But rather than fight with him, after he'd so generously opened his painful past, I sat back in the chair. One battle at a time, I told myself.

"We had an agreement," I calmly reminded him.

He hesitated. I knew it was because he was terrified of seeing something happen to me, of sending me to my death, or perhaps something worse. His wife had died in his arms, on a blood-soaked field of failure. And I knew he was determined that my fate would not follow hers. Hadn't I already seen him respond violently when I was threatened? And I was not even his daughter by blood.

This must be the Maevan in him, which I had also seen in Luc. Maevan men did not tolerate any threat toward their women.

Which meant *I* needed to become more Maevan. I needed to learn how to wield a sword, how to set these stubborn men in order.

"Our agreement was for you to have a voice in the plans, which I fully intend to see done, and for you to bestow the stone to the queen," Jourdain replied. "We said nothing of you going to Maevana and retrieving the stone."

He was right.

I choked back a retort, washed it all the way down with cordial, and then said, "So who is that man? The stranger?"

"One of my faithful thanes," Jourdain responded. "He served me when I was lord."

My eyes widened. "Does it alarm you that he found you here?"

"Yes and no. It means I am not as hidden as I once thought," he said. "But he has been searching for years. And he knew me very well. He knew how I would think, how I would hide and act far better than Lannon's cronies would."

There was a soft rap on the door. A moment later, Luc peered in, saw me sitting before Jourdain, the cordial in our hands, the emotion still bright in our eyes.

"Dinner at Laurents'," he announced, gaze roving from Jourdain to me, back to Jourdain with countless questions.

"Amadine will accompany us," Jourdain said.

"Excellent," Luc stated. "Liam is in the kitchen, having his fill of Pierre's cooking."

I took it that Liam was the thane. But who was Laurent?

Before the inquiry could even flicker over my face, Jourdain said, "The Laurents are the Kavanaghs."

There were a lot of names to keep up—Maevan names hidden within Valenian names—but I began to draw a lineage in my mind, a tree with long branches. One branch was MacQuinn, who I would continue to call Jourdain for protection. One branch was Laurent, who were the long-hidden Kavanaghs. And the last branch was for Lord Morgane, who I had yet to meet and learn his alias.

"Do you need to freshen up before we depart, Amadine?" Jourdain asked, and I nodded and slowly rose.

I was about to pass Luc on the threshold when I paused, helplessly turned back around. "I thought the Laurents had settled in another town."

"They did," Jourdain responded. "They moved here not long ago. To be closer."

Closer to the heart of the plans that had unexpectedly changed with my arrival.

I mulled on all of this, the excitement threading through

my heart, my stomach, my mind. I washed my face, changed my dress—Jourdain had been true to his word and procured me new clothes—and then tamed my hair in a braided crown.

Jourdain and Luc were waiting for me in the foyer, and wordlessly, we stepped out into the night and walked to the Laurents' town house.

They lived three streets east on the edge of town, a quiet sector, far from the market and from curious eyes. Jourdain didn't bother with the bell; he knocked, four times fast. The door opened at once, and an older woman with a linen wimple and a ruddy face let us in, her gaze hovering on me as if I might be dangerous.

"She is one of us," Jourdain said to the chamberlain, who stiffly nodded and then led us down a narrow corridor to the dining room.

A long, oaken table was lined with candles and scattered with lavender, the plates and pewter glasses glistening as morning dew. An older man was sitting at the head of the table, waiting for us. He stood when we entered, a welcoming smile on his face.

He was white-haired and tall, broad-shouldered and cleancut. He might have been pressing late sixties, but sometimes it is difficult to tell with Maevan men. They age faster than Valenians, with their love of the outdoors. His eyes were dark, gentle, and they found me at once.

"Ah, this must be your passion daughter, Jourdain," he said, extending his large, scar-ridden hand to me.

That's right; Maevan men shook hands. It went back to fiercer days, to ensure your guests were not hiding blades up their sleeves.

I smiled and let my hand rest in his. "I am Amadine Jourdain."

"Hector Laurent," the man replied with a bow of his head. "In another time, I was Braden Kavanagh."

To hear the name come from his lips gave me chills, made the past suddenly seem closer and clearer, like the days of queens were gathering in my shadow.

But I didn't have time to respond to him. A soft tread came up behind me; a lithe figure brushed my shoulder to stand beside Hector Laurent. A young woman, not much older than me, her hair a wild tumble of dark red curls, her freckles as stars across her cheeks. She had doe eyes—large and brown—and they crinkled at the edges as she tentatively smiled at me.

"Yseult, this is my daughter Amadine," Jourdain introduced. "Amadine, allow me to introduce you to Yseult Laurent—Isolde Kavanagh—the future queen of Maevana."

# ⊷ SEVENTEEN ⊷

# A SWORD LESSON

How did one greet a Maevan queen?

I didn't know, and so I fell back to my Valenian upbringing and curtsied, my heart pounding wildly.

"I have heard so many wonderful things about you, Amadine," Yseult said, her hands reaching for mine as I straightened.

Our fingers linked, both pale and cold, a passion and a queen. For one moment, I imagined she was a sister, for here we stood among a room of men, daughters of Maevana who had been raised in Valenia.

I vowed in that moment that I would do everything I could to see her reclaim the throne.

"Lady Queen," I said with a smile, knowing the Maevans

didn't bother with "highness" and "majesty." "I . . . I am honored to meet you."

"Please call me Yseult," she insisted, squeezing my fingers just before she let go. "And sit beside me at dinner?"

I nodded and followed to a chair beside hers. The men filled the spaces around us, and the ale was poured and the dinner platters set along the spine of the table. Again, I was surprised by the sentiments of a Maevan dinner—there were no courses set down and taken away before us in orderly fashion. Rather, the platters were passed about, and we filled our plates all at once to overflowing. It was a casual, intimate, natural way to partake in a dinner.

As I ate, listening to the men speak, I marveled at how well they had forced their accents into hiding, how Valenian they truly seemed. Until I saw little glimpses of their heritage—I heard a slight brogue emerge in Jourdain's voice; I saw Laurent draw forth a dagger from his doublet to cut his meat, instead of using the table knife.

But for all the Maevan air that had settled about the table, one thing I could not help but notice: Yseult and Luc still maintained the strict posture, the correct handling of their forks and knives. For, yes, they had been born in Maevana, but they had both been very young when their fathers fled with them. Valenia, with her passion and her grace and etiquette, was the only way of life they knew.

No sooner had I thought such did I glance down to see a dagger belted to Yseult's side, nearly hidden in the deep pleats of her simple dress. She felt my stare and glanced at me, a smile hovering just over the edge of her goblet as she prepared to take a sip of ale.

"Do you fancy blades, Amadine?"

"Never held one," I confessed. "You?"

The men were too absorbed in their conversation to hear us. All the same, Yseult lowered her voice as she responded, "Yes, of course. My father insisted I learn the art of swordsmanship from an early age."

I hesitated, unsure if I had the right to ask such of her. Yseult seemed to read my thoughts though, for she offered, "Would you like to learn? I could give you a few lessons."

"I would love to," I answered, feeling Luc's gaze shift over to us, as if he knew we were making plans without him.

"Come tomorrow, at noon," Yseult murmured and winked, for she felt Luc's interest as well. "And leave your brother at home," she said loudly, only to rile him.

"And what are you two planning?" Luc drawled. "Knitting and embroidery?"

"How did you ever guess, Luc?" Yseult smiled demurely and returned to her dinner.

No plans or strategies for recovering the throne were discussed that night. This was merely a reunion, a pleasant gathering before a storm. The Laurents—Kavanaghs—did not ask me at all about my memories, about the stone, although I could sense that they knew every single detail. I felt it every time Yseult looked at me, a hoard of curiosities and intrigue in her eyes. Jourdain had said she had a trace of magic in her blood; I was about to recover the stone of her ancestors, set it about her neck. Which meant I was about to bring forth her magic.

It was my all-consuming thought as we prepared to leave, bidding the Laurents good-bye in the foyer.

"I shall see you tomorrow," Yseult whispered to me, folding me in an embrace.

I wondered if I would ever feel comfortable hugging her, the future queen. It went against every Valenian sentiment in me, to touch a royal. But if there was any time to shed my mother's heritage, it was now.

"Tomorrow," I said with a nod, bidding her farewell as I followed Jourdain and Luc into the night.

The following day, I returned to the Laurents' a few minutes shy of noon, Luc on my heels.

"I am not opposed to this," my brother insisted as we stood on the front door and rang the bell. "I only think it best that we focus on *other* things. Hmm?"

I had told him about the sword lessons but not that my foremost motivation was to convince Jourdain that I could protect myself, that I could be sent to Maevana for the stone's retrieval.

"Amadine?" Luc pressed, wanting an answer from me.

"Hmm?" I lazily returned the hum, to his amused annoyance, as Yseult opened the door.

"Welcome," she greeted, letting us inside.

The first thing I noticed was she was wearing a long-sleeved linen shirt and *breeches*. I had never seen a woman wear pants, nor look so natural in them. It made me envious that she could move so freely while I was still encumbered by a flurry of skirts.

Luc hung his passion cloak in the foyer, and then we followed her down the hallway into an antechamber at the back of the house, a room with a stone floor, mullioned windows, and a great oaken chest. Atop the chest were two wooden long-swords, which Yseult gathered.

"I must confess," the queen said, blowing a stray tendril of her dark red hair from her eyes, "I have always been the student, never the teacher."

I smiled and accepted the scuffed training sword that she extended to me. "Don't worry; I am a very good pupil."

Yseult returned the smile and opened a back door. It led into a square courtyard enclosed by high brick walls, sheltered overhead by woven wooden rafters that were thickly knotted by vines and creeping plants. It was a very private space, only a few splotches of sunlight caressing the hard-packed ground.

Luc overturned a bucket to sit against the wall while I joined Yseult at the center of the courtyard.

"A sword has three foremost purposes," she said. "To cut, to thrust, and to guard."

So began my first lesson. She taught me how to hold the pommel, then the five primary positions. Middle, low, high, back, and hanging guard. Then she transitioned to the fourteen essential guards. We had just perfected the inside left guard when the chamberlain brought us a tray of cheese, grapes, and bread, along with a flask of herbal water. I hadn't even been aware of the hours that had slipped by, fast and warm, or that Luc had fallen asleep against the wall.

"Let's take a break," Yseult suggested, wiping the sweat from her brow.

Luc woke with a start, wiping drool from the corner of his mouth as we approached him.

The three of us sat on the ground, the tray of food in the center of our triangle, passing the flask back and forth as we ate and cooled off in the shade. Luc and Yseult teased each other with a familial affection, which made me wonder what growing up in Valenia must have been like for them. Especially Yseult. When had her father told her who she was, that she was destined to take back the throne?

"A ducat for your thoughts," Luc said, flicking a coin from his pocket my way.

I caught it on reflex as I said, "I was just thinking of how you were both raised here. How difficult that must have been."

"Well," Luc said, popping a grape into his mouth. "In many ways, Yseult and I are very Valenian. We were raised in your customs, your politeness. We don't remember anything of Maevana."

"Our fathers have not let us forget it, though," the queen added. "We know what the air tastes like, what the land looks like, what a true brogue sounds like, what our Houses stand for, even though we have not yet experienced it wholly for ourselves."

An easy lull came about us as we each took a final swig from the flask.

"I hear you are Maevan on your father's side," Yseult said to me. "So you are similar to Luc and me. You were raised here, you love this kingdom, embrace it as part of yourself. But there is more to you, which you cannot begin to fully know until you cross the channel."

Luc nodded his agreement.

"Sometimes I imagine it will be like our time here was all just a dream," the queen continued, glancing down to a stray thread in her sleeve. "That when we return to our fallen lands, when we stand in our halls among our people once more . . . it will feel like we have finally woken."

We were silent again, each of us lost to our own thoughts, our own imaginations quietly blossoming as to what it would be like to see Maevana. Yseult was the one to break the reverie, brushing the crumbs from her shirt, and then she tapped me on the knee.

"All right, let's do one more guard, and then we will call it a day," Yseult said, drawing me back into the center of the dirt. We gathered our swords, Luc lazily chewing the last of the bread as he watched us with hooded eyes. "This is called the close left guard, and . . ."

I lifted my practice sword, to mirror her as she demonstrated the guard. I felt the wooden hilt slide in my sweaty palms, a steady ache drum up my spine. And then she was suddenly, unexpectedly lunging for me. Her practice sword shed its wood and shimmered into steel as it cut for me. I lurched back, fear piercing my stomach as I tripped and heard an irritated male voice snap, "*Hanging* left, Tristan! Hanging left, *not* close left!"

I was no longer standing in an enclosed courtyard with Yseult. The sky was cloudy, troubled above me, and a cold wind washed over me, smelling like fire and leaves and cold earth. And him— the one cutting his sword at me, the one who had barked at me as if I were a dog. He was tall and dark-haired, young but not quite a man yet, as his beard was still trying to fill in along his jaw.

"Tristan! *What* are you doing? Get up!"

He was talking to me, pointing the sharp tip of his sword at me. I now realized why he looked so irritated; I had tripped and sprawled out on the grass, my backside throbbing and my ears ringing, my practice sword fallen uselessly beside me.

I clambered for the discarded sword, wooden and scuffed, and that's when I noticed my hands. Not mine, but the uncertain, grubby ones of a ten-year-old boy. There was dirt under his nails and a long scratch across the back of his right hand, still swollen and red, as if it wanted to break its scab.

"Get up, Tristan!" the older one shouted, exasperated. He took hold of Tristan's collar—my collar—and hauled him up to his feet, lanky legs kicking momentarily before boots found the earth. "Gods above, do you want Da to see you like that? You'll make him wish we were daughters and not sons."

*Tristan's throat tightened, his cheeks flushed with shame as he retrieved his sword and stood before his older brother. Oran always knew how to make him feel worthless and weak—the second-born son, who would never inherit or amount to anything.*

*"How many times are you going to get that guard wrong?" Oran insisted. "You realize I nearly cut you open."*

*Tristan nodded, angry words swarming in his chest. But he kept them locked away, bees buzzing in their hive, knowing Oran would hit him if he talked back, if he sounded the least bit defiant.*

*It was days like that one when Tristan fervently wished he had been born a Kavanagh. If he had magic, he would blast his brother* into pieces like a broken mirror, melt him into a river, or turn him into a tree. The mere thought, however impossible with his Allenach blood, made Tristan smile.

Of course, Oran noticed.

"Wipe that off your face," his older brother sneered. "Come on, fight me as a queen would."

The anger stirred, dark and blazing. Tristan didn't think he could hold it in much longer—it made his heart rot when he held it in—but he settled into middle guard, just as Oran had taught him, the neutral guard that could shift into offense or defense. It wasn't fair that Tristan was still forced to wield a wooden blade, a child's blade, while Oran, who was only four years older, was holding steel.

Wood against steel.

Nothing in life was ever fair, was always set against him. And Tristan longed, more than anything, to be inside the castle, in the library with his tutor, learning more about history and queens and literature. Or exploring the castle's hidden passages and finding secret doors. Swords had never been what he wanted.

"Come on, maggot," Oran taunted him.

Tristan shouted as he lunged forward, bringing his wooden sword down in a powerful arc. It lodged into Oran's steel, stuck, and Oran easily twisted the hilt from Tristan's hands. Tristan stumbled and then felt something hot on his cheek, something wet and sticky.

"I hope that scars," Oran said, finally yanking Tristan's wooden sword off of his blade. "It'll make you at least look half a man."

Tristan watched as his brother tossed his training sword in the grass, lifting his fingers to his cheek. They came away bloody, and he felt a long, shallow cut down his cheekbone. Oran had purposely cut him.

"Are you going to cry now?" Oran asked.

Tristan turned and ran. He didn't run toward the castle, which sat on the crest of the hill as a dark cloud that had married earth. He ran past the stables, past the weaver's guild, past the alehouse to where the forest waited with dark green invitation. And he could hear Oran pursuing him, shouting at him to stop. "Tristan! Tristan, stop!"

Into the trees he went, weaving deep within them, bounding like a hare, or like the stag of his heraldry, letting the forest swallow him, protect him.

But Oran still trailed him; he had always been fast. His older brother rudely broke branches, blundering through the pines and alders, the aspens and hickories. Tristan could hear Oran gaining on him, and he nimbly jumped a little creek and shot through a thicket, finally reaching the old oak.

He had found this oak last summer, after he had fled from another one of Oran's brutal lessons. Quickly, Tristan scaled her branches, going as high as he could, the leaves beginning to thin with autumn's glamour.

Oran reached the clearing, panting beneath the massive branches. Tristan held still in the crook of his chosen branch, watched as his older brother walked all the way around the tree, only then conceding to glance up with a squint.

"Come down, Tris."

Tristan made no noise. He was nothing more than a bird roosting in a place of safety.

*"Come. Down. Now."*

*He still didn't move. Didn't so much as breathe.*

*Oran sighed, jerked his fingers through his hair. He leaned against the trunk and waited. "Hark, I am sorry for cutting your cheek. I didn't mean to."*

*He did too mean to. He always meant to these days.*

*"I'm only trying to train you the best way I know how," Oran continued. "The way Da taught me."*

*That made Tristan sober. He could not imagine Da training him. Ever since their mother had died, their father had been ruthless, sharp, angry. No wife, no daughters, two sons—one who was trying desperately to be like him, the other who couldn't care less.*

*"Come down, and we will go steal a honey cake from the kitchens," Oran promised.*

*Ah, Tristan could always be bribed with something sweet. It reminded him of the happier days, when their mother was alive and the castle was filled with her laughter and flowers, when Oran was still his playmate, when their da still told stories of brave and heroic Maevans by the hearth in the hall.*

*Slowly, he climbed down, landing right before Oran. His older brother snorted, made to wipe the blood away from Tristan's cheek.*

"Wake her up."

*Oran's lips were moving, but the wrong words, the wrong voice, came out. Tristan frowned, frowned as Oran's hand faded, the invisibility eating up his arm, turning his brother into a swirl of motes. . . .*

\* \* \*

"Amadine? Amadine, wake up!"

The trees began to bleed, the colors dripping as paint off a piece of parchment.

I didn't realize my eyes had been closed until they opened, and I looked up into two worried faces. Luc. Yseult.

"Saints, are you all right?" the queen asked. "Did I hurt you?"

It took me a moment to fully shift my mind back to the present. I was lying on the dirt, my hair spread out around me, the wooden sword at my side. Luc and Yseult hovered over me as protective hens.

"What happened?" I asked, my voice croaking as if the dust of a century still crowded my throat.

"You fainted, I think," Luc said, a frown creasing his forehead. "Maybe it's the heat?"

I took in this morsel of news—I had never fainted before, and to think the shifts might cause such was troubling—but then I remembered what I had just seen, the new memory finding space among my own.

A smile curled on my lips. I tasted the dirt and my sweat, reaching for each of their hands. Luc took my left, Yseult my right, and I said, "I know exactly how to find the stone."

# —✦ EIGHTEEN ✦—

# OBLIQUE

On the last day of August, the first planning meeting was to be held over dinner at Jourdain's, an exact fortnight since the most crucial of memories had manifested at my first sword lesson. As that date drew near, I continued to meet with Yseult every other day, to broaden my swordsmanship. Jourdain permitted it, thinking another memory might jar forward. But I knew that Tristan Allenach had not been fond of spars or his sword lessons, at least as a ten-year-old boy.

So I continued my sword lessons to improve my skill and to learn more of the queen.

Yseult was older than I'd first thought her to be, ten years my senior. She was friendly and talkative, patient, and graceful, but every now and then, I could see her eyes dim, as if she battled worry and fear, as if she was overcome with the feeling of inadequacy.

She opened up to me during our fifth lesson, when the chamberlain brought us our usual refreshments. We were sitting face-to-face, just the queen and me, sharing ale and mutton pies and sweating in the heat, when she said, "It should be my sister. Not me."

I knew what she was implying, that she was thinking of her older sister, who had ridden beside her father the day of the massacre, who had been slain on the royal castle's lawn.

So I said, very gently, "Your sister would want you to do this, Yseult."

Yseult sighed, a sound inspired from loneliness, from inherited regrets. "I was three the day of the massacre. I should have been killed with my mother and sister. After the slaughter in the field, Lannon sent his men door to door of those who had rebelled. The only reason I was spared was because I was at the estate with my nurse, who hid me when Lannon's men came for me. They killed her when she would not give me over. And when my father finally arrived, thinking I was dead . . . he said he followed the sound of a child weeping, believing he was hallucinating in his distress, until he found me hidden in an empty cask outside the alehouse. I don't remember any of it. I suppose that is a good thing."

I rested in all she had just revealed to me, wanting to speak and yet wanting to remain silent.

Yseult traced a fingertip through the dust coating her boots and said, "In this time of day, it is dangerous to be a daughter of Maevana. My father has spent the past decade preparing me for that moment when I will finally stand before Lannon, to take back the crown and the throne and the land. And yet . . . I do not know if I can do it."

"You will not stand alone, Isolde," I whispered, using her Maevan name.

Her eyes flickered to mine, dark with fear, with anxious longing. "In order for us to be victorious, we need the other Houses to follow us, to stand with us. But why would the other lords gather behind a girl who is more Valenian than she is Maevan?"

"You are two in one," I replied, thinking of Merei, of how my arden-sister had known my heart so thoroughly. "You are Valenia as you are Maevana. And that will shape you into an exquisite queen."

Yseult mulled on that, and I prayed my words would find their mark. Eventually, she said with a smile, "You must think me weak."

"No, Lady. I think you everything you ought to be."

"I grew up here without friends," she continued. "My father was too paranoid to let me get close to anyone else. You are the first girlfriend I have truly ever had."

Again, I thought of my arden-sisters, thought of how much my life was enriched because of them. And I understood her loneliness then, felt it as if I had been socked in the stomach.

I reached out my hand, let my fingers link with hers.

*You are enough*, my touch assured her. And when she smiled, I knew she felt my words, let them settle in the valleys of her heart.

But for all my encouragement, I was just as anxious as she was, my mind impatient for the first strategic meeting, when the plans to recover the stone and take back the crown would finally become tangible.

The last day of August finally arrived, and I helped Agnes set the table for seven people. It was to be Jourdain, Luc, me, Hector and Yseult Laurent, Liam the thane (who had remained with us, safely tucked away on the third floor), and Theo d'Aramitz, who was the last piece of our puzzle and the final rebelling lord I had yet to meet, his Maevan name being Aodhan Morgane.

The Laurents arrived, right on time, and Liam descended the stairs to enter the dining room. We gathered about the table, only one chair vacant: Theo d'Aramitz/Lord Morgane's.

"Should we begin without him?" Jourdain asked from his place at the head of the table. The platters had been set down, the fragrance of the food taunting all of us as we waited for the third lord. Agnes was filling our goblets with ale, discreetly reaching between us.

"He's coming from Théophile," Hector Laurent commented. "That is not too far away, but perhaps there was trouble on the road."

"Hmm," Jourdain hummed, no doubt thinking of our own escapade with the thieves.

"He wouldn't want us to wait," Luc insisted, but probably because he was hungry, his eyes on the meat platter.

"Let us go ahead and eat, then," Jourdain decided. "We shall hold off on planning until after the meal, until d'Aramitz arrives."

The platters were passed about, and I filled my plate with far too much food. But Pierre had truly outdone himself with preparing the Maevan-inspired meal, and I couldn't resist taking a little spoonful of everything. We were halfway through dinner when there was a knock on the door.

Luc stood instantly. "That would be d'Aramitz," he said, disappearing down the hall to greet the lord.

Hector Laurent was in the middle of telling us the story of how he'd met his wife when Luc returned, alone. But a piece of paper was unfolded in his hands, and he paused on the threshold of the dining room, his eyes scanning the letter's contents. Jourdain noticed this at once, the conversation dying at the table as my patron father demanded, "What is it?"

Luc glanced up. The tension had woven around us as a rope, cutting off our air as we all thought the worse, as we all imagined we were caught before we had even started.

"D'Aramitz has business in Théophile that he cannot abandon," Luc explained. "He writes an apology, saying he can arrive in two weeks' time."

Jourdain relaxed, but there was still a deep furrow in his brow, his displeasure evident.

"Should we postpone the first meeting, then?" Hector inquired, his white hair gleaming in the candlelight.

"The question is," Luc said, folding d'Aramitz's letter, handing it to Jourdain. "Do we feel comfortable forging plans without him?"

Jourdain sighed, burdened, and read the letter for himself. I was sitting at my patron father's left, Yseult beside me, and I exchanged a glance with the queen. This should be her call, I thought. And as if reading my mind, Yseult cleared her throat, drawing all the men's gazes to her.

"The rest of us are here," she said. "It is unfortunate d'Aramitz is absent, but since he is only one and we are six, let us begin with the plans."

Jourdain nodded, pleased with her decision. We finished our dinner, and then Agnes quickly took up the plates and platters, and Jean David brought forth the map of Maevana. It was unrolled over the heart of the table, the land we were about to reclaim. A reverent quiet settled over the six of us as we studied that map.

And then, to my surprise, Yseult turned to look at me. "Amadine?"

I felt the men's gazes, like sunlight, bright with curiosity. My hands were cold as I brought my right forefinger to the map, to the Mairenna Forest.

"My ancestor was Tristan Allenach, who took and buried the Stone of Eventide in 1430. I know the very tree he has buried the stone at, which would be in this segment of the forest, about two miles into the woods."

The men and the queen looked to where I pointed.

"That is near Damhan," Liam spoke up. He no longer looked like a bedraggled beggar. His hair was washed and slicked back, his beard trimmed, and his face had filled out from eating proper meals once more.

"Damhan?" I echoed, shivering as that name tickled my tongue. I had never heard the name, yet it pulled along my bones in recognition.

"Lord Allenach's residence during summer and autumn," Liam continued. His insight was about to be extremely valuable to us, as he had only been gone from Maevana for six years, as opposed to the twenty-five that Jourdain and Hector had experienced. "He should be there now, preparing for the annual hunt of the hart."

Now that definitely caressed my memory. My mind searched furiously through the past few weeks, then months, wondering why this felt so familiar. I finally rested on the afternoon when Oriana had sketched me as a Maevan warrior, when Ciri had said something I never thought I would need again: *My father used to visit once a year, in the fall, when some of the Maevan lords opened their castles for us Valenians to come stay for the hunt of the white hart.*

"Wait . . ." I said, my eyes fastened to the forest, to where my finger still rested. "Lord Allenach invites Valenians to partake in the hunt, does he not?"

Liam nodded, his eyes sparkling with something that looked like vengeance. "He does. Makes quite a fuss over it. One year he invited as many as sixty Valenian nobles, all who paid a hefty price to hunt his forest, all who needed a letter of invitation."

"Which means they will be hunting in the Mairenna," Luc said, his fingers trailing through his hair.

"Which means the door into Maevana is about to be open,"

Liam added, glancing to Luc. "Lannon keeps the borders closed, save for a few occasions. This is one of them."

"When would be the next?" Jourdain asked.

Liam sighed, his eyes wandering back to the map. "The spring equinox, maybe. Many Valenians like to go to watch the jousting, and Lannon welcomes them, if only to shock southerners with our bloody sports."

I did not want to wait for spring. The thought of it made it seem like bricks were hanging from the eaves of my shoulders. But autumn was so close . . . just a few weeks away. . . .

"Yseult?" I murmured, eager to hear her thoughts.

Her face was placid, but her eyes were also glittering with something that looked hungry, vicious. "Allenach's hunt sets us right where we need to be. At Damhan, on the edge of the Mairenna."

She was right. We fell silent, wondering and fearing. Could we move so quickly?

"And how would we solicit an invitation?" Hector Laurent asked quietly. "We cannot simply go and knock on Damhan's door, expected to be let in."

"No. We will need a forged invitation," Yseult stated.

"I can forge one for you," Liam offered. "I wrote plenty of the invitations when I was held under Allenach's House."

I was hung on what Liam had said—when he was *held* under Allenach's House?—but the conversation kept moving.

"We forge an invitation," Jourdain said, linking his fingers. "We pay the hefty sum. We send one of our men into Damhan.

He partakes in the hunt; he recovers the stone."

"Father," I interrupted, as pleasantly as I could. "I need to be the one to recover the stone."

"Amadine, I am *not* sending you to Maevana."

"Jourdain," Yseult said, also as pleasantly as she could. "The stone is Amadine's to find and reclaim. None of us will be able to locate the tree as swiftly as she can."

"But we cannot send Amadine to the *hunt*," Luc protested. "These are Valenian men who are invited, not women. She would undoubtedly raise suspicions."

"One of you men will go to partake in the hunt," I said. "I shall arrive after you."

"How?" Jourdain responded, a bit sharply. But I saw the fear haunting his eyes when he looked at me.

"I want you to hear this with an open mind," I said, my mouth going dry. I was nervous to share my scheme, which I was spinning as the evening deepened. This was not one of Abree's lighthearted plays; I was not plotting a way out of a dungeon. I was conspiring against a king; multiple lives were about to be involved and put at risk.

With an ache in my stomach, I remembered that old skit of mine, the one where every character perished save for one. But I felt Yseult close at my side, knowing the queen was my ally. And Jean David had set down a small purse of cheques by the map, which would help me illustrate my plans with pawns.

I opened the purse and took out the first pawn, inevitably thinking of Merei and all the evenings we had played each other in cheques and marques. *You never protect your side, Bri. It's your one true weakness,* she had once said to me. She only defeated me when she took me by surprise, when she made the oblique move—distracting me with one obvious, powerful pawn and championing me with a stealthier, lesser pawn.

Drawing in a deep breath, I took my obsidian pawn and set it on Damhan.

"One of our men goes to Damhan as a Valenian noble, under the pretense of enjoying the hunt." I took the next pawn, carved from blue marble. "I arrive to Lyonesse, as a Valenian noble-woman. I go directly to the royal hall, to make a request to King Lannon." I set my pawn down on Lyonesse, the royal city. "I ask the king to pardon MacQuinn and grant him admittance to the country, that my patron father would like to return to the land of his birth and pay the penance for his past rebellion."

Luc sat back in his chair, as if his stomach had melted down to the floor. Yseult didn't move, didn't even blink as she stared at my pawn. But Jourdain's hand curled in a fist and I heard him draw in a long, conflicted breath.

"Daughter," he growled. "We have already discussed this. Asking for a pardon will *not* work."

"We discussed what would happen if *you* asked for the pardon, not me." Our gazes locked—his was that of a father who knew his daughter was about to defy him. My fingers still held to my pawn, and I looked back to the map. "I make a request before a royal hearing, before the soon-to-be-dethroned king. I speak the name MacQuinn, a name that has haunted Lannon for twenty-five years. I make it known that I am his passion daughter, under MacQuinn's protection. Lannon will be so fixated on MacQuinn's return that he will not see the Kavanaghs sneak over his border." I took a red pawn, which represented Yseult and her father, and moved them over the channel, into Maevana, into Lyonesse.

"An oblique move," Yseult said with a hint of a smile. So she had played cheques and marques before, and she recognized my bold, risky strategy.

"Yes," I agreed. "It will raise Lannon's suspicions, but he will not think we are so foolish to announce our presence before a revolt. We play into his beliefs."

"But how does that get you to Damhan, sister?" Luc gently asked, his face pale.

I looked to Liam. The next phase of my plans was contingent on whatever the thane could tell me. "If I am making a request in the royal hall, would Lord Allenach be present?"

Liam's salt-and-pepper eyebrows rose, but he finally understood where my plans were heading. "Yes. Lord Allenach is Lannon's councillor. He stands to the left of the throne, hears everything the king hears. Royal hearings take place every Thursday."

"So I arrive on Thursday," I said, daring to look at Jourdain. He was all but glaring at me. "I speak your name before the king and before Lord Allenach. Lord Allenach will be unable to resist offering me sanctuary while I wait for you to cross the channel, since the two of you are archenemies. The lord takes me to

Damhan." I slid my pawn to where the castle sat on the edge of the forest, next to the black pawn. "I recover the stone. MacQuinn and Luc," I said and drew forth a purple pawn, moving it over the water, into Maevana, "cross the channel and arrive to Lyonesse. We are all in Maevana at this point, ready to storm the castle."

"And what if Lannon kills you on the spot, Amadine?" my patron father demanded. "Because as soon as my name flies from your mouth, he will want to behead you."

"I think what Amadine says is truth, my lord," Liam cautiously spoke up. "She is right when she says that Lord Allenach—who has overtaken your House and your people—will want to host her until you arrive. And while Lannon is paranoid these days, he does not kill unless Allenach blesses it."

"So we are gambling on Allenach having a gracious day?" Luc spurted.

"We are gambling on the fact that Lannon and Allenach will be so absorbed with MacQuinn's reckless return that they will never see the Kavanaghs and Morgane coming," I said, trying to keep the heat from rising in my voice.

"There is another advantage to this," Hector Laurent spoke, his eyes on the pawns I had arranged. "If Amadine announces MacQuinn's name at court, his return will spread like wildfire. And we need our people to be alert, to rise at a moment's notice."

"Yes, my lord," Liam agreed with a nod. "And your Houses have been scattered for twenty-five years. Allenach took Mac-Quinn's House, Burke took Morgane's, and Lannon, of course, took Kavanagh's. Your lands have been divided, your men and women dispersed. But if they so much as hear the name of Mac-Quinn spoken again . . . it would be the spark to a dry pasture."

My patron father groaned, knowing this was a very good argument in favor of my plan. He covered his face and leaned back, as if the last thing he wanted to do was acknowledge this. But he did not have the final say. The queen did.

"Once we have all returned home," Hector Laurent spoke up, his eyes fastened to something on the map. "We gather our people and converge at Mistwood. We storm the castle from there."

The mood in the room changed at the sound of that name. I cast my eyes to the map, searching for the place he spoke of. I finally found it, a slender strip of woods on the Morgane, Mac-Quinn, and Allenach border, a forest that stood in the royal castle's shadow.

"I think this is a good start," Yseult said, the trance of Mistwood broken. "It's very risky, but it's also bold, and we need to move bravely if we are going to do this. What Amadine is offering is selfless and invaluable. And the plans cannot move forward without her." She drummed her fingers on the tables, staring at my pawns. "I say Liam needs to begin the forgery of the invitation. As to which man will go under pretense of the hunt . . . that can be decided later, although I have a good inkling as to who it should be."

I looked helplessly across the table at Luc. It obviously would have to be him, since the three lords would be easily recognized. Again, Luc looked ill, like his dinner wanted to come back up.

"Liam, we also need to arrange a list of safe houses, should something go wrong after we cross the channel," the queen continued, and Liam nodded. "All of us need to be aware of Maevans who would be ready to house us—to hide us at a moment's notice—if plans are uncovered and pursuit is employed. Let's plan to meet two weeks from now, when d'Aramitz will be present, and we can finalize the plans."

Because autumn was on the horizon. We would have to weave our plans together and strike quickly.

A chill danced down my spine as I met Yseult's gaze. There was a question in her eyes, solemn as it was desperate. *Are you certain, Amadine? Are you certain that you desire to do this?*

Was I certain that I was brave enough to stand before a corrupt king and speak the name of MacQuinn, a name that would undoubtedly bear a cost? Was I certain that I wanted to go stay at Lord Allenach's castle, knowing my father might be one of his thanes, one of his servants, one of his cronies? Knowing that my heritage was rooted in that land?

But I was ready, ready to find the stone and redeem my ancestor's past transgressions. To set a queen upon the throne. To return to Cartier and gain my cloak.

And so I whispered, "Let it be done, Lady."

## → NINETEEN ←

# SUMMER'S END

*September 1566*

Two days before our second strategic meeting, I came down with a fever. Agnes commanded me to remain in bed, where in vain I drank every healing tonic, ate every nutritious root possible, and sipped copious amounts of slippery elm tea. But it was to no avail; I burned steadily off and on, as if I were a fallen star trapped on Earth.

Luc came and saw me, right before he, Jourdain, and Liam were to leave for the Laurents' dinner. He laid his hand on my brow and frowned. "Saints. You're still burning, Amadine."

"I can go," I panted, weakly attempting to push the heap of quilts away. "I can go to the meeting."

I was worried Jourdain would try to upend my plans, and

Luc saw it in my glassy eyes.

"You are not going anywhere," he insisted, sitting beside me on the bed, tucking the blankets firmly about me. "Don't worry; I will make sure your plans are upheld."

"Jourdain will try to undo them," I croaked, which prompted Luc to reach for my cup of lukewarm tea.

"He will try, but he will not go against the queen," my brother said, tilting the cup to my lips. "And the queen is drawn to your ideas."

I took one sip and then had to lie back on my pillows, my strength fading.

"Now rest," Luc ordered, rising from the bed, setting my tea on the table. "It's more vital that you heal from this so you are ready to cross the channel soon."

He was right.

I didn't even remember hearing him leave my room. I fell into a tangle of dark, feverish dreams. I was at Magnalia again, standing in the gardens, the fog thick on the ground, and a man was coming toward me. I wanted it to be Cartier; I nearly ran to him, my heart overflowing with the joy of seeing him again, until I realized it was Oran—Tristan's older brother. He was coming to cut me down for stealing pieces of his brother's memories. And I had no weapon but that of my two feet. I ran through a never-ending maze for what felt like hours and hours, until I was ragged and exhausted, until I was ready to kneel down and let Oran cut me in two, until light seeped into my eyes.

I woke, achy and drenched, but the sunlight that streamed in through my windows was pure and sweet.

"She's woken!"

I turned my head to see Agnes there, her rosy, plump cheeks trembling as she jumped up from her chair. "Monsieur! She's awake!"

I winced at her hollering, winced at the urgent creaking of the stairs as Jourdain appeared, halting on my threshold, as if he was too embarrassed to enter my room.

"Tell me," I tried to say to him, but my voice cracked into pieces.

"I'll go fetch you some water," Agnes promised, touching my brow. "Ah, the fever has finally broken. Praise Ide." She scurried from the room, which enabled Jourdain to ease inside, still a bit hesitant.

He finally settled in the chair Agnes had abdicated, at my bedside.

"What did I miss?" I croaked again, feeling as if coals had been raked down my throat.

"Shh, just listen," Jourdain said. He acted like he wanted to reach for my hand, but was too shy to do it. "Everything you planned is going to occur. The invitation has been forged; we have the sum of money Allenach requires for the hunt. D'Aramitz is going to cross the channel next week. He will be staying at Damhan under the pretense of the hunt, but he is also there to quietly gather and ready my forces. In addition to that, I have requested that he keep an eye on you, that he be your shield, your protection, your ally should you need him."

"But, Father," I rasped, "I do not know what he looks like."

"As I know. We prepared for this, though. The first night you are at Damhan, when you go into the hall for dinner, wear this in your hair." Jourdain retrieved a delicate silver rose from his pocket, the edges crusted with tiny rubies. He set it into my palm. "This is how d'Aramitz will identify you, although you will likely be one of very few women there. He will be wearing a red jerkin with this emblem stitched over the center." He withdrew a piece of parchment. I blinked, my vision still blurry from the illness, but I could see it was a drawing of a great oak, encompassed in a circle. "We discussed this at length, and everyone has come to the conclusion that it is best that once you make the acknowledging eye contact with him the first night, you avoid d'Aramitz the remainder of the time. Should he be caught, I do not want you to be caught with him. Do you understand?"

Ah, fatherly orders. He sounded so stern, so formidable. But that gleam was in his eyes again, that star of worry. I wished I could extinguish it somehow.

"Yes," I said.

"Good. Now, another conclusion we made the other night: when you go to Lyonesse, to appeal to Lannon . . . if Allenach is not present when you enter the royal hall, do *not* make the appeal for my admittance. You will have to wait until the following Thursday, and Liam has a list of safe houses we still need to get you. . . ." He patted his pocket, frowning. "All this has been decided because if you make the admission before Lannon, without Allenach's presence, you will most likely be held in the keep of the castle. You understand? You move forward only if you see Allenach, and he stands to the left of the throne and will be wearing his coat of arms. You remember the Allenach coat of arms?"

I nodded, my voice too withered to try to speak, even though countless questions began to flood my mind.

"Good. Very good." His gaze softened, as if he was seeing something in the distance, something I could not discern. "You will cross the channel the last day of September, which will have you reaching Lyonesse the first of October. A Thursday. The royal hearings typically take all day, but I would recommend you go early, because it is a six-hour trip from Lyonesse to Damhan."

"Don't worry," I rasped, to which he gave me a wry look.

"That is like telling me not to breathe, Amadine. I will worry every moment you are away."

"I can . . . handle a sword now."

"So I hear. And I am glad you brought that up because . . ." He reached inside his doublet, brought forth a dagger in a leather sheath. "This is for you, what we Maevans call a dirk. To be worn about your thigh, beneath your dress. Wear it at all times. Do I need to tell you where the best places to stab are?" He set it in my other hand, so I now held a silver rose ornament and a dirk. Quite the contradiction, but a flame of anticipation warmed my chest.

"I know where," I struggled to say. I could have pointed to all the vital blood flows of the body, the ones to cut to make a person bleed out, but I was too weak.

"Liam is going to plan a time to talk with you about the best ways to move in and out of Damhan," Jourdain continued. "You will need to recover the stone at night, when the castle slumbers. We think it is best if you disguise yourself as a servant, and use the servant quarters to slip in and out."

I didn't let him see how the mere thought of this terrified me . . . the idea of wandering alone in unfamiliar woods at night . . . the threat of being caught trying to leave and enter the castle. Surely there was another way I could accomplish this. . . .

"I also hear your birthday was yesterday," Jourdain said, which startled me.

How long had I been sleeping?

"You slept for two days," he replied, reading my mind. "So how old are you now? Sixteen?"

Was he teasing me? I frowned at him and said, "Eighteen."

"Well, I hear there is to be a party of some sorts, most likely tomorrow, after you have rested."

"I don't . . . want . . . a party."

"Try telling that to Luc." Jourdain stood just as Agnes returned with a bowl of broth and a jar of rosemary water. "Rest, Amadine. We can tell you the remaining plans when you have recovered."

Indeed, I was very surprised that he had already told me so much, that my original plans had been honored.

After Jourdain left, Agnes helped me to a bath and clean clothes, and then stripped my linens. I sat by the window, the glass cracked open so I could breathe fresh air, my hair wondrously damp on my neck.

I thought of everything Jourdain had just told me. I thought of the Stone of Eventide, of Damhan, of what I should say when I stood before Lannon and made my request. There were so many unknown things, so many things that could go wrong.

I watched as the first golden leaves began to drop from the trees, one by one as gentle promises. My birthday marked summer's end and autumn's beginning, when warm days slowly faded and cold nights became longer and longer, when trees gave up their dreams and only the hardiest, most determined of flowers persisted to bloom from the earth.

Summer was over. Which meant Cartier had discovered my mysterious departure by now.

I let myself think on him, something I had not allowed my heart or mind to do since I had taken the mantle of Amadine. He would be at Magnalia, preparing to teach the next passion cycle, preparing for his next ten-year-old arden of knowledge to arrive. He would stand in the library and see half his books on the shelves, knowing I had put them there.

I closed my eyes. What constellation had he chosen for me? What stars had he plucked from the firmament? What stars had he captured with a bolt of the finest blue fabric, to caress my back?

I had to tell myself in that moment, that moment of in-between—in between seasons, in between missions, in between seventeen and eighteen—that I would be at peace even if I never received my cloak. That seven years at Magnalia was not in vain, because look where it had brought me.

"There's someone downstairs waiting to see you."

I opened my eyes and turned to see Luc standing in my room, that impish smile on his lips, his cinnamon hair standing up at all the wrong angles.

For one heady moment, I thought it was Cartier waiting down-stairs. That he had found me somehow. And my heart danced up my throat, so wildly that I could not speak.

"What's the matter?" Luc asked, that smile fading as he stepped closer to me. "Do you still feel unwell?"

I shook my head, forced a smile to my lips as I brushed the damp hair away from my eyes. "I'm fine. I . . . I was just thinking of what will happen if I fail," I said, glancing back to the window, to the trees and the twirling descent of the leaves. "There is so much that can go wrong."

Luc put his hand on my knee. "Amadine. None of us is going to fail. You cannot cross the channel with such shadows in your thoughts." When he squeezed my knee, I relented to look back at him. "We all have doubts. Father does, I do, Yseult does. We all have worries, fears. But what we are about to do is going to carve our names into history. So we rise to the challenge knowing that the victory is already ours."

He was so optimistic. And I could not help but smile at him, rest in the assurance he gave me.

"Now, do you want to come downstairs with me?" he inquired, holding out his hand.

"I hope it is not a party," I said warily, letting him draw me to my feet.

"Who said anything about a party?" Luc scoffed, leading me down the stairs.

It was a party.

Or as much of a party as they could manage with our secret lives.

Pierre had made a grand Valenian cake, three layers deep with wispy butter icing, and Yseult had hung ribbons from the dining room chandelier. Agnes had cut the last of summer's flowers and scattered them down the table. And they were all waiting: Jourdain, Agnes, Jean David, Liam, Pierre, Hector Laurent, and Yseult.

It was odd to see them gathered in honor of me. But it was even stranger how my heart affectionately tightened at the sight of them, this mismatched group of people who had become my family.

Luc played a lively tune on his violin as Pierre cut the cake. Yseult gave me a beautiful shawl, spun from midnight wool with threads of silver—just like stars—and Agnes gave me a box of ribbons, one for each color of passion. That was enough, I thought. I did not want any other gifts.

But then Jourdain came up behind me, next to my shoulder, and held out his palm. A shimmering silver chain rested there, waiting for me to claim.

"For your pendant," he murmured.

I accepted it, felt the delicate silver in my fingers. It was beautiful and deceptively strong. This will not break, I thought and met Jourdain's gaze.

He was thinking the very same.

Nine mornings later, I began my four-day journey in the coach to Isotta, Valenia's northernmost harbor. Jourdain accompanied me, and he did not waste a minute of that trip. It seemed he had a mental checklist, and I listened as he moved from point to point, his dry lawyer tone emerging, which made me fight yawn after yawn.

He went through the plans, from start to finish, yet again, for each member of our group. I patiently soaked it in, thinking back to my pawns moving on the map, so I could know each person's location. Then he gave me the list of safe houses that Liam had made, for me to memorize before he burned it.

There were five in Lyonesse—two bakers, a chandler, a silver-smith, and a printmaker—and two yeomen on the way from the royal city to Damhan. All these people had once served beneath Jourdain's House, and Liam swore they were still secretly loyal to their fallen lord.

Then Jourdain launched into his opinions of Lannon, of what I should and definitely should not say when I made the appeal. But as for the subject of Allenach, my patron father remained quiet.

"Was I right to call the two of you archenemies?" I dared to ask, weary of listening and bumping along in this coach.

"Hmm."

I took that as a yes.

But then he surprised me by saying, "Under no circumstance should you tell him that your father, your real father, serves his House, Amadine. That you are actually an Allenach. Unless you are in a deadly situation and it is the only hope you have of getting out alive.

"For this mission, you are wholly Valenian. Stick to the history we gave you."

I nodded and finished memorizing the safe houses.

"Now then," Jourdain cleared his throat. "There is no telling what will happen when I cross the border. Allenach may insist on keeping you at Damhan, or he may bring you to me in Lyonesse. If he should hold you at Damhan, you need to leave with d'Aramitz on the third night after my arrival. That is when we are converging at Mistwood, to storm the throne. We will prepare for battle, but hopefully Lannon—coward that he is—will abdicate when he sees our banners rise and our people gather."

Mistwood. That name was like a drop of wonder to my heart. "Why Mistwood?"

"Because it borders mine and Morgane's lands, where most of our people still dwell, and it's at the back gate of the royal castle," he gruffly explained. But I saw how Jourdain glanced away from me with a sheen in his eyes.

"Was this the place . . . ?" My words died when he looked back at me.

"Yes, it is the place where we failed and were slaughtered twenty-five years ago. Where my wife died."

We didn't speak much after that, reaching the city of Isotta at dawn on the last day of September. I could smell the brine of the sea, the cold layers in the wind, the bittersweet smoke trickling from tall chimneys, and the damp patches of moss that grew between the cobblestones. I breathed it in, savored it, even if they did make me shiver, these final fragrances of Valenia.

My good-byes to Luc and Yseult had been built on hope,

bound with embraces and poorly cracked jokes, crowned with smiles and thundering hearts. Because the next time we reunited, we would be storming the castle.

But my good-bye to Jourdain was a completely different experience. He refused to go all the way to the harbor with me, for fear of being recognized by some of the Maevan sailors who were unloading casks of ale and bundles of wool. So Jean David halted the coach in one of the quieter side streets, in view of the ship I was to leave on.

"Here is your boarding pass, and here are your Valenian papers," Jourdain said briskly, handing me a carefully folded wad of forged papers that he had made. "Here is your cloak." He handed me a dark red woolen cloak. "Here is the food Pierre insisted you take. And Jean David will carry your trunk to the docks."

I nodded, quickly knotting my new cloak about my collar, pinning my travel papers beneath my elbow as I took the small knapsack of food.

We were standing on the road, shadowed by tall town houses, the echoes of Isotta's fish market carrying on the sea gusts.

This was it, the moment when I finally crossed the channel, the moment I—*at last*—saw the land of my father. How many times had I imagined it, watching those green Maevan shores come into view through the channel's notorious fog? And somehow, this felt like the summer solstice all over again . . . that sensation of time quickening, moving so quickly that I could scarcely catch my breath and absorb what was about to befall me.

I self-consciously felt for Cartier's pendant beneath the high neck of my traveling gown, strung on Jourdain's chain. I would think of Cartier, my master as he was my friend, the one who had taught me so much. The one who had granted me passion. And I would think of my patron father, who had accepted me for who I was, who loved me in his own gruff way, who was letting me go despite his better judgment. The one who was granting me courage.

My heart pounded; I drew in a shallow breath, the sort of breath one might take right before battle, and looked up at him.

"You have your dirk on you?" Jourdain asked.

I pressed my hand to my right thigh, feeling the dirk through the fabric of my skirts. "Yes."

"You promise me that you will not hesitate to use it. That if a man so much as looks at you the wrong way, you won't be afraid to show your steel."

I nodded.

"I say this to you, Amadine, because some Maevan men look upon Valenian women as . . . coquettes. You must show such brutes otherwise."

Again I nodded, but a horrible feeling had crept up my throat, nestled on my voice box. Was that what happened to my mother? Had she come to visit Maevana and been looked at as a coy, flirtatious woman who was eager to slip into a Maevan man's bed? Had she been abused?

Suddenly, I realized why my grandfather might have hated my father so much. For I had always believed I had been conceived in love, even if it was forbidden. But perhaps it had been completely different. Perhaps she had been forced against her will.

My feet turned to lead.

"I'll be awaiting your letter," Jourdain murmured, taking a step back.

The letter I was supposed to write when Lannon gave him admittance. The letter that would bring him and Luc over the waters to a dangerous homecoming.

"Yes, Father." I turned to go, Jean David patiently waiting with the typical stern expression on his face, holding my trunk.

I made it four steps before Jourdain called me.

"Amadine."

I paused, looked back at him. He was in the ribs of shadows, gazing at me with his mouth pressed in a tight line, the scar on his jaw stark against the paleness of his face.

"Please be careful," he rasped.

I think he wanted to say something else, but I suppose fathers often struggle in saying what they truly want when it comes to farewells.

"You too, Father. I will see you soon."

I walked to my ship, handed my papers to the Maevan sailors. They frowned at me but let me board, as I had paid quite a sum of money for passage on this ship and the borders were legally open.

Jean David set my trunk down in my cabin and then left without a word, although I did see the farewell in his eyes before he disembarked.

I stood at the bow of the ship, out of the way from the wine being loaded into the hold, and waited. The fog sat thick over the waters; my hands moved along the smooth oak of the rails as I began to prepare myself to see the king.

Somewhere, in the shadows of a side road, Jourdain stood and watched as my ship left the harbor, just as the sun burned away the fog.

I did not look back.

# TWENTY

# TO STAND BEFORE A KING

*Lord Burke's Territory, Royal City of Lyonesse, Maevana*
*October 1566*

The legends claim that the fog was spun from Maevan magic, from the Kavanagh queens. That it was a protective cloak for Maevana, and only the foolish, bravest of men sailed through it. These legends still rang true; magic was dormant, but as soon as the Valenian mist blissfully burned away, the Maevan fog fell upon us as a pack of white wolves, growling as we sailed closer to the royal port at Lyonesse.

I spent most of the short voyage staring into it, this infuriating white void, feeling it gather on my face and bead in my hair. I didn't sleep much in my cabin that night as we crossed the channel; the rocking of the ship made it feel as if I were being held in a stranger's arms. I longed for land and sun and clear winds.

Finally, at dawn, I caught the first glimpse of Maevana through a hole in the fog, as if the misty clouds knew I was a daughter of the north.

The city of Lyonesse was built on a proud hill, the castle resting at the top like a sleeping dragon, scaled in gray stones, the turrets like the horns along a reptile's formidable spine, draped in the green-and-yellow banners of Lannon.

I stared at those banners—green as envy, yellow as spite, emblazoned with a roaring lynx—and let my gaze trickle down through the streets that ran as little streams around stone houses with dark shingled roofs, around great big oaks that sprouted throughout the city, bright as rubies and topaz in their autumn splendor.

A sharp wind descended upon us, and I felt my eyes water and my cheeks redden as we eased into the harbor.

I paid one of the sailors to carry my trunk, and I disembarked with the sun on my shoulders, vengeance in my heart as my papers were cleared for admittance. The first place I went was the bank, to have my ducats exchanged for coppers. And then I went to the nearest inn and paid a servant girl to help me dress in one of my finest Valenian gowns.

I chose a gown the color of cornflowers—a blue that smoldered, a blue for knowledge—with intricate silver stitching along the hem and bodice. The kirtle was white, trimmed with tiny blue stones that glistened in the light. And beneath that, I wore petticoats and a corset, to hold me together, to blatantly define me as a Valenian woman.

I drew a star mole on my right cheek with a stick of kohl, the mark of a Valenian noblewoman, and closed my eyes as the servant girl carefully gathered half of my hair up with a blue ribbon, her fingers carefully pulling through my tangles. She hardly spoke a word to me, and I wondered what was flickering through her mind.

I paid her more than necessary and then began my ascent up the hill in a hired coach, my luggage in tow. We clattered beneath the oaks, through markets, passing men with thick beards and braided hair, women in armor, and children hardly clothed in tattered garments as they rushed to and fro with bare feet.

It seemed that everyone all wore some mark of their House, whether it was by the colors of their garments or the emblem stitched into their jerkins and cloaks. To proclaim which lord and lady they served, which House they were faithful to. There were many who wore Lannon's colors, Lannon's lynx. But then there were some who wore the orange and red of Burke, the maroon and silver of Allenach.

I closed my eyes again, breathing the earthen scent of horses, the smoke of forges, the aroma of warm bread. I listened to the children chanting a song, to women laughing, to a hammer striking an anvil. All the while, the coach trembled beneath me, higher, higher, up the hill to where the castle lay waiting.

I opened my eyes only when the coach stopped, when the man opened the door for me.

"Lady?"

I let him help me down, trying to adjust to the ambitions of my petticoats. And when I looked up, I saw the decapitated heads, the pieces of bodies staked on the castle wall, rotting, blackening in the sun. I stopped short when I saw the head of a girl not much older than me on the closest spike, her eyes two holes, her mouth hanging open, her brown hair blowing like a pennant in the breeze. My gorge rose as I stumbled back, leaning against the coach, trying to take my eyes from the girl, trying to keep my panic from splitting a hole in my exterior.

"Those would be traitors, Lady," my escort explained, seeing my shock. "Men and women who have offended King Lannon."

I glanced to the man. He watched me with hard eyes, with no emotion. This must be a daily occurrence to him.

I turned away, leaned my forehead against the coach. "What . . . what did she do to . . . offend the king?"

"The one your age? I heard she refused the king's advances two nights ago."

Saints help me. . . . I could not do this. I was a fool to think I could ask a pardon for MacQuinn. My patron father had been right; he had tried to express this to me. I may walk into the royal hall, but I most likely would not emerge in one piece.

"Should I take you back to the inn?"

I drew in a ragged breath, felt my sweat run cold down my back. My eyes wandered to the coachman, and I saw the mockery in the lines of his face. *Little Valenian coquette*, his eyes seemed to say. *Go back to your cushions and your parties. This is no place for you.*

He was wrong. This was my place, by half. And if I fled,

more girls would end up with their heads on spikes. So I gave myself only a moment more to breathe and calm my pulse. Then I pushed away from the coach, standing in the shadow of the wall.

"Will you wait for me here?"

He tipped his head and went to stand by his horses, stroking their manes with a chapped hand.

I trembled as I approached the main gate, where two guards in gleaming plate armor stood armed to the teeth with weapons.

"I am here to make a request before the king," I announced in perfect Dairine, drawing forth my papers once again.

The guards only took in my tightly strung waist, the glistening blue of my gown, the poise and the grace of Valenia that softened my edges and abolished any semblance of a threat. The wind played with my long hair, drawing it over my shoulder as a shield of golden brown.

"He's in the throne room," one of them said, his eyes lingering on my décolletage. "I will escort you."

I let him lead me through archways burnished with antlers and vines, through a bare courtyard, up the stairs to the royal hall. The doors were massive, carved with intricate knots and crosses and mythical beasts. I would have liked to stand and admire those carvings, listen to the quiet story they told, but the two other guards saw my approach and wordlessly opened the doors for me, the old iron and wood groaning in welcome.

I entered a pool of shadows, my dress whispering elegantly over the patterned tiles as my eyes adjusted to the light.

I felt the weight of the ancient dust as I approached that

cavernous hall. There was the sound of voices, one pleading, one scathing, bouncing off the impressive height of the ceiling, which was upheld by crosshatched timber rafters. I rose up on my toes, trying to see over the heads of those gathered. I could just barely discern the dais, where the king sat on his throne of welded antler and iron, but more important . . . there was Lord Allenach. I caught the dark brown of his hair, the flash of his maroon doublet, as he stood by the throne. . . .

Relief rippled down my bones, that I would not have to delay. But before I could enter the hall, I had to stop before a white-haired man dressed in Lannon green, his eyes going wide at the unexpected sight of me.

"May I inquire why you are here, Lady of Valenia?" he whispered to me in heavily accented Middle Chantal, my mother tongue. He had a scroll before him, a quill in his veiny hand, a list of names and purposes scrawled on the paper.

"Yes," I responded in Dairine. "I have a request for King Lannon."

"And what might that request be?" the chamberlain asked, dipping his quill into the ink.

"That is for me to say, sire," I answered as respectfully as I could.

"Lady, it is merely protocol that we announce your name with your purpose for seeking the king's aid."

"I understand. My name is Mistress Amadine Jourdain of Valenia. And the purpose must come from my tongue alone."

He hefted a sigh but relented, writing my name out on the list. Then he wrote my name on a small scrap of paper, which he passed to me, instructing me to hand it to the herald when my time arrived.

A wake of quiet followed me as I entered the back of the hall, as I walked the aisle. I could feel the eyes of the audience rivet to me, drenching me like rain, and then threads of whispers as they wondered why I had come. Those whispers flowed all the way to the throne on the dais, where King Lannon sat with heavy-lidded eyes, blatantly bored as the man before him knelt, begging for an extension on his taxes.

I stopped, two men waiting to appeal between me and the king. That's when Lannon saw me.

His eyes sharpened at once, taking me in. It felt like the point of a knife rushing over my body, testing the firmness of my skin, the layers of my gown, the nature of my forthcoming request.

Why, indeed, had a Valenian come to him?

I should not stare at him. I should lower my eyes, as a proper Valenian always does in the presence of royalty. But he was not royalty to me, and so I returned his stare.

He was not what I expected. Yes, I had seen his profile on a copper, which had depicted him as handsome, mythically godlike. And he truly might have been handsome for a man in his mid-fifties, had the scorn not soured the lines on his face, trapping his expressions in sneers and frowns. His nose was elegant, his eyes a vivid shade of green. His hair was pale, light blond melting amid the white of age, resting to the tops of his angular shoulders, a few Maevan braids beneath the twisted silver and glittering diamonds of his crown.

It was Liadan's crown; I recognized it from the illustration I had once admired of her, the woven branches of silver and buds of diamonds, a crown that looked as if the stars had come about her. And he was wearing it. I almost frowned, angered at the sight.

*Look away*, my heart commanded when Lannon began to shift on his throne, his eyes suddenly assessing my pride as a threat.

I looked to the left, straight to Allenach.

Who was also staring at me.

The lord was elegant, well built and groomed, his maroon jerkin capturing his heraldic stag and laurels on his broad chest. His dark brown hair was tempered with a few threads of gray; two small braids framed his face, and a thin golden circlet sat on his forehead to denote his nobleness. His jaw was clean-shaven, and his eyes gleamed like coals—a flicker of blue light that made me shiver. Was he also seeing me as a threat?

"My lord king, this sigil was found among this man's possessions."

I looked away from Allenach to see what was unfolding at the footstool of the throne. The man in front of me was kneeling, bowing his head to Lannon. He looked to be somewhere in his sixties, weathered and worn and trembling. At the man's side stood a guard dressed in Lannon green, accusing him of something before the king. I let my focus home in on them, especially when I saw a small square of blue fabric dangling from the guard's fingers.

"Bring that to me," Lannon requested.

The guard ascended the dais, bowed and then gave the king the blue fabric. I watched as Lannon sneered, as he held the fabric up for the court to see.

There was a horse, stitched in proud silver thread, over the blue fabric. At once, my face blanched, my heart began to pound, for I knew whose sigil that was. It was Lord Morgane's mark. Lord Morgane, who was disguised as Theo d'Aramitz, who was currently at Damhan for the hunt. . . .

"Do you know the price for bearing the traitor's sigil?" Lannon calmly asked the kneeling man.

"My lord king, *please*," the man rasped. "I am faithful to you, to Lord Burke!"

"The price is your head," the king continued, his voice bored. "Gorman?"

From the shadows, a hulk of a man wearing a hood emerged, an axe in his hands. Another man brought forth the chopping block. I was crushed with shock, with horror, when I realized they were about to behead the man in front of me.

The hall had gone painfully quiet, and all I could hear was the memory of Jourdain's words . . . *I watched it, afraid to speak out. We were all afraid to speak out.*

And so now I watched as the old man was forced to kneel, to lay his head upon the chopping block. I was one breath from stepping forward, from letting my entire façade shatter, when a voice broke the silence.

"My lord king."

Our eyes shifted to the left of the hall, where a tall, gray-haired lord had stepped forward. He wore a golden circlet on his head, a bright red jerkin pressed with the heraldry of an owl.

"Quickly speak what ails you, Burke," the king impatiently said.

Burke bowed, and then held up his hands. "This man is one

of my best masons. It would hurt my household to lose him."

"This man also harbors the traitor's mark," Lannon spouted, holding the blue fabric up again. "Do you mean to tell me how to dole my justice?"

"No, my king. But this man, long ago, once served the traitor before the rebellion. Since the victory of 1541, he has served under my House, and he has not once spoken the fallen name. It is, most likely, by accident that this sigil has endured."

The king chuckled. "There are no accidents when it comes to traitors, Lord Burke. I would kindly remind you of that, and I will also say that if any more traitorous marks arise from your House, you will have to pay for it with blood."

"It will not happen again, my lord king," Burke promised.

Lannon propped his jaw on his fist, his eyes hooded as if he was bored again. "Very well. The man will be given thirty lashes in the courtyard."

Burke bowed in gratitude as his mason was hauled up from the chopping block. The man wept his thanks, thanks that he was going to be scourged instead of beheaded, and I watched as they passed me, heading for the courtyard. Lord Burke's face was ashen as he followed them, and he brushed my shoulder.

I took note of his expression, of his name. For he was bound to become an ally.

"Lady?" the herald was whispering to me, waiting for my name card.

I handed it to him, my mouth going dry, my pulse spiking through my mind. Saints, I could not do this. *I could not do this. . . .* It was folly to mention MacQuinn's name right on the heels of Morgane's. And yet . . . I was here. There was no going back.

"May I present Mistress Amadine Jourdain, of Valenia, to his royal Lordship, King Gilroy Lannon of Maevana."

I stepped forward, my kneecaps turning to water, and presented him with a graceful, fluid bow. For once, I was grateful for the rigid stays about my waist; they kept me upright and transformed me from an uncertain girl to a very confident woman. I thought of Sibylle and her mask of wit; I let such a mask come over my face, over my body as I waited for him to address me, my hair flowing around my shoulders, wavy from the ocean breeze. I hid the worry deep within me, let assurance hold my expression and posture, just as Sibylle would do.

This encounter would not come unraveled, like the summer solstice had months ago. This encounter was made from my creation and plotting; I would not let the king steal it from me.

"Amadine Jourdain," Lannon said with a dangerous little smile. He seemed to say my name only to taste it as he caught Morgane's sigil on fire from a nearby candle. I watched as the blue and the silver horse burned, burned and became ash as he dropped it to the stone floor beside the throne. "Tell me, what do you think of Maevana?"

"Your land is beautiful, my lord king," I answered. Perhaps the only truth I would ever speak to him.

"It has been a long time since a Valenian woman has come to make a request of me," he continued, drawing a finger over his lips. "Tell me why you have come."

I had woven these words together days ago, forged them in the warmth of my chest. I had carefully selected them, tasted them, practiced them. And then I had memorized them, spoken them facing a mirror to see how they should influence my expression.

Even so, my memory wilted when I needed it most, the fear like a spider crawling up my voluptuous skirts when all I could see was the girl on the spike, when all I could hear was the faint lash of the whip from the courtyard.

I linked my trembling hands together and said, "I have come to ask your graciousness to grant passage to Maevana."

"For whom?" Lannon asked, that insolent smile still curling the ends of his mouth.

"My father."

"And who is your father?"

I drew in a deep breath, my heart thundering through my veins. I looked up at the king beneath my lashes, and proclaimed loud enough so every ear in the hall could hear: "I know him as Aldéric Jourdain, but you will know him as the lord of the House of MacQuinn."

I expected there would be silence when I spoke the fallen name, but I did not expect it to last so long or cut so deep. Or for the king to rise with slow, predatory grace, his pupils turning his eyes to a near black as he glared down at me.

I wondered if I was about to lose my head, right here at the footstool of the antler-and-wrought-iron throne that had once been Liadan's. And there would be no Lord Burke to stop it.

"The name 'MacQuinn' has not been spoken here for twenty-five years, Amadine Jourdain," Lannon said, the words twisting as a long vine of thorns throughout the hall. "In fact, I have cut out many tongues who dared to utter it."

"My lord king, allow me to explain."

"You have three minutes," Lannon said, jerking his chin toward one of the scribes who sat further down the dais. The scribe's eyes widened as he realized he was appointed to time how long I got to keep my tongue.

But I was calm, collected. I felt the pulse of the earth, buried deep beneath all of this stone and tile and fear and tyranny, the heartbeat of the land that once was. The Maevana that Liadan Kavanagh had created so long ago. *One day, a queen will rise,* Cartier had once said to me.

That day was coming on the horizon. That day gave me courage when I needed it most.

"Lord MacQuinn has spent twenty-five years in exile," I began. "He once dared to defy you. He once dared to take the throne from your possession. But you were stronger, my lord king. You crushed him. And it has taken nearly a quarter of a century for him to strip his pride to its bones, for him to soften enough to recognize his mistake, his treachery. He has sent me to ask you to pardon him, that his exile and his loss have been a great price he has paid. He has sent me to ask you to allow him back into the land of his birth, to once more serve you, to show that while you are fierce, you are also merciful and good."

Lannon stood so still and quiet he could have been carved

from stone. But the diamonds in his crown sparkled with malicious glee. Slowly, I watched his leather jerkin rustle with his breathing, and he stepped down the dais, his boots hardly making noise on the tiles. He was coming—stalking—to me, and I held my ground, waiting.

Only when he was a handbreadth away, looming over me, did he ask, "And why has he sent *you*, Amadine? To tempt me?"

"I am his passion daughter," I answered, helplessly looking at the broken blood vessels around his nose. "He has sent me to show his trust in you. He has sent me because I am of his family, and I have come alone, without an escort, to furthermore show his good faith in his king."

"A passion, is it?" His eyes roved over me. "What sort?"

"I am a mistress of knowledge, my lord king."

A muscle feathered along his jaw. I had no inkling as to what thoughts swarmed his mind, but he didn't seem pleased. Knowledge, indeed, was dangerous. But he finally turned away, walking back to his throne, his long royal robes of amber dragging behind him on the floor, rippling as liquid gold as he ascended the dais stairs.

"Tell me, Amadine Jourdain," he said, resuming his seat on the grand throne. "What would your passion father do upon returning to the land of his birth?"

"He would serve you in whatever manner you would ask of him."

"Ha! That is rather interesting. If I remember correctly, Davin MacQuinn was a very proud man. Do you recall, Lord Allenach?"

Allenach had not moved, not an inch. But his eyes were still on me, circumspectly. And that was when I remembered what Liam had said, the dynamic between the king and his councillor. That it was more important for me to get Allenach's blessing, for Allenach influenced the king like no other.

"Yes, my lord king," Allenach spoke, his voice a deep set baritone that moved through the hall like darkness. "Davin MacQuinn was once a very proud man. But his daughter speaks otherwise, that twenty-five years have finally cured him."

"It does not strike you odd that he would send his passion daughter to come make atonement for him?" Lannon questioned, the amethyst ring on his forefinger catching the light that poured in through the windows overhead.

"No. Not at all," Allenach eventually responded, those eyes still weighing me, trying to measure my depth. Was I a threat, or wasn't I? "As Amadine has stated, he has sent his most precious resource, to exemplify the honesty of his request."

"And what of the others, Amadine?" Lannon asked brusquely. "The other two lords, the two cowards who have slipped through my nets, just as your father? I just burned one of their sigils. *Where* are the others?"

"I know of no others, my lord king," I answered.

"For your sake, I hope you speak truth," the king said, leaning forward. "Because if I find out otherwise, you will regret ever stepping into my hall."

I had not prepared to be threatened so many times. And my voice had fled, turning to dust in my throat, and so I gave him another curtsy, to acknowledge his cold statement.

"So you believe we should allow him to return home?" Lannon crossed his legs, glancing back to his councillor.

Allenach took one step closer, then another, until he was standing at the edge of the dais. "Yes, my king. Let him return, and let us hear what the traitor has to say. And while we wait for him, I will take his daughter to my holding."

"I would prefer his daughter to remain here," Lannon objected, "where I can keep an eye on her."

My jaw clenched; in vain, I tried to look pleasant. I tried to look as if I did not care who hosted me. But I almost fell to my knees in profound relief when Allenach said, "Amadine Jourdain is a Valenian, my lord king. She will feel more at home with me, with the hunt of the hart ongoing at Damhan, and I swear to keep an eye on her at all times."

Lannon cocked his nearly invisible eyebrow, thrumming his fingers on the armrest of his throne. But then he declared, "So be it. MacQuinn may cross the border unscathed, and will come appeal to me in person. Amadine, you will go with Lord Allenach for the time being."

I pressed my fortune one final time. "My lord king, may I write the letter to my father? So he knows he may cross the channel?" I was to use two phrases in that letter, one that would secretly alert Jourdain to just how agitated Lannon had been with my request, and one that would assure him that I had made it to Damhan. And at this precarious point in time, I didn't dare to send a letter over the channel without the king's permission.

"Why of course you may." Lannon was mocking me when he motioned for the scribe to bring his desk, his paper, and his ink to me in the middle of the aisle. "In fact, let us do that now, together." The king waited until I had dipped the quill in the ink, and then he stopped me, just before I began to write. "I will tell you exactly what to say to him. How is that?"

I couldn't refuse. "Yes, my lord king."

"Write this: *To my Dearest, Cowardly Father . . .*" Lannon began in an animated voice. And when I hesitated, the ink dripping on the parchment as blackened blood, the king ground out, "Write it, Amadine."

I wrote it, bile rising up my throat. My hand was trembling—his entire court could see me quiver like a leaf. And it didn't help when Lord Allenach came to stand at my side, to make sure I was writing what the king dictated.

"*To my Dearest, Cowardly Father,*" Lannon continued. "*His most gracious lordship, the king of Maevana, has agreed to allow your treacherous bones to cross the channel. I have bravely arranged it for you, after realizing how magnanimous the king is, and how much you have deceived me with stories of your past woes. I believe you and I will have to have a little talk, after the king speaks with you, of course. Your obedient daughter, Amadine.*"

I signed it, signed it with tears in my eyes as the court laughed and chuckled at how cleverly scathing their king was. But I swallowed those tears; this was no place to appear weak or frightened. And I did not dare imagine Jourdain reading this, didn't dare imagine how his face would contort when he read these words, when he realized the king had mocked and coerced me before an audience.

I addressed the letter to Isotta's wine port, where Jourdain was keeping an eye on the deliveries. And then I stepped back, feeling as if I might collapse until a strong hand wrapped about my arm, holding me upright.

"The letter will be sent on the morrow," Allenach said, peering down into my pale face.

His eyes were crinkled at the edges, as if he was fond of smiling, laughing. He smelled like cloves, like burning pine.

"Thank you," I breathed, unable to stifle yet another shiver.

He felt it and gently began to escort me from the hall. "You are brave indeed coming here for a man such as MacQuinn." He studied me, as if I were some complicated puzzle he needed to solve. "Why do that?"

"Why?" My voice was going hoarse. "Because he is my father. And he longs to return home."

We walked out to the courtyard, into the sun; the brightness and cool wind nearly brought me to my knees again, the relief snapping my joints. Until I saw that the old man was still being whipped, tied between two posts a few yards away. His back was flayed open, his blood spilling over the cobbles. And there stood Lord Burke, witnessing the punishment, cold and silent as a statue.

I forced my eyes away, even though the crack of the whip made me jump. *Not yet*, I told myself. *Do not react until you are alone.* . . . "I need to thank you," I said to Allenach. "For offering me a place at your home."

"Although the royal castle is beautiful," he replied, "I think you will find Damhan far more enjoyable than remaining here."

"Why is that?" As if I truly needed to ask.

He offered me his hand again. I took it, his fingers politely holding mine as if he understood Valenian sensibilities, that a touch was supposed to be delicate as it was elegant. He began to lead me away, blocking my view of the flogging.

"Because I have forty Valenians lodging at my castle, for the hunt of the hart. You will feel right at home among them."

"I have heard of the hart," I said as we continued to walk in perfect stride with each other; I was mindful of the sheathed sword swinging at his side, as he was careful with the swell of my skirts. "I take it your forests are full of them?"

He snorted playfully. "Why do you think I invite the Valenians every autumn?"

"I see."

"And you have come alone, with no escort?"

"Yes, my lord. But I have a coach waiting outside the gates. . . ." I led him to it, where the coachman all but blanched at the sight of Lord Allenach with me.

"My lord." He hurried to bow. I noticed he wore a green cloak, which meant he must be one of Lannon's.

"I would like you to bring Amadine to Damhan," Allenach said to him as he helped me up into the coach. "You know the way, I trust?"

I settled on the bench as the lord and the coachman spoke. So I appeared at ease when Allenach leaned into the cab.

"It's several hours of travel to Damhan," he said. "I'll be riding behind you, and will greet you in the courtyard."

I thanked him. When he finally latched the door and I felt the coach bump forward, I slid deeper into the cushions with a shudder, the last of my courage slowly crumbling to ash.

# PART THREE

# ALLENACH

## —⊰ TWENTY-ONE ⊱—

# THE MADEMOISELLE WITH
# THE SILVER ROSE

*Lord Allenach's Territory, Castle Damhan*

I arrived to Damhan just as evening bruised the sky. The courtyard was teeming with life; liveried servants rushing about
with lanterns to transport food from the storerooms, fetching
water from the well and carrying stacks of firewood in prepara-
tions for the feast that night. The coachman opened the door for
me, but it was Allenach who eased me to the ground.

"I'm afraid it is getting too late for a tour," he said, and I
stopped to breathe the air—burning leaves, roasting wood, and
the smoke from the kitchen fires.

"A tour tomorrow, perhaps?" I requested just as a monstrously
large dog came trotting up to us, nuzzling into my skirts. I froze;
the dog looked like a wolf, wiry-haired and vicious. "Is . . . is that
a wolf?"

Allenach whistled, and the wolf dog at once stepped away from me, blinking up at her master with liquid brown eyes. He frowned down at her. "That is odd. Nessie hates strangers. And no, she is a wolfhound, bred to hunt the wolves."

"Oh." I still felt a bit shaky, although Nessie looked back at me, tongue lolling, as if I was her greatest friend. "She seems . . . friendly."

"Not usually. But she does seem quite taken with you."

I watched as Nessie trotted off, joining her pack of three other wolfhounds, who were trailing a servant carrying a shank of meat.

Only then did I turn to gaze at the castle.

I recognized it.

Tristan had likened it to a storm cloud that had married the earth. And I found that I agreed with him, for the castle was built of dark stones, reaching upward as a thunderhead. It felt primitive and old—most of the windows were narrow slits, built during a fierce time of constant war, the time before Queen Liadan. And yet it was still welcoming, like a gentle giant opening his arms.

"I might be able to give you a tour tomorrow," Allenach said, speaking in Middle Chantal even though his brogue caught roughly on the words. And then, as if he wanted to appear more Valenian than Maevan, he offered his hand again and walked me into his home.

He was saying something about dinner in the hall when I noticed that the sconces on the walls began to flicker with heated sparks, as if the flames were being pulled through hundreds of years. My heart quieted when I realized it was old light battling present light, that Tristan was about to summon me to his time. I must have seen something, smelled something in this castle to trigger it, and for half a moment I almost submitted to him, let his memory swarm me. It would be about the stone—a vision I undoubtedly needed to see—yet when I imagined fainting or going into a trance in Allenach's presence . . . I could not allow that.

I inadvertently tightened my hold on Allenach's hand, cast my eyes to the stone floors, to the way the light tumbled off my dress. Anything to evade the shift, anything to keep my ancestor at bay. It was like trying to smother a sneeze or a yawn. I watched the walls ripple, eager to melt back in time, watched the shadows try to catch me. And yet I would not submit to them. I felt as if I were tumbling from a tree and I caught myself on a branch—a weak yet stubborn one—just before hitting the ground.

Tristan relented; his grip faded, my pulse throbbing in relief.

"There is the door to the hall," Allenach said, pointing to a set of tall double doors christened with his armorial banner. "Breakfast and dinner will be served in there for all my guests. And here are the stairs. Let me show you to your room."

I walked beside Allenach up a long flight of stairs, a maroon carpet rolled out like a tongue to lick every step, up to the second floor. We passed several Valenian men who looked at me with interest but said nothing as they continued on to the hall. And then I began to notice the carvings over the doors, that the threshold of each guest room was dedicated to something, whether it was a phase of the moon, or a certain flower, or a wild beast.

He saw my interest, slowing his pace so I could read the emblem of the closest threshold.

"Ah yes. When my forefather built this castle, his wife had every room blessed," Allenach explained. "See, this guest room is given to the fox and the hare." He pointed to the baroque carving of a fox and a hare running in a circle, each chasing the other.

"What does that mean?" I inquired, fascinated with how the fox's sharp mouth almost clamped on the fluffy tail of the hare, and how the hare almost bit the generous tail of the fox.

"It harkens back to a very old Maevan legend," Allenach said. "One that warns of stepping through a door one too many times."

I had never heard of such lore.

He must have sensed my intrigue, for he stated, "To protect oneself against the wiles of thresholds—to ensure a man knew where it would lead him every time he passed from one room to another—it became wise to mark, or bless, each room. This room grants stamina to the Maevan who never let one's enemy out of sight."

I met his gaze. "That is fascinating."

"So most Valenians say, when they stay here. Come, this is the room I think will best suit you." He led me to an arched door, latticed with iron, blessed with the carving of a unicorn wearing a chain of flowers around its neck.

Allenach took the candle from the nearest sconce and opened the door. I waited as he lit candles in the darkened room, a warning brushing against my thoughts. I was hesitant to be alone with him in a chamber, and my hand drifted to my skirts, feeling the shape of the hidden dirk.

"Amadine?"

I let my hand fall from my gown and tentatively passed beneath the unicorn's blessing, standing a safe distance from him, watching as the light roused the chamber to life.

The bed was covered with silk embroidery, curtained with red sendal. An old wardrobe sat against one wall, carved with leaves and willow branches, and a small round table held a silver washbasin. There were only two windows framing a stone hearth, both war-inspired slits of glass. But perhaps more than anything, it was the large tapestry hanging from the longest wall that drew my admiration. I stepped closer to look upon it, the endless number of threads coming together to depict a rearing unicorn amid a colorful array of flowers.

"I thought that might catch your eye," Allenach said.

"So what blessing does this room give?" I asked, warily glancing back to him just as one of his servants brought in my trunk, carefully setting it at the foot of the bed.

"Surely you know what the unicorn embodies," the lord said, the candle faithfully flickering in his hand.

"We have no unicorn myths in Valenia," I informed him mournfully.

"The unicorn is the symbol of purity, of healing. Of magic."

That last word felt like a hook in my skin, his voice pulling on me to see how I would respond. I glanced back to the tapestry, only to shift my eyes from his, remembering that while this lord was appearing friendly and hospitable to me, he was not easing his suspicions. He was not forgetting that I was MacQuinn's daughter.

"It's beautiful," I murmured. "Thank you for choosing it for me."

"I'll send one of my servant girls to help you change. Then come down and join us for dinner in the hall." He departed, closing the door with hardly a sound behind him.

I hurried to unpack my trunk, locating the homespun servant's dress, apron, and shawl that I would wear two nights from now, when I would sneak out of the castle to find the stone. In the deep apron pocket was my digging spade, and I quickly bundled it all together and hid it beneath the bed, a place the chambermaid would not think to look. I was leisurely unpacking the remainder of my clothes, hanging them in the wardrobe, when the servant girl arrived. She helped me shed the blue gown and white kirtle, refastened my corset even though I was aching to peel it away after wearing it all day. And then she re-dressed me in a gown of silver that bared my shoulders and gathered in a scintillating bodice. The dress flowed like water when I moved, the train following me like spilled moonlight. I had never worn something so exquisite, and I closed my eyes as the girl gathered and pinned my hair up from my neck, leaving a few tendrils loose about my face.

When she left, I reached deep within my trunk to find the silver rose I was to wear in my hair. I twirled it in my fingers, watching the candlelight breathe fire over the small rubies, wondering how simple it would be for me to locate d'Aramitz. A man I had never met, who I was supposed to recognize by a crest. Well, he was here somewhere, I thought and moved to stand before the hanging copper plate that served as a mirror. I watched my dim reflection as I pinned the silver rose behind my ear, and then I wiped away my star mole and redrew it on the ridge of my cheekbone.

Oh, d'Aramitz would know it was me, even without the rose. I was going to stand out like a sore thumb in a hall full of men, even if they were predominantly Valenian.

I began to walk to the door, but I paused, my eyes catching on the unicorn tapestry once more. I had won two victorious battles that day. I had gained passage for Jourdain, and I had made it to Damhan. I let that sink into my heart, let that courage rekindle. Tonight should be very simple, perhaps the cleanest branch of my mission. I did not even have to speak to the third lord, just make eye contact.

I left my room and found the stairs, following the trickle of laughter and the rich aromas of a promising feast all the way to the hall.

I was impressed by it, perhaps even more so than the royal hall. Because Damhan's hall was some sixty feet long, the high ceiling crafted from exposed wooden beams that arched in complexity, darkened from habitual smoke. I admired the tiles on the floor, which led me to the fire in the middle of the hall, raised on flagstones. The light illuminated the heraldry that guarded the four walls—stags that leaped through crescent moons and forests and rivers.

This was the House I had come from.

Shrewd blessings and leaping stags.

And I savored it, this Maevan hall and all its charms and life, knowing that long ago Tristan had once sat in this hall. I felt close to him, as if he might materialize any moment, might come and brush my shoulder, this man I had descended from.

Yet it wasn't Tristan who brushed past me, but servants rushing to set platters of food, glazed wine jugs, and ale flagons upon the long trestle tables.

D'Aramitz, I reminded myself. He was my mission tonight.

Most of the Valenian nobles were milling toward the center of the hall while the tables were prepared, holding silver cups of ale and reliving the day's events to one another. There were also seven thanes of Allenach, intermingling with the Valenians, but I easily identified them by the leather jerkins pressed with the stag.

So I began to quietly move about the clusters of men, my eyes modestly coasting over their chests as I sought the crest of the tree. A few of the men, naturally, tried to catch me in conversation, but I merely smiled and continued on my way.

It felt as if I had wandered about aimlessly for a good while when I finally came upon a gathering of men I had yet to peruse. The first couple were certainly not d'Aramitz. I stopped in weary frustration, until I began to imagine how he should look in my mind. If he was one of the lords, he would be older, around Jourdain's age most likely. So perhaps a few wrinkles, a few gray hairs.

I had just sketched a very ugly lord in my mind when my eyes were suddenly drawn to a man standing with his back to me. His flaxen hair was bound in a ribbon, and something about his height and manner of stature seemed strangely comforting to me. He was dressed in a dark red jerkin and white long-sleeved linen shirt, his breeches a simple black, yet the longer I looked upon his backside, the more I realized there was no chance for me to unobtrusively circumvent the crowd to see his crest.

He must have sensed my gaze, for he at last turned about and glanced at me. My eyes immediately fastened to the emblem imprinted on the breast of his jerkin. It was the tree Jourdain had shown me. This was d'Aramitz. But he had become very still, so still that it was unnatural.

My gaze slowly moved from the crest to his face—which was in no manner ugly and old but young and handsome. Eyes blue as cornflowers. A mouth that rarely smiled.

I was broken, I was mended as I stared at him, as he stared at me.

For he was not just d'Aramitz, the third fallen lord. He was not just an unfamiliar man I was supposed to make eye contact with and then drift away from.

He was Cartier.

# — TWENTY-TWO —

# D'ARAMITZ

For a moment, all I could do was stand and breathe, my hands pressed to the silk of my bodice, to the stays of my corset. This could not be, I thought, the protest filling my mind as rain in a river. Cartier was a passion. Cartier was a Valenian.

And yet, all this time, he had been something else.

Cartier was Theo d'Aramitz . . . Aodhan Morgane . . . a fallen Maevan lord.

I could not take my eyes from him.

The sounds of the hall began to melt away as frost in sun, the firelight flickering into a dark gold, as if it were laughing, laughing at Cartier and me. Because I saw it in his gaze too, the longer he drank me in. He was shocked, alarmed that I was the mademoiselle with the silver rose, that I was Amadine Jourdain, the one to retrieve the Stone of Eventide, the one he had been admonished to keep an eye on, to assist if trouble should befall her.

His eyes rushed over me, hung upon that rose in my hair as if it were a thorn, something akin to pain flaring across his expression. And then his gaze returned to mine, the distance between us thin and sharp, like the air just before a steep incline.

Oh, how, *how* had this happened? How had we not known about each other?

The shock of this was about to blow our covers.

I turned away first and stepped directly into a man who caught me by the arm before I spilled his chalice of ale down his doublet.

"Careful, Mademoiselle," he said, and I forced a shy smile to my lips.

"Forgive me, Monsieur," I rasped, then darted away before he could hold me captive.

I was seeking a place to run, to hide until I could recover—I wanted shadows and quiet and solitude—when I heard Cartier following me. I knew it was him; I recognized the heady sensation of distance closing between us.

I stopped before one of the empty trestle tables, pretending that I was admiring the heraldry on the wall, when I felt his leg brush my skirts.

"And who might you be, mademoiselle?"

His voice was soft, agonized.

I should not look at him, should not talk to him. If Allenach happened to glance this way, he would know. He would know there was something between Cartier and me.

And yet I could not resist it. I turned to face him, my body waking to how close he was to me.

"Amadine Jourdain," I responded—polite, detached, disinterested. But my gaze was bright, my heart smoldering, and he knew it. He knew it because I saw the same in him, as if we were mirrors, reflecting each other. "And you are . . . ?"

"Theo d'Aramitz." He gave me a bow; I watched as his blond hair gleamed in the light, as his body moved with grace. Beneath that polish and passion, he was steel and cold wind; he was the blue banner and the horse of the House of Morgane.

A rebelling House. A fallen House.

His father must have been the lord to join with MacQuinn and Kavanagh, because Cartier would have been only a child twenty-five years ago. And even as I began to weave together the threads, I knew there was still more that I needed to know. He and I needed to find a way to speak, alone, before the mission completely rotted beneath our feet.

"Which room is yours?" I whispered, and enjoyed the way his face flushed from my brash inquiry.

"The flying stoat," he returned, so low I almost didn't hear him.

"I will come to you, tonight," I said, and then turned away, as if he had lost my interest.

I merged back into the crowd just in time, because Allenach entered the hall, his eyes finding me immediately. He strode toward me, and I waited, hoping that the color in my face had cooled.

"I would like for you to sit at my table, at the place of honor," Allenach said, offering me his hand.

I took it, let him walk me to the dais, where a long table sat heavily laden with chalices, plates, flagons, and platters of steaming food. But it wasn't the feast that drew my attention; it was the two young men who sat waiting for us there.

"Amadine, allow me to introduce you to my oldest son, Rian, and my youngest son, Sean," Allenach said. "Rian and Sean, this is Amadine Jourdain."

Sean nodded politely at me, his hazelnut-colored hair cropped short, his face freckled and sunburned. I guessed him to be a little older than me. But Rian, the firstborn, merely looked at me with eyes of flint, his thick eyebrows cocked, his dark brown hair loose and long at his collar as he impatiently tapped his fingers along the table. I made a note to avoid him in the future.

I curtsied to them, even though it felt awkward and unnecessary in such a hall. Rian sat at Allenach's right—signifying he was the heir—and Sean sat on his left. I was to sit on the other side of Sean, which was probably the safest seat in the entire hall for me at the moment. I was cushioned from Rian's suspicious gaze and Allenach's inquiries, and I was on the other side of the hall from Cartier.

But as I sat in my appointed chair of honor, my gaze helplessly roamed the trestle tables set before us, seeking my master out despite my better judgment. He was sitting to the left of the hall, three tables away, yet he and I had a perfect view of each other. It felt like a chasm had opened up, cracking the tables, the pewter and silver, the tiles that stretched between us. His eyes were on me; my eyes were on him. And he raised his chalice ever so slightly and drank to me. Drank to my fooling him, drank to my reuniting with him, drank to the plans that entwined us not as passions but as rebels.

"So, my father says you are a passion of knowledge," Sean said, trying to engage me in polite conversation.

I glanced at him, granted him a little smile. He was regarding me as if I were a flower with briars, the grandeur of my dress obviously making him slightly uncomfortable.

"Yes, I am," I replied, and forced myself to take the platter of dove breasts that Sean handed me. I began to fill my plate, my stomach revolting at the sight of everything as it had been crunched all day by my corset. But I had to appear at ease, grateful. I ate and spoke to Sean, slowly adjusting to the cadence of the hall.

I was just asking Sean about the hunt and the hart when I felt Cartier's gaze on me. He had been staring at me for a while, and I had stubbornly resisted, knowing that Allenach was also watching me from the corner of his eye.

"Has anyone seen the hart yet?" I asked Sean, dicing my potatoes and finally meeting Cartier's gaze from beneath my lashes.

Cartier inclined his head, his eyes flickering to something. I was just about to follow his silent order to look at whatever he was perturbed about when the warmth of strings filled the hall. A violin.

I would know her music anywhere.

Startled, I glanced to the right, where a group of musicians—passions of music—had gathered with their instruments, their music beginning to claim the hall. Merei sat among them, her violin obediently propped on her shoulder, her fingers dancing along the strings as she began to harmonize with the others. But her eyes were on me, dark and lucid, as if she had just woken from a dream. She smiled, and my heart about escaped my chest.

I was so overcome I knocked over my chalice of ale. The golden liquid spilled down the table, onto my dress, onto Sean's lap. The youngest son bolted upright, but I could hardly move. Merei was in the hall. Merei was playing. *In Maevana*.

"I am so sorry," I panted, trying to catch my breath as I began to mop up the ale.

"It's all right; these were my old breeches anyway," Sean said with a crooked smile.

"Does music always affect you like that, Amadine?" Rian drawled from his end of the table, leaning over to watch as I helped Sean clean up the mess.

"No, but it is a pleasant surprise to hear it in a Maevan hall," I replied as Sean resumed his seat, looking as if he had wet his pants.

"I like for my Valenian guests to feel at home," Allenach explained. "The past few years, I have invited a consort of musicians for the season of the hunt." He took a sip of ale, motioned for a servant to come refill my chalice although I was utterly finished with eating and drinking and trying to appear normal. "As one passion to another, they should make you feel at home."

I chuckled, unable to help myself. Steam had been building in my chest ever since I had come face-to-face with Cartier. And now it was escaping, along with Merei's music.

I had known she would travel the realm with her patron. But never had I imagined that she would cross the channel and play in a Maevan hall.

*Merei, Merei, Merei,* my heart sang along with its pulse. And as her music flowed over me, explored every corner and eave of the grand hall, I suddenly realized how dangerous it was for her to be there. She was not to know me; I was not to know her. And yet how could I sleep under such a roof, knowing she and Cartier were both here, so close to me?

Cartier must have already experienced this, the first night at Damhan, when Merei had unexpectedly emerged with Patrice Linville's consort to play in the evening. Cartier must have told her to pretend that she did not know him, and so all I could do was pray she extended the same act toward me.

I thought of a myriad of ways to approach her under pretense, to find a way to speak to her alone, to explain to her why I was here. But all I could do was sit and listen to her, the hall growing quiet in appreciation of the music, my heart thrumming with longing and fear. Should I move or remain frozen?

I wanted to look at her; I wanted to rush to her. But I rose to my feet and glanced to Lord Allenach, smiling as I requested, "Will you escort me to my room, my lord? I fear I am exhausted from a long journey."

He stood at once, the golden circlet over his forehead winking in the firelight. As he led me down the aisle, my eyes brushed over the tables to the left of the hall, one by one.

Cartier had disappeared.

## ↠ TWENTY-THREE ↞

# TO PASS THROUGH A TAPESTRY

I did not expect to see a guard posted at my door. But as Allenach escorted me back to the unicorn chamber, I realized that I was to be watched *and* guarded. My face betrayed nothing, but my heart was tripping over my ribs as I realized there would be no way for me to sneak out to Cartier's room, for me to sneak out of the castle to get the stone.

"For your protection, Amadine," Allenach said when we came to the door, the guard standing as determinedly quiet as a statue. "With so many men in the castle, and you without an escort, I would not want you to come to harm."

"How thoughtful, my lord. I shall sleep peacefully tonight," I lied and gave him a sweet smile.

He returned it, although the smile didn't quite reach his eyes as he opened the door for me. "I'll send the chambermaid to come assist you."

I nodded and entered the room, the candlelight sighing with my return. Everything was crumbling, I thought as I sat on the edge of my bed. Was this why secret missions always failed, because it was impossible to prepare for every little twist in the road?

I had planned to sneak out the following night, to give myself time to locate the servant doors Liam had described to me, the doors I should use to move in and out of Damhan. And if I couldn't find a way out of this room . . . I was going to have to adjust my plans. I was going to have to recover the stone during daylight. And that was going to be risky, with the men hunting in the woods.

I needed to conjure a reason to either join the hunt or to be near the woods tomorrow. Both seemed impossible at the moment, when I was tired and overwhelmed and guarded.

The chambermaid finally arrived, to help me undress and stir a fire in the hearth. I was grateful when she left, when I was finally alone wearing nothing but my chemise, my hair loose and tangled. And then I collapsed on my bed and stared at the unicorn tapestry, my head aching.

I thought of Tristan. He had once lived here. Maybe he had once been in this room.

That prompted me to sit forward. I began to pick apart every memory of his I had inherited, searching them until they were softened from so much handling. He had shared a thought with me about Damhan, the day he sparred with his brother. He had thought about the nooks and crannies, the secret passages and hidden doors of this castle.

I rose from the bed and began to access the room. I was instantly drawn to the tapestry. Gently, I pulled it aside and looked at the stone wall beneath. My fingertips began to trace the mortar lines, seeking, seeking . . .

It took me a while. My feet had gone cold on the stone floors by the time I felt a strip of mortar catch beneath my nails. I eased it forward, felt the wall shift as a narrow, ancient door opened into a dark inner corridor that smelled of mold and moss.

A hidden web. An intricate branching of the castle's veins and arteries. A way to move about without being seen.

I hurried to gather my slippers and a candelabra. And then I dared to step into the passage, letting the shadows swallow me, my candlelight hardly making a splash amid the darkness. I didn't latch my door, but I did close it as much as I dared. And then I mulled over thresholds, how they were portals and each chamber needed a blessing. If the main doors had signifiers, then surely a hidden door would, as well?

I raised my candelabra, scrutinizing the roughened arch of this door. And there . . . the unicorn was carved, rather crudely, but it was marked.

I could find Cartier's room like this, I thought, and before my courage could wane, before my better sense could dampen my impulse, I began to walk the passage. I wondered if I could also find a way out of the castle by these routes, and then shivered when

I imagined getting hopelessly lost in this dark, twisting maze.

I went cautiously, as if I were a child just learning to walk. I paused every time I heard a sound . . . echoes from the kitchen, doors banging beneath me, the wind howling as a beast on the other side of the wall, peals of laughter. But I began to find the other doors, and I read their blessings. This portion of the castle was the guest wing, and as the inner passage began to curve, I took note of every bend and turn I made, praying Cartier's chamber would have an inner door.

I lost track of time. I was just about to relent, my feet as ice, the cold air seeping through my thin chemise, when I found his door. Under different circumstances, I would have laughed that Cartier's room was blessed by a winged weasel. But my heart, my stomach, my mind were all tangled in a knot, and I was trembling, trembling because I was about to see him. Would he be angry at me?

I lifted my fingers and flipped the latch. The secret door opened into the passage, most likely so it wouldn't scuff the chamber floors. A heavy tapestry met me, to guard the passage as mine had been covered.

I could hear Cartier's boots on the floor, although he was not coming to me. He was pacing, and I wondered how to greet him without frightening him.

"Master."

My voice melted through the tapestry, but he heard. And he must have felt the draft. He all but yanked the tapestry from the wall as his eyes fell on me in the yawning of the secret door. For the second time that night, I had rendered him speechless, and I invited myself into his chamber, brushing past him and all but groaning at the warmth and rosy light of the fire.

I stood in the center of his room, waiting for him to come to me. He took the candelabra from my hands and roughly set it on a table, his fingers pulling through his loose hair. He kept his back to me, looking everywhere but at me, until he finally turned. Our eyes locked.

"Amadine Jourdain," he said with a sorrowful smile. "How did you slip past me?"

"Master Cartier, I am sorry," I rushed to say, the words tumbling over one another. I think he must have heard the pain in my voice, the pain of having to leave Magnalia so quietly. "I wanted to tell you."

"And now I understand why you didn't." He sighed and noticed my shivering, that I was wearing nothing but my chemise. "Here, come sit by the fire. You and I need to have a little talk." He drew two chairs before his hearth, and I sank into one, easing my feet forward to catch the warmth. I felt him watching me, that space between us tender and confusing. For I might have left Magnalia without a trace, but he had been keeping secrets as well.

"So," he said, casting his gaze to the fire. "Jourdain is your patron."

"Yes. And you are Aodhan Morgane." I whispered that forbidden name, as if it were honey on my tongue, as if the walls might hear us. But the sound of it seemed to electrify the air between us, for Cartier looked at me, his eyes wide and bright as midsummer, and he gave me a tilt of a smile.

"So I am. And so I am also Theo d'Aramitz."

"As well as Cartier Évariste," I added. Three different names, three different faces. All one man.

"I don't even know where to start, Brienna," he stated.

"Start at the beginning, Master."

He seemed to hang on that last word—"master"—as if it reminded him of what our relationship was still supposed to be. But then he found his voice, and his story woke as an ember.

"My father defied Lannon twenty-five years ago, a story you no doubt know very well by now. I was so young I do not remember anything, but my mother and my older sister were slaughtered, and my father ran with me before the same fate could befall me. He came south to Delaroche, became a scribe, and raised me up as a Valenian. About the time that I began to beg him to let me passion, he told me who I truly was. I was not Theo d'Aramitz, as I'd thought I was. I was not Valenian. I was Aodhan, and he was a disgraced Maevan lord who had a score to settle."

He paused. I could see him remembering his father. Cartier's face hardened, as if the pain of that loss was still keen.

"He met with Jourdain and Laurent once a year. They began to plan, but everything they thought of was weak. All the while, I thought it was ridiculous. We all had fine, good lives in Valenia. We were safe. Why were the lords still trying to return? Then my father died, eaten up by his grief. I became a master of knowledge, and I took up a new name. I didn't want to be found. I didn't want to be drawn into some foolish plan for vengeance. I became Cartier Évariste, and I chose to go to Magnalia because the Dowager had given us aid when we'd crossed the border. I didn't expect her to recognize me; I had only been a small child when she had sheltered us, but all the same . . . I felt drawn there."

"Did you tell her who you were?" I asked. Surely, she would have wanted to know it was him. . . .

"I wanted to tell her," he replied. "I wanted to tell her that I was little Aodhan Morgane, the son of a fallen lord, and that I was alive because of her goodness. But . . . I never found the courage. I remained Cartier, as I wanted, even though I began to change. I began to think more and more of Jourdain, of Laurent, of Luc and Yseult. Of why they wanted to return. I began to think of my mother, my sister, whose blood still cries out from the ground, of the Morgane people, who have been persecuted and scattered while their estranged lord hid. I realized that to stay in Valenia, pretending that Lannon's atrocities were not happening, was cowardly.

"I almost left Magnalia before my seven-year contract was up. I almost left, hardly able to bear my secrets, my past. Until you asked me to teach you."

I drew in a slow, deep breath. My gaze was on his face, but he was still looking to the fire, his chest gently rising and falling.

"You asked me to teach you knowledge in three years," he recounted, and that smile returned. He finally met my gaze, and my heart began to unravel. "You were the very challenge I needed, Brienna. I remained for you, telling myself that after you passioned, I would rejoin Jourdain and Laurent's efforts to return north. What you asked was nigh impossible, but I was determined to see you gain what you wanted, to see you passion. You kept me so distracted I could hardly think of anything else."

I glanced down to my hands. There was so much I wanted to say to him, and yet somehow, no words seemed worthy.

"Master Cartier," I finally breathed, looking at him.

He was about to keep talking, his lips forming a word I would never hear. There was a soft, patterned knock on the door, and Cartier was up from his chair in a blink, motioning for me to follow him.

"You need to leave," he whispered to me as I trailed him across the room. "This is one of Jourdain's thanes, and for your protection . . . I do not want him to know of you." He handed me my candelabra and drew back the tapestry.

I had all but forgotten that d'Aramitz also had a mission here, to secretly rally the remnants of Jourdain's people. I pushed open the door and stepped into the inner passage, turning to look back at him. There was still so much we had not resolved. And he must have seen the lingering questions and desires in my gaze, for he whispered, "Come to me again tomorrow night?"

"Yes," I murmured.

"Be careful, Brienna." And then he lowered the tapestry and I shut the inner door.

I paused only long enough to ensure that I could not hear anything through the wall as he met with the thane, and then I began to wend my way back to my room. I had not once thought of our conversation being overheard. But I should have. He should have. Because one careless move, and Cartier and I would both be dead.

And I still had to retrieve the Stone of Eventide.

## ⟶ TWENTY-FOUR ⟵

# THE HUNT

The following morning, I ate a hasty breakfast in the hall and then followed the trail of Valenians out to the court-yard as they waited for their horses. The mist was just beginning to burn away, and I stood off to the side and watched as Dam-han's sprawling lands woke with sun and gleaming dew.

There was the alehouse, the servants' quarters, the stables, the sparring turf where Tristan and Oran had once practiced. And just on the rim of the pasture, there sat the Mairenna Forest, swathed in dark green pines and yellow aspens, crowned with fog. Not much had changed over the past one hundred and sixty years. It was a gentle reminder that this land, this people, was built in fortitude and tradition, that change happened slowly, gradually.

My plans were to get near the forest by requesting a tour, a tour I expected would be deterred since all of the men were going to be hunting. But I needed to show my curiosity in the land so it would not appear strange to see me walking about on my own.

I felt the weight of the spade in my dress pocket; I felt the weight of the rebellion in my heart.

I shivered against the uncertain chill and told myself that if these plans failed, I would revert back to exploring the secret passages that night, even though I had no knowledge on how to navigate them and there was a greater risk of me opening the wrong door than the right one. . . .

I was imagining the horror of getting lost within those dark passages when I heard the lilt of a beloved voice behind me.

"I hear that you are a passion of knowledge."

I turned to look at Merei, fiercely suppressing the urge to throw my arms about her. I think we had the same expression on our faces, for her dimples set little valleys in her cheeks as she tried to restrain herself.

"I am. And you are a mistress of music?"

"Yes. Merei Labelle." She swept me a little curtsy.

"Amadine Jourdain," I returned, just as graceful. I felt Allenach's eyes on me from the other side of the courtyard. Good, I thought. Let him see me introduce myself.

"Well, Amadine, it seems that we are vastly outnumbered by men. Perhaps you and I might spend the day together?" Merei asked, her eyes bright with questions.

I held my breath, my mind rushing through the sudden

possibilities. I had not planned on Merei's involvement—the last thing I wanted was to risk her safety—but I suddenly realized how much I could use her assistance.

"Yes, I would love to. But I planned to ride the land today," I said as we meandered back into the crowd of men, toward Allenach. From the corner of my eye, I saw Cartier standing in a loose circle of Valenians. My heart quickened as I asked Merei, "Perhaps you could ride with me?"

"Of course!" Merei agreed as we came to stand before Allenach.

"My lord," I greeted him, dropping a dutiful curtsy. "I was hoping for that promised tour of the land today."

"I fear that I must ride with the men and lead the hunt," he replied.

"Would one of your sons be willing to escort me?" I inquired, praying that he would give me gentle, polite Sean, not Rian, who I had sensed was suspicious of me last night.

As if he felt the tugging of my hopes, Sean appeared in the courtyard with sleep still in his eyes, his short hair ruffled. He was wearing his father's colors, a maroon shirt beneath a leather jerkin, and black breeches tucked into knee-high boots. A quiver of arrows was slung over his shoulders, as was a long yew bow. When he felt my stare, he glanced to me, and I smiled at him. Just like that, he approached us.

"Good morning," he greeted. "I did not think you were a hunter, Amadine."

"I am not," I concurred. "But I was hoping to tour the property today, to see more of your father's lands."

Allenach was very quiet, watching this interaction between me and his youngest son. I couldn't tell what he was thinking, but my stomach clenched as I realized that the lord scarcely let me drift from his sight. I yearned for a shield, a flicker of magic, a way to hide myself from him and his keen observations.

"Your father is unable to escort me, though," I said. "So I guess I shall have to wait for tomorrow?"

Sean shifted his weight. "I could take you," he said, looking to his father. "Couldn't I, Father?"

And here came Rian. He moved like a snake in the grass, as if he could smell my secret intentions from across the courtyard.

"What is this about?" the oldest brother inquired, his eyes remaining on me, hard and dark and suspicious.

"Sean is going to take Amadine on a tour," Allenach stated, and again, I could not decipher if he was annoyed or bored. His words were carefully articulated.

"What?" Rian objected. "No, not Sean. Let me take her."

My palms began to sweat, but I held my ground, praying, waiting. . . .

"You are supposed to lead the hunt with Father," Sean objected.

"And you are supposed to bring up the rear."

"Enough," the lord said, a quiet but sharp word. His sons instantly obeyed. "Rian, you will come with me. Sean, you will take Amadine."

I scarcely could believe it, that the lord of the House of

Allenach was playing directly into my hands, directly into my wishes.

Sean nodded, evidently pleased, but Rian scowled, his face darkening as he finally removed his gaze from me. But I heard what he said to Allenach, his words striking me as pebbles as he muttered, "You are treating MacQuinn's wench like a princess."

I didn't hear Allenach's response, but my throat tightened.

"Come, mademoiselles," Sean said, holding out an arm for each of us. I took his left, Merei his right. "And you would be?"

"Merei Labelle," she said. "I just met Amadine a few moments ago."

He guided us to the open gates of the courtyard, where Allenach's servants were starting to bring the horses up to the Valenians.

"Give me just a few moments, to go fetch two palfreys for you," Sean said. "Wait here. I shall return."

We moved out of the way, watching Sean jog down the path to where the stables lay in the palm of the valley. I took this moment—the courtyard was humming with activity and movement as the men mounted their horses to leave—to ease Merei to a quiet pool of morning light.

"Act as if I am telling you something pleasant," I whispered to her. Her face was exposed to the men, while my back was turned, so someone like Rian couldn't read my lips.

"Very well," Merei said, giving me that *I just met you* smile. "Tell me what is going on."

"Shh. Just listen," I murmured. "At some point in this ride, I am going to give you a hand signal. When you see me lay my hand over my collar, I need you to pretend that your horse has spooked. Ride as far away from the forest as you can. You must distract Sean for as long as you are able."

Merei was still smiling at me, tilting her head as if I had just told her something wonderful. But her eyes widened, fixated on mine.

"I cannot tell you the details," I whispered. "It's best that you do not know."

She wanted to say my name. I saw her lips, wanting to form *Bri*. But she laughed instead, remembering my coaching. And it was good she did, because I felt the grease of Rian's stare again as he rode out of the courtyard.

"Be careful of the dark-haired brother. He looks at you in a way that angers me," she whispered, hardly moving her lips so they could not be read as the last of the men departed.

"Don't let him anger you." I linked my arm with hers, the courtyard feeling vast and lonely now that it was empty. We walked back to the gates, watching the groups of men ride across the lush meadows, toward the forest. "I promise you when all this is over, I will tell you everything."

Merei glanced to me, just as Sean emerged from the stables with three horses in tow.

"You had better," she playfully admonished. "Since you-know-who is also here."

I couldn't help but smile at the reference to Cartier. "Ah yes. That was a surprise."

The curiosities crowded her eyes, desperate to spill as tears, but I didn't dare say anything more about him. All I said was, "Continue to play along with me."

She nodded, and we greeted Sean with excited smiles. He gave Merei a bay mare while I took a roan gelding. And then we were mounted, following Sean as he led the way on his black stallion.

"Now, what should I show you first?" he asked, turning in the saddle to regard us riding side by side.

He had definitely chosen palfreys for us. These horses were extremely mellow, clopping along at a disinterested speed. Merei's mare looked half-asleep, and my gelding was determined to taste every blade of grass we plodded by.

"Perhaps we could start with the alehouse?" I offered.

"Excellent choice," Sean declared, and as soon as he turned back around in the saddle, I gave Merei a knowing look. She was going to have to switch the mare to get her to "spook."

We rode the short distance down the hill, leaving our horses tethered outside the alehouse. It was evident Sean was thrilled to show us around; he told us every bit of the history of the stone-and-timber building, which I half listened to. I was more worried about making sure Merei found an appropriate switch, so when I saw her discreetly slip a slender branch into her skirt pocket, my heart finally settled back into my chest.

Now. I needed to go now, while I was still near the portion of forest that Tristan had once darted into, while the men were still pressing deep into the woods for the hunt, before they started to trickle back to the castle.

We mounted our horses, and Sean began to trot us along the

wood line, chattering about the mill, which he was taking us to next. We were nearly upon the portion of forest that I needed to enter. I looked at Merei, laid my right hand over my left collar. She nodded and brought forth her switch. She gave her mare a hearty tap on the rump, and blessed saints, that horse bolted, just as I'd hoped.

We had all been taught how to ride at Magnalia. Even so, Merei almost lost her seat as the mare pulled back in a rear and then lurched into a furious gallop. I screamed after her, which startled Sean and sent him in hasty pursuit after her, across the wide pasture.

My gelding, old stalwart, watched with a little nicker. I nudged him into the woods, which he opposed until I kicked him harder. We trotted among the trees, the branches clawing us, my eyes hungrily taking it in. Faster, faster, I coaxed the horse, and he shifted into a rolling canter.

The branches swatted my face, yanked through my hair, kissed me with sap. But I continued to weave through them, my heart pounding as we drew near. I was letting the memory guide me, Tristan's ten-year-old memory, and I felt the oak's presence. Its roots were groaning beneath the ground, recognizing me, drawing me in as if I were on a tether.

The gelding jumped the little creek, and then we came to the clearing.

The years had shifted the forest, widening the arc about the oak. It stood alone, defiant, its long branches rustling in the gentle breeze. But it also meant I would be clearly exposed as I dug.

I dismounted on tingling legs and hurried to the tree. I knew this was the one, yet I couldn't help but run my hands over the massive, furrowed trunk. And there, nearly worn away by years and seasons, was the carving of *T.A.*

I fell to my knees, searching my pockets for the little spade. I began to dig, settling into an urgent rhythm, feeling the muscles burn between my shoulder blades. The earth was soft; it spilled around my skirts as chocolate cake, stained my fingers as I continued to seek the locket and the stone.

My ears suddenly popped, and there was the sound of thunder, although it had been a perfectly clear morning. I felt the shift starting to happen, Tristan taking over. I couldn't allow him to overcome me, and I dug faster, harder, and bit down on my lip until it bled, the pain and the metallic flow over my tongue keeping me anchored to my time and place.

Again, it took all of my focus to fend him off, to resist surrendering to him. It was like swimming against a strong current; I felt ragged, exhausted, when I finally tamped his urging by addressing him.

"What you have done, I will undo," I whispered to him, my ancestor who had started the decline of Maevana.

I almost felt his surprise, as if he were standing behind me. And then he faded, giving way to my persistence.

There was a hollow thud at the tip of my spade.

And deep within the hole lay the wooden locket.

I had been prepared for it to have rotted away, but it was whole and well; the years of burial had not affected it, as if it had charmed itself to survive. Carefully, reverently, I reached down and took the chain, bringing the locket into my palm. My fingers were shaking as I worked the latch open.

The stone was just as I remembered, even though the memory had not been mine. It was smooth, luminescent, like a moonstone. Until it sensed my presence, and a blue light cascaded through it, like sun shining through rain. The awe poured over me like honey, thick and sweet. I wanted to sit and watch the magic dance through the stone. And I might have done so, fallen shamelessly captive to the quiet beauty of it. But the colors melted away, leaving the stone pearly white again, dim and mournful.

I was no Kavanagh. There was no trace of magic in my blood, and the stone had gone dormant after sensing me. It wanted Yseult, I thought, and thinking of her brought me back to the urgency, the danger I was flirting with.

As I latched the locket, I heard voices, the crunching of horses trotting through the woods. I was trembling as I shoved the wooden locket down the front of my dress, into the cage of my corset. Then I sent the spade tumbling down the hole and furiously refilled it, patting the earth firmly, scattering leaves and acorns and twigs over it. Just as Tristan had done one hundred and thirty-six years ago.

I heard the breaking of a stick, the swishing of feet in grass, just behind me.

Frantic, I tried to form a response for why I was kneeling here, beneath a tree, my fingers lined with dirt. I waited for a hand to fall on my shoulder and spin me about, to demand to know what

I was doing. But it was a wet nose instead, nudging beneath my elbow. I sat down, the relief hot and prickly beneath my skin, as the wolfhound Nessie nudged me again, as if she wanted to play.

"Amadine!"

Now it was Sean, nearly upon me.

With what little time I had left, I ripped the hem of my dress, wiped the dirt from my hands onto the skirts, and tucked a twig into my hair. Nessie watched me with solemn eyes, as if she sensed my distress. Then I stumbled to retrieve the gelding, who was munching on the thin grass that flourished here. The locket pressed against my stomach, uncomfortable, but it would hold steady.

"Sean!" I called out to him, leading the horse back into the woods, Nessie on my heels.

"Amadine?"

We continued to call to each other until we met in the woods. His face went pale at the sight of me; he dismounted in a rush.

"What happened? Are you all right?"

"My horse spooked, right after Merei's," I said, making my voice waver. "He went for the woods."

"Gods above, did you break anything?" He was looking at my lip, which I had forgotten about. A little trickle of blood had dribbled down my chin.

"No, it just rattled me a bit," I said. "How is Merei?"

"She's well."

I glanced over his shoulder to see her and the mare approach us. Her gaze took me in, my dirt and my torn dress and my blood. Her fear finally roused, crossing the space between us as a shadow.

*Bri, Bri, what are you doing?*

"I swear that I chose the steadiest of horses for this tour," Sean said with a shake of his head. "I cannot believe they both spooked. I apologize."

"It's not your fault," I said, laying my hand on his arm. "All the same, do you mind taking me back to the castle?"

"Of course," Sean said, offering his knee to help me mount.

We rode back to the courtyard, where Merei's consort was about to go on a walk. They eagerly invited me to join them, but I declined. All I could think of was two things: I needed to change my dress and scrub the dirt from my nails before Allenach returned. And I needed the privacy to cry in relief that I had the Stone of Eventide.

I did both, and then made myself scarce until dinner, giving my heart and mind plenty of time to settle and realign to what now was to come. Not until after dinner, when I was back in my chamber pacing, trying to give Cartier enough time to leave the hall before I met him in his room, did a knock sound on my door.

Cautiously, I went to answer it, finding my chambermaid standing at the threshold with an envelope.

"One of the mistresses of music has invited you to join her in the library this evening," the girl said, dutifully handing me the letter.

I took it, fully aware that the guard beside me was watching. "Thank you."

The chambermaid was off before I could shut my door. I knew Merei wanted to discuss what had happened this morning, that this was her attempt to let me explain myself.

I eased the envelope open; a square of parchment slipped out. My heart swelled when I recognized her handwriting:

*Meet with me?*

I hesitated, wanting nothing more than to go to her. But before I could make up my mind, I watched as Merei's elegant penmanship began to slide around on the paper. My breath caught as it slithered about like a black snake, eventually resting on the paper in slanted Dairine.

*Meet with me.*

Tristan's memory unexpectedly captured me. I was too late to save myself from succumbing this time, and I sighed, watching as his hand crumpled the message, as he strode to the fire blazing in his hearth and tossed the parchment to the flames.

*He had been waiting two days for her to finally send him this message.*

*Tristan had invited Princess Norah Kavanagh to Damhan under the pretense of loyal hospitality. She had agreed to stay at his castle, and both of them knew it was only to make plans about stealing the Stone of Eventide from her mother, the queen, before war was unleashed on western Maevana.*

*Tristan slipped from the chamber. The corridor was quiet, dark. Only a few sconces continued to burn, casting monstrous light on the walls as he began to walk.*

*He had wondered how the queen's magic would corrupt in*

battle. He had read only one story about it, a story Liadan had ensured was passed down as it described what battle magic had done. Uncontrollable storms, unearthly creatures that rose up from the shadows, swords that stole sight when they pierced flesh, arrows that multiplied and returned to their archers . . .

He shuddered, hoping that Norah was ready to do what he suggested, that she would obtain the Stone of Eventide before the war came.

Tristan ascended the stairs to the third floor, silently padded down a narrow hallway to the door that led out to the northern parapet.

He stepped outside on the parapet walk, easing into the cold night.

His lands were drowning in moonlight. Everything looked so small, a quilt of dark greens and umbers and steel blues knit together with celestial light. The moon was swollen with gold, full and generous, the stars scattered about her as sugar spilled over black velvet.

From the corner of his eye, he saw a shadow shift, and he knew it was her.

"Shouldn't we find a better place to meet?" he asked.

"And why would I meet with you?" A man's voice.

Tristan's heart plummeted; he turned to look closer at the moving shadow. It was Norah's face, her dark hair streaming loose around her shoulders. And her mouth was moving—she was saying something— and he couldn't hear her. . . .

"Answer me," Norah snapped, but it was a masculine, suspicious voice that was shaped by her lips. And that was when the princess's face split down the middle, leaving Rian Allenach behind in her dust.

## ⊸⊱ TWENTY-FIVE ⊰⊷

## THE WARNING

"What are you doing here?" Rian snarled.

For a moment, all I could do was gape at him as my ears popped, as a shiver pulled over my skin, as horror rooted in my heart. Tristan had completely disintegrated, leaving me behind to mend this disaster.

"I . . . I am sorry," I panted, pulling my shawl tighter about my shoulders. "I was exploring and I—"

"Who were you exploring with?"

I swallowed, the suspicions in his dark gaze piercing me. "One of the musicians. We thought it would be nice to see a castle view."

"You don't have castles in Valenia?"

I stared at Rian, trying not to flinch when he stepped closer to me.

"Why don't you and I wait together for your friend to arrive," he murmured, tilting his head to the side as his eyes roamed over me.

I wanted to turn and flee. I almost did, my right foot beginning to slide on the stone floor when Rian moved to purposely block the path to the door.

"This will give us a good chance to get to know each other," he continued, crossing his arms. "Because ever since you arrived here, my father has been all out of sorts."

"Wh-what?" My pulse was wild, pounding like a drum in my ears.

"You heard me, Amadine Jourdain."

I took a step back, to put some space between us. The parapet wall jarred into my back, the mortar picking at my dress.

"Why have you come here?" Rian questioned.

Before the words could crumble in my throat, I said, "I came here for MacQuinn."

He smiled down at me—we were close to the same height, and yet I felt small in his shadow. It was evident my fear was like wine to him.

"Let's play a little game." He withdrew a sheathed dirk from his belt.

"I don't want to play," I rasped and tried to slip away.

His arm extended, his hand resting on the wall to keep me standing before him. "I'm not going to hurt you . . . unless you lie. In fact, we'll play the game equally. If I lie, you get to wield the blade. But if you lie . . ."

I stared at him. I thought of what Jourdain had said to me,

just before I departed Valenia. And I told myself to be brave, that Rian was fueling off my fears and helplessness. "Fine, but my friend will arrive any moment. . . ."

"We get three questions each," he all but spoke over me, flicking the end of the blade. "I'll go first." He set the point of his dirk at my throat. I didn't dare move, breathe, as the steel hovered over my pulse. "If you are a passion of knowledge, where is your fancy cloak?"

I swallowed, fear wedging in my throat like splintered bone. "My cloak was burned in a house fire a month ago. My mistress is currently having it replicated."

I waited, praying he would believe me. He clearly enjoyed making me worry and suffer, but eventually he lowered the blade and gave it to me. I didn't want to hold a dirk to him; I didn't want to stoop to his level of cruelty. And yet I thought of what might have happened to my mother. I took the point of the blade and aimed at his crotch.

Rian glanced down at it and smirked. "You're a vicious little thing, aren't you?"

"Why do you feel threatened by a woman?" The question flowed like fire from my mouth, anger curling the words.

His eyes sharpened over mine; his smirk shifted into a sinister expression. "I do not feel threatened by a *woman*. I question one who would come and appeal for a known traitor and coward."

He didn't give me time to weigh his response, to test if he was lying. He swiped the blade from me and pressed it against the bodice of my dress, just below my right breast. He was one inch from pointing it at the Stone of Eventide, which began to hum within my corset, as if the stone were waking with ire.

"The dark-haired musician," Rian snarled. "What's her name? Merei, I think. You know her. You knew her before you arrived here. How?"

Sweat began to trace down my back as my mind whirled, trying to weave a plausible lie. My hesitation fanned his contempt. He began to press the blade deeper; I felt the outer layer of my gown tear, my corset bend . . .

"There is camaraderie in passion, in sisterhood," I answered hoarsely. "This is something I do not expect you to understand, but there are binds between anyone who wears the cloak, even among strangers."

He paused, his eyes cold as they traced the lines of my face. I thought he believed my answer. I was about to extend my hand for the dirk when he shoved the blade into me.

My body went rigid, stiff with the sudden flare of pain in my side. And then came the terror as I acknowledged that he had stabbed me, that a dirk was embedded in my flesh.

"No, Amadine," Rian whispered bitterly. "That's a lie." And he withdrew the blade from me, so quickly that I staggered, sinking to my knees. "You lose."

My fingers curled into the stone floor, trying to find something to anchor me, to give me courage to face him. I was violently trembling when he knelt in front of me, when his fingers brushed the hair away from my face. The sensation of his skin touching mine made me want to retch.

"Let me give you some advice, little Valenian lass," he said, wiping my blood off the dirk before sheathing it back into its scabbard. "If you have come here for one like MacQuinn, if you plan to do something foolish . . . you had better have all your lies figured out. Because King Lannon is a hound when it comes to falsehood. And that wound in your side? That is only a foretaste of what he will do to you if you lie. So you can thank me for the warning."

Rian stood. I felt a cold whisper of air, heard the howling of the wind as he moved to leave the parapet walk. I was still on my hands and knees when he turned and said, "If my father finds out about this lesson, I can promise you that your little musician friend will pay for it. Good night, Amadine."

The door closed.

Alone, I began to gulp in air, trying to sear my distress before the shock overcame me, before I lost my composure. I slowly sat back on my heels, my eyes clenched shut. I didn't want to look; I didn't want to see what he had done to me. I wanted to melt and vanish; I wanted to go home, but I didn't even know where home was.

The stone was growing warmer against my stomach, so warm I realized it might burn me through the wooden locket, as if it were angry for me, for what had been done to me. I opened my eyes and glanced down to my bodice.

My blood was trickling down the pale blue of my gown and kirtle, dark as ink in the moonlight. He had stabbed me just below my breast, within my rib cage. I numbly tried to examine my puncture—how deep had the dirk gone into me?—but the layers of my dress . . . I couldn't access anything, only feel the pain begin to gradually ease as the shock overcame me.

I took my shawl and tied it around my middle, to conceal the blood.

I hurried back inside, down the corridor, down two flights of stairs. I could feel the blood flowing, leaving me. I could feel my panic gnaw around my mind as I held it together, long enough to pass my guard and slip into my chamber.

I locked the door. I tore away the shawl.

My blood was bright red in the firelight.

I stumbled to the tapestry, snagging a candelabra on my way. Into the dark I went. The inner passageway felt like I was roaming the endless bowels of a beast. I went from door to door, my head becoming fuzzy, the shadows whispering and nipping at my dress as I searched for the symbol for Cartier's room.

I could hardly remain upright, my heart thundering in my ears, my feet tripping over themselves. But like the night before, his door appeared to me just before I gave up, just before I melted to the floor.

The winged weasel flickered with blessing in my candlelight as I opened the inner door, as I pushed against the tapestry.

He was sitting at his desk, writing. My unexpected entrance startled him; he jerked, his quill streaking across the parchment as I came to stand in the heart of his room.

"Brienna?"

The sound of my name, the sound of his voice, was my undoing. I took my hand from my wound, my blood dripping from my fingers onto the rug.

"Cartier," I whispered just before I collapsed.

## ❧ TWENTY-SIX ☙

# WOUNDS AND STITCHES

H e moved faster than I had ever seen, nearly overturning his desk as he caught me just before I hit the ground. The candelabra spilled from my grip, clanging against the floor, the flames going out one by one, but Cartier held me to him, his eyes riveted to mine. I watched that Valenian elegance and poise dissipate from his demeanor as he took in my blood, as he took in my wound. Fury darkened his gaze, a fury found in battles and steel and moonless nights.

Gently weaving his fingers into my hair, he asked, "Who did this?"

I saw the Maevan in him rise, saw it overtake him at the sight of me bleeding in his arms. He was ready to crush whoever had hurt me. I had seen it before, in Jourdain and in Luc. But then I remembered that I was half Maevan. And I let that part of me answer.

"It's not deep," I murmured, taking hold of the front of his shirt, taking the helm of this problem. "I need you to undress me. I did not want to call the servant girl."

We stared at each other. I watched my words expand in his mind—he was about to take off my clothes—and his fingers loosened in my hair.

"Tell me what to do," he finally said, his gaze straying to the complicated mystery that man calls a woman's dress.

"There are laces . . . at the back of my gown," I panted, my breath coming short and shallow. "Loosen them. The gown comes off first. . . ."

He turned me in his arms, his fingers finding the knotted laces, unraveling them quickly. I felt the gown begin to loosen, felt him pull it off of me.

"What next?" he asked, his arm wrapped around my waist to support me.

"The kirtle," I murmured.

He slid it off, my body beginning to feel light. Then he unlaced my petticoats; they fell to my ankles in a wide hoop.

"My corset," I breathed.

His fingers fought with the stays, until my corset at last relinquished me and I could sag and breathe. I forgot all about the Stone of Eventide until I heard the wooden locket clink among the layers of fabric at my feet.

"The stone, Cartier . . ."

His arm tightened about me; he spoke into the tangles of my hair, "You found it?"

I heard the desire and the fear in his voice . . . like the thought of the stone being so close was as terrifying as it was marvelous. I leaned back against him, drawing on his strength, and smiled when I realized that he was feeling two conflicting things at once.

And then reality seemed to weave between us; he was holding me, and I was wearing nothing more than my undergarments, and the magical stone was somewhere at our feet, hidden in my clothes. I didn't know which one was more astonishing. By the pressure of his hands on my waist . . . neither did Cartier.

"Yes. I've been hiding it in my corset."

At once he knelt and took the locket, setting it on his writing desk. I was amazed at his disinterest in it, that he treated it like any other piece of jewelry. Until his gaze returned to mine, to my wound, and I saw how pale he was, how stressed.

All I wore was my sleeveless chemise, which reached my knees, and my woolen stockings, which had itched their way down my calves. And my blood bloomed bright and angry over the white linen, which I couldn't lift to examine unless I wanted to utterly bare myself to Cartier.

He must have read my mind. He moved to his wardrobe and brought me a pair of his breeches.

"I know, these are far too big for you," he said, holding them up to me. "But slip them on. I need to examine your wound."

I didn't protest. He guided me to his bedside and turned his back to me, leaving his pants in my hands. I sat on the mattress, unbuckled the dirk from my thigh, and began to pull my legs through his breeches, wincing when the pain echoed through my abdomen.

"All right," I said. "You can look."

He was at my side in an instant, guiding me to lie down over his blankets, resting my head on his pillow. Then, gently, he rolled up my chemise to expose my stomach, his fingers carefully probing my wound.

"It's not deep," he said, and I watched the tension ease from his face. "But I need to stitch this."

"I think my corset saved my life," I breathed, and then laid my head back and laughed.

He did not think that was amusing. Not until I had him fetch my corset, and he held it up. We both saw that the thick material, torn and bloodied, had taken the brunt of the blade, had protected me from a deeper piercing.

He cast my corset back to the floor and said, "I was about to empathize, for society dictating that you wear a cage like that. Not anymore."

I smiled as he walked to the desk, rummaging through his leather satchel. My eyes half-closed, I watched as he brought forth a pouch of herbs, as he sprinkled them into a goblet of water.

"Drink this. It'll help with the pain," he said, easing me up so I could drink.

I spluttered after the first sip. "This tastes like dirt, Cartier."

"Drink it."

I glared at him. He returned the glare, until he ensured that I had swallowed three more mouthfuls. Then he swept the goblet from me and I lay back down so he could clean my wound.

"Tell me," he said, kneeling at my side, threading his needle. "Who did this to you, Brienna?"

"Does it matter who did it?"

Cartier's anger kindled, his gaze like the blue heart of a flame. That Maevan lord had returned; I saw it in the set of his jaw, in the taut muscles of his posture, in the vengeance that gathered about him as shadows. In my mind's eye, I could see him standing in his reclaimed hall with a circlet of gold upon his head, walking through morning light, and beyond the windows his green meadows flourished, brightened by the Corogan flower. . . .

"It matters," he said, breaking my vision. "Who stabbed you? And why did they do it?"

"If I tell you, you must swear not to retaliate," I said.

"Brienna . . ."

"You will make it worse," I hissed impatiently.

He dabbed the blood from my skin and began to stitch me. My body went rigid at the bite of the needle, at the pull of my flesh as he brought me back together.

"I swear I will not do anything," he promised. "Until this mission is over."

I snorted. It was suddenly difficult to picture him holding a sword, returning the favor to Rian. Until I remembered that day in the library, when Cartier and I had stood on chairs with books on our heads. He had bled through his shirt.

It might have been the shock, or the northern air, or the fact that he and I were reunited. But I lifted my hand and traced my fingertip down the sleeve of his upper arm, where he had once bled. He stilled as if I had charmed him, pausing halfway through the stitching, and I realized this was the first time I had ever touched him. It was wickedly delicate; it was fleeting, a star moving over night. Only when my hand returned to the quilt did he finish his stitches and cut the thread.

"Tell me your secrets," I whispered.

"Which one?"

"Why did you bleed that day?"

He rose and took the needle and spool of thread to his desk. Then he wiped the blood from his fingers and drew a chair to the bedside. He sat down, folded his hands, and looked at me. I wondered what crossed his mind at the sight of me lying in his bed, my hair spread out over his pillow as I wore his pants and his stitches.

"I cut my arm," he answered. "During a spar."

"Spar?" I repeated. "Tell me more."

He chuckled. "Well, long ago, I made a pact with my father. He would let me study to become a passion as long as I also took sword lessons. I continued that promise, even after he died."

"So you must be very proficient with a blade."

"I am very proficient," he agreed. "Even so, I still get cut from time to time."

We both fell quiet, listening to the crackle and pop as the fire burned in the hearth. My wound had gone numb beneath his careful stitches; I hardly felt the pain anymore, and my head was beginning to feel airy, as if I had breathed in a cloud.

"So . . . how did you not know that I was Amadine?" I finally asked; it was the foremost question that continued to sift through my thoughts. "And why were you absent for the first planning meeting?"

"I missed the first planning meeting because of *you*, Brienna," he said. "I had just discovered your disappearance. I forced myself to wait all summer, I forced myself to stay away, thinking you did not want to see me after my letters began to go unanswered. But I finally roused the courage to go to Magnalia, believing that I had time before I needed to be in Beaumont for the meeting. The Dowager informed me you were gone, that you had left with a patron, that you were safe. She wouldn't tell me anything more, and I spent the next week searching Théophile, thinking you were there since it's the closest city to Magnalia. It obviously made me late."

I stared at him, my heart twisting in my chest. "Cartier . . ."

"I know. But I couldn't rest if I didn't at least try to find you. I originally worried that your grandfather had come for you, and so I went to him. But he had no inkling of your whereabouts, and that only quickened my fears. There were so many nights that I thought the worst had befallen you, and the Dowager was merely trying to shield me from such a blow. All the while, she kept insisting that you would contact me when you were ready."

"And so you finally gave up the search, and came to Beaumont for the second meeting," I murmured.

"Yes. And Jourdain sat across the table from me and said he

had adopted a daughter, a young woman named Amadine, who had passioned beneath Augustin House, who had inherited the memories we needed to find the stone. I was so worn and vexed, I took it all for truth, not once suspecting he was feeding me your alias."

"But I still don't understand," I softly argued. "Why wouldn't Jourdain tell you who I was, where I came from?"

Cartier sighed and leaned deeper in the chair. "All I can figure is Jourdain didn't wholly trust me. And I don't blame him. I had evaded him for the past seven years. He had no idea I had taken the name Cartier Évariste and was teaching at Magnalia. And when I missed the first planning meeting . . . I think he worried I might bolt on the mission. So when the plans were divulged to me, I volunteered to be the one to infiltrate Damhan under pretense of the hunt. It was supposed to be Luc, but I offered myself, to show my commitment."

I thought on what he had just told me, the pieces finally coming together. Slowly, I sat up, propping myself on the pillows, and eased my chemise down, covering my stomach and wound.

"Now," Cartier said, "tell me your side of the story."

I told him everything. I told him about each of my shifts, I told him about the Dowager's decision to contact Jourdain, of arriving to Beaumont and desperately trying to force another bond. Of my discovery of who Jourdain was, of the planning meeting, of my fever and my crossing of the channel. Of recovering the stone.

He didn't say a word, his gaze not once straying from me. He could have been carved from marble until he suddenly leaned forward, his brows pulling in a frown, his fingers brushing over his jaw.

"You tried to tell me," he whispered. "You tried to tell me about the first shift. The last day of lessons. *The Book of Hours.*"

I nodded.

"Brienna . . . I am sorry. For not listening to you."

"There is nothing to be sorry over," I said. "I didn't exactly give you details."

He remained quiet, staring down at the floor.

"Besides," I whispered, drawing his eyes back to mine, "it no longer matters. You and I are here now."

"And you have found the Stone of Eventide."

The corner of my mouth curved with a smile. "Don't you want to see it?"

A mirthful glimmer returned to his gaze as he stood to retrieve the stone. Then he came to sit beside me on the bed, his thumb opening the locket. The stone writhed with gold, with ripples of blue and petals of silver that wilted to red. We both watched it, mesmerized, until Cartier shut the locket with a graceful snap, gently easing it over my head. It came to rest above my heart, the stone thrumming with contentment through the wood, warming my chest.

"Jourdain should arrive to Lyonesse tomorrow morning," Cartier said quietly, his shoulder nearly touching mine against the headboard. At once, the mood shifted in the room, as if winter had chewed through the walls, coating us in ice. "I have a feeling that Allenach may keep you here. If he does, you need to ride with me to Mistwood, in three nights."

"Yes, I know," I whispered, my fingers tracing the locket. "Cartier . . . what is the story behind Mistwood?"

"It was where the three rebelling lords gathered with their forces twenty-five years ago," he explained. "They emerged from the forest to ride across the field, to reach the back castle gates. But they never made it to the gates. That field is where the massacre occurred."

"Do you think it foolish that we are planning to ride out from the same place?" I questioned. "That it might be unwise for us to meet there before we storm the castle?" I knew it was the superstitious Valenian speaking in me, yet I couldn't wash away the worry I felt over this arrangement, that we were storming from a cursed forest.

"No. Because Mistwood is more than the ground where we first failed and bled. It used to be a magical forest where the coronations for the Kavanagh queens were held."

"They were crowned in the woods?" I asked, intrigued.

"Yes. At dusk, just when light and darkness are equal. There would be lanterns hovering in the branches, magical flowers and birds and creatures. And all of Maevana would gather in the woods, woods that seemed to never end, and watch as the queen was crowned first with stone, then with silver, and last with cloak." His voice trailed off. "Of course, that was long ago."

"But perhaps not as distant as we think," I reminded him.

He smiled. "Let us hope."

"So when we gather in Mistwood in three nights . . ."

"We gather on ancient ground, a place of magic and queens and sacrifice," he finished. "Others who want to join our rebellion will inherently know to meet there. When you spoke MacQuinn's name at the royal hearing, you began to stir not only his House, but mine, and what little remains of Kavanagh. You stirred people beyond our Houses. I don't know how many will appear to join us in the fight, but Mistwood will undeniably draw them, especially when you bring the stone there."

I wanted to ask more—I wanted him to tell me of those ancient, magical days. But I was exhausted, as was he, each of us feeling the weight of the days to come. I shifted on the bed until the breeches tried to slip farther down my waist.

"Let me return your pants, and then you can escort me to my room," I said, and Cartier rose to angle his back to me. I removed the breeches, refastened my dirk, and carefully set my feet on the floor, my chemise tumbling back down to my knees. Those herbs he had given me must have spread into my blood, for the pain was but a dull itch in my side.

We gathered the pieces of my gown, and then Cartier took a candelabra and I led him through the winding inner passages, showing him the way to the unicorn chamber. Only when I had opened the hidden door to my room did he say, "And how did you discover these doors and secret paths?"

I turned to look at him through the candlelight, one foot in my chamber, one foot in the inner passage, billows of my gown crumpled to my chest. "There are many secret doors around us, in plain sight. We just don't take the time to find and open them."

He smiled at that, suddenly looking worn and tired, as if he needed sleep.

"Now you know where to find me, should you need to," I whispered. "Good night, Theo."

"Good night, Amadine."

I closed the inner door, smoothed the wrinkles from the tapestry. I changed into my night shift, hid my bloodied clothes at the bottom of my trunk, and crawled into bed, the Stone of Eventide still about my neck. I watched as the fire in my hearth began to fade, flame by flame, and thought of Jourdain.

Tomorrow.

Tomorrow he would return home.

I closed my eyes and prayed, prayed that Lannon still had a merciful bone in his body.

But all my dreams were consumed with one chilling image I could not break: Jourdain kneeling at the footstool of the throne, his neck being severed by an axe.

# TWENTY-SEVEN

# THAT WHICH CANNOT BE

Allenach was absent the next morning.

I felt it when I entered the hall, the lord's absence like a gaping hole in the floor. And there were Rian and Sean, sitting in their usual places at the table on the dais, mopping their porridge up with clumps of bread, too hungry for spoons, as Allenach's grand chair sat empty between them.

Rian saw me first, his eyes going at once to my bodice, as if he hoped that I might bleed through the fabric. "Ah, good morning, Amadine. I trust you had a good night?"

I sat in the chair beside Sean, smiling gracefully at the servant who brought my bowl of porridge and sliced plums.

"The best sleep I have had in a while, Rian," I responded. "Thank you for asking."

Sean said nothing, but he was stiff as a board as the tension between me and his older brother grew taut.

"You have noticed that my father is away," Rian continued, glancing down the table at me.

"Yes. I see that."

"He has gone to Lyonesse, to bring MacQuinn before the king."

I was just raising a spoonful of porridge to my mouth. And my stomach clenched so violently I thought I might heave. But somehow, I swallowed the porridge, felt it clog all the way down my throat to my roiling stomach.

Rian was smiling at me, watching me struggle to eat. "You know what the king likes to do to traitors, Amadine? He cuts off their hands first. Then their feet. Then he gouges out their tongues and eyes. Last, he severs their heads."

"Enough, Rian," Sean hissed.

"Amadine needs to prepare herself," Rian countered. "I would hate for her to think this story has a happy ending."

I looked to the hall, my eyes going right to Cartier. He was sitting in his usual place with a bowl of porridge before him, Valenians chattering about him like birds. But he was solemn and still, his eyes on me. And then they slid to Rian, and he knew. I watched that Maevan stealth and that Valenian elegance merge, watched as Cartier's gaze marked Rian as a dead man.

"Did you hear me, Amadine? Or has one of the Valenians caught your interest?"

I set down my spoon and looked at Rian again. "What did you say?"

"I said perhaps I could finish the tour you so wanted yesterday,"

Rian said, shoving the last of his bread and porridge in his mouth.

"No thank you."

"Pity," he spoke through the crumbs, rising from the table. "I would have loved to show you around."

Sean and I watched as Rian sauntered from the hall. Only then did I breathe, did I let myself sink deeper in the chair.

"I do hope that your father is pardoned," Sean murmured, and then he rushed to his feet and left, as if he was embarrassed he had made such a confession.

I forced down a few more bites of porridge and then nudged my bowl aside. My eyes rested on Merei, who was sitting at a table with the rest of her consort, their purple cloaks like gemstones in the gentle light. They were laughing, enjoying the morning, nothing dark on their horizon. And I wanted to go to her, the friend of my heart, and I wanted to tell her everything.

She felt my gaze, looked to me.

She would meet me, if I signaled her. She would come right away, no doubt wondering why I hadn't met her the night before.

But I had promised that I would not risk her safety, not after I had already endangered her with my wild ploy to fetch the stone. And I was so burdened at that moment, I would undoubtedly tell her everything I shouldn't.

I rose and quitted the hall, leaving Cartier among the Valenians and Merei among her consort. I returned to my room, so overcome with fear and worry that I lay facedown on my bed. At this very moment, Jourdain was being brought before Lannon in the royal hall. And I had wrought this plan. I had strung it together, using Jourdain as the distraction. But what if I had planned wrong? What if Lannon tortured my patron father? What if he cut him into pieces and staked him on the wall? And what of Luc? Would Lannon punish him too?

It would be my fault. And I could hardly bear it.

My heart beat low and heavy as the hours continued to burn, as morning gave way to afternoon, as afternoon molted into evening. I hardly moved, growing weak with dread and thirst, and then came a knock on my door.

I stood and walked to it, my hand trembling as I swung the door open.

It was Allenach, waiting on my threshold.

I told myself to stand tall, to bear whatever he would say, that no matter what had happened, the mission must continue. We would still storm the castle, with or without Jourdain.

"May I come in?" the lord asked.

I stepped aside so he could enter, shutting the door behind him. He paced to my hearth, stopping only to turn back around, to watch me slowly close the gap between us.

"You look ill," he stated, his eyes sweeping me.

"Tell me." I didn't even try to sound polite or poised.

"Sit down, Amadine."

No, no, no. My heart was screaming, but I sat, preparing for the worst.

"I won't lie to you," he began, gazing down at me. "Your father nearly lost his head."

My hands were gripping the armrests of the chair, white-knuckled. "He is alive, then?"

Allenach nodded. "The king wanted to behead him. Took the axe up to do it himself. In the throne room."

"And why didn't he?"

"Because I stopped him," the lord replied. "Yes, MacQuinn deserves death for what he did. But I was able to grant him a little more time, to convince the king to give him a proper trial. The lords of Maevana will judge him in two weeks' time."

I covered my mouth, but tears began to spill from my eyes. The last thing I desired was to cry, to look weak, but it only brought Allenach to his knees before me, a sight that made the shadows and the light gather close around us.

"Your father and your brother have been taken to a house ten miles from here," he murmured. "They are on my land, in one of my tenants' houses. They are guarded and under orders not to leave, but they should rest in safety every night until the trial."

A sound of relief broke from me and I wiped my cheeks, the tears on my lashes casting prisms about Allenach's face when I looked at him.

"Would you like to remain here, or would you like to go to them?" he asked.

I could hardly believe he was being so kind, that he was giving me a choice. A warning bell rang at the back of my mind, but my relief was so strong it drowned out my suspicions. Everything I had planned had come to pass. Everything was moving forward as we wanted.

"Take me to them, my lord," I whispered.

Allenach stared at me, and then he rose and said, "We'll leave as soon as you pack your things."

He departed and I rushed to shove all my belongings into my trunk. But before I left the room, before I departed the blessing of the unicorn, I laid my hand over my corset, over the stitches that itched at my side, over the stone that had become my closest companion.

This was truly happening. We were all here. I had recovered the stone. And we were ready.

Allenach had a coach drawn for me in the courtyard. I walked through the blue shadows of evening at his side as he escorted me out. I thought he would grant his good-byes there, on the cobblestones of Damhan. But he surprised me when a groom brought his horse, tacked and ready.

"I will ride behind you," the lord said.

I nodded, concealing my shock as he shut the coach door. When Cartier realized I was gone during dinner in the hall that night, he would know that I had been taken to Jourdain. I wouldn't see him again until we converged in Mistwood, and I prayed that he would remain safe.

Those ten miles seemed to stretch into a hundred. The moon had risen over the tree line by the time the coach came to a halt. I broke my manners and let myself out, stumbling over a thick tussock of grass as I soaked in my surroundings by moonlight.

It was a yeoman's house, a long stretch of building that resembled a loaf of bread—white cob walls, a thatched roof like scorched crust. Smoke dribbled out from two chimneys, tickling the stars, and candlelight breathed on the windows from within.

There was nothing else around save for the valley, a gloomy barn in the distance, the white speckles of sheep as they grazed. And a dozen of Allenach's men, guarding the house, stationed by every window and door.

Allenach's horse came to a stop behind me just as the front door of the house swung open. I saw Jourdain, etched in the light as he stood on the threshold. I wanted to call out to him, but it hung in my throat as I began to walk, began to run to him, my ankles sore as my feet crushed the grass.

"Amadine!" He recognized me, shoved past the guards to reach me, and I fell into his arms with a sob, despite my promise not to cry again. "Shh, it's all right now," he whispered, the brogue rising in his voice again now that he was home. "I'm safe and well. Luc is too."

I pressed my face to his shirt, as if I were five years old, and breathed in the salt from the ocean, the starch in the linen, as his hand gently touched my hair. Despite the fact that we were under house arrest, that he had almost lost his head that morning and I had been stabbed the night before, I had never felt safer.

"Come, let's get you inside," Jourdain said, ushering me to the house.

It was only then that I remembered Lord Allenach, who I had never thanked for saving my patron father's life.

I turned out of Jourdain's arms, my eyes seeking the man on horseback. But there was nothing but the moonlight and the wind dancing over the grass, the imprints of hooves from where he had once been.

I cried again when I saw Luc waiting for me in the hall. He

crushed me to his chest and rocked me back and forth, as if we were dancing, until I laughed and finally cried the last of my tears.

Jourdain shut and bolted the front door and the three of us stood in a circle, our arms wound about one another, our foreheads pressed together as we smiled, as we silently claimed this victory.

"I have something to tell you both," I said, at which Luc quickly covered his mouth with a finger, indicating I should be quiet.

"I bet you enjoyed Damhan," my brother said loudly, walking to a table that was tucked out of sight from the windows. There was a sheet of paper on it, a quill and ink. He made the motion for me to write, and then pointed to his ear and then the walls.

So the guards were eavesdropping. I nodded and chattered about the grandeur of the castle as I began to write.

*I have the stone.*

Jourdain and Luc read it at the same moment, their eyes affixing to mine with a joy that made the stone hum again.

*Where?* Luc hastened to write.

I patted my corset, and Jourdain nodded, and I thought I saw the silver of tears line his eyes. He turned away before I could affirm it, to pour me a cup of water.

*Keep it there*, Luc added to his sentence. *It is safest with you.*

I accepted the cup of water Jourdain handed me and nodded. Luc took the paper and set it in the fire to burn, and we sat before the hearth and talked of safer, inconsequential things that would bore the guards who listened beyond the walls.

\* \* \*

The following day, I swiftly learned that being under a strict house guard was stifling. Everything we said was capable of being overheard. If I wanted to step outside, the eyes of the guards followed me. The greatest challenge would be the three of us overtaking the twelve of them when it was time to ride to Mistwood in two nights.

So that afternoon, Luc wrote out a plan, which he gave me to read. He and Jourdain had arrived to Maevana completely weaponless, but I still had my dirk strapped to my thigh. It was our one and only weapon, and after I read the plan of escape, I set my little blade into Jourdain's hands.

"Did you have to use it?" he whispered, tucking it away in his doublet.

"No, Father," I said. I still had yet to tell him about the stabbing incident. I began to reach for the paper, so I could write it all down for him to read. . . .

There was a knock on the door. Luc jumped up to answer it, returning to the hall with a basket of food.

"Lord Allenach has been quite the generous host," my brother said, rummaging through loaves of oat bread, still warm from the oven, a few wedges of cheese and butter, a jar of salted fish, and a pile of apples.

"What is that?" Jourdain questioned, noticing a flash of parchment tucked among the bread.

Luc plucked it from the linen as he bit into one of the apples. "It's addressed to you, Father." He handed it to Jourdain, and I saw the red wax that held the parchment together, pressed with a leaping stag.

Distracted from writing about the stabbing, I joined Luc,

exploring the basket of food. But just as I was unpacking the bread, I heard Jourdain's sharp intake of breath, I felt the room grow dark. Luc and I turned at once to look at him, watched him crumple the parchment in clawlike hands.

"Father? Father, what is it?" Luc quietly demanded.

But Jourdain did not look at Luc. I don't think he even heard his son as he set his eyes to me. My heart plummeted to the floor, breaking for a reason it didn't even know.

My patron father was staring at me with such fury that I took a step back, bumping into Luc.

"When were you going to tell me, Amadine?" Jourdain said in that cold, sharp voice that I had heard only once before, when he had killed the thieves.

"I don't know what you speak of!" I rasped, pressing harder against Luc.

Jourdain took hold of the table and hurled it over, spilling the candles, the basket of food, the paper and ink. I lurched back as Luc cried out in surprise.

"Father, return to yourself!" he hissed. "Remember where we are!"

Jourdain slowly fell to his knees, that parchment still caught in his fingers, his face pale as the moon as he stared at nothing.

Luc rushed forward to snag the paper. My brother became very still, and then he met my gaze, wordlessly handed the letter to me.

I didn't know what to expect, what could infuriate Jourdain so swiftly. But as my eyes moved over arches and valleys of the words, the world around me cracked in two.

*Davin MacQuinn,*

*I thought it best to tell you that I extended your life for one purpose, and it has nothing to do with how well you begged yesterday morning. You have something that belongs to me, something that is precious, something that I want returned unto my care.*

*The young woman you call Amadine—who you dare to call your daughter—belongs to me. She is my rightful daughter, and I ask that you relinquish whatever binds you have on her and allow her to return to me at Damhan. The coach will be waiting outside the door for her.*

*Lord Brendan Allenach*

"It's a lie," I growled, crumpling the paper in my hands, just as Jourdain had done. "Father, he is *lying* to you." I stumbled over the apples and bread to kneel before Jourdain. He looked as if he had broken, his eyes glazed over. I took his face in my hands, forcing him to look at me. "This man, this Lord Allenach, is *not* my father."

"Why did you keep this from me?" Jourdain asked, ignoring my impassioned statements.

"I kept nothing from you!" I cried. The anger bloomed in my heart, crowding it with thorns. "I have never seen my blood father. I do not know the man's name. I am illegitimate; I am unwanted. This lord is playing a game with you. I do not belong to him!"

Jourdain finally focused on my face. "Are you certain, Ama-dine?"

I hesitated, and the silence pierced me, because it made me see that I was not at all certain.

I thought back to the night I had asked the Dowager to conceal my father's full name from Jourdain. . . . She had not wanted to, but yet she had, because I insisted upon it. And so Jourdain had believed—as I had—that my father was a mere servant beneath the lord. We had never entertained the idea that he might be the lord.

"Did you tell him that you hail from his House?" Jourdain asked, his voice hollow.

"No, no, I told him nothing," I stammered, and that's when I realized it. How on earth would Allenach know to claim me?

This cannot be. . . .

Jourdain nodded, reading my painful trail of thoughts. "He is your father. How else would he know?"

"No, no," I whispered, my throat closing. "It cannot be him."

But even as I denied it, the threads of my life began to pull together. Why would my grandfather be so adamant to hide me? To keep my father's name from me? Because my father was a powerful, dangerous lord of Maevana.

But perhaps, more than anything . . . how did Allenach know who I was?

I stared at Jourdain. Jourdain stared at me.

"Do you want to know why I hate Brendan Allenach?" he whispered. "Because Brendan Allenach was the lord to betray us twenty-five years ago. Brendan Allenach was the one who plunged his sword into my wife. He stole her from me. And now he will steal you from me as well."

Jourdain rose. I remained on the floor, sitting on the backs of my heels. I listened to him retreat to his bedchamber, slam and lock the door.

I was still holding the letter. I shredded it, let it fall around me as snow. And then I stood.

My gaze strayed to Luc. He was staring at the mess on the floor, but he lifted his eyes to mine when I approached him.

"I am going to prove that this is a lie," I said, my heart pounding. "I will ride with d'Aramitz to Mistwood."

"Amadine," Luc whispered, cradling my face. He wanted to say more to me, but the words turned to dust between us. He gently kissed my forehead in farewell.

I hardly felt the ground beneath me as I left that house, as I stepped out into the afternoon rain. There was the coach that Allenach had promised, waiting to cart me back to Damhan. I walked to it, my hair and my dress drenched by the time I sat on the cushioned bench.

As the rain pounded the roof and the coach bumped along the road, I began to think of what I should say to him.

Lord Allenach believed that I was his illegitimate daughter.

I did not believe such, yet the lingering doubt was worse than the blade Rian had pierced me with. Most likely, the lord was taunting his old enemy and using me to do it. So I would walk into his hall tonight and let him believe that I was pleased with his claim on me. And when I asked for proof, which he would be powerless to give, I would deny his claim.

It took me ten miles, but by the time I arrived to Damhan's courtyard, I was ready to face him.

I stepped out into the rain, lightning flickering overhead, splitting the night sky in two. As am I, I thought, walking into the castle corridor. I am Brienna, two in one.

I followed the music, Merei's music, to the light and warmth of the hall. The Valenians were gathered at their tables for dinner. The fire was roaring, the heraldic stags gleaming from their carved places in the walls. And so I walked the aisle of the great hall, my dress dragging along the glazed tiles, leaving a trail of rain behind me.

I heard the men go quiet, the laughter ease as the Valenians noticed my entrance. I heard the music painfully end, Merei's strings clang as her bow jerked. I felt Cartier's gaze, like sunlight, but I did not respond. I felt all of them watching me, but my eyes were only for the lord who sat on the dais.

Allenach noticed me the moment I had entered. He had been waiting for me; he watched me approach him, setting his chalice down, the ruby on his forefinger glittering.

I walked all the way to the dais stairs, and there I came to rest, standing directly before him. I opened my palms, felt the rain drip from my hair.

"Hello, Father," I said to him, my voice soaring like a bird up to the highest rafters.

Brendan Allenach smiled. "Welcome home, Daughter."

# —❖ TWENTY-EIGHT ❖—

# A DIVIDED HEART

"Rian? Give my daughter her rightful seat."

I watched Rian jerk, astounded by his father's request. I watched Rian's face contort in rage, rage toward me, for his greatest fear had just been cloaked in flesh and blood.

The lost daughter had come to take back her inheritance.

I let him rise, just to see if he would do it. And then I lifted my hand and said, "Rian may keep his seat, for now. I would like to talk privately with you, Father."

Allenach's eyes—a pale shade of blue, like deceptive ice on a pond—flickered with curiosity. But he must have been expecting I would say such, because he stood without qualm, extended his right hand to me.

I ascended the dais, walked around the table, and set my fingers in his. He escorted me from the hall, up the stairs, down a corridor I had not ventured yet. He took me to his private wing, a vast connection of chambers that were lavishly furnished.

The first chamber was something I would call a parlor, a place to sit with guests and close friends. There was a large hearth, alight with a roaring fire, and several chairs overlaid with sheepskin. On one wall was a grand tapestry of a white stag, leaping with arrows lodged in his chest, and so many mounted animal heads that I felt as if they were all watching me, the firelight licking their glassy eyes.

"Sit, daughter, and tell me what I can get you to drink," Allenach said, dropping my fingers so he could walk to a bureau that sparkled with bottles of wine, ceramic pitchers of ale, and a family of golden chalices.

I sat in the chair closest to the fire, shivering against my wet dress. "I am not thirsty."

I felt him glance at me. I kept my gaze to the dance of the fire, listening as he poured himself a drink. Slowly, he walked back across the floor, sat in the chair directly across from mine.

Only then, when we were both still, did I meet his gaze.

"Look at you," he whispered. "You are beautiful. Just like your mother."

Those words angered me. "Is that how you knew it was me?"

"I thought you were your mother at first, the moment I saw you step into the royal hall. That she had come back to haunt me," he replied. "Until you looked at me, and I knew it was you."

"Hmm."

"You don't believe me?"

"No. I need proof, my lord."

He crossed his legs and took a sip of wine, but those shrewd blue eyes of his never broke from mine. "Very well. I can give you all the proof you desire."

"Why don't you start by telling me how you came to know my mother."

"Your mother visited Damhan with your grandfather for one of my hunts some eighteen years ago," Allenach began, his voice smooth as silk. "Three years before that, I had lost my wife. I was still grieving her death, thinking I would never look at another woman. Until your mother arrived."

It took everything within me to conceal my scorn, to suffocate my sarcasm. I held it at bay, forcing myself quiet so he would keep talking.

"Your mother and grandfather lodged here for a month. During that time, I came to love her. When she left with your grandfather to return to Valenia, I had no inkling that she was carrying you. But she and I began a correspondence, and once I learned of you, I asked her to return to Damhan, to marry me. Your grandfather would not allow it, thinking I had ruined his daughter."

My heart was beginning to pound deep in my chest. Everything he had shared *could* be taken for truth—he had mentioned my grandfather. But still, I held quiet, listening.

"Your mother wrote to me the day you were born," Allenach continued. "The daughter I had long waited for, the daughter I had always wanted. Three years after that, all your mother's letters ceased. Your grandfather was gracious enough to inform me that she had died, and that you were not mine, that I had no claim on you. I waited, patiently, until you were ten. And I wrote you a letter. I figured your grandfather would withhold it from you, but still I wrote to you, asking you to come visit me."

When I was ten . . . when I was ten . . . when Grandpapa had flown to Magnalia with me, to hide me. I could hardly breathe. . . .

"When I still failed to hear from you, I decided that I should grant your grandfather a little visit," Allenach said. "You were not there. And he would not tell me where he had hidden you. But I am a patient man. I would wait until you came of age, until you turned eighteen, when you could make your own decisions. So imagine my surprise when you walked into the royal hall. I thought you had at last come to meet me. I was about to step forward and claim you until one particular name came off your tongue." His hand tightened on his chalice. Ah, the jealousy, the envy, began to tighten his face like a mask. "You said *MacQuinn* was your father. I thought perhaps I had mistaken it—perhaps my eyes were fooling me. But then you said you were a passion, and it all came together; your grandfather had hidden you by passion, and MacQuinn had adopted you. And the longer you stood there, the more certain I was. You were mine, and MacQuinn was using you. So I offered to host you here, so I could learn more of you, so I could protect you from the king. And then that skittish dog confirmed my suspicions."

"Dog?"

"Nessie," Allenach said. "She has always hated strangers. But she was certainly attracted to you, and it made me remember . . . when your mother was here all those years ago, one of my wolf-hounds refused to leave her side. Nessie's dam."

I swallowed, told myself that a dog couldn't have known. . . .

"Why let me return to MacQuinn, then?" I asked, the words too hot to hold any longer in my chest. "You let me reunite with him, only to tear me away."

Allenach tried not to smile, but the corners of his mouth revealed his twisted pleasure at the thought. "Yes. Perhaps it was cruel of me, but he was trying to wound me. He was—still is—trying to turn you against me."

How wrong Allenach was. Jourdain hadn't even known whose daughter I truly was.

And then I stared at his hand—his right hand, holding his chalice—and remembered. That hand had cut down Jourdain's wife. That hand had betrayed them, brought their wives and daughters to their deaths.

I rose, my anger and distress a marriage of horror in my blood. "You are mistaken, my lord. I am not your daughter."

I was halfway to the door, the air squeezing out of me as if iron fingers had wrapped about my chest. The Stone of Eventide felt it, spread a comforting warmth against my middle, up to my heart. *Be brave*, it whispered, and yet I was all but running from him.

My hand was reaching for the door handle when his voice pierced the distance between us.

"I am not finished, *Brienna*."

The sound of it stopped me short, sealed my feet to the floor.

I listened to him as he stood, as his tread moved into one of the adjoining chambers. When he returned, I could hear the rustling of papers.

"Your mother's letters," was all he said.

It turned me about. It dragged me back across the floor to him, where he had set a thick bundle of letters in my chair. It made me reach for them, this tiny remnant of her, the mother I had always longed for.

I began to read them, my heart completely sundered. It was her. It was Rosalie Paquet. My mother. She had loved him, then, even though she had no inkling as to what he had done.

In one of the letters was a tiny lock of hair. My hair. A soft golden brown.

*I named our daughter Brienna, out of honor for you, Brendan.*

I sank to the floor, my strength leaving me. My very name was inspired by his—this devious, murderous man. I looked up at him; he stood near, watching me absorb the truth.

"What do you want with me?" I whispered.

Allenach knelt on the floor before me, took my face in his hands. Those treacherous hands. "You are my one and only daughter. And I will raise you up to be queen of this land."

I wanted to laugh; I wanted to weep. I wanted to peel this day back, burn it, forget it had ever happened. But his hands held me steady, and I had to reckon with this wild claim he was making.

"And how, my lord, would you make me a queen?"

A dark light gleamed in those eyes. For one moment, my heart stopped, thinking he had discovered I was carrying the stone. But we were not Kavanaghs. The stone was useless to us.

"Long ago," he murmured, "our ancestor took something. He took something that was vital for Maevana to remain a queen's realm." His thumbs gently caressed my cheeks as he smiled down at me. "Our House has hidden the Queen's Canon for generations. This very castle holds it, and I will resurrect the Canon to put you on the throne, Brienna."

I closed my eyes, trembling.

All these years, the House of Allenach had been holding the Stone of Eventide *and* the Queen's Canon. My House had destroyed a lineage of queens, had forced magic to fall dormant, had enabled a cruel king such as Lannon. The weight of what my ancestors had done bowed me down; I would have completely melted to the floor if Allenach had not been holding me upright.

"But I am half Valenian," I argued, opening my eyes to look at him. "I am illegitimate."

"I will legitimize you," he said. "And it does not matter if you are only Maevan in part. Noble blood flows in your veins, and as my daughter, you have a rightful claim to the throne."

I should have denied him right then, before the temptation could set down roots within me. But the Queen's Canon . . . we needed it. We had the stone, but we also needed the law.

"Show me the Canon," I requested.

His hands slowly drifted from my face, but he continued to

stare at me. "No. Not until you pledge allegiance to me. Not until I know that you fully deny MacQuinn."

Oh, he was playing with me. He was manipulating me. It made me despise him all the more, that he felt the need to compete with Jourdain. That he only wanted me to flex his own power.

I will not rush into this, I thought.

So I took a deep breath, and said, "Give me the night to ponder this, my lord. I will give you my answer in the morning."

He would respect that. He was Maevan, and a Maevan's word was their vow. Valenians had their grace in etiquette and politeness, but Maevans had their words. Simple, binding words.

Allenach helped me to my feet. He called for a warm bath to be drawn for me back in the unicorn chamber and left me for the night. I soaked in the water until I was wrinkled, staring at the fire and hating my blood. Then I rose and dressed in the sleeping shift he had provided for me, since I had left all of my belongings with Jourdain.

I sat before the fire, the stone and locket hidden beneath the soft wool of my nightdress, and I fell captive to my own horrible thoughts.

I had arrived to Damhan tonight believing Allenach was taunting Jourdain with his claims on me. But now I knew better. . . . I was blood of his blood, a stag leaping through laurels, a cruel man's only daughter.

And he wanted to make me into a queen.

I closed my eyes and began to draw my fingers through the tangled web that had become my life.

In order to resurrect the Canon, I would have to pledge myself to Allenach.

If I pledged myself to Allenach, I would either follow him, let him place me on the throne, or betray him and take the Canon with me to Mistwood.

If I refused to pledge myself to Allenach, I would not recover the Canon. I would still ride to Mistwood with the stone, as planned. That is, if Allenach didn't lock me away in Damhan's keep.

"Brienna?"

I glanced to the right, saw Cartier standing in my chamber. I had not even heard him enter through the secret door, so lost was I in my own dark contemplations. He came to my chair, knelt before me, set his hands on my knees as if he knew that I was drifting, as if he knew his touch would bring me back.

I watched the firelight kiss the golden threads of his hair, and I let my fingers rush through it, his eyes closing in response to my caress.

"He's my father," I whispered.

Cartier looked at me. There was such sadness in his eyes, as if he felt every blister of pain within me.

"Did you know it was him?" I persisted.

"No. I knew your father was Maevan. I was never told his name."

I let my fingers slip from his hair and I leaned my head back in the chair, stared up at the ceiling. "He has the Canon. And he wants to make me queen."

Cartier's fingers tightened on my knees. I brought my gaze back to his; his eyes revealed nothing, even as I spoke betrayal. There was no horror, no greed in his eyes. Only a faithful shade of blue.

"Cartier . . . what should I do?"

He stood and pulled a chair close to mine, to sit directly across from me, so I had no other place to look but at him. I watched the fire spill light over one side of his face, shadows on the other.

"Four months ago," he said, "I thought I knew the best path for you. I had come to love you, so deeply, that I wanted to make sure you chose the branch that would keep you close to me. I wanted you to go with Babineaux, to teach as I had done. And when summer's end came, when I discovered you had disappeared without a trace . . . I realized that I could not hold you, that I could not decide for you. Only when I let you go did I find you again, in the most marvelous of ways."

He grew quiet, but his eyes never left mine.

"I cannot tell you what to decide, what is best," he stated. "That is for your heart to choose, Brienna. But I will say this: no matter which path you choose, I will follow you, even unto darkness."

He rose, his fingers gently tracing my hair, down the sharp line of my jaw to the tip of my chin. A touch of promise, a touch of consecration.

*I will follow you.*

"You know where to find me, should you need to," he whispered, and then left before I could so much as breathe.

* * *

I waged a war that night, for my heart was divided. Which father should I betray? The one bound by passion, or the one bound by blood? Did Jourdain hate me now, knowing whose daughter I truly was? There were some moments I thought my patron father had come to care for me, had come to love me. But he might never look at me the same, now that he knew.

I was the daughter of the man who had destroyed him.

I battled all night . . . pacing, doubting, agonizing. But when dawn breathed lavender light upon the windows, when the morning stole into my room, I had finally chosen my path.

## —✦ TWENTY-NINE ✦—

# THE WORDS WAKE FROM THEIR SLUMBER

I met Allenach at the doors of the hall, just before breakfast. He had been waiting for me, leather gloves on his hands, a fur-lined cloak knotted at his collar. I was wearing a Maevan dress that he had provided—a red woolen gown that fit comfortably close to the body, a dress for exploring and riding, with white, billowy sleeves—and a warm cloak and leather boots so fresh they still creaked.

I raised my brows when I saw him. Did he truly desire me to tell him my answer outside the hall?

"I want to take you somewhere," he said before I could utter anything. "We can break our fast afterward."

I nodded and let him escort me out to the courtyard, worried as I wondered why he wanted to draw me away from the safety of the castle. Two horses were already tacked, waiting for us. Allenach mounted his chestnut stallion while I took the dapple mare, and I followed him, cantering up a mountain that lay to the east of his lands. The fog was slowly burning away, minute by minute, as we continued to ride higher, the air becoming sweet and sharp.

The cold had sunk into my bones by the time he came to a stop. My mare eased to a halt beside his stallion, and I watched as the fog receded, brushed by the wind, leaving the two of us behind on a great summit. If I had thought the view from the castle parapet was breathtaking, this changed my mind.

The lands of Allenach stretched down before us, hillocks and streams and forests, green and blue and umber, docile patches mixed with wild meadows. My eyes soaked it in, this bewitching land. This loam was in my blood, and I felt it, felt it tug and pull along my heart.

I had to close my eyes.

"This is your home, Brienna," he said, his voice rasping, as if he had not slept last night either. "Anything you want, I can give you."

Land. Family. A Crown.

My eyes opened once more. I could see Damhan below, a smudge of dark stones, the smoke rising up from her chimneys.

"What of your sons?" I asked, finally taking my gaze from the beauty to look at him.

"My sons will have their portion of inheritance." The horse shifted beneath him, pawing the earth. Allenach looked at me, the wind playing with his loose, dark hair. "I have waited for you a long time, Brienna."

I looked back to the sprawling land, as if my answer lay hidden in her streams and shadows. I had set my mind, determined my course. I had gone to Cartier at dawn to tell him my choice, to spin together a final plan with him. Even so, I was astounded by how doubt still set a crater in my heart.

But I rested my eyes upon him, the lord who was my father, and I said, "I choose you, Father. I choose the House of Allenach. Set me upon the throne."

Allenach smiled, a slow warm smile that made him look ten years younger. He was thrilled, his eyes praising me as if I had no faults, as if I were already his queen rather than his long-lost daughter.

"I am pleased, Brienna. Let us return to the castle. I want to show you the Canon." He was turning his horse around when I stopped him with my voice.

"Perhaps, Father, we can plan to look at the Canon tonight, after dinner?"

He paused, glancing over his shoulder at me. "Tonight?"

"Yes," I said, forcing a smile to the corners of my mouth. "You have the Valenians here, remember? I can wait until tonight."

He contemplated my words. I prayed he would take the bait.

"Very well," he finally conceded, then inclined his head in invitation for me to follow him back.

I was heartsick and sore by the time we clattered into the courtyard. I dismounted with as much grace as my tight legs would allow and took Allenach's hand, letting him guide me to the hall.

Breakfast was still thriving when we entered, the warmth like a tingling balm to my frozen hands. I noticed that Rian was nowhere to be seen, that his chair was empty. And Allenach took me to it, giving me the seat at his right hand.

"Good morning, Sister," Sean greeted, his eyes suddenly wary of me, like he couldn't believe this was happening.

"Good morning, Brother," I returned just as our father took the chair between us.

I made myself take three swallows of porridge before I found Cartier in the thinning crowd. He was looking my way with heavy-lidded eyes, as if he was bored, but he was intently waiting.

Discreetly, I stroked my collar.

He returned the motion, the air shimmering between us, like a cord made of magic was strung from me to him.

There was no going back from this.

I waited until dinner was nearly over, the hall buzzing with stories, ale, and music. I had forced myself to eat until my stomach wound into a tight knot. Only then I looked to the left, to Allenach as he sat at my side, and said, "Perhaps you could show me now, Father?"

He still had food on his plate, a chalice brimming with ale. But if there was one thing I was learning, it was that a father liked to indulge his daughter. Allenach stood at once, and I slipped my hand in his, glancing over my shoulder just before we disappeared from the hall.

Cartier watched us leave. He would wait ten minutes after our departure, and then he too would slip away.

I inwardly counted my own steps as Allenach led me back to his private chambers, the order of numbers strangely comforting as my boots pressed into the carpet.

This was the part of the plan that had been wholly un-predictable—the actual location of the Canon. Allenach had said it was hidden somewhere in the castle, and so Cartier and I had taken our chances with that. I had predicted it was probably in the lord's wing, the very chambers that had once been Tristan Allenach's.

I had presumed right.

I followed Allenach through his parlor, through his private dining room, into his bedchamber. There was a grand bed, cov-ered with quilts and furs, and a large stone hearth that was cold with ashes. A trio of stained-glass windows lined one wall, candle-light illuminating the dark-colored glass.

"Tell me, Father," I said, waiting patiently as he vanished into an adjoining room. "How did you know about the Canon?"

He remerged holding a long, skinny piece of iron with a curved head. For a moment, my heart struck my breastbone, thinking he was about to wield it as a weapon. But he smiled and said, "It is a secret that has been passed from father to inheriting son ever since the Canon was hidden here."

"Does Rian know, then?"

"He knows. Sean does not."

I watched as he began to use the iron pick to uproot one of the stones of the hearth. It was a long slab, stained from years of soot and the scuff of logs, and as he worked to bring it up, I thought of Tristan. I could almost see my ancestor employed with the same movements, the same motions as Allenach, only Tristan had labored to hide rather than to liberate.

"Brienna."

I moved forward when he spoke my name, the sound of his voice breaking sightless fetters about my ankles. He was holding the stone slab up, waiting for me to come and see what lay beneath, waiting for me to come and claim it.

Quietly, I walked to Allenach's side and peered down at the depression in the floor.

Cartier had once described it to me. He said that Liadan had used her magic to carve the words into stone. The sight of it stole the very breath from me, made the Stone of Eventide flare unbearably hot in its locket, still tucked away in the bodice of my dress. The stone's awakening forced me to kneel, and with trembling hands I reached for the stone tablet.

Liadan's words glimmered, as if stardust had been resting in the grooves. The tablet was deceivingly light, a rectangle of white stone, the size of a large book cover. I wiped away the dirt and dust, the words responding to my strokes, lighting up from within. I knew it was the stirring magic; the Canon was responding to the proximity of the Eventide. And sweat began to prickle at the nape of my neck when I realized Allenach saw the celestial light coming from within the Canon, as if the tablet's veins had been filled with nourishment.

I stood and took a few steps away, angling my back to him, cradling the tablet as a child in my arms, silently ordering the

Canon to swallow that alluring gleam, for it was about to give me away.

And as if the Canon had heard me, the light from within died as an ember, and the Stone of Eventide also cooled. I could only imagine what this experience would have been like had I but one drop of Kavanagh blood.

"Read it to me, daughter," Allenach said as he lowered the hearthstone back into place.

I cleared my throat, willing my voice to be steady.

Liadan's words flowed off my tongue, ethereal as a cloud, sweet as honey, sharp as a blade:

> "I, Liadan Kavanagh, the first queen of Maevana
> hereby proclaim that this throne and this crown
> shall be inherited by the daughters of this land.
> Whether they be Kavanaghs, or whether they
> hail from one of the other thirteen Houses,
> that no king shall sit upon this throne
> unless the queen and people choose it to be so.
> Every noble daughter has a contention for
> the crown I leave behind, for it is by our
> daughters that we live, that we flourish,
> and that we endure.
> Carved this first day of June, 1268"

The room became quiet as my voice eased to the shadows, the words hanging like jewels in the air between Allenach and me. I had once believed that only a Kavanagh daughter had the right to the throne. Now I realized that Liadan had opened the crown to any noble daughter of the fourteen Houses.

Allenach was right; I did have a legitimate claim.

And then he stepped forward, his hands framing my face again, the lust for power and the throne glittering in his eyes as he stared down at me, as he saw the shade of my mother within me.

"So the House of Allenach rises," he whispered.

"So it does, Father."

He kissed my forehead, sealing me to his plans of destiny. I let him lead me out to the parlor and sat in the chair before the lit hearth while he poured me a chalice of wine to celebrate. I kept the Canon on my lap, let it rest along the length of my thighs, my fingers still caressing the carved words.

That was when the urgent pounding on his door finally came.

Allenach frowned, setting his bottle of wine down with a flash of irritation in his face. "What is it?" he called with pointed annoyance.

"My lord, the fields are burning!" a voice returned, muffled through the wood of the door.

I watched Allenach's perturbed expression transform to shock as he strode across the chamber and swung open the door. One of his thanes stood there, his face smudged from smoke and sweat.

"What do you mean the fields are burning?" the lord repeated.

"The entire field of barley is taken by fire," the thane panted. "We cannot contain it."

"Rally all the men," Allenach ordered. "I will be right there."

I rushed to my feet, leaving the Canon on the chair. Allenach was striding back across the room to a door off to the side of the parlor, a door that blended into the wall, so I had not noticed it before. I trailed him, wringing my hands.

"Father, what can I do?" I asked, realizing he had stepped within his own private armory. Swords, shields, maces, spears, bows, quivers full of arrows, and axes gleamed from their places on the wall when the firelight touched them.

Allenach belted a sheathed long-sword at his side, and then he was moving back into the parlor, all but forgetting about me until he saw me standing there.

"I want you to remain here," he said. "Do not leave my chambers."

"But, Father, I—"

"Do not leave my chambers, Brienna," he repeated, his voice rough. "I shall be back as soon as it's safe."

I watched him leave, listened to him shut the door. This was exactly as I'd hoped. Until I heard him turn a key, the sound of the door locking me into Allenach's wing.

*No*, my heart pounded as I rushed to test the door, the only way out. The iron handles held fast, married to the threshold, holding me captive in my father's chambers. I still pulled, fighting the door. It hardly budged.

I had to get out. And I had only a few ordained moments to do it.

My mind swelled with panic until I remembered the steps I had planned. I left the doomed doors and hurried to Allenach's bedroom, straight to his wardrobe. I rummaged through his things, his clothes organized by color and fragranced with cloves and pine, and found a leather bag with a buckle and drawstrings. Back to the parlor I hurried, easing the Canon into the satchel, slipping the straps onto my shoulders, and buckling it tight to my back.

Then I went to his armored room. I chose a slender sword with an extraordinary hilt—there was an orb of amber in the pommel, and in the amber there was a black widow, frozen in time. Widow's Bite. This sword shall suit me, I thought and belted it about my waist. I also grabbed the closest axe and returned to the locked door, swinging the blade into the wood about the iron handles. In a matter of moments, I knew this was futile. It was draining my strength and this door was hardly splintering beneath my swings.

It would have to be the window.

I returned to Allenach's bedchamber, to the stained-glass windows. Through the colors, I could see the fire burning in the distant field, the glass translating it to an eerie green light. I held up my axe, drew in a long breath, and swung.

The window exploded around me, rained upon my shoulders and the floor as crunching teeth of color. Cold night air howled in, carrying the smoke from the fire Cartier had set, carrying the calls of Allenach's thanes and vassals as they rushed to put it out. I worked furiously to clear all the shards of glass from the sill, and then I leaned forward to see how far I was from the ground.

This was the second floor of the castle, and still a fall like that would break my legs.

I had to return to the armored room, to snag a coil of rope. I liked to pretend that I knew what I was doing as I knotted one end of the rope to Allenach's bedpost, which was thankfully bolted to the floor. I liked to pretend that I was calm as I eased myself to stand on the windowsill, the world beneath me a swirl of darkness, of bittersweet decisions, of broken vows, of treacherous daughters.

I couldn't hesitate. I only had a matter of moments.

And so I began to scale down the castle's wall, the rope burning my hands, the Stone of Eventide humming in my dress, the Queen's Canon a shield at my back, my hair loose and wild in the smoky wind. My poorly wound knot came undone from Allenach's bedpost, because I was suddenly falling, flailing through darkness. I hit the ground with a bark of pain in my ankles, but I had landed on my feet.

I began to run.

As the fire raged through the field, blessing my escape and signaling Jourdain's people to *rise, rise and fight*, I darted through shadows to the alehouse, which sat quietly in the early hours of night. I was almost there, the grass whisking about my dress, when I heard the pounding gait of a horse.

I thought it was Cartier. I stopped to turn toward the sound, my heart in my throat, only to see Rian furiously cantering toward me, his face a blaze of anger in the starlight. And in his hand was a morning star, a thick wooden club embedded with spikes.

I hardly had time to catch my breath, let alone dodge his death swing. The only shield I had was at my back, the tablet of magical stone, and I turned it to him, felt his morning star slam into the Canon.

The impact rattled my bones as I fell facedown in the grass, believing he had just obliterated the tablet. Numb, I reached back, felt a solid piece of stone within the satchel. It was still whole—it had just saved my life—and I crawled to my feet, tasting blood on my tongue.

The clash of morning star and Canon had split his weapon in half, the way lightning slices a tree. And the impact had ripped him from the saddle; it made me think that even after all this time, Liadan's words still protected her Maevan daughters.

I was trying to decide if I should run, my breath still wheezing from my fall, or if I should face him. My half brother was lying in the long grass, staggering up to his feet. He caught sight of me, my hesitation, and took a portion of his split weapon.

I only had a matter of moments to fumble for the sword sheathed at my side, but I could feel the air spark with warning, because he was about to give me a deathblow before I could defend myself.

He loomed over me, blocking the moon, and raised one half of his severed weapon.

But his blow never came. I watched, wide-eyed, as he was suddenly rocked off his feet by a leaping beast, a dog that looked like a wolf. I stumbled back, shocked, as Nessie tore his arm open. He let out one strangled scream before she was at his throat. The dog was quick; I watched as Rian went still, his eyes open to the night, his blood spilling into the grass. And then Nessie moved to nuzzle me, whining into the folds of my skirts.

"Easy, girl," I whispered, shivering. My fingers stroked her head, thanking her for saving me.

He was my half brother, and yet I felt no remorse that he had been killed by his father's hound.

I turned my back to him and hurried the rest of the way to the alehouse, Nessie trotting at my side.

Cartier was waiting for me at the back door of the building, the shadows of the heavy eaves nearly concealing him from my sight. But he stepped forward when he saw me coming, two horses saddled and ready, the moonlight like spilled milk around us.

I walked right into his embrace, his arms coming about me, his hands touching my back to feel the Canon that I carried. I would have kissed the smile that graced his mouth when he looked down at me, but the night demanded that we hurry. And then I saw that we were not alone.

From the shadows, Merei emerged with a horse in tow, the starlight limning her face as she smiled at me.

"Mer?" I whispered, slipping from Cartier's arms to reach her. "What are you doing?"

"What does it look like I'm doing?" she teased me. "I'm coming with you."

I glanced to Cartier, then back to Merei, just now realizing that she had been involved from the very beginning, that she was part of our plans.

"How . . . ?"

"When I volunteered to be the one to go to Damhan," Cartier explained quietly, "I contacted Merei. Asked if she could convince Patrice to come north, to play in Damhan's hall. I honestly didn't think she would be able to sway her patron . . . and so I said nothing of it to Jourdain, in case my idea never materialized."

"But why?" I persisted.

"Because I knew Amadine Jourdain would need help on her mission," Cartier replied with a smile. "Little did we know it was you, Brienna."

And how right he had been. Without Merei, I would have never been able to recover the stone.

I took both of their hands. "To Mistwood?"

"To Mistwood," they whispered in unison.

We had a six-hour ride ahead of us, through the deepest stretch of night. But before we reached Mistwood, there was one more place we needed to visit.

"Whose dog?" Cartier asked, finally noticing the large, wiry-haired hound who waited at my heels.

"She's mine," I replied as I mounted my horse. "And she goes with us."

Five hours later, I found the safe house on a dark street corner, just beneath one of the oaks that flourished through Lyonesse. Cartier and Merei followed me, their boots hardly making noise on the cobblestones as we moved from shadow to shadow, from road to road, all the way to the printmaker's front door.

We had left our horses hidden outside the city, guarded by Nessie, who had kept up with our pace, so we could silently travel on foot, to avoid being discovered by Lannon's night patrol, who enforced a strict curfew. Even so, I still felt a shudder rack my spine as I lifted my knuckles to quietly knock on the door.

The three of us waited, our breath escaping our lips as plumes of smoke in the cold night.

By the moon's position and the deep chill in the air, I guessed it to be around three in the morning. Again, I dared to rasp my knuckles upon the printmaker's door, praying that he would hear and answer.

"Brienna," Cartier whispered. I knew what he was telling me; we had to hurry. We had to reach Mistwood before dawn.

I sighed, about to turn away when the front door unlocked and creaked open, just a sliver. Wide-eyed with hope, I looked to the man who had answered us; his frown was lit by a solitary candle.

"Evan Berne?" I murmured.

His frown deepened. "Yes? Who are you?"

"I am Davin MacQuinn's daughter. Will you let us in?"

Now he was the one to go wide-eyed, his gaze assessing me, assessing Cartier and Merei. But cautiously, he opened the door and let us enter his home.

His wife was standing a few paces back, clutching a woolen shawl about her shoulders, her terror evident. Flanking her were two sons, one who was obviously trying to conceal a dirk behind his back.

"I am sorry to come at such a time." I rushed to apologize. "But Liam O'Brian marked you down as a safe house for our mission, and I must ask something of you."

Evan Berne came to stand face-to-face with me, his gaze still wide and frightened. "Did you say you were . . . *MacQuinn*'s daughter?"

"Yes. My father has returned to Maevana. By dawn, the three

fallen Houses will rise and take back the throne."

"How?" one of the sons sputtered.

I glanced to him before letting my eyes return to Evan, slipping the satchel from my back. "You are a printmaker?"

Evan gave a sharp nod, the candle trembling in his hands as he watched me pull the Queen's Canon from the bag.

He hardly breathed as he moved closer, to let his light shine upon the carved words. His wife gasped; their sons stepped forward with entranced gazes. They gathered about me, reading the words Liadan had carved so long ago. With every moment, I felt the hope, the wonder, the courage weave through their hearts.

"Where did you find that?" Evan's wife whispered, tears filling her eyes when she looked at me.

"It is a long story," I responded with a flicker of a smile. One day, I thought, I will write it all down, of how this came to be. "Can you print this Canon on paper? I want it posted on every door of this city, every street corner, by dawn."

Evan grew very still, but he met my gaze. Again, I watched years of fear, years of oppression and estrangement melt from him. This was one of Jourdain's most beloved thanes, a man who had watched his lord fall decades ago, thinking he would never rise again.

"Yes," he whispered, but there was iron within his voice. At once, he began to give out orders, for his sons to drape blankets over the shuttered windows so no candlelight could leak out, for his wife to ready the press.

Cartier, Merei, and I followed him into the workroom, where

the press sat as a sleeping beast. I set the Canon down on a long table and watched as Evan and his wife began to line the letter plates up, copying Liadan word for word. The air was rich with the scent of paper, with ink as he wet the metal words with it, as he set down a square of parchment.

He began to pump the press, and I watched as the Queen's Canon was inked on paper, over and over, as quickly as Evan Berne could move. Before long, there was a glorious stack of them, and one of the sons gathered it with reverent hands.

"We will post these everywhere," he murmured to me. "But tell me . . . where is the rising happening?"

From the corner of my eye, I saw his mother glance up from her place at the ink roller, her mouth pressed in a tight line. I knew what she was thinking, that she was worrying about her sons fighting.

Cartier answered before I could, coming to stand close behind me. "We ride from Mistwood at dawn." His hand rested on my shoulder, and I could feel the urgency in his touch: we needed to depart. Now.

Evan shuffled to us, gently handing the Canon to me. The tablet went back into my satchel, tethered to my shoulders. He guided us to the front door, but just before we left, he took my hands.

"Tell your father that Evan Berne stands with him. Come darkness or light, I will stand with him."

I smiled and squeezed the printer's hands. "Thank you."

He opened the door, just a sliver.

I slipped out into the streets, Cartier and Merei at my sides, our hearts pounding as we once again ran from shadow to shadow, creeping around enforcers who milled in their dark armor and green capes. I prayed the Berne sons would be careful, that the night would protect them as they too ran the streets with an armful of Canons.

I felt ragged and worn by the time we returned to our horses. Dawn was close; I could feel her sigh in the air, in the crinkling of the frost over the ground as my gelding followed Cartier's up the road that would lead us safely around Lyonesse's walls, deep to the heart of Mistwood, Nessie close behind us.

The forest waited, etched in moonlight, sheltered by a thick cloak of fog. Cartier slowed his horse as we approached, our mounts easing into the earthly cloud as if it were foamy water. We rode deep into the trees before we finally saw the torchlight, before we were greeted by men I had never seen before.

"It's Lord Morgane," a voice murmured, and I had the prickling suspicion that we had just had notched arrows lowered from us. "Welcome, my lord."

I dismounted in tandem with Cartier, my back sore, my legs tight as harp strings. A man took my horse as Merei and I began to walk deeper into the forest, Nessie stuck to my side. We wove around tents and clusters of people, people who had joined us for the rising, utter strangers who wore armor and the colors of the fallen Houses.

Blue for Morgane. Crimson for Kavanagh. Lavender for Mac-Quinn.

Yet I could hardly soak this in as I continued to search for the queen, for my patron father, weaving through the trees as a needle in fabric, around stacks of swords, shields, and quivers brimming with arrows.

Jourdain had been right: we were prepared to wage war. If Lannon did not yield, if Lannon did not abdicate his throne for Yseult, we would clash with sword and shield.

We were here, and we would fight until the last of us fell. And while I had been told such, I found that I was not prepared for the thought of war.

This all felt like a dream, I thought, the exhaustion knotting in my muscles, in my blurred vision. But then I heard his voice, and it snapped every yawn, every desire for sleep.

"She is not here yet," Jourdain said. "She was going to ride with Morgane, from Damhan."

His voice pulled me, drew me closer as I waded through the mist.

"Will she come?" Yseult asked. But I could hear the words she did not say, pitted in the valley of her voice. *Will she still choose us, or will she join Allenach?*

I finally saw them, standing in a clearing. Jourdain, Luc, Yseult, Hector Laurent. Their armor glistened like the scales on a fish in the torchlight as they stood in a weary circle. Their heads were bowed, their swords sheathed at their sides, and the shadows seemed to feed off their doubt, the darkness rising higher as they contemplated what to do.

"We have told our people the Stone of Eventide would be here," Hector said quietly. "They all believe that when we ride out to defy Lannon, the stone will be in our possession. Do we continue this belief, even if she doesn't come?"

"Father," Yseult said, reaching out to touch his arm. "Yes, the stone is life for us. The stone is what makes us Kavanaghs. But it is not what makes us Maevans." She paused, and I watched as all the men, one by one, raised their eyes to look at her, their queen. "I am not going to ride out wearing the stone come dawn."

"Isolde . . ." her father warned, his displeasure evident.

"If Lannon does not abdicate peacefully," she continued, "we will fight, we will wage war, and we will take back the throne with steel and shield. I am not going to awaken magic only to let it go corrupt in battle. Magic has been dormant for over a hundred years. I need to learn how to wield it in peace."

"But all of these people who have rallied behind us," Hector softly argued. "They have done so because of the stone."

"No," Luc countered. "They have done it because of Isolde. Because we have returned."

I held my breath, waiting to see what Jourdain would say, what Jourdain thought.

But he never spoke.

And so I stepped forward, breaking the fog as I said, "I am here."

## ⭒ THIRTY ⭒

# THE THREE BANNERS

The four of them spun to look at me, the relief making them sag within their breastplates. It was Yseult who came to me first, her hands outstretched to link with mine in welcome, a smile blooming across her face.

"Amadine," she greeted, turning me away before I could so much as make eye contact with Jourdain. "Come, I have something for you."

Luc stepped forward next, noticing Merei's passion cloak instantly, capturing her in conversation as Yseult guided me through the trees, the torches hissing from their pegs in the trunks. She brought me to a tent, parting the cambric flaps to slip inside. Nessie lay down outside, the wolfhound exhausted from her long run, as I followed the queen, breathing in the scent of pine, smoke, and polished steel.

In one corner of the tent was a cot, rumpled with furs and quilts. In the other corner there was a set of armor. This is where the queen guided me, bringing forth a breastplate fashioned like dragon scales.

"This is for you," Yseult said. "And I have a shirt and some breeches here as well."

I unbuckled the satchel from my shoulders, saying, "And I have something for you, my lady." My hands were trembling as I brought forth the Queen's Canon, the white stone soaking in the candlelight as if the words were thirsty.

Yseult went very still when she saw it. She eased my breastplate to the ground and accepted the tablet, and I saw that she was trembling too.

"Amadine . . ." she whispered, her eyes rushing over the carved declaration, the declaration that was going to liberate this country. "Where? Where did you find this?"

I began to unlace my boots, unbuckle Allenach's sword from my waist, unwind from my dress. "I fear that I have descended from a House of traitors. The Allenachs not only buried the stone; they took the Canon as well."

The cold sent ripples over my skin as I pulled on the breeches and the linen shirt. The wooden locket clinked over my chest, and I felt Yseult's gaze rest upon it, the stone stirring.

I was one moment from taking it from my neck, to give her the Eventide, when she stepped back.

"No," Yseult whispered, holding the tablet to her breast. "I want you to wear the stone, Amadine. Do not give it to me yet."

I watched the shadows and light dance over her face, her red hair loose about her shoulders.

"If I take the stone now," she said, "then magic will return in the heat of battle. We both know that is dangerous."

Yes, I knew. It was the very reason why the stone had been buried to begin with.

"Wear it for me, just one more day," Yseult murmured.

"Yes, Lady," I promised.

We both became quiet as Yseult set the Canon on her cot and lifted my breastplate once more. She buckled it snugly about me, and then dressed my forearms with leather vambraces, studded with little spikes that made me think of dragon teeth. I knew she had chosen this armor for me, was dressing me for battle. She plaited a river of braids about my face, to knot back, to keep my eyes clear for the fight. But the rest of my hair flowed around my shoulders, wild and brown and free.

A daughter of Maevana.

I could feel dawn creeping closer, trying to peek within the tent; I could feel the uncertainty in the queen, in me, as we both wondered what the light would bring. Would we have to fight? Would we fall? Would Lannon surrender to us?

Yet the questions faded, one by one, when Yseult brought forth a shell filled with blue. My heart brimmed with emotion when I saw her dip her fingers within the woad.

This is how we prepare for war, I thought as a dark peace wove between the queen and me. This is how we face the unexpected—not by our swords and our shields and our armor. Not even by the woad we paint upon our skin. We are ready because of sisterhood, because our bonds go deeper than blood. We rise for the queens of our past, and for the queens to come.

"This day, you fight at my side, Amadine," she whispered and began to grace my brow with a steady line of blue dots. "This day, you rise with me." She drew a line down my cheeks . . . steady, resolute, celestial. "This day would have never dawned without you, my sister, my friend." And she set the shell in my hands, silently asking me to mark her as she had marked me.

I dipped my fingers in the woad, drew them from her forehead down across her face. As Liadan had once worn her war paint. As Oriana had once painted me that day in the art studio, long before I knew who I was.

The dawn was seeping through the mist when we at last emerged from the tent, armed and ready for battle. I followed Yseult through the woods, to where the trees began to thin, the crowd of men and women bowing their heads to her as she passed.

Just before the forest gave way to the field, three horses stood, saddled and waiting for their riders. Then I saw the three banners.

A red banner for Kavanagh, graced with the black dragon.

A blue banner for Morgane, graced with the silver horse.

A purple banner for MacQuinn, graced with the golden falcon.

Yseult went directly to the horse waiting in the middle, mounting with a flash of her armor, a man handing her the red banner.

This is it, I thought. The fallen Houses are about to rise from their ashes, brave and unyielding, ready to bleed again.

I turned away, overcome, until I saw Cartier striding to me. His armor gleamed like a fallen star as he walked, a long-sword sheathed at his side, his blond hair tamed by plaits, the right side of his face consumed by blue woad. He looked nothing like the master of knowledge I had known for years; he was a lord, rising.

He had never seemed so fierce and wild, and I had never wanted him more.

He framed my face with his hands, and I thought my heart had surely melted to the grass when he breathed, "When this battle is over, and we set the queen upon the throne . . . remind me to give you your cloak."

I smiled, the laughter hanging between my lungs. I rested my hands upon his arms as he leaned his forehead to mine, the moment before battle quiet, peaceful, and aching. A bird sang above us in the branches. The mist flowed away as a tide about our ankles. And we breathed as one, holding every possibility deep in our hearts.

He kissed my cheeks, a chaste farewell that promised more when night fell, when the stars aligned.

I stood among his people and watched as he walked to the horse on the left, mounting with Valenian elegance, taking up his blue banner. Merei emerged from the crowd to stand at my side, her presence a balm to my fear. Someone had fitted her with armor, and she stood as if she had worn linked steel all her life, a quiver of arrows over her shoulder.

The third horse was still waiting, flicking her black tail. It was the horse for MacQuinn, and I wondered who would ride with the queen and Cartier, who would ride to defy Lannon with that forbidden purple and falcon streaming at their shoulder.

No sooner had I thought such did I see Luc carrying Mac-Quinn's banner, his dark hair standing up in all the wrong angles, streaks of woad down his cheeks as he looked for something. As he looked for some*one*.

His eyes fell upon me, and there they remained. Slowly, my knees popping, I walked forward to meet him.

"Amadine. I want you to carry our banner, in memory of my mother," he said.

"Luc, no, I couldn't," I hoarsely whispered in response. "It should be you."

"My mother would want it to be you," he insisted. "Please, Amadine."

I hesitated, feeling the warmth of countless gazes upon us. I knew Jourdain was among them, standing in the crowd watching Luc make this request, and my chest tightened. Jourdain might not want me bearing his banner; he might not want me to claim his House. "Your father . . . he might not . . ."

"Our father wills it," Luc murmured. "Please."

Luc could be making a claim just to get me to acquiesce, but I could not let the morning continue to slip away from us. I reached forward and took the slender pole, felt the gentle weight of the purple banner become mine.

I walked to the horse as the third and final rider, mounting with a tremor in my legs. The saddle was cold beneath me as I settled my feet in the stirrups, as my left hand took up the reins while my right held to the pole. The velvet banner stroked my back, the golden-stitched falcon perching upon my shoulder.

I looked to Yseult, to Cartier, who both sat watching me, the morning light flickering across their faces. The wind came about us, tugging at my braids, stroking our banners. And the peace that came over me was like a warm cloak, guarding me against the fear that howled in the distance.

I nodded to the queen and the lord, my gaze proclaiming that I was ready, that I would ride, that I would fall at their side.

Yseult broke from the forest, the fire. *Kavanagh the Bright.*

Then Cartier, the water. *Morgane the Swift.*

And last, I emerged, the wings. *MacQuinn the Steadfast.*

We rode close together, the queen as the point of an arrow, Cartier and I at her flanks, our horses galloping in perfect stride. The fog continued to burn away as we claimed the field piece by piece, the grass glittering with frost, the earth pounding with the song of our redemption.

This was the same field that had witnessed the massacre, the defeat twenty-five years ago. And yet we took it as if it was ours, as if it had always been ours, even when the royal castle loomed in the distance with the green and yellow banners of Lannon, even when I saw that the king was waiting for us with a horde of soldiers lining his back as an impenetrable wall of steel and black armor.

He would know that we would come for him. He would know because he would have been woken just before dawn to find the Queen's Canon had fallen upon Lyonesse as snow. He would know because Lord Allenach—I imagined—had stormed to the royal hall after discovering I had fled from his lands, along with Jourdain's people.

There would be no doubt in Lannon's narrow mind, not when he saw the three forbidden banners billowing at our shoulders.

We were coming to wage war.

Yseult eased her horse to a canter . . . to a trot. Cartier and I mirrored her, reining our horses slower, slower, as the distance between us and Lannon closed. My heart was throbbing as our horses came to an elegant halt, a stone's throw from where the king sat upon his stead, flanked by the captain of his guard and Lord Allenach.

Oh, his eyes fell upon me as poison, as a blade to my heart. I met my father's gaze, MacQuinn's banner gracing my shoulder, and watched the hatred set upon his handsome face.

I had to look away before the grief cleaved me.

"Gilroy Lannon," Yseult called, her voice sharp and rich in the air. "You are an imposter to this throne. We have come to claim it from your unrighteous hands. You can either abdicate now, peacefully, on this field. Or we will take it forcefully, by blood and steel."

Lannon chuckled, a twisted sound. "Ah, little Isolde Kavanagh. However did you escape my blade twenty-fire years ago? You know that I drove my sword into your sister's heart on this very field. And I can easily do it to yours. Kneel before me, deny this folly, and I will bring you and your disgraced House back into my fold."

Yseult didn't so much as flinch, as he was hoping she would. She didn't let her emotions visibly gather, even though I could feel them, like a storm was brewing overhead.

"I do not kneel to a king," she declared. "I do not kneel to tyranny and cruelty. You, sire, are a disgrace to this country. You are a dark blemish, and one that I am about to purge. I will give you one final chance to surrender before I rend you in two."

He laughed, the sound taking to the air as crows, dark and cawing. I felt Allenach staring at me; he had not taken his eyes from me, not even to look at Yseult.

"Then I fear that we have come to an impasse, little Isolde," Lannon said, the crown on his head snaring the sunlight. "I will give you a count of fifteen to ride back across the field and ready yourselves for battle. One . . . two . . . three . . ."

Yseult whirled her horse about. Cartier and I remained on either side of her, her buffers and her support, as our horses began to gallop the way we had come. I could see the line of our people as they strode over the grass, their shields locked and ready, to meet us in the middle and wage the battle we predicted would unfold.

I should have been counting. I should have kept track of the fifteen seconds. But time in that moment went shallow and thin, brittle. We were almost rejoined to our group when I heard the whizzing, as if the wind were trying to catch us.

I never turned about, not even as the arrows began to sink into the ground before us. There was a shout from one of our people—it sounded like Jourdain. He was screaming orders, and I watched as the wall of shields opened in the center, ready to swallow the three of us as we tore across the field.

I didn't even realize I had been hit, not until I saw the blood begin to pour down my arm, red, eager. I glanced at it like I was looking at a stranger's arm, saw the tip of an arrow protruding from my bicep, and the pain quivered deep in my bones, up to my teeth, stealing my breath.

You can make it, I told myself, even as the stars began to speckle the edges of my vision, even as I watched as Yseult and Cartier pulled ahead of me.

You can make it.

But my body was melting like butter in a hot skillet. And it wasn't just the sharp pain of the arrow. I realized too late what was happening. . . . The pressure clenched around me, popping my ears, scraping my lungs.

No, no, no . . .

My hands went numb. MacQuinn's banner slipped from my fingers just as the sky above me blackened with a storm, just as my body began to fall from the saddle.

I hit the ground as Tristan Allenach.

# THIRTY-ONE

# A CLASH OF STEEL

Tristan eased up from the ground, the arrow lodged in his left thigh. As the rain poured, forming bloody puddles on the dirt around him, he broke the fletching and shoved the arrowhead cleanly through his leg, clenching his jaw to contain his scream. The sky was black, the clouds swirling as the eye of a terrible storm, limned with an eerie green light.

He had broken from the line of his warriors, broken from the orders to remain waiting a mile from battle. Because of such, he had been shot; he was now vulnerable, exposed, alone.

But he had to get to the queen, before she sundered the land to pieces.

His horse cantered away, ears back in terror as a boom shuddered from the sky to the earth. His ears were ringing as he limped up the hill, scrambling to find Norah, the quiver of arrows at his back rattling, his bow bent from his fall. He screamed for her as he wove through the dead bodies of the Hilds, their limbs broken in unnatural pieces, gnawed to the bone by some magical creature of the queen's creation, their faces split in two with the skin peeled back.

He reached the crest of the hill, gazing down at the land that stretched before him, once so beautiful and verdant. It was now scorched, the ashes blowing as will-o'-the-wisps. And there was Norah, her long black hair flowing like a midnight banner as she ran, bearing sword and shield, blue woad blazing on her face.

"Norah!" he shouted, his wounded leg keeping him from pursuing her.

She somehow heard him despite the thunder and rain. The princess whirled among the ashes and corpses and saw Tristan. He stumbled across the distance to reach her, and before he could stop himself, he grasped her arms and shook her.

"You must get the stone, Norah. Now. Before your mother's magic consumes us all."

Her eyes widened. She was afraid; he could feel her quivering. And then she looked to the next summit, where they could see the outline of her mother the queen, standing as her magic waged a battle that spun and spun, knowing no depth and no end.

Norah began to move, heading to the hill, Tristan in her shadow. A shower of arrows began to rain down on them, shot from desperate Hild bows in the valley, and Tristan waited for the impact. But the arrows split in two, turning back on themselves, hurling to return to their archers. Screams punctured the air, followed by another resounding boom that brought Tristan to his knees.

But Norah was walking, stealing up the summit. The wind gathered about her as she prepared to face her mother with only sword and shield. Tristan crawled to a rock, embraced it, and waited, watching her reach the crown of the hill.

He couldn't hear their voices, but he could see their faces.

The queen had always been beautiful and elegant. In war, she was terrifyingly so. She smiled down at Norah, even as Norah opened her arms and screamed at her.

Tristan had read that magic in war easily went astray, that it fogged the wielder's mind, that it fed off the bloodlust and hatred it found when two rulers clashed to kill and conquer. Liadan had written documents about it, how magic should never be used to harm, to kill, to annihilate. And Tristan was witnessing it firsthand.

He watched as the queen struck her daughter across the face— something she would never have done had the battle magic not corrupted her mind. The blow made Norah stagger backward, made her drop her sword. Tristan felt his blood simmer as the queen brought forth a dirk and reached for Norah. He responded without thinking, drawing an arrow, notching it to his bow, aiming for the queen. And he shot it, watched the arrow spin gracefully through storm and rain and wind, lodging in the queen's right eye.

The dirk fell from her grip as she crumpled to the ground, the blood streaming down her face, down her dress. Norah crawled to her, weeping, cradling her mother as Tristan rushed to the summit.

He had just killed the queen.

His knees turned to water when Norah glared up at him, the magic gathering about her as sparks of fire, her mother's blood smeared over her hands. And at the queen's neck, the Stone of Eventide had turned purple and black, bruised with fury.

"I will cut you in two," Norah screamed, rising and running toward him, her hands lifting to summon her magic.

Tristan grabbed her wrists and the two of them tumbled to the ground, rolling over each other down the summit, over bones and rocks and streaks of blood. She was strong; she nearly overcame him, her magic eager to break him apart, but Tristan found himself on top when they finally came to a halt. He yanked out his dirk and pressed it to the pale column of her neck, his other hand crushing her fingers into submission.

"Bring this battle to an end, Norah," he rasped, telling himself that he would not hesitate to kill her should she threaten him again. "Stop the storm. Tame the magic the queen has set loose."

Norah was panting beneath him, her face twisted in pain, in agony. But she returned to herself, slowly. It was like watching rain fill a cistern, and Tristan shuddered in relief when she finally nodded, tears flowing from her eyes.

He let her hands go, and he warily observed as she murmured the ancient words, her fingers flickering to the sky. Gradually, the magic unraveled and weakened, breaking like plates on a floor, leaving behind its residue as dust and gossamer in an abandoned house.

The storm clouds began to dissipate, revealing ribs of blue, and the wind eased, but the corpses remained. The destruction and the dead and the consequences remained.

*Gently, he rolled off her, drew her to her feet. The dirk in his hand was slick, with sweat, with blood.*

Kill her, *a voice whispered.* She will betray you. She is like her mother. . . .

*"You want to kill me," she whispered, reading his mind.*

*He held her by her wrist, and her eyes were fearless as she looked at him. He could feel her magic brush his bones . . . like autumn's first frost, like a slow-consuming fire, like the seductive texture of silk . . .*

*He tightened his hold and lowered his face to hers, until their breaths intermingled. "I want you to disappear. I want you to vanish, to deny your right to the throne. If you come back, I will kill you."*

*He shoved her away, even though the motion tore what little remained of his heart. He had come to admire her, respect her, love her.*

*She would have made an exquisite queen.*

*He expected her to fight, to summon the magic, to raze him to the earth.*

*But Norah Kavanagh did none of those things.*

*She turned and walked away. And she went five steps before she pivoted to look at him one final time, her dark, blood-matted hair the greatest crown she had ever worn. "Heed this, Tristan Allenach, lord of the shrewd: you have bought my House to ashes. You have taken the life of the queen. And you will steal the Stone of Eventide. But know that one day, a daughter will rise from your line, a daughter who shall be two in one, passion and stone. And she will bring down your House from within and undo all your crimes. But perhaps the greatest wonder of all? She shall steal your memories to do it."*

*She set her back to him and walked, walked until the mist came about her.*

*He wanted to brush aside her words. She was trying to rattle him, make him doubt himself. . . .*

Brienna.

*Somewhere, a voice that reminded him of midsummer stars spoke within his mind. An echo trembled through the earth as Tristan began to ascend the summit once more.*

Brienna.

*He came to kneel at the queen's side, her blood beginning to cool and darken, his arrow protruding from her eye.*

Brienna.

*The Stone of Eventide was his.*

Just as Tristan reached for the stone, I opened my eyes, leaving his battle for mine.

The earth was hard and cold beneath me, the sky remarkably cloudless and blue as I squinted up at Cartier, the sun like a crown behind him. I drew in a long breath, felt the stabbing pain in my left arm, and remembered. The banners, the arrows, the fall.

"I'm all right," I rasped, my right hand fluttering over my chest, finding his. "Help me up."

I could hear the clashing of steel, the shouts and screams that preceded blood and death. Lannon and Allenach's forces had broken through our wall of shields, and Cartier had carried me as far back to the line as he could, trying to rouse me. I glanced to my arm; the arrow was gone, a strip of linen fastened about the wound. My blood still seeped through it as he raised me up to my feet.

"I'm all right," I repeated, and then drew my own sword, the widow in the amber. "Go, Cartier."

His people were pressing forward, fighting without him. And it was evident to see we were outnumbered. I shoved him gently in the chest, smearing his breastplate with my blood.

"*Go.*"

He took a step back, his eyes riveted to mine. And then we both turned at the same moment, taking up wooden shields and wielding our steel. While he moved toward the warriors in blue, I moved toward the warriors in lavender, the House that was mine, that I wanted to belong to.

I tripped over a body, one of ours, a young man whose eyes were glassy as he stared at the sky, his throat shredded. And then I tripped over another, one of theirs, a green cloak about his neck. I began to step over death, wondering if she was also about to trip me. No sooner did I sense the brush of death's wings than did I feel a cold gaze touch me.

I looked forward, into the fray, to see Allenach a few yards away.

Blood was splattered on his face, his dark hair blowing in the breeze beneath his golden circlet. Calmly, he began to walk forward, the battle seeming to flow away from both of us, opening a chasm of passage between the lord and me.

He was coming for me.

There was a side of me that begged me to run, to hide from him. Because I could see it in the dark glitter of his eyes, in the bloodlust that swarmed him.

My father was coming to kill me.

I stepped back, tripping, regaining my balance before I told myself to stand firm, steadfast. When that gap closed between us, my sword the only thing preventing him from reaching me, I knew that only one of us was going to walk away from this encounter.

"Ah, my traitor of a daughter," he said, his eyes going to the long blade in my hand. "As well as a thief. Widow's Bite suits you, Brienna."

I held my tongue, the battle raging around us, raging but not touching us.

"Tell me, Brienna, did you cross the channel to betray me?"

"I crossed the channel to set a queen upon the throne," I said, thankful my voice was steady. "I had no inkling who you were when I first saw you. I was never told the name of my father."

Allenach gave me a malicious little smile. It seemed as if he was weighing my soul in that moment, weighing how valuable I was to him. His eyes flickered from my bloodstained boots up to the woad on my face, the braids in my hair, the wound in my left arm, the sword in my right hand.

"You are brave, I will give you that," the lord said. "If I had raised you, you would love me. You would serve me. You would fight *with* me, not against me."

And how different my life would be, if Allenach had raised me from the very start. I saw myself standing at his shoulder, a cold warrior of a girl, taking life and taking the throne with no regrets. There would have been no Magnalia, no Merei, no Cartier. Just me and my father, sharpening each other into vicious weapons.

"I will give you one final chance, Brienna," he said. "Come to me, and I will forgive you. I know MacQuinn has clouded your judgment; he has stolen you from me. Join me, and we will take what is rightfully ours." He dared to extend his left hand, palm upward, as a Valenian would offer their allegiance and their heart.

I stared at the lines of his palm, the lines my own life had grafted from. And I remembered Tristan's memory, the one I had just tasted. *But know that one day, a daughter will rise from your line, a daughter who shall be two in one, passion and stone.* Norah Kavanagh had seen me coming in the features of Tristan's face, had predicted my life and my purpose.

I had descended from selfish, ambitious blood.

And I was Norah Kavanagh's vengeance. I would redeem myself.

"No," I said, a simple yet delicious word.

Allenach's pleasant façade shattered. His hatred returned, burning bright, his face like a stone that had cracked, turning itself into dust. Before I could so much as breathe, he growled—the beast within him coming unleashed—and cut his sword at me.

It was all I could do to block his blade, to protect myself from being split open by his wrath. I stumbled again, my exhaustion my slow undoing, the impact of clashing steel rattling up my fingers, up my arms, setting my teeth in a grimace.

I fell into a dangerous dance with him, over blood and death,

Yseult's training rising in me, keeping me alive as I deflected and blocked and twisted away from the edge of his blade.

I needed to pierce him with my steel. I needed to sever one of his vital blood flows. And yet . . . I couldn't bring myself to do it. I had never taken life. I had never killed. And I wanted to weep, to know that I had reached this moment, this moment when I would have to kill the man who had made me, or let him extinguish my life.

Those thoughts were haunting me when an arrow hissed through the air, so unexpectedly that it took Allenach a full breath to realize he had been shot in his thigh, the very place Tristan had been pierced, the fletching trembling as he took a step back. The lord looked down at it, stunned. And then we both glanced up, following the path the arrow had flown to see a girl with dark hair and elegant fingers standing a few yards away, lowering her bow, her eyes gleaming as she defied Allenach.

"Run, Brienna," Merei ordered me, notching another arrow on her bow, calm and poised as if she were about to play me a song on her violin.

I felt stricken as our gazes met. She was ordering me to run while she stayed. She was offering to kill him, so I would not have to.

But my father was charging to her now, his sword flashing in the sunlight. And all she had was her bow and arrows.

"No!" I screamed, chasing after him, trying to catch him before he could reach her.

Merei stepped back, her arm quivering as she shot at Allenach again, a brave one aimed at his face. He ducked, narrowly missing her lethal shot, and then swung his blade. I bit through my lip trying to intercept him. But there was a sudden gleam of armor, a blur of dark red and silver as someone came between Allenach and Merei.

Sean.

His face was trapped in a grimace as his sword clashed with Allenach's, as he shifted his blade to push the lord away from Merei. I didn't know if I should wholly trust him: my half brother was wearing the colors and sigil of Allenach. But Sean continued to spar our father back, until Allenach was trapped between us, his son and his daughter.

"Enough, Father," Sean rasped. "This battle is lost. Surrender, before more lives must fall."

Allenach chuckled bitterly. "So my son is also a traitor." He glanced between us. "You choose your illegitimate sister over *me*, Sean?"

"I choose the queen, Father," Sean said, his voice steady. "Surrender. Now." He extended the point of his blade, until it rested against Allenach's neck.

I was struggling to breathe, to stand as my legs went numb. I could not imagine one as gentle and polite as Sean killing his father.

The lord laughed, no fear in the sound, only disgust and fury. In one bold move, he disarmed my brother. In one breath, he plunged his sword into Sean's side, through the weak seams of his armor.

A scream clawed its way up my throat, but all I could hear was the roar of my own pulse as I watched Sean fold and tumble down to the grass. My eyes were fixed upon his blood, blood that began to coat Merei's hands as she frantically tried to help him.

And then Allenach turned that bloodstained sword on me.

He disarmed me swiftly, the pain a vibrant sting up my arm. I watched Widow's Bite sail through the air, falling a great distance from me. And then I felt his knuckles as he backhanded my face, my cheek blistering with his spite. He hit me again, again, and my eyes blurred as I felt the blood flow from my nose, from my mouth.

I tried to bring my shield between us, but he wrenched it from my wounded arm, and I at last surrendered to the grass, to the solid push of earth against my spine.

Allenach stood above me, his shadow cascading over my burning face. I could hear Merei screaming my name, over and over, trying to rouse me. But she sounded far away, and I could only watch as he raised his sword, preparing to pierce my neck. I drew in a deep, calm breath, resting in the belief that Yseult would make it. She would reclaim the throne. And that was all that mattered. . . .

Just before Allenach's steel drank away my life, a shadow overcame both of us, raging and swift. I watched, disbelieving, as Allenach was jarred backward, his grace dissipating as he tripped, as Jourdain stood over me.

"Davin MacQuinn," Allenach hissed, spitting a stream of blood from his mouth. "Get out of the way."

"This is my daughter," Jourdain said. "You will not touch her again."

"She is *mine*," Allenach growled. "She is mine, and I will take back the life I gave her."

Jourdain had the defiance to chuckle, as if Allenach had said the most foolish of things. "She was never yours to begin with, Brendan."

Allenach lunged at Jourdain, their swords meeting in a high guard. My heart felt wrenched from my chest as I watched the two lords fight, their swords tasting the sunlight, tasting blood as they nicked and sliced through each other's arms and legs.

"Bri? Bri help me!"

I began to crawl to where Sean lay, where Merei knelt beside him, frantically trying to stem his blood. I finally reached her side, and my hands joined with hers as we tried to calm his bleeding.

I didn't have the strength to meet his gaze, but when he whispered my name—*Brienna*—I had no other choice. I looked at him, my hope breaking when I saw the starkness of his face.

"Why are brothers so foolish?" I cried, desiring to smack and embrace him all at once for his courage.

He smiled; I wanted to weep, for him to die just as I was beginning to know him. Merei wrapped her arm around me, as if she felt the very same.

"Do you hear that?" Sean whispered.

I thought he was about to surrender his spirit, that he was hearing the song of the saints. And I would have begged them to let him stay with me, when I realized that I heard something too.

A shout coming from the south, a shout of people emerging from Lyonesse, bearing swords and axes and pitchforks, whatever weapons they could find. I knew that they had found the Canon on their doors, on their street corners. They had come to stand and fight with us. And from the east came another shout, a song of triumph and light, another banner, orange and red. Lord Burke had brought his warriors, had come to give us his support and his aid.

I was about to tell Sean what I was seeing as I watched the tide of the battle change; I was just about to open my mouth when there came a painful sound from behind me, a gurgle of surprise. I knew it was one of them; it was either Jourdain or Allenach. And I could hardly bring myself to turn, to look and see who had fallen.

But I did.

Allenach was staring at me, his eyes wide as the blood bloomed from his neck, pouring like rain as he sank to his knees. I was the last thing of living earth he saw as he lay facedown in the grass at my feet, as he breathed his last.

I remained seated on the ground by Sean and Merei, my hand clasped with hers, my gaze transfixed with how still death was, how the wind continued to blow over Allenach's dark hair. And then there was warmth at my side, arms coming about me, fingers wiping the blood from my face.

"Brienna," Jourdain said, his voice cracking as he wept beside me. "Brienna, I just killed your father."

I held to him as he held to me, our hearts aching. Because

vengeance doesn't taste quite how you imagine it will, even after twenty-five years.

"No," I said, as Lannon's men began to surrender and retreat, leaving us behind on a field of blood and victory. I laid my palm to Jourdain's cheek, to his tears. "You are my father."

# PART FOUR
# MACQUINN

## — THIRTY-TWO —

## LET THE QUEEN RISE

The red banners were soaring as Yseult walked the remaining strip of field, as we followed her to the castle gates that sat open as a yawning mouth. Lannon had fled to the royal hall, had barricaded himself behind the doors. Yet we came as a mighty river, growing in number with every step we took, reclaiming the castle courtyard. When the doors of the hall held fast, two men brought forth axes and began to chop. Piece by piece, we whittled and we hacked and we splintered until the doors came down.

The first time I had stepped into this cavernous hall, I had done so as a Valenian girl in an exquisite dress, alone.

I now entered it as a Maevan woman, covered in blood and

woad, Merei on my left, Luc on my right, Jourdain and Cartier at my back.

Lannon was sitting on the throne, his eyes wide, his fear like a stench in the air as his hands gripped the antler armrests. He had only a few men remaining around him, standing, watching as we strode closer, closer. . . .

Yseult finally came to stand before the dais. The hall grew quiet as she opened her arms, victorious, the light glistening down her dragon-inspired armor.

"Gilroy Lannon." Her voice echoed up to the rafters. "Maevana has weighed you and found you wanting. Come and kneel before us."

He wasn't going to move. His face had gone pale, the ends of his hair quivering as he tried to swallow his fear. He might have sat there stubbornly, but then the men standing around him knelt before her, leaving Lannon exposed, leaving him on his own.

Slowly, as if his bones might break, he stood and descended the dais. He came to kneel before her, before all of us.

"Father?" Yseult murmured, glancing to where Hector stood near her elbow. "Take the crown from him."

Hector Laurent rustled forward, lifted the crown from Lannon's head.

There was a moment of silence, as if she was pondering how to punish him. And then Yseult struck Lannon across the face, lightning swift. I saw the former king's head snap to the side, watched his cheek begin to welt as he gradually brought his eyes back to hers.

"That is for my sister," Yseult said. And then she struck him again, on the other cheek, drawing blood. "That is for my mother."

She struck him again.

"That is for Lady Morgane." Cartier's mother.

Again.

"That is for Ashling Morgane." Cartier's sister.

Again, the crack of bone, the crack of twenty-five years.

"And that is for Lady MacQuinn." Jourdain's wife, Luc's mother.

For the women who had fallen, who had paid in blood.

"Now lie prostrate before us," she demanded, and Lannon did. He slithered forward and lay facedown on the tiles. "You will be bound and held in the keep, and the people of Maevana will decide your fate in trial, fourteen days from now. Do not expect mercy, O Cowardly One."

Lannon's wrists were bound behind his back by Yseult's men. He was dragged away, and a cheer resounded in the hall as thunder, rumbling deep in my chest where my heart continued to pound in awe.

That was when Yseult turned to find me in the crowd, wedged between my father and my brother. Her eyes were lined with tears, her hair flowing as fire when I stepped forward.

The hall grew quiet, like the first falling of snow, as I brought the wooden locket out from beneath my armor. Reverently, I unlatched the locket and let the wood fall between our feet.

The Stone of Eventide swung gracefully from its chain as it hung from my fingers. It rippled with color, with crimson and blue and lavender, like a pebble influenced the surface of a quiet lake. I smiled at her, my friend and my queen, and carefully raised the stone higher.

"My Lady," I said. "May I present to you the Stone of Eventide."

She knelt before me, closing her eyes as I set the stone about her neck, as the Eventide came to rest over her heart.

I had long imagined how magic would awaken. Would it return gently, quietly, like winter gradually melting into spring? Or would it come violently, like a storm or a flood?

The stone glimmered to liquid gold as it rested against her, as it basked in the glory she granted it. I waited, hardly breathing as Isolde Kavanagh stood and opened her eyes. Our gazes locked; she smiled at me, and that was when the wind blew into the hall, carrying the scent of forests and lush meadows, of summits and valleys and the rivers that flowed between shadows and light.

I felt warmth radiate from my arm, like honey was rushing along my skin, like sunlight had kissed my wound. I felt her heal me, weld my broken veins back together, seal the arrow's puncture with magical threads.

She didn't even know that she was doing it, that I was the first one to feel her magic.

And so it would return gently, naturally as sun and blissful warmth, as healing and mending.

I watched as she walked among her people, reaching out to hold their hands, to learn their names. Isolde Kavanagh was surrounded as men and women gathered about her as if she were a cup of everlasting water to quench their thirst; they laughed and cried as she blessed them, as she brought us together as one.

All eyes were on her, save for one gaze.

I felt his draw, let my eyes drift to where the lord of the House of Morgane stood, half in the shadows, half in the light.

The world grew quiet between me and Cartier, as he looked to me, as I looked to him.

It was only when he smiled did I realize tears were streaming down his face.

Hours after Lannon fell, I returned to the battle green with a flask of water as I began to search for wounded survivors. A few healers had already set up tents to work in the shade; I could hear their weary voices as they labored to stitch wounds and set broken bones. I knew Isolde was among them, drawing magic into her hands as she touched to mend, for I could feel it again: her magic stirred a gentle, fragrant breeze over the blood and gore of the field.

I didn't know if I should ask after his name, or keep searching on my own, desperately hoping he had survived. Eventually, I approached one of the healers, her dress smudged with blood, and inquired.

"Sean Allenach?"

The healer pointed to a distant tent. "The traitors are over there."

And my throat tightened to hear it. *Traitors*. But I swallowed and made my way carefully to that tent, unsure as to what I would find.

Men and women were laid out on the grass, shoulder to

shoulder. Some looked to have already died before a healer could tend to them. Others were moaning, broken and weak. All of them wore the Lannon green or the Allenach maroon.

I found Sean on the outskirts. Carefully, I knelt at his side, believing he was dead until I saw his chest rise and fall. His armor had been unbolted, and I could see the severity of the wound in his side.

"Sean?" I whispered, taking his hand.

His eyes opened slowly. I tilted his head up so I could trickle some water into his mouth. He was too weak to talk, so I merely sat at his side with my fingers linked with his, so he would not have to die alone.

I don't know how long I sat there with him before she came. But that breeze blew into the tent, lifting the matted hair off my neck, and I turned to see Isolde was standing among us, her eyes focused on me and my brother.

She walked to us, kneeling at my side so she could look at Sean.

"Lady?" one of the healers respectfully murmured to the queen. "Lady, these are traitors."

I knew what the healer was implying. These are traitors, and they deserve to die as they lie, without the queen's healing magic. And I yearned to tell Isolde that Sean was not a traitor, that Sean had chosen to fight for her.

"I know," Isolde answered, and then she gently took Sean's hand from me.

My brother's eyes fluttered open, riveted to the queen. I

watched the air shimmer around our corners and edges as Isolde traced Sean's wound. The sunlight fractured as if she were a prism, and Sean's breath caught as the queen slowly, achingly knit him back together with sightless threads.

My feet were prickling with pins and needles by the time she finished, offering him a cup of water.

"You will be weak for a few days," she said. "Rest, Sean Allenach. When you are stronger, we can talk about the future of your House."

"Yes, Lady," he rasped.

Isolde stood and laid a reassuring hand on my shoulder. And then she moved on to the others, healing the traitors one by one, not seeing their faults but seeing their possibilities.

And while I could not heal, I could do other measures of service. I began to pass out bowls of soup, chunks of bread, listening as stories began to unwind about me, stories of bravery and stories of fear, stories of desperation and stories of redemption, stories of loss and stories of reunion.

I fed, I buried, and I listened until I was so exhausted I could hardly think, and night had drawn her cloak over the sky, dusted with a multitude of stars.

I stood in the field and drank the darkness, the grass still crimped and stained with blood, and gazed at the constellations. Weeks ago, I would have wondered straightaway which one was supposed to be mine. But now, all I could wonder was where I was to go, where I was to remain. I had done almost everything I had set out to do. And now . . . I did not know where I belonged.

I heard the gentle footsteps of a man walking through darkness to find me. I turned, recognizing Jourdain at once, the starlight catching the silver in his hair. He must have read my thoughts, or read my face with ease.

He drew me to his side so we could admire the stars together. And then, so quietly I almost didn't hear, he said, "Let's go home, Brienna."

# —❧ THIRTY-THREE ❧—

## FIELDS OF COROGAN

*Lord MacQuinn's Territory, Castle Fionn*

Three days later, I rested in the dappled shade of a lonely oak, the dust of travel still clinging to my breeches and shirt, Nessie panting at my side. The surrounding fields had just been harvested, the air smelling of candied earth, the grass golden from the songs the men had chanted while their sickles had swung.

Jourdain's—*MacQuinn's*—castle sat in the heart of the meadow, the shadows of the mountains only touching the roof early morning and late evening. It was built of white stone, a modest holding, not as grand or large as some of the others, like Damhan. But the walls were seasoned with fire and stories, with friendship and loyalty.

Steadfastness.

And the rightful lord had finally come home.

I had watched as his people greeted him, as they gathered about him in the courtyard, which was strewn with wildflowers and herbs and ribbons. And it had taken me by surprise, the longing for Valenia in that moment. It might have been the ribbons, the colors of passion tangled over the cobblestones. Or it might have been the wine they brought us, which I knew came from a bottle that had crossed the channel.

I had chosen to walk the fields and found this tree not long after the introductions were made and I became known as MacQuinn's daughter. I was content to watch the sun continue her arc across the sky, weaving long tendrils of grass together as I reflected on all that had come to pass, a faithful dog at my side.

"I think you should pick the eastern chamber," Luc declared. I glanced up to see him walking toward me. "It's spacious and has bookshelves. And a beautiful view of the sunrise."

I smiled as he sat beside me, ignoring Nessie's protective growl. It was difficult to think about which room I should pick when there was still so much to come . . . Isolde's coronation, Lannon's trial, trying to mend a world that had continued to spin beneath tyranny. I wondered how the coming days would gather, how they would feel as I tried to settle into my new life.

"Although," Luc said, flicking a beetle from his sleeve, "I have a feeling you won't remain at this castle for long."

I shot him a curious glance. He was ready for it, cocking his brow at me with that arrogant, brotherly confidence.

"And what is that supposed to mean?" I countered.

"You know what I mean, Sister. Shall I give him a hard time?"

"I have no inkling as to what you speak of." I plucked another blade of grass and twisted it, feeling Luc's gaze on me.

"It doesn't surprise me," he said. "The old legends claim that nearly all of the Maevan lords fall hard."

"Hmm?"

Luc sighed, plucking a clover. "I suppose I shall have to challenge him to a spar. Yes, that is the best way to handle this."

I shoved him in the arm and said, "I think you have counted your eggs before they hatch, dear brother."

But the smile he gave me told me otherwise. "I hear Aodhan Morgane is an expert sword master. I should probably practice."

"All right, *enough*." I laughed and nudged him again.

I had not seen Cartier since three days ago in the hall, which already felt like a year. But he was a lord now. He had his people, his lands to restore. I told myself I would not see him until Lannon's trial, which would come the end of next week. And even so, we would be consumed with the task.

Before Luc could tease me anymore, a group of children ran through the field, searching for him.

"Lord Lucas!" one of the little girls cried excitedly when she spotted him in the shade of the oak. "We found you a lute! It's in the hall."

"Oh, excellent!" My brother rose, brushing stray clover buds from his clothes. "Care to join us for some music, Brienna?"

Music made me think of Merei, which made my chest feel far

too small for my heart. Yet I smiled and said, "Go on without me, brother. I shall be along shortly."

He hesitated; I think he was about to ask me again when the little girl boldly grabbed his sleeve and tugged on him, giggling.

"Last one to the courtyard has to eat a rotten egg," Luc challenged, and the children squealed in delight as they tore across the field, as he chased them all the way to the courtyard.

I waited until I saw that he was, indeed, the last one to the courtyard—I would have loved to see Luc eat a rotten egg—but my heart was still restless. I rose and began to walk toward a copse of trees that grew along the river, Nessie trotting at my side as we followed the silver thread of water, eventually coming to a mossy bank.

I sat in a patch of sun and dipped my fingers to the rapids, trying to identify why I felt a shade of sadness, when I heard his soft tread behind me.

"This was where I married my wife."

I glanced over my shoulder to see Jourdain leaning against a river birch, quietly regarding me.

"No grand celebration?" I asked, and he moved forward, sitting beside me on the moss with a slight grunt, as if his joints were sore.

"No grand celebration," he said, propping his elbow on his knee. "I married Sive in secret by handfasting, on this riverbank by the light of the moon. Her father didn't particularly care for me, and she was his one and only daughter. That is why we married in secret." He smiled as he reminisced, staring into the distance as if his Sive were standing on the other side of the river.

"What was she like? Your wife?" I asked gently.

Jourdain looked down to the water, and then to me. "She was graceful. Passionate. Just. Faithful. You remind me of her."

My throat tightened as I glanced to the moss. All this time, I worried he would look at me and see Allenach. And yet he looked at me as if I truly were his daughter, as if I had inherited his wife's attributes and character.

"She would have loved you, Brienna," he whispered.

The wind rustled the branches above us; golden leaves drifted loose and free, eventually caught by the river to be carried away downstream. I wiped a few tears from my eyes, thinking he would not notice, but not much escapes a father.

"I miss Valenia too," Jourdain said, clearing his throat. "I didn't think that I would. But I find myself longing for those vineyards, for that politeness, for a perfectly tailored silk doublet. I even miss those eels upon sops."

I laughed, and a few more tears escaped me. Eels upon sops *was* disgusting.

"I know that you still have family there," he continued, serious once more. "I know you may choose to return to Valenia. But always know that you have a home here, with Luc and me."

I met his gaze as his words settled like gentle rain over me. I had a home, a family, and friends on *both* sides of the channel. I thought of my brave Merei, who had departed Maevana to return to Valenia, despite my begging her to stay. She still had obligations, a four-year contract with Patrice Linville to uphold. But when those four years were over . . .

I had shared my idea with her, hoping it would eventually draw her back. It was a purpose that had begun to blossom in the far reaches of my mind, one I was almost afraid to speak aloud. But Merei had smiled when I told her; she even said she might return for such a purpose.

"Now," Jourdain said, rising to his feet, offering his hand to pull me up along with him. "There is a horse saddled and ready for you."

"For what?" I asked, letting him guide me from the copse of trees.

"Lord Morgane's holding is only a short ride from here," Jourdain explained, and I swear I saw a gleam of mischief in his eyes. "Why don't you ride there now, invite him for a celebratory feast in our hall tonight?"

I had to hold back another laugh, but he saw the helpless crinkling of my nose. I was surprised by how he knew it too, this irresistible draw between Cartier and me. As if it were obvious for the world to see when I stood near my former master, like the desire was a catching flame between our bodies. But perhaps I shouldn't be shocked; it had been evident even before the solstice, before I had come to wholly realize it.

Jourdain led me to where he had the horse waiting, in the cool shadows of the stables. I pulled myself up in the saddle, felt the wind sigh golden with hay and leather in my hair as I looked down at my father.

"Take the western road," he said, patting the mare's withers.

"Follow the Corogan flowers. They shall guide you to Morgane."

I was just about to nudge my horse onward, my heart like an eager drum, when Jourdain took the reins, forced me to look at him.

"And be back before dark," he admonished. "Or else I will worry."

"Don't worry, Father," I replied, but I was smiling, and he gave me a pointed look that said I had better not go off and hand-fast without his knowing.

Nessie sat obediently at his side, as if she knew I needed to take this ride alone.

The mare and I took to the fields, chasing after the sun in the west, following the promise of blue wildflowers.

# THIRTY-FOUR

# AVIANA

*Lord Morgane's Territory, Castle Brígh*

Castle Brígh stood in a grove of oaks, a beautiful crumbling estate built in the foothills of the Killough Mountains. My mare slowed as I approached the trees, as I realized that Cartier's homecoming had been nothing like Jourdain and Luc's.

It was quiet, dilapidated. For twenty-five years, the Morgane holding had been left to fall apart, abandoned, given back to the earth.

I slid from the horse and left her tethered in the shade of one of the oaks, next to Cartier's gelding. And then I began to walk to the courtyard, my fingers brushing over the tips of the long grass, where the Corogan faithfully bloomed in a glory of cold-loving petals. I followed the narrow trail that Cartier had blazed through the thicket, stopping to pick several of the flowers, careful to avoid the thorns on their stems.

I remembered how he liked my hair down and loose, how he had once crowned me with wildflowers. So I took out my braids and let my tresses fall wild and free, tucking a few of the Corogan flowers in my windblown hair.

I looked down at my breeches, my boots, the loose draws of my linen shirt, the pendant that gleamed silver over my heart. This is who I am, all I have to give him.

I ascended the broken steps of his courtyard.

It was quiet. Nature had gradually regained much of the terrace; vines weaved down walls, through the broken windowpanes. An assortment of weeds worked their way up to fearsome bullies through the cracks in the stones, provoking me to sneeze when I passed them. But I could see the path Cartier had taken. He had chopped and beaten his way through the tangling greenery to the twin front doors, which hung at sad angles from their iron hinges.

The shadows of the interior were refreshing to my face—which would undeniably gain a sunburn come evening—and I walked carefully through the foyer, taking heed of the vines and plants that had claimed shattered pieces of the floor. Somehow, the disaster was beautiful to me. The furniture still stood, coated with dust and taken by cobwebs. I stopped at a chair in the foyer, and as my fingers touched a pattern in the dust, I imagined Cartier had once sat in it as a child.

"I wondered when I would see you again."

His voice startled me. I jumped upright, my hand pressed to

my heart as I turned to see him standing halfway down the grand staircase, watching me with a hint of a smile.

"You know better than to startle me like that!" I scolded.

He continued descending the stairs, through streams of sunlight that illumined the arched windows.

"Welcome," he greeted. "Would you like the grand tour?"

"Yes, Lord Morgane."

He wordlessly held his hand out for me, and my fingers wove among his. "Let me show you the second floor," Cartier offered, guiding me back up the stairs, pointing to broken stones I should avoid.

"Do you remember living here?" I asked, my voice filling the corridor as I let him pull me through cobwebs and dust, through the places where he had once lived.

"Sometimes I think I do," he replied, pausing. "But honestly, no. I was just a child when my father and I fled. Here, this is my favorite room."

We walked into a wide chamber, open and full of light. Dropping his hand, I passed through the room, taking in the marble bookshelves built into the walls which still held an impressive collection of books, the cracked mirror that hung upon the rose-stoned hearth, the furniture that sat exactly as it had been left over two decades ago. I went directly to the wall of large mullioned windows, pieces of broken glass remaining as jagged little teeth, admiring the view of the pastures.

"Where are your people, Cartier?" I asked, unable to hold my curiosity.

"They will arrive tomorrow. I wanted to see the castle for myself, alone."

And I could understand. I appreciated solemn, private moments, ones where I could reflect and think. But perhaps more than that, I realized that he had wanted to see his parents' room, his sister's room, without an audience.

Before the melancholy could creep upon us, I stated, "I think I could look at this view every day and be content."

"You missed the best part of the room," Cartier remarked, and I frowned and turned on my heel.

"What? The books?"

"No, the floor."

I glanced down. Through the marks our boots had made in the dirt, I saw the amazing pattern of the tiles. I knelt beside him, and we both used our hands to smooth away the years of dust. The colors still thrived, each tile intricate and unique, beauty spilling from one square to the next.

"My father told me that he had many arguments with my mother about these floors," Cartier explained, sitting back on his heels.

"Why?"

"Well, he had them laid for her, because she loved art. And she had always told him that floors were sorely unappreciated. But the conflict lay in that she wanted to be able to admire them, and he wanted rugs. Stone and tile floors are miserably cold during autumn and winter in Maevana."

"Yes, I can imagine," I said.

"So they argued about the floors. To cover them with rugs, or to suffer cold feet for half of the year."

"I imagine your mother won?"

"You imagine right." Cartier smiled. He brushed the dirt from his hands and stood. "So, my little passion. I surmise you have come to my lovely home because I still have something of yours?"

I stood, feeling my muscles pull sore and tight from the ride. I walked to the bookcases, suddenly needing something solid to lean on. My pulse was skipping, anxious, hungry, as I leaned against the wall, as I turned and looked at him, through sunlight and dust motes.

"Yes, Master Cartier," I said, knowing it was the last time I would ever address him as such.

I watched as he moved to the other side of the room, where his satchel rested on a desk. My fingers spread behind me on the cold marble of the shelves as I waited for him. When I saw the color of blue in his hands, I closed my eyes, listened to my heart dance steady and slow.

"Open your eyes, Brienna."

When I did, the cloak unfolded in his hands, rippling to brush the floor as the tide of the ocean.

"Aviana," I whispered, my fingers moving to catch the rich tumble of the cloak that was mine. He had chosen Aviana for me, the constellation that accompanied his own. They were stars that, like his Verene, bespoke of bravery in darkness, of triumph. Of steadfastness.

"Yes," he said. "And we both know that Verene would have no hope of light without Aviana."

I stepped forward as he brought the cloak about my shoulders, as he fastened the draws at my collar. Then his hands gently gathered my hair, lifting it up and letting it fall down my back, the Corogan flowers casting a sweet fragrance between us.

A master and his passion. A passion and her master.

I met his gaze and breathed, "This is all that I am, all that I can offer you . . ."

I am broken and treacherous, I am divided . . .

But the words faded when he touched me, when his fingertips traced my cheek, down my neck, stopping when he reached my cloak strings, the very knot he had made.

For once, he gave me no words, this master of knowledge, this lord of the Swift. But he answered me. He kissed the left corner of my mouth, the girl I had once been who he had first loved, Valenian grace and passion. And then he kissed the right corner of my lips, the woman I had become, who had risen from ashes and steel, courage and fire.

"I will take and love all of you, Brienna MacQuinn, your shadows and your light, for you have challenged me; you have captivated me. And I desire no other but you," he whispered, his fingers tangling in my hair, in my wildflowers, as he drew me close to him.

He kissed me in the quiet shadows of his house, in the sweetest hour of afternoon, when light desires to surrender to evening. His fingers trailed down my back, touching every star he had given me. And I let the wonder cascade around us as I tasted each of his promises, as I woke the fire that he had long tempered in wait for me.

Time became luminous, as if the moon had married the sun, the minutes eventually tugging on my heart to make me see how late it was, that night had almost fallen. And I remembered that I had someplace to be, that I had a father and a brother who would be watching the door for my return. Only then did I break our kiss, although Cartier's hands pressed to my back, keeping me close.

I laid my finger over his lips and said, "My father has invited you to dinner in our hall. We had better leave now, or else he will think the worst."

Cartier dared to steal one more kiss and then he let me go, gathering his cloak and his satchel. We stepped out into the dusk together, weaving back through the weeds; the nightingales sang for his return, the crickets chirped one final melody before the frost could officially silence them.

I mounted my horse and waited as Cartier saddled his gelding, looking up as first star winked in the fading sunset. And that was when I stated, "I am going to build a House of knowledge here."

This was what I had told Merei before she left Maevana, hoping it would draw her back, hoping she would unite her passion with mine.

I felt Cartier's gaze shift to me, and I turned in the saddle to meet it.

"I only want the very best of arials to teach my ardens," I continued. "Do you know where I may find one?"

The wind tousled his hair as he smiled at me, a gleam of midnight in his eyes as he rose to my challenge. "I know of one."

"Tell him to apply at once."

"Don't worry. He will."

I smiled and nudged my horse forward, leaving Cartier behind to catch me on the road.

I wondered if I could truly do this, if I could build the first House of knowledge in Maevana, if I could inspire the passions in a land of warriors. When it felt daunting, when it felt like I was pressing against immovable stone, I imagined a group of bright-eyed Maevan girls becoming passions of knowledge, girls who wore swords at their sides beneath blue cloaks. I imagined picking their constellations from the sky, and realized that Cartier had been right at the solstice; I was a historian as I was a teacher, and I was about to carve my path.

*I will raise this House.* I breathed my promise to the wind just as I heard Cartier's horse cantering behind me, closing the distance between us.

I eased, just a bit, to let him catch me.

Above us, the stars burned, slow and steady. Their light guided me home.